Werewolf

and Idol

LANCE TAIT

Werewolf

and Idol

LANCE TAIT

Metropole Books

New York

CHAPTER 1

A month had passed since spring began but when night came ice formed again. Smoke and soot from stoves and incinerators burning wood, coal, and garbage spiked the damp air.

Shimizu, the quickly built neighborhood for nights out, was plain. And if no Americans showed up one night, it was like a ghost town.

Tonight, Bar Eden was empty except for two G.I.s.

Their combat duty in Korea the previous year brought them a reward: they were transferred to peaceful postwar Japan to finish their military service. They were stationed on a base on Hokkaido. Though sparse in population, this northern island was huge: roughly the same size as the state of Maine.

Fernandez and Kelso, both White, and twenty-one years old, had never been abroad before they were drafted.

Their overcoats hung by the door. They had unhandsome crew cuts. They were still in their fatigues. The freezing temperature had reddened the sharp tip of Bob Fernandez's nose. Lloyd Kelso's large ears were colorless.

Most troops in Camp Chitose (or "Chitose I" as it soon would be called) were continuing with the past two weeks' military exercises. It was the snow, the drifts of it, and its melting. It was training for possible action on Soviet terrain during winter—hopefully that would never come to pass. Fernandez and Kelso were not part of it; they and a few others would never be sent back into combat. Korea was enough. They were assigned secretarial work in offices, for officers in admin. The U.S. military was ramping up its presence in Chitose. A new army base four miles away would open in ten weeks. The local populace welcomed the growth. It meant dollars. It meant yen. It meant money.

The two buddies had gotten liberty passes for the evening whereas the grunts engaged in the exercises could go no farther than the on-post recreation halls.

Bar Eden was just another one of the oversized dollhouses like many other places in Shimizu: the establishment had six stools at a bar counter, three small standing tables that were round, and a couple of sit-down ones. The place smelled from thousands of cigarettes having been smoked in it. The pine-scented air freshener—of U.S. military origin, acquired by swapping Japanese souvenirs—couldn't cover it up. The bar's owner, Mommy Eri, coughed discreetly after exhaling smoke, contributing her part to the aggregate smell of the room. The hand she held her cigarette in trembled as she glanced at the soldiers, who might be her only customers that night.

Something was missing from Bar Eden and its owner, worn by her forty-seven years, knew it. It was the bar's main attraction. It was not an "it"—it was a "she".

She fought the urge to get away from standing behind the bar. Except for the vestibule leading to the toilet and the back door, Bar Eden had no extra spaces. Because she couldn't escape for any length of time, she had a routine that helped her to avoid the young men: she attended to her prize possession, her record player. Whenever a song ended, she hurried over to it. But tonight her hand quivered so much that she scraped the needle on the record when picking it up or setting it down. The harsh sound detracted from her intention: the flow of music to distract her customers.

Fernandez and Kelso settled into their chairs at one of the sit-down tables. They didn't focus any of their attention on her—not directly, at least. But at the same time, Bob

Fernandez's body language couldn't help but warn her he was displeased.

She placed "Too Young" by Nat King Cole on the turntable. It was a hit the year before, and exactly the kind of mushy serenade she liked.

> *They say that love's a word,*
> *A word we've only heard*
> *But can't begin to know the meaning of.*
> *And yet we're not too young to know.*

A schmaltzy, romantic song like that was a universe away from the blood-soaked bodies, the excrement and dying that the unseasoned platoons experienced after they'd hit the ground in Korea. For the troops that came out of that alive, this type of song meant less now.

Mommy Eri reached for the needle and scratched the record again. She couldn't help it.

"So, where's Kiriko?" Fernandez, the G.I. who grew up on a farm in the San Joaquin Valley asked. He was staring just to the space on the right side of Mommy Eri, not looking her in the eyes. The Californian made his question sound casual.

Eri carried on as though she hadn't heard him clearly. She coughed and took another cigarette out of the pack.

"We like you, but… she's cute," he added. Maybe the playful approach would help with the forbidding woman behind the bar.

A shadow crossed Mommy Eri's face. She struck a match and lit another cigarette. She was cornered. She needed words but they didn't come. She stared at the floor.

"She's a keeper," Bob pressed on, his voice ringing out. "There's a big hole here now. What the hell happened?" He glanced around the bar and then at Lloyd Kelso. "Am I speaking in tongues or what?" Lloyd, who came from a small town in central New York State, laughed nervously. His friend Bob was being an abrasive hick. Lloyd knew all about

3

hicks; he considered himself one of the polite specimens of them.

Mommy Eri didn't move. She thought to herself: I wish there was a big hole in the floor I could crawl into and then hope I'd never see either of you again.

Bob made it no secret to anyone who would listen that he was in love with Kiriko. It was a love that wasn't reciprocated. Kiriko was in her late teens and Bar Eden was her first real job. She was always attentive to customers; not one of them was any different than the other.

"So," Bob Fernandez said, stretching his toes in one motion inside his boots. "Um…" He softened his voice, trying to sound as friendly as possible, "So where is she?" Mommy Eri didn't respond, and she acted as if there was some small thing that was incredibly fascinating on her side of the bar.

Eri had dismissed Kiriko Wada from her job three days before. It was difficult to do, especially since Eri was afraid it would kill business. She wanted the Eden to stand out and Kiriko Wada made it do just that. The girl had excellent manners like so many other girls but there was something about her face. Mommy Eri thought she looked Eurasian. She was hoping the girl's round, hazel eyes and her naturally wavy hair would prove to be attractive to the Americans.

Sure, there were other local girls like Naomi Fujimoto and Shiori Ando. They were pretty, but not distinctly so, and their English was better than Kiriko's. Anyway, they would never work at Eden. They knew where the money was. They worked in brothels nearby where they earned ten times more than they could at her bar.

What an agonizing decision to let Kiriko go, but it was the right one, the only one. Something happened when she was heading home after closing.

Chitose's streets are laid out in a regular grid pattern. The area is as flat. That night a full moon whitened a murky sky. No one was around. From a dark space between two buildings, a human-sized figure wrapped in animal skins and fur appeared. It moved toward her. She couldn't discern its face. The farmers outside Chitose are simple people, not at all self-conscious; they improvised all sorts of get-ups to protect themselves against the cold, but nothing ever as strange as the figure's coverings. In addition, they wouldn't be in town at that hour.

The figure seemed to know exactly who she was. The closer it got to her, the more animal it became—or so it seemed to her. She was sure when it was three feet away it raised a *paw* to strike her. She shrieked and ran away—there were patches of snow and jagged clumps of frozen slush underfoot—she almost slipped and fell. While she hurried away, not once did she look back to see if she was being followed—she was too scared. Only after scurrying and panting a half a mile, then opening her door, did she peek back into the darkness. She saw nothing.

Once inside her house she continued to shake in terror. Would it appear at her door, force it open, violate her, tear her to pieces?

And, what *was* it?

Gradually it came to her: the figure was the Ainu man, Shigeru Akiyama.

From time to time you'd see him in town buying supplies. He lived in the woods, alone in a cottage; the terrain rose steadily to the northwest of Chitose; his cottage was on a patch of level ground up there. He'd been in town a lot more since the earthquake. People figured his house had been damaged.

What was he doing in Chitose so late into the night? Why had he approached her? Had he intended to do her harm? He certainly was unkempt. His long, unruly hair and his abundant beard—Japanese men don't have such beards—all swaddled in savage coverings.

It had to be something to do with Kiriko. He must know she'd hired her to work in her bar. But when she hired her, she didn't know she'd been born up in that cottage, that Akiyama was her father, that the Wada family had adopted her when she was seven. If she'd known those things, she wouldn't have taken her on.

Mommy Eri's heart pounded. What a shock to realize that crazy Akiyama knew that his natural daughter had been under her employ. One would think the ties between them had been cut. Maybe—she could only conjecture—he wanted to harm her because he thought she hired Kiriko to work as a prostitute in her bar. But no, he did not understand. Kiriko was just a bar hostess, a waitress.

She felt that Akiyama had touched her, even though he hadn't *physically*. What a repulsive creature he was. You could be dirtied, corrupted, by being close to him.

That night, tossing and turning, she couldn't make up her mind. When morning broke, she knew she had no alternative. Her life was in danger so long as the girl worked in her bar. She thought back and saw the facts as they were; she'd dismissed from her mind the reasons why Kiriko's features were as they were: the sheen of her hair, her naturally long eyelashes, her eyes—why had Eri blocked out acknowledging that Kiriko was a pretty Ainu girl? And she should've imagined Kiriko could be related to Akiyama—the Ainu people in Chitose were a tiny minority—they were all probably related to each other in one way or another. What a stupid idea it was to hire her! So much for exotic looks! But so many Japanese girls are so plain...

Mommy Eri stubbed out her cigarette. It wasn't possible any longer to avoid the two young men. She needed their business. She glanced over at Lloyd. He was safer to speak to. She made a stab at conversation, asking him, "Keeping warm at the base?"

"Yeah," he responded curtly.

She went on in a halting voice, "Working hard?"

"As always, each of us does the work of four."

"That's an earthquake for you," she retorted slowly.

"It's got nothing to do with the earthquake. The base only needed a week to recover from that."

"We're understaffed," Bob broke in. Yes, the men were pressed to do mountains of clerical work as fast as they could in overheated offices with the majors and sergeant majors ignoring they were inexperienced at their jobs.

She finally felt forced to address Bob. She lied, saying, "It's good to see you."

In truth, it was only good to see people in her bar buying drinks.

"It would be better to see Kiriko," Bob said emphatically.

She flinched at the sound of the girl's name. It was unsettling to be spoken to by a young man who showed no respect for his elders. Her face flushed when he pressed on and said, "You haven't answered my question."

She rephrased his confrontational words in her mind. She thought to herself: No, it would *not* be better to see Kiriko.

Bob pulled his legs in from their stretched position. "Don't know why she's not here!" He shifted himself in his chair, sat up more and practically sang the words, "If she's not coming back, it's your loss!" He rocked his heels underneath him a couple of times.

"Excuse me, please," Mommy Eri said. She pretended there was something to do near the back door that led to the alley. She slinked off down the short passage, opened the wooden door and went out. The vapor from her lungs hung in the air in front of her. Her breathing was uneven. She was seen by a *tanuki*—a small Japanese mammal, a carnivore—it looks like an American raccoon, eats like one, but the two species aren't closely related. (Many Japanese believed *tanuki* had shapeshifting abilities and they'd take on quasi-human traits. To her, they were just pests.) The *tanuki* was going through garbage. Once it saw her it scampered away. No surprise it was hungry. Likely it had emerged recently from a winter's sleep *(tanuki,* unlike raccoons, hibernate during the winter).

Eri stood in the alley until she couldn't take the cold and damp anymore.

Back in the bar, Bob said loudly, "Strange."

Eri pretended she didn't hear.

The music on the phonograph had ended. There was silence.

It was a good bet that nobody else was going to come into the bar that night. Yes, indeed, few G.I.s would come into town that night.

The boys ordered another round. Sure, Kiriko wasn't there but the weather put them off from going to any other bar.

Eri got them another two beers and resumed her pantomime, putting records on the turntable. The young men sipped their beers and looked around, each seeing mental pictures of how different it was when Kiriko was there.

At one moment when it was taking Eri some time to figure out which record to put on next Bob said, "Game starts in three and a half hours."

An afternoon game between the Brooklyn Dodgers and the Boston Red Sox was due to begin at 1 p.m. It would be broadcast live on the radio, at 2 a.m. Japanese time.

"I'm tired," Lloyd said. "I don't know if I can stay up."

"It's only the Red Sox. They'll get beat again," Bob said smugly. "The Dodgers are great. They can play anybody, and I'm interested."

"The Giants!" Lloyd blurted out wistfully. He ran through the players' names as if they were spirits from an enchanted land: "Willie Mays, Whitely Lockman, Al Dark, Don Mueller, Bobby Thomson."

Bob countered proudly with his own set of Dodger heroes: "Roy Campanella, Gil Hodges, Jackie Robinson, Pee Wee Reese." He needled his buddy. "The Giants can't make up their minds. As excellent as they are, there's always something wrong. Like, they can't get enough fans to come see them. Or one-year spring training camp is in Phoenix and the next it's in Florida!"

The world was paradise so long as the young men could immerse themselves in baseball. Six months before, the Dodgers and Giants had played each other in a three-game series to break the tie between them to decide who would go onto the World Series. Those playoffs produced some of the most dramatic moments in baseball history, including the "Shot Heard Around the World" in which a skinny outfielder, Bobby Thomson, hit a home run that got the pennant for the Giants in the game's last moments. The tall, self-effacing "Staten Island Scot" hit big, with Willie Mays on deck.

Lloyd Kelso heard the celebrated home run live on radio while hunched in a freezing combat bunker on a hill in Korea. Disobeying orders, knowing the sound could tell the enemy exactly where he was and at any moment a grenade might blow him to pieces, he had the radio turned up loud enough for him to be able to hear every word. Who would've thought that Thomson would smack it like that—sure, he was a pro, but he wasn't a star player, was the least likely one you'd think would hit a game-changer. When he thought about it, he could almost hear the ball crack off the bat. It was the most euphoric moment in Lloyd Kelso's life. He wanted to jump up and cry out in joy. But the stench and the darkness surrounding him told him it could be fatal to do that. Then a mortar shell whistled over him and he turned the radio set off.

Mommy Eri was relieved the soldiers were discussing something that had nothing to do with her or Kiriko. She put on "Jezebel" by Frankie Laine. It was rambunctious music and the soldiers liked it. After "Jezebel" she only played "raucous" records she couldn't stand, like Rosemary Clooney's "Come On-a My House" and Les Paul-Mary Ford records. She followed that with Dinah Shore's comic "Sweet Violets". The boys ordered two whiskeys for the road.

Eri fantasized that even though the bar no longer had the young Ainu girl's appealing eyes, the boys were happy to stay right where they were.

The two soldiers downed their shots, put on their coats, and left—with only Lloyd saying good-bye to Eri. Immediately she became nervous that they'd pass the word on about Kiriko. Once they were gone, she slid over to the player and put on her favorite record one more time.

They say that love's a word...

She felt defeated.

The coldness walloped the two young men when they stepped outside. It was like walking into the interior of a vast air balloon filled with frigid, lung-stopping gas. The freeze had solidified the slush and mud, creating a kind of pitted skating rink for them to fall on. Shimizu was desolate. There was no sign of soldiers going in or coming out of any of the other small bars.

Planks served as sidewalks. They were laid down in parallel pairs, none too flat or level. They weren't even easy to negotiate when sober. Fernandez and Kelso walked, slipped, and grabbed at timber poles (that carried electrical lines) spaced at irregular intervals along the streets.

A couple of minutes before they got to the lot where they'd parked their car (it wasn't their car; they'd borrowed it from a friendly sergeant on base) a figure appeared ahead of them on their right, near the side of a wooden building. Lloyd saw it first. It stood motionless in the glimmering haze, watching them. Were it not for vapor in the air near its mouth, it might have gone unnoticed. Next to its body, leaning against a shabby wall was... some sort of long stick.

Lloyd became agitated as soon as he saw the figure which was covered with layers of hide and fur. He believed the figure was a man—and the man was a dangerous threat to them. Lloyd was troubled that he couldn't see the man's hands and forearms. Possibly they concealed a gun, a knife, or a grenade.

The figure stood there still, almost like an animal hoping a predator wouldn't notice it. Bob saw it but wasn't fazed. He was soused; a lone figure in the night couldn't cause any trouble now. It was peacetime Japan. But then he noticed fear on Lloyd's face. So he spoke up, muttering, "What's going on, buddy?"

Kelso thought to himself, there's no time to tell Bob. The man is going to kill us.

Kelso instinctively reached for the knife on his belt. But his hand wouldn't move and there was no knife there anyway.

Shocked that his hand wouldn't move, a deep moan of dread escaped Lloyd's chest. He glanced over to the spot where the figure's frosty breath was seeping out. A fog closed in on Lloyd. Bob Fernandez drunkenly guided his friend to keep him moving but Lloyd was slowing down, getting ready to stop. Bob moved closer to him and asked, struggling to keep his voice down, "What's the matter, Lloyd?"

Lloyd's vocal cords were paralyzed. Bob could only search Lloyd's face for a response that wasn't there.

Lloyd's eyes darted around looking for somewhere to take cover. There wasn't one. He grimaced. We have no way to defend ourselves. We're going to die, he told himself.

Bob was smart enough to know that you don't feed panic at a time like this, and in any case, he'd seen Lloyd act strangely before. So, Fernandez played the steady, unflappable one.

"Keep your eyes on the ground, Lloyd, or you'll slip on the ice."

Kelso's throat loosened just enough to groan, "Over there. He's got a weapon and he's going to kill us!"

Vehicles large and small had shifted the surface of the dirt street into furrows and crowns, and at night a nervous young G.I. who had put too much away, might see the frozen humps and valleys in the road and think they covered up a curdled sea creature or an unexploded artillery shell.

Bob assumed Lloyd was hallucinating that there was a

threat a short distance away.

"Just keep looking at your feet, Lloyd. If there's anything going on around here, it's no business of ours."

"That man. Over there," Lloyd motioned with his head in the direction of the strange figure in the shadows. Bob refused to look.

"It's no business of ours. Let's go." Bob gently nudged his friend.

There was pain in Lloyd's voice when he whispered, "Don't you see, he's going to kill us!"

Bob was unwavering, "We're going to the car and then we're driving back to post."

"He won't let us. He's here for us."

"He doesn't know us, Lloyd."

"He does, he does." Lloyd felt a sharp ache in his chest. The soreness in his throat traveled down to his heart. "Can't you see he's not a civilian? He's got something under his coat."

As a newly arrived recruit in Korea, Lloyd Kelso could only look on as police and military authorities, selectively stopped and searched townspeople and refugees. Sometimes they found guns or explosives beneath civilian clothes. Some of those caught were Communist combatants who intermingled with the crowds. One bright July afternoon Lloyd was walking down a road when fifty yards away a grenade went off in a thick crowd. It was a suicide attack. Twenty people were killed.

Soon after that Lloyd was ordered to the Jamestown Line, notorious for its trench warfare. Three months later, on his twenty-first birthday, he was the last soldier left alive in his trench on the side of a hill. For a month, alone, he endured bombs shaking the ground and gunfire rattling through the air. He survived on the cans of tuna fish the Army dropped to him. With nothing else to eat, his body began to fall apart; his gums bled and slowly turned black.

Now, on this wretched street, in this terrifying situation,

his gums started to bleed from the stress.

Kelso's panic continued with no sign of diminishing. Feeling the guilt of having survived Korea when so many of his buddies hadn't, he exclaimed at a hoarse, higher pitch: "It's my time now!"

His face contorted. "I don't want to die here!" he cried. "We don't know *anybody* here!"

Fernandez stayed calm. "What do you need, Lloyd? Tell me what to do."

"You can't do anything. We need to take cover and we can't."

"We'll get out of here, don't you worry."

Kelso's body tensed more. "I don't want to die. I don't want to die!" He jerked his head far to his right and looked back in desperation at the unstable ground they'd already covered. Go back there, he thought, was that an option?

Bob Fernandez tried to summon a soothing voice, "You made it. You're alive. You're out of there."

Kelso wept. "Frank isn't. Bruce isn't. Jack isn't. Alden, too." Then he screamed in alarm, "My hands! Where are my hands? I can't feel my hands!"

Fernandez didn't know what to do. He started to tear up, too, feeling what his friend was going through. He struggled against his tears. "Listen, last year was one of the greatest years in the history of baseball! This year will be even better. You watch. Hang in there, you'll see. Willie Mays is getting more a-*mazing* with each game. The Giants will win the series this time!"

Doom gripped Lloyd Kelso. He knew he was targeted. He'd be dead any second.

Fernandez was so boozed up his spinal cord took over the thinking from his brain. There was no other conceivable action that might work: he slugged Kelso hard in the gut. Maybe it would stun him out of his current state.

Lloyd Kelso crumpled, fell to the ground, and wept twice as much. It was awful and impossible to resist—Bob

Fernandez broke out in full tears. When he saw Kelso's pale face was slimy with blood darkening it from the cleft beneath his nose down to the tip of his chin, his knees buckled. He collapsed on top of his friend. He felt sick. The alien landscape spun around him. He'd gotten off easy in Korea compared to Lloyd. Man, the horrible things people do to each other, he thought, as he glued himself to Kelso as if to safeguard them both and to try to stop it all from spinning.

Between Kelso's spasms of crying, Fernandez muttered, "Hang in there, buddy. Don't give up. We'll make it."

Bob Fernandez spread over Lloyd Kelso like he'd been tackled. He repeated over and over, "I'm sorry, Lloyd. I'm sorry." There was no relief in sight. Neither soldier could vomit.

How frightening it is to be a man.

The two G.I.s passed out. For how many minutes, it was not known. When they came to, they were numb and needed warmth fast. Bob pulled himself off Lloyd. The two men staggered to their feet as soldiers do after surviving an artillery explosion. The blood around Lloyd's mouth had dried. It looked like he'd eaten a freshly killed animal.

Neither one of them looked over to the spot where the mysterious figure had been standing. The parking lot was only forty yards ahead. Lloyd grabbed Bob's coat sleeve and held it. They were watchful with each step.

The Chrysler Windsor sedan they came in was the only vehicle left in the lot. Fernandez climbed into the driver's side. After he pulled the choke and turned the ignition key the motor belts squeaked, and the engine roared to life. The chill inside was as bad as that outside, and ice crystals covered the windshield. Kelso got in the passenger side and sat there silently, too stunned to shiver, hanging his head down. After Fernandez turned on the fan and the heat full blast, he hung his head down, as well. They waited in that position for the car to warm up. They sat there in a daze, grieving. They grieved for what they'd done, for their buddies who didn't make it, and the innocence they'd lost.

When the Chrysler was ready to go Bob said, "All right, buddy, let's get on back to base." He put the car in gear and lurched it forward.

CHAPTER 2

An hour later a passenger train with a steam locomotive at the front pulled up to Platform 2 at Chitose Station, the last stop on the line. It was the final train of the day; only four passengers were aboard. The station, a half mile from Shimizu, was dimly lit. A squiggly network of steel rails took up most of the rail yard, which was dark. By day, these tracks served trains coming from Sapporo (where the factories were) in the north, from Muroran (where the coal mines were) in the south and from Ashagawa (where the sawmills were) in the east.

Noboru Nakano, a young man of seventeen, was the only rider in the last car of the train. He'd fallen asleep. He worked in a coal mine in Muroran. When the train's engineer looked out his window at the three men leaving the train, he assumed they were all that was left of his passengers. The locomotive's fireman had the same idea. The train had no conductor in the evenings—riders bought tickets on the honor system.

The two men shut the train down, left the driver's cab, and glancing at the cars to make sure all the doors were closed, walked over to the stationmaster's office. The stationmaster locked up the station and the three railway workers left together.

In the rail yard, patches of ice solidified on the rail ties and their gravel beds.

A strange figure wrapped in hide and fur picked his way over the network of tracks, not casting a shadow. He used a pole to help support himself as he advanced, with a single mind, to his purpose: to get inside a train car while it was still warm.

The long pole he carried was an Ainu bear-spear. There were no bears in town. But the spear wasn't only a useful walking stick—it could be used as protection against aggressive spirits and demons.

The man began carrying the spear at night soon after the earthquake struck, five and a half weeks earlier. It had damaged his cottage outside town, forcing him to sleep elsewhere. An invasion of evil spirits, too, had come with the physical destruction. There were times he visited his property, but he would never go into the house.

Akiyama steadied himself and climbed up from the yard to Platform 2. He opened the door of the last car. His face flushed when it met the warm air. He shut the door behind him. All was pitch dark. He took off his gloves and felt his way with his naked hands into the aisle and shuffled slowly down it to reach the mid-section, the warmest part of the car.

To his dismay he heard a voice in his head, and it told him there was a ghost present. It told him directly to his left was where the demonic ghost was pretending to be asleep. It was a malignant spirit; it could easily kill Akiyama. If it woke up and he wanted to survive, he would have to outwit it— quickly. This sudden information was distressful to him. He was very tired. The only thing he could do was bring his body to a halt.

Unconsciously, he let his left hand hover and touch… a padded *something*… a shoulder?—at least that was the thought after it came to him a moment later—the shoulder of a demon, he suspected. He took his hand away carefully, in fear, but while doing it grazed the cap the demon was wearing. Between his naked fingers he felt something that had the consistency of coal dust—he'd gotten the stuff on his hand when it had touched the cap. That was bad. It meant this demon lived in the underworld where coal was plentiful.

Usually, the gods remained below and concerned

themselves with governing in the Afterlife. But humans above—on this earth—had been disrespectful of the divine order and it had upset them. It was clear to Akiyama they'd sent a being from the depths of the earth, to mete out punishment, to teach reverence. A large fissure caused by the earthquake was its pathway. Humans would be dealt harsh justice—they would pay for their disrespect. The havoc and suffering the quakes caused them already weren't enough.

Ah, Akiyama so well understood the reasons for the gods' wrath! However, he, a human, would not accept being chastised without at least first putting up a good fight—he *must* do this—he shouldn't be blamed for it—after all, the instinct of self-preservation is in all creatures.

The thing was, you couldn't kill a demon, ghost or spirit. They could only be frightened, or you could run away from them.

While Akiyama struggled to think exactly what he might do, the voice speaking in his head was joined by another—and then another. The voices grew in number and got louder but they didn't offer him advice. What were the voices saying? It was gibberish for the most part. He could make out only a few words. The underlying violence was plain.

He needed to act. I could make a wound in the demon, he thought. It would nurse it while I make my escape.

The Ainu man grasped the shank of his bear spear just below the blade. His slash skimmed the demon with injurious effect, it seemed. He tried not to shiver in fright. This was an awesome move on his part; it was a strike against a spirit from the Other World. It was bold. Unnerved, he hurried out of the dark train car, his body tense with distress.

Noboru Nakano felt warm liquid slowly seeping from inside his neck. In his dream the calm, warming syrup was welcome because he felt cold. His dream was making him suspicious though—there was an indescribable sensation that came along with it. Reflexively, he slowly woke up, needing to know more about the strange feeling he was experiencing. He passed through a limbo of intense vagueness and opened his eyes. It was completely dark. He was blind; he could not perceive where he was.

His arms were crossed against his chest. One leg was folded underneath him and the other dangled, almost touching the floor. He was half-curled up on a bench of some kind, the air was still and cold. He felt the bulk of a wool coat around him. As he became more conscious it occurred to him that he must be indoors, not outdoors. Then he realized he was in a public place. Fuzzily, he recollected boarding the train for home. He supposed that he must have fallen asleep, and no one noticed he didn't leave the train at its last stop. He wanted to shiver but fortunately he didn't. Instead, he yawned but immediately had to catch himself—opening his jaw brought with it a bolt of hair-raising pain. His eyes widened in alarm: something was terribly wrong.

He asked himself: what is this warm liquid? He raised his arm from his chest and made his hand touch his neck gently. The liquid was sticky. He put his fingers to his nose. He couldn't smell it, but he knew it had to be blood. Why was there blood on his neck? Drowsiness hadn't fully left him yet. That was good, otherwise he might have moved too quickly.

He touched his neck again, lightly. Yes, it was wet and sticky there. There was no mistake about it. He then realized the warm liquid was oozing over his collar and down onto his coat.

He carefully unfolded his limbs. He gently rose. His hands guided him down the aisle past the seats of the car. He reached the door, his head throbbing. He feared his neck was throbbing, too. When he turned the handle of the door, he felt blood drip down on his hand.

He stepped down from the door and onto the station platform. His mind refused to feel the pain coming from his neck. He held one of his hands on the spot where most of the blood was flowing. His back and other parts of his body felt numb--this raised his degree of alarm to a new level.

He could see more now that he was out of the train. He looked over at the station office. No lights were on. It was closed. He'd have to find help elsewhere. His ears were ringing. He recognized it was imperative to leave the platform and get to the police booth that was adjacent to the rail station. It would be open—it never closed.

Noboru had grown up in Chitose and was used to what a late freeze could do. With experienced wariness, he ambled, in as straight a line as possible, over the frozen rail ties and the lumpy ice. He reached the police booth in less than two minutes.

The lone policeman on duty was seated, reading a newspaper. He lowered it and glanced up over the countertop that separated him from the rest of the world. He found himself looking at a young man with a gash in his neck, wearing a wool coat whose front was drenched with blood. The officer's hand automatically reached for the phone on the shelf just below the countertop.

CHAPTER 3

Noboru remained unconscious until noon. The doctors didn't know what to make of the wound. A blade caused it, but they didn't know what kind.

The Sheriff's Office started investigating at the first light of day. Police officers combed the railway tracks and rail yard. They found Noboru's blood where he'd stepped from the train and followed its faint trail to the police booth. No evidence was found of who assaulted him. They only saw human and a few dog footprints leading nowhere in particular, and they were melting. They dusted all handles of the train cars—and everywhere else a human hand might touch—for fingerprints. Since many people took the train, fingerprints on top of smudged prints, with glove prints into the bargain, were available for their confusion. After they got the phone call from the hospital saying the boy was unlikely to be of any help for at least a day, the police were left with little or nothing to go on. A mysterious, late-night attack with no witnesses confronted them; they decided that releasing information about the incident to the press would only frighten Chitose's residents. They needed to wait and interview the boy.

The driver of the train that night, Takuma Hara, was beside himself with guilt, knowing he was entirely at fault for not making sure the train was empty. Hara expressed to the police that he wished to kill himself—he was quite serious on that point. But before he did it, he wanted his employer, the Hokkaido Railway Company, to fire him.

Hara had been with the company for many years; his employers liked him. It took an official from the company, Mr. Ototaro Hasegawa, to come up with a plan acceptable to the poor man: he would fire Hara if he would promise not to take his life. Mr. Hara promised.

He was fired and a day later the company re-hired him, but it was a desk job. Though Hara wasn't pleased with the outcome, his family was.

The sun made feeble attempts to shine that day in late April. Chitose was cold and sooty. The ice was thawing again. Walkways were slippery and muddy. American planes droned and helicopters whirred above.

Mommy Eri had an errand to run before she opened the bar: her clock had been shaken off the mantel by the earthquake and was being repaired in a shop in Shinonome ward. It was ready for her to pick up. Eri set out over Shinbashi Dori bridge to get it.

Once she was inside the clock shop, she bowed to the proprietors, Mr. and Mrs. Sugawara—he in a simple dark kimono, she in a brighter one; both were diminutive and in late middle age. The closing of the shop's door completely banished the noise of the outside world.

Thirty clocks of different sizes and shapes ticked away. They were throughout the room, on various shelves, ticking in sync in various groups. The pitch of each clock was different. It seemed as though the walls hid insects that had banded together to produce a soft concert of metronomic languor.

Mr. Sugawara took Eri's clock from the shelf behind him. He turned it over in both hands, explaining what had been damaged and repaired, and then, effortlessly, the clock moved from his hands into those of his wife. Before Mrs. Sugawara wrapped it in old newspaper she apologized profusely for the delay. There'd been so many clocks to fix since the earthquake. She and her husband had never been so busy.

As she finished folding the paper around the clock her husband reached over with twine between his fingers to help tie the package up.

There was gossip. What would a visit to a neighborhood shop be without hearing the latest?

Like the Sugawara Clock Repair Shop, Chitose Hospital was also in the small ward of Shinonome. Mrs. Sugawara's cousin worked in the hospital as a receptionist. She'd just visited the shop during her lunch break. Confidentiality in Chitose Hospital was selectively practiced. When something as unusual as what happened to Noboru occurred, discretion not only went by the wayside. Word of the patient and his or her circumstances escaped quickly.

"It was a cut. A long, thin one," Mrs. Sugawara said.

"All the way from one side of his neck to the other," her husband added for effect.

Mommy Eri gasped.

Mr. Sugawara continued, "A straight line."

Mrs. Sugawara said that after stitching the wound, the doctors told the boy's family he'd survive, that they were hoping the scar wouldn't be too bad. With the mention of stitches, Mommy Eri smelled the light odor of clock repair oil for the first time since she came in the shop. It smelled like oil used on a sewing machine.

"But how was he cut, with a knife or a razor?" Eri queried.

No one knew for sure, the couple answered.

Mommy Eri was worried. The idea of a midnight attack… Chitose was not a violent place. There were dozens of bars and many servicemen, but her place was practically empty last night and the town was quiet. She declared, "How could somebody from Chitose do such a thing! Do the police have any idea who did it?"

The Sugawaras replied in one voice, "We don't know."

Maybe the assailant wasn't from Chitose. Maybe it was an American soldier—this wasn't a far-fetched idea. But what people in town didn't know was the Chitose police had spoken with Camp Chitose and all U.S. personnel were on post by curfew, 11 p.m., and the attack occurred sometime after the train pulled into the station at 11:43.

Mr. and Mrs. Sugawara mentioned the name of the boy. He wasn't known to either them or Mommy Eri—though Eri did know a *Toshi* Nakano—this she kept to herself. She hoped the crime would be solved quickly and all matters surrounding it would vanish like old, forgotten news. If Chitose were seen as a dangerous place, soldiers would stay on base more, business would drop off. It would be the end, she thought to herself. By and large people were orderly and good. They got on with their business. As for Toshi Nakano, he was a delinquent, and the less said the better.

Eri carefully took the package containing the clock from the counter. The couple bowed and thanked her repeatedly. She said goodbye, bowed and left the shop.

Imagine, in Chitose, Mommy Eri thought. There's somebody who would attack an innocent young man, nearly killing him. An instant later she pictured Akiyama in animal skins, lurking in the cold night. Catching her breath, she thought, *Shigeru Akiyama!* Her heart skipped a beat. Should she go to the police to tell them about her encounter with him a week before? Yes, she decided. He could be the one responsible for the attack!

There was a telephone booth just over the bridge, not far from Bar Eden. Mommy Eri's call was brief. She said someone had told her about last night's attack; that she'd seen the Ainu man, Shigeru Akiyama, on the street not long before it happened—which wasn't true because she'd seen him the week before, not the previous night. She told the police he'd acted strangely and was aggressive toward her. She refused to give her name—she knew that Toshi Nakano dealt in Chitose's black market and if Noboru was related to Toshi, she didn't want to be named in an investigation that might ultimately involve him.

Kiriko heard the front door close. She listened as her aunt took off her boots in the entryway and hung up her coat. They each called out hello, Kiriko referring to her aunt as "mom." Satomi was a switchboard operator at the local phone company and her workplace was close enough for her to come home for lunch. It was just past noon.

In those days, every telephone call needed an operator for it to be completed, someone who manually inserted the phone plug into the board. Often the operator caught parts of people's conversations.

Kiriko's aunt had heard about the attack.

Satomi padded into the kitchen softly, saw the lunch Kiriko had prepared, and stood a few feet behind the girl as Kiriko washed the pot that had been used to cook the rice. "I'm afraid I have some bad news, dear," Satomi whispered. Though she was reluctant, she felt there was no other choice but to get right to the point.

Kiriko set down the pot and turned around to her aunt whose kind face was long and full of care. Knowing she was about to hear unwelcome news, Kiriko couldn't look her aunt straight in the eyes.

"Last night, Noboru Nakano fell asleep on the last train. He didn't leave when it shut down at the platform. Somebody came into the car he was in and attacked him."

Kiriko had met Noboru when she was ten years old and had come to live with Satomi and her husband, Kenshin Wada. The Nakanos occupied a spartan, small wooden house, like the Wadas. Kenshin Wada was a junior manager at Chitose's only department store.

Kiriko said nothing. She avoided looking at her aunt and waited for her to say more.

"His neck got cut pretty badly," she added. "It's serious but the doctors at the hospital say he'll fully recover."

The only thing Satomi was glad about was that she, not

someone else, had been the first one to break the news to Kiriko. The girl and Noboru had been childhood playmates. It was a diverse neighborhood that included newcomers to town (like the Nakano family which had moved from Osaka), established Chitose working class families, and a few families of mixed Japanese-Ainu blood—though if somebody was part Ainu, they didn't mention it.

After the girl reached puberty the two spent far less time together. It was normal. There was no decrease in affection between the two. It was just that the sexes were more separated.

Kiriko was as much shocked to hear that Noboru had been attacked, as she was to hear of an act so violent occurring in Chitose. Until now, the recent earthquake was the scariest thing she'd ever experienced in town.

Noboru! Who would attack *him?* Her mind flashed back to the last time she'd seen him: it was a few weeks ago. He had his work clothes on. She knew he'd gotten a job in Muroran. He was on his way to catch a train there.

Kiriko's stomach sank. She asked, "How did it happen? Who did it?"

"The police are investigating. That's all that's known."

Satomi had been protective of Kiriko since she moved in. Kiriko had arrived from one dire situation and was being thrust into another that had its own set of serious complications. For example, many Japanese parents wouldn't let their children play with other children who had more than just a trace of Ainu blood in them. Aunt Satomi, who was half-Ainu, passed as Japanese.

Kiriko came to her speaking like a child younger than her real age and lacking education. Satomi herself tutored her for two years until she could keep up with her class. Satomi was aware that the girl could be made fun of, be an easy target of prejudice, and be shunned.

There were some things Satomi could do about Kiriko's appearance. Her hair, for one. Every Sunday evening, she would pull, comb, and brush Kiriko's hair. She would bind it overnight so it would be straight for her week at school.

When Kiriko arrived at the Wada home—which was childless for reasons the couple did not know—she was shy but inquisitive. When she first asked questions like, "Why do some people whisper when they talk about Ainu people?" and "What are Ainu people?" she got brief, unsatisfying replies. It pulled at Satomi's heart she couldn't answer in any other way.

Satomi was sorry for Noboru Nakano but also sorry about the effect the attack on him was going to have on Kiriko. Enough had gone wrong for her lately with Eri Maeda's dismissing her from work at Bar Eden, a job Satomi regarded at first with apprehension but was later persuaded to allow her to take because she could practice English there.

Satomi was convinced Kiriko's dismissal had to do with her being Ainu. Three days ago, the girl went over to The Swan—another bar in Shimizu—to see if they were hiring. She thought since she had some experience as a hostess, why not ask around at other places. It looked like The Swan might try her out.

"I would like to go see him," Kiriko spoke softly to her aunt, still dumbstruck at the news.

"They'll let us know when it's possible to visit Noboru," her aunt said, adding sympathetically, "Poor boy."

Aunt Satomi had never had many concerns about safety in Chitose after dark. Now, she was worried. She wasn't about to voice them aloud. She only said to her adopted daughter, "It's terrible. Terrible things happen sometimes. I'm sure this'll be the first and last time."

"Auntie, I can't eat lunch. I don't feel hungry." Kiriko was trying to calm herself.

"I understand." Satomi reached out and held the girl's hand for a moment.

"But I'll have lunch, *musume san,*" Satomi said thoughtfully.

Satomi's years as a phone operator had made it easier for her to deal with some of the harsher realities of life.

CHAPTER 4

Akiyama spent the rest of the night scrambling in the intense cold, in the hilly land west of Chitose that climbed steadily. Sometimes patches of lingering snow slowed him down.

After getting to where the forest was level and snowless and the trees were sparse and grew low, he set his sights on reaching a shallow, teal-colored pond. In ten minutes he was there. Low evergreen trees and spindly, leafless deciduous ones wreathed the odd-colored body of water. The mud at the shoreline of the hot spring pool was marked with bird tracks and bore evidence of visits by many small animals which also left their feces behind. Vapor rose from the water and released a sulfurous odor.

Akiyama laid his belongings on top of a large rock. He took off every piece of clothing he had on and slipped into the cloudy pungent water at an edge of the pool where the water was deepest. At first it felt dangerously hot. Then he fell asleep for four hours and woke up, his body tingling.

His mouth was dry, and he feared he might pass out quickly again. Pulling himself out of the reeking pool, feeling stimulated but also intensely thirsty, he went to his belongings and drank from his canteen. Then he went back to sit, still naked, half in the pool and half on the bank.

Steam surrounded him—it hid the day's leaden sky. His mind drifted back to the time when his son was still alive.

He'd only received a single letter from Fumito, who served in the Japanese infantry in the equatorial Pacific during World War II. In the letter, which Akiyama had to have read to him, Fumito said it was very hot and humid where he was, that he was sleepwalking through the days. One day was just as the next, though it rained more on some than others. He told his father that people in Hokkaido have never seen anything like the twenty-four-hour-a-day heat he was enduring. His stomach was often sick from it. He was always light-headed. One way Hokkaido people might envisage such cruel weather was to image steam on a very hot day permanently wrapped around you no matter where you went.

To enslave, to torture a boy like that, and to make him do battle at the same time, Akiyama lamented. At home on their native soil of Hokkaido, the Ainu were harassed and maltreated. Then the Japanese expanded their empire, and another abomination was laid on: they forced young Ainu to fight *their* war, far away, overseas. The Ainu had remonstrated for centuries, "The Japanese use us whenever they like. When they don't use us, we mean nothing to them."

"Cunning Japanese!" Akiyama mused bitterly—this was an invective the Ainu often used. Akiyama had heard Ainu elders say it thousands of times… "The cunning Japanese, our only choice is to die or become one of their henchmen. They trick our men into filling our stomachs with women's rice when once, all men had to use their wits and spears to negotiate with our animal cousins. Now we're sick on this rice, our minds are dulled. We live without physical power, so we are prey to disease and extinction."

Fumito had never gotten a proper burial. The Ainu custom was to dress the dead in their best clothes, which were, as part of the funeral ritual, carefully torn or cut. The body was then laid out next to a fire. Fuji, the fire goddess, was first among the Ainu gods. It is this same Fuji that the Japanese named *their* sacred mountain after—and that mountain is on Japan's main island, a mere eighty-five miles southwest of Tokyo.

A second, better life awaited the deceased in the Other

World. But Fumito's body had never been returned. Akiyama's son's spirit still roamed this world. It roamed in rags and was greatly distressed.

Akiyama rose from the bank and crept over to the bulky flat-topped rock. All his belongings—deerskins, furs, his spear, and a loosened bundle—were spread over it. He slowly dressed himself.

His family was scattered, gone. His parents died just after he turned sixteen. His sister Akemi married a Japanese and the husband forbade her to see him. Nine years ago his wife died. Soon after that, Kiriko was taken away by a couple he didn't know—but her mother knew them vaguely. Sometime after that, Fumito died.

There was another loss that Akiyama sustained which modern people can't grasp because there's nothing in their experience like it. The loss occurred even before he was born. It was a grave loss for all the Ainu of his clan and one that had taken place long ago, in 1889. In that year the last living wolf in Hokkaido was killed. Japanese authorities had succeeded in finally eradicating the whole species from the island, by providing poison—strychnine—to the island's Japanese-settler dairy farmers. The farmers laced venison or rabbit with the poison, placed the meat in steel-jaw traps and the wolves took the bait and died. (Japan isn't the sole country that's undertaken a campaign to rid itself of *Canus lupis*. In England, that claims that animal husbandry required the extirpation of wolves led to the last wild wolf dying there in 1590.)

What happens when a clan loses all the living specimens of their animal-ancestor? Akiyama was of the Wolf Clan.

In Hokkaido, there are Ainu of the Bear Clan, the Fox Clan, the Fish-Owl Clan, the Clan of the Killer Whale, and others. The members of these clans identify with their totem animals and draw from them great practical and spiritual meanings. When their totem is exterminated, their life is profoundly affected. Life becomes directionless, chaotic.

The effects of the sulfur pool on his body still lingered. He still wasn't completely dressed and had to lean against the cold stone, with his head slumping toward his chest. Strangely though, the vitality sparked inside him by the mineral bath was strong in his eyes.

Cast down, but fully open, his eyes saw hyper-lucidly. He studied in intense detail a beetle crawling on the mud between his feet. He could sense its iron will to move, to persevere. He was also acutely attentive to the creature's smallness, and that the creature was at the mercy of so much around it.

He was unwell. He knew it. But the warmer season meant he could look forward to moving around more freely. He would be able to gain strength, hunt with fewer difficulties and, instead of running away from them, even help the emerging *kamuy* (spirits) from the underworld in some small but important way.

He took his eyes off the beetle and noticed he'd already put his leather leggings on. He took another layer of deerskin off the rock and slipped his arms into it. His eyes dulled. In between the vapor clouds he made out a fuzzy, unnatural landscape, full of confusing shapes. Then, certain patches of the haze took on form. No! Swarms of bad *kamuy* had arrived!

He let out a cry, fearing he was going to be ambushed, and his life would end right there.

The pestilent spirits were hiding in hundreds of flying lice. Their buzzing grew deafening as they came nearer. Once this built to an excruciating crescendo, the noise switched off. Vision replaced it. A hideous formless display mixed unstable colors, decaying green and diabolical brown together; there were intense flashes of blinding light that interrupted this miasma.

Then in an instant the mass of dark colors was just black. He let out a moan of anguish; he knew what was going to happen next.

The mass picked off tiny pieces of flesh from his neck and nose. He clenched his eyelids shut as the bites stung like drops of aconite poison. What a venomous force these spirits were! Were they the same as what was on the train with him? They'd followed him. He was astounded. He shouldn't have been because they were capable of anything. He let loose a scream that sounded like the cry of an animal pierced by pain. Throwing off the top layer of deerskin on his back, he ran to the hot spring pool, and plunged in.

The onslaught started again whenever he raised his head above the surface of the water.

But he couldn't keep his head in the water without coming up for air.

It could not last. This pool was no refuge. He crouched in the water and thought.

He knew he risked his whole body being devoured, but he rose anyway. He shook the water from his hair. He threw his head back; somehow his eyes were able to pierce through the cluster of spirit invaders and see the sky. He shouted up at it, "What must I do?"

The sky was silent long enough for Akiyama to blink twice in agony. Then the sky answered in a voice like that from an old tree, "Summon your ancestor."

The sky did not mean his human ancestor. It meant he must summon his ancestor the Wolf.

Akiyama dragged himself to the bank of the pool, got his footing and stood up straight. With the hot, stinking water dripping off of him, his jaws spread and his eyes grew fierce. "Ah-oowh," he howled, to summon the Wolf.

After he had howled like a wolf as many times as he could, he teetered into the mud at the pool's edge and fell unconscious.

While he was passed out, peaceful flies, not flesh-eating ones, and young bees, flew between the newly blooming wildflowers—yellow *fukujyuso* and pink *katakuri*—in the meadow between the muddy ground and the pine and birch woods.

When Akiyama came to, his hair was dry. At first he didn't know where he was. The left side of his field of vision was blurry. He recalled the evil spirits attacking him. *They* had put the blurriness there. But he and his ancestor had scared them off. He, though slightly wounded, had survived and would heal quickly. He knew this because he felt the protection and the support his spirit animal, the wolf, was providing him.

Once he finished dressing himself, he gathered all his belongings and left the thermal pool.

The farther he got away from it, the better his vision became.

How is it possible that Akiyama howled like a wolf when wolves had been eliminated in Hokkaido years before he'd been born?

Chitose had three movie houses. Since Akiyama could not read, movies could speak to him. He wasn't allowed into two of the theaters because he was scruffy, smelled and besides, he was an Ainu. But the other theater let him in, making him sit up front, as far away as possible from the rest of the customers—the owner profited greatly from him—he was in the black market fur trade.

Both Japanese and American movies were shown in Chitose. The U.S. Occupation authorities had deemed Hollywood Westerns politically safe. They were popular with the Japanese, and Akiyama liked them, too. Also popular were horror movies. Akiyama had seen a few of them. Once he'd stayed through three consecutive showings of *The Werewolf of London*. It was from that movie he learned what a wolf howl was supposed to sound like.

CHAPTER 5

Though Lloyd was worn out from work and still hadn't recovered from the trip to Mommy Eri's two nights before, he did his best to imitate the play-by-play of a baseball radio announcer: *"It's three balls, two strikes. He knows he's got to get a hit to break the tie. He steps up to the plate. He raises his bat. There's the wind-up, the pitch. A curveball? He swings! It's a hit! He starts running …AND HE RUNS DIRECTLY TO THIRD BASE!"*

Bob sat across from Lloyd in the barracks, drinking coffee from a metal cup. "Very funny," he said begrudgingly—because it was clever what Lloyd said, and he didn't like being outshone.

"Glad you think so," Lloyd said quickly, and then wondered to himself, what part of my brain did *that* come from?

Bob couldn't resist adding with a sting, "Hm, actually, I think you should take up calisthenics as a hobby. That would be very funny to watch."

Lloyd was trying to put Bob in a better mood. He was attempting to put himself in a better one, as well. He was drinking orange soda, not coffee, and he wasn't going to have any alcohol tonight. He was going to stay on post. The panic attack he'd had in town still spooked him.

The sun was headed down. You could see the light fading in the window across from their bunks. They were in their barracks. They'd just come back from a full day at their respective offices. The falling temperature outside was doing its best to work its way into their "palace," as they sometimes humorously called it.

Lloyd said: "Maybe you'll find her tonight. You'll see. It's just that Kiriko found a job at another bar that pays more." As he spoke, he realized he shouldn't have brought the subject up.

"Yeah, that would explain why Mommy Eri didn't want to talk about it," Bob retorted brusquely. His eyes were bloodshot from drinking three six packs of beer there in the Quonset, smoking and talking endlessly.

Lloyd knew that only Bob was allowed to broach the subject of Kiriko and then blab on and on about her. Really, Bob knew nothing about the girl. She was his blank canvas on which he could paint anything.

He was going back into town tonight to see if he could find her. That's why he was drinking coffee now. He needed to pull himself together if he was going to make it through the evening. The coffee irritated him. He was aggressive: "By the way, thanks for snoring last night," he said sarcastically to Lloyd. "I really appreciate it."

It was Saturday. Buses ("liberty buses") ran from 5 p.m. until 11. Four hundred and fifty G.I.s were issued passes to go into town. It was important to keep up the soldiers' morale—after all, most of the guys were draftees.

After arriving in town Bob Fernandez had beers in three different bars in quick succession. He was unable to learn anything regarding Kiriko's whereabouts. When he asked after her, he tried to make it sound like small talk, like it wasn't important, that it was just one of many things he happened to be wondering about that night.

As far as he knew, no bar was looking to hire a new hostess, but what did he know? He debated whether to go to The Swan, a haunt which none of his buddies cared for and one he'd never heard anything especially good about.

Bar Tomy was his next stop. Kiriko wasn't going to be there, that was for sure. But if he got drunker, he'd be more at ease showing up alone at The Swan where he knew he wouldn't know a soul.

Even though it was called Bar Tomy, nobody there was named Tomy, or Tommy. Ryuichi Gibo, its owner, was a strong, sturdy fellow from Okinawa. He gained experience working in G.I. bars there. He aimed to own a collection of bars and cocktail lounges in Sapporo, where the economy was big and bustling. Bar Tomy was his start.

Walking into the bar felt at first like entering a basement coat check in a club in New York or Chicago. It was small and cave-like. Then the darkness hit you. There was so little light—you knew there were walls somewhere but you didn't know exactly where they were. The bar could hold around fifteen customers, even though fifteen customers never visited Bar Tomy all at once. The coat check ambience was bolstered by the customers' coming in in overcoats, tracking in mud and feeling through the dark to locate a hook on a clothes tree that they could hang their coats on.

Once your eyes adjusted to the dimness you could see Ryuichi had given the bar a tropical décor, which meant forty bamboo sticks lined up, side by side, glued together to create a wall below the bar counter, with a few brown coconuts hanging together in bunches at the corners. A fake potted plant resembling some unknown species of dwarf palm rounded out the décor. The centerpiece of the bar, aside from the shelves of many different bottles, was a large aquarium that glowed phosphorescently. It received more electric light than anything else in the room. Light gleamed from the tubular bulb under the aquarium's cover to illuminate its occupants—colorful fish, seashells and coral, and a thick thread of spindly seaweed. Oxygen bubbled out of a vertical tube sticking up from the white sandy bottom. The aquarium provided shimmering entertainment that unfolded slowly. You had to fix your gaze at it to see if anything besides the bubbles were moving.

The real draw of Bar Tomy was neither its décor, nor the

sleepy Hawaiian songs that played on the record player, but its selection of different kinds of rum. The other bars in Shimizu only served shots of rum and the rum was always one of the same three brands. Bar Tomy had a dozen different labels, and mixers of various kinds.

Bob Fernandez was uncharacteristically quiet. The darkness probably had something to do with it. Normally after a couple rounds, he'd be jabbering on about one of his favorite topics. Sometimes he'd interrupted the subject of other people's conversations and inject his own. There was one spiel of his he was particularly fond of. It would go something like this: "We got to get beyond ourselves, go out and meet new people. It's dumb to look back. We're young. We grab the future by the throat! We get things we never could ever imagine." He would peer briefly into the distance then continue, "We're experiencing many firsts. This is the first time, for example, that most of us have been overseas."

"Yup. *Moto, koto, sota, deska?*" a soldier nearby would break in, mocking Bob by throwing around scraps of words he heard from the Japanese around him.

Bob wouldn't let that stop him.

"I'm serious. This is the first time I've eaten rice—I'm not kidding—if you don't count rice pudding, I never ate rice before I went into the army." Bob wouldn't mention, though everyone knew he could, that two firsts he shared with a lot of the guys standing close by, was one, they had shot and killed one man or more, and two, that they had sex with one woman or more—paid sex, but even so.

But tonight his talk about meeting new people and grabbing the future by the throat was taking a break: the pot of coffee, the beers that followed, the tiredness that trailed him into town…

…Now, rum.

He stood at a high table in Bar Tomy while the music twanged, looking at the fish tank while three soldiers rattled on about the other night's baseball game. Just as he was finishing his first rum cocktail the songs stopped; Ryuichi had gotten into a conversation with the soldiers and was too occupied to tend to the music. A quietness descended. The voices went momentarily softer. Then Bob heard Ryuichi's voice ring out.

"Yeah, guys, something happened the night before last. Nobody from the base did it. It was after curfew. But you know how people in town can get—they start accusing even though something might be impossible."

"What? What are they accusing us of?" one of the soldiers said, raising his voice at Ryuichi.

"A boy fell asleep on the last train into Chitose and got his throat slit. Things like that don't happen in Chitose. I'm only telling you this in case you find that people aren't treating you as nicely as they were before. It'll blow over, especially when they find out who did it."

The same soldier, observably drunk, grunted, "They got a lot of nerve!" He acted as though he personally bankrolled some of the businesses in town and expected the Japanese to be grateful for the American presence, with its soldiers coming into Chitose to drink, to blow off steam, to find girls, and forget about what was going on in Korea.

"I just wanted you to know," Ryuichi said defensively.

One of the soldiers, less drunk, asked him if the police had any idea who did it. Ryuichi peered into the darkness of the room and said, "It's a mystery."

With that, the bar owner's news bulletin was over.

But the three G.I.s and Ryuichi continued their conversation. It just turned to other matters. Bob tuned it out and paid closer attention to the fish tank. His pick-me-ups hadn't picked him up. His eyes roamed the peaceful aquarium, following an angelfish calmly coasting left to right, its lips pursing and unpursing every few seconds. He studied the angelfish's gills opening and closing: the gills were bloodless, crude beating slits. He wondered what it would be like to slit a man's throat. He'd never done that. Luckily, he'd never been in hand-to-hand combat. Hopefully he never would be. He shook himself to take his mind off the subject. Then, he felt the need to close his eyes.

At quarter to eleven one of the G.I.s shook Bob's shoulder and told him to look lively. The soldiers all hustled out of the bar together to catch the last bus back to base.

The boss at The Swan said he'd give Kiriko a try on Saturday night, if she worked for free. It was going to be their busiest night in the last three weeks.

Kiriko worked the shift, got along with everyone, and was happy the place was bigger than Mommy Eri's. She was able to put her English to work—that was most important. Of course, the boss made her stay to help with the clean-up. At midnight when they closed, he told her he was pleased with her and he'd like her to work on Friday and Saturday nights, plus Thursdays—which normally was also a busy night.

She started homeward on Koen Dori Street in her dour gray, thick wool coat, her woolen mittens, and a fur cap. She passed a small shop—a shack with a big front window, selling only ramen soup. A faint yellow glow came from inside. Only the couple that ran it were there, cleaning up after closing time.

The temperature was just above freezing. She walked carefully on the wooden planked sidewalk, passing the few shops that continued to stay open and sell hot food and snacks. Each shop had old steel barrels out in front, with scraps of pine blocks and plywood burning in them. The heat and the blaze of the flames were meant to attract people who still might be out at that hour.

Shimizu, and the rest of Chitose's business district with it, soon petered out as she walked. The air was dank. There were no streetlights. All the light Kiriko had to go by was from the half moon rising in the east, shining through gauzy clouds drifting northward. She reached Chuo Odori. It was a broad thoroughfare that ran parallel to the train tracks. She thought of Noboru. She crossed the bland boulevard with its boxy prefabricated warehouses and small businesses. Though everything was closed, one business kept its high, dimly lit sign on all night long. Why? Few people were awake to see it.

The cold chilled her; she adjusted her scarf and went down a small street that had a green painted storehouse at its corner. Instantly she was in a residential part of Chitose. She walked by a house with large timbers on the outside. It reminded her of Noboru's home. She pushed Noboru out of her mind, visualizing the front door of her own house, and then her bed, and how pleasant it would be to slip under the quilt and sleep.

No traffic or people were around, so when Kiriko got near to home, she cut diagonally through the intersection of Nakanobashi Dori and New Sun Road. But just when she was in the middle of the crossroads, a large, mangy Akita dog charged at her, seeming to come from out of nowhere. There weren't many stray dogs in Chitose and Kiriko had never seen this one before. Its fur was unkempt, and its bear-like face was scraggy.

In no time it was blocking her way. It snarled and barked, and incredibly—she'd done nothing to provoke it—it bared its teeth, threatening to bite. Perhaps she'd invaded its territory, she thought. Maybe it was sick. She had to act quickly. She looked straight into the eyes of the poor animal, stamped her right foot hard against the ground and shouted, "No!"

The big-boned dog stopped abruptly, held back a couple of yelps and became quiet. It stepped back meekly, then turned and scampered away into the shadows.

She caught her breath, collected herself, and began walking again, wanting nothing more to happen, wanting to be home. So many things had been upsetting her: changing jobs, Noboru being attacked, the harsh winter that had included an earthquake, now, a crazed dog that came out of nowhere to attack her. She sighed: just three more blocks to go before she needed to cross the only paved road in Chitose—Sapporo Road, or as the Americans called it, Route 36—to be on the final stretch home.

Then there was a low, distant roar. With each house she passed, the noise grew louder. The ground trembled, also, and the trembling increased with each of her steps. The din separated into sounds: engines hummed, tires could be heard rolling over crusty asphalt, metal parts clattered.

She could see Sapporo Road in the distance. The closer she got, the more she was able to see icy particles in the air lit up by the headlights of the U.S. army cargo trucks in their convoy. She wouldn't be able to cross the road until it passed. She stopped walking. There was an undeveloped lot ahead, at the corner. Tall mounds of gravel had been dumped there, ready to be used in construction.

She walked in the direction of the lot, reaching one tall mound. She stood next to it. The huge pile towered above her, and she positioned herself in its shadow to take in the spectacle of trucks trundling by. She saw fifty or so trucks pass her before the convoy ended. As the American two and one-half ton trucks passed, sometimes she imagined she could see the face of a young driver gazing sleepily ahead.

These motorized embodiments of power and wealth came through only at night, often originating from Otaru, a port more than an hour to the north. These massive processions fed the hopes of many Chitoseans that their town had an even more lucrative future in front of it.

No one at home awoke when Kiriko arrived.

It was cold in the house. The girl heated water on the stove to put into her hot water bottle. This was one of the last nights she'd have to be doing this. The weather would soon break. The season would change

CHAPTER 6

Mommy Eri's anonymous phone tip about Shigeru Akiyama made the police notice that since the attack, he hadn't been seen in town or anywhere. It could be he was the attacker, or maybe he'd been attacked himself; he'd died, his body taken away somewhere. The Sheriff's Office had little to go on. No witnesses, no solid leads.

Soon after leaving the hot springs, Akiyama entered a liver-colored section of woods, and among the leafless deciduous trees there, encountered an old alder tree. It spoke to him. It told him to not lag, to keep to a steady pace to avoid adversarial spirits that could strike at him. Ah, Akiyama thought, the alder tree is actually a wolf spirit, perhaps the Great Wolf himself, endeavoring to protect me from further harm.

He looked down to the ground and a stick lay there. It was part of tree limb. He picked it up and thought: he's even providing me with a sturdy walking stick.

The stick was a replacement for his bear hunting spear, which he couldn't remember where he'd lost.

Settling into his measured march-like steps, thoughts raced through his mind. Many were thoughts of self-reproach. From time to time he dug his walking stick into the ground to help propel himself forward in his journey.

Akiyama reproached himself for thinking he was strong enough during these past days to undertake such a strenuous activity as hunting bear. It was a springtime tradition among the Ainu to lead their dogs in the hunt for bears in their dens, bears weakened after months of hibernation; they would capture them and later ritually sacrifice them. For the Ainu, a bear hunt was considered most manly, not to say thrilling. It called upon great reserves of bravery to attack such a dangerous creature with such a simple weapon.

It was a mistake to venture out, spear in hand, to find a bear den—and he didn't have a dog with him! No wonder his actions were all missteps, and he had confrontations with malevolent spirits.

The morning sun seemed to promise a gift of warmth and strength.

He spotted a fine willow tree. It beckoned him to linger, and he accepted its offer. He stopped and took out a knife. He cut some skin and body—that is, bark and wood—from the willow. He sat down and made a bandeau, the bark becoming a strip of cloth for his headband. From the wood he made shavings and attached them to it. He took a wooden medallion out of his pocket that he'd carved several weeks before: on it was the face of a wolf. Once he'd fastened the medallion to the willow headband, he rose from the ground and got back on his march.

In a half hour he arrived at his destination. He didn't set up camp. He stuffed his bundle of belongings in a snug recess in the ground and left the clearing to search for deer.

Sometime later his poison tipped arrow struck near the brain of a four-year-old buck. It had been feeding on the buds of an ash tree. He wasn't strong enough to drag the dead animal back to camp, so he cut it into pieces, hacking off its legs and head. But still, the torso was too heavy to drag. Come back later, he told himself, I'm too weak right now. He cut the buck's chest open and took out the liver, kidneys, and heart, stuffing them into his shirt. There was no other way to carry them. "I must grow stronger!" he said out loud.

As soon as he made it back to his camp, he made a fire and cooked the deer offal. Colors from the final two hours of daylight lent a strange gloss to his meal. He filled his hungry stomach; that he might die before he met the Great Wolf in its original, untransformed shape distressed him.

He got up from the fire and found another willow tree. He stripped a branch from it and whittled an *inau* (prayer stick). He sat down cross-legged by the smoking fire, his face pale, his willow headband on his head. With the *inau* in his hand he improvised a prayer, not to the monotheistic sky god of the Mediterranean peoples, but to the humble deity that inhabited the willow tree.

> "O dear deity, when man was created,
> His spine was made of your wood.
> I beseech you, with this *inau* before me,
> To listen, and hasten to heal me.
> My backbone is weak, and so too is my body.
> I am ill.
> Please, make me strong.
> Dear deity, help me.
> I am forever at your service."

At one end of the area of his camp there was a rocky out crop. Akiyama had previously dug out a niche between three large slabs of rock there—he let those rocks serve as a roof and two walls. Among the basic supplies he stored there were rolled up animal pelts. He unrolled and arranged the pelts on the ground inside the rough-hewn lair. He would sleep now.

After waking the next morning Akiyama hauled the torso of the buck back to camp. He finished butchering it and whenever he felt pangs of hunger, he roasted some meat and ate.

He grew stronger with each passing day, he believed. His daily routine was leisurely, although at times there were interruptions.

One day at sunset he was out walking simply for the sake of exercise. At one point in his ramble, a powerful cloud of red mist assaulted him, blinding him. He fell to his knees.

Once the mist cleared, he discovered that his headband of bark and willow wood shavings had disappeared, along with the wolf medallion. He panicked, threw himself to the ground, and cried into the twigs and dead leaves that covered the ground: "What will become of me, I am not growing strong!"

He found another willow tree. He fashioned a new prayer stick and prayed to God. He prayed for more strength, then fashioned a new headband out of willow, yet this time there was no medallion.

Days passed. When he'd eaten all the venison he went back to the same spot in the woods where he killed the first buck. There he found another deer, a buck of about the same age. It was already dead; it lay there freshly killed. He didn't know who had killed it and, surprisingly, he didn't care. All he knew was there would be no further need to hunt for a while. He dismembered the animal on the spot and dragged its torso back to camp.

One morning he awoke and felt a craving for wild, tasty *gobo* (burdock) root to mix with the venison. He knew *gobo* grew best in sunny places with a little shade.

There was an airy clearing farther up a slope from where he slept. He climbed to that spot and remained on his feet to catch his breath. As he stood, he let the sun's rays penetrate his body. With the heat, his senses sharpened. He looked out upon the vast open sky and noticed an eagle gliding over the tops of the trees above a forested cliff a mile away. A curious thing, he thought, because it was a large sea-eagle, and such birds usually didn't come this far inland—the sea was eighteen miles away. Akiyama peered intensely at it, tweaking his vision telescopically. The animal's black and white wings were spread out, riding a current of air. What a glorious creature, he thought, marveling at it.

He closed his eyes briefly to stop focusing so energetically on the bird. Then, after this short rest, he opened them. The eagle had shifted its course—it now glided in his direction, though perhaps it was making its way to a nearby stream where the fishing was easy. Yet it was strange it was flying still farther inland, away from its normal prey, marine life.

He thought of the seashore and the times he'd spent there. He thought of the coastal towns, Tomakomai and Shiraoi. He thought about the jobs he'd had with the Japanese when he was young, working with a team of Ainu men spreading out fishing nets in ocean waters just beyond the beach and its crashing waves. Other months of the year he, along with a crew of Ainu, would gather seaweed for the Japanese. Some of Ainu men's hair would change color in the summer, from black to inky brown or reddish.

With the flight the eagle, he forgot he'd come up the slope to gather burdock.

The eagle rode the air currents, always steering itself to sustain its trajectory toward him. Sea-eagles were known for their inquisitiveness. Eighteen miles is a small distance for a bird that can fly as high as ten thousand feet. But maybe it wasn't looking for prey. He focused on the eagle's head and saw it was pointed downward—yet its eyes weren't scanning for prey.

So, there had to be something else on its mind. Could this bird possibly be the roaming spirit of his son Fumito, who had never received his send-off to the Other World? Could he be flying over and pining after the land where he was born? What would this spirit do when it reached him, Akiyama—it was coming in his direction.

He tracked the bird's gaze down to exactly where he believed it was looking at that moment. To his surprise he found its gaze was fixed on a man in green fatigues and a parka, who was standing behind a tripod. He then noticed the man had a companion, positioned some two hundred yards away from there. He saw that the two men had reached the lower flat grassy land by jeep. The vehicle was parked by a brook not far from them.

It anguished him to discover people in the valley below.

Though it was more than a mile away, it was too close to him. To be safe he needed to be alone. He hoped the spirit of Fumito would swoop down and frighten them off. If the men didn't go, he might have to kill them.

But then all at once the eagle vanished from the sky. Where did it go? Its disappearance set off a chain reaction in Akiyama.

Though it was a bright day, now everything was too bright. Akiyama became conscious of his heartbeat, which grew louder and louder. His blood vessels twitched and pinched, and his feet and hands throbbed. The sun shouldn't be affecting him in this way, he thought. His lungs pressed against his ribcage as if they wanted to burst.

A feeling of foreboding came over him. Then he felt his muscles and organs struggling against his bones.

Violent pushes, jabs, growths—the changes struck one after another. His bones, organs and limbs rearranged themselves in altered sizes, his feet and legs shrank. The adaptations did not hurt, though. Parts of him got thicker, others thinner; others were replaced by features his body had never known before. Flaps of skin grew from his arms. Were they to be wings?

An uncontrollable energy coursed through him.

The two soldiers below faced each other in such a manner that it looked as though an invisible straight line in space was connecting them. They were land surveyors in the U.S. Army Corps of Engineers, recording topographic details of the area that was going to be developed into a third army base, Camp Chitose III.

Akiyama's body was lighter. Air flowed into his lungs with ease now. With his transformed shape quaking, he leapt. Almost immediately he was down below, in the meadow where the surveyors were. The meadow and sky were intensely bright, with the jeep standing out in the brightness, reflecting light despite retaining its dull green color.

More change racked Akiyama's body. His legs and arms

swiftly grew to become roughly the same length. Akiyama could only stand on all fours. He scurried to hide himself behind one side of the jeep so as not to be seen by the two men.

From this vantage point he watched the surveyor closest to him who was peering through an instrument fixed atop a surveying stand. He thought to himself: it might not be so easy to chase these men away. They're dressed as soldiers. If they are soldiers it means they have weapons, they feel superior, they'll bravely resist anyone trying to overcome them. Akiyama reprimanded himself: I should've looked closer before coming here. I didn't see the danger.

Great agitation rose inside him. He spoke aloud to himself, "What am I to do?"

He recoiled in surprise when a large wolf approached him, creeping quietly around the front of the vehicle so it could speak to him face to face.

"You cannot be effective here," the wolf said calmly to Akiyama. The wolf's voice was feminine, yet deep. It was a very old voice. All around, the light was so intense and penetrating that the stiff hairs of the animal's outer coat were almost transparent.

Akiyama gaped in awe. He could not answer.

The wolf resumed, "Stop your wandering. You can't build your strength if you're taking shelter in a different place every few nights. We know you've fled from your cottage because you feel it's different than what it used to be. Nonetheless, you have supplies there that shouldn't be abandoned."

"I, I…," Akiyama stammered like a nervous child. He was filled with great respect and with even greater trepidation. He was ashamed he even felt the need to speak at all.

The wolf tried to make him feel less awkward. "You wonder if you'll be protected on your way there?" The wolf did not move a hair. "We'll protect you as long as you conduct yourself peacefully."

The wolf walked away in the direction of the nearby

brook and vanished into a patch of effervescent light.

Once it had gone, the radiant day around Akiyama dimmed in increments until a breezy dullness surrounded him, though the sun was still perceptible. He regained all his human features and hiked back to camp. The going was slow.

He was exhausted. He passionately hoped that the last few days had been nourishing and healthful. He broke camp and got on his way. He dreaded visiting his cottage. It was full of voices inside and out, all of them scolding and threatening him.

Though he believed he'd spent fourteen days at his camp, only four nights had passed.

CHAPTER 7

The same day that Akiyama left his makeshift camp for his cottage, Lloyd Kelso went to Tsuru Lanes, the only bowling alley in Chitose.

It was evening. Bob wasn't with him—Bob had been there without him two nights before and afterward when he came back on the last liberty bus too drunk, he said he was going to take a rest from Shimizu for a couple of days. (Bob was in the barracks tonight, already on his second six pack of beer, trying to bury his uncharacteristic moodiness. Apparently he'd put his search for Kiriko momentarily on hold.)

Tonight was the first night Lloyd felt like drinking again since his panic attack five nights before.

Tsuru Lanes was the only nightspot in town where G.I.s and Japanese men mingled with any regularity. There could be trouble with the two crowds in bars and billiard halls. An abundance of machismo and a habit of betting money in those places easily caused turmoil. The bowling alley's spacious layout and the constant need to get on with the matches were important ingredients in the recipe that made for a straightforward atmosphere at Tsuru.

G.I.s typically bowled against one another in informal teams but when there weren't enough Americans to fill out a team, they'd ask a Japanese to join. The main reason for the Japanese to be there wasn't to bowl; rather it was to get their hands on American goods that had been bought by the G.I.s at Camp Chitose's Base Exchange ("the BX"), or by

American mail order.

There was, however, something that the Japanese could offer the Americans in return, that otherwise wasn't readily available. It was *shabu* (crystal methamphetamine), the number one illicit drug in Japan. Men took it so they might work long hours. American soldiers took it to endure life away from home, life in the army, the life they did not choose.

Toshi Nakano, Noboru Nakano's older brother by five years, was decked out in a brown sport coat and beige trousers that went up past his navel. A turquoise and white necktie with ivory-colored flowers flowed down his light blue dress shirt. It wasn't easy to look sharp in Hokkaido in winter. No dowdy overcoat ever covered him—he had to maintain his look. If he could have, he would've liked to have looked like a new, jazzy Japanese.

He sat at the Tsuru Lanes bar, high on *shabu,* with a beer in front of him, drumming his fingers against his upper trouser legs. The clatter of bowling pins tumbling to the floor was underneath the din of young men talking all at once. Out of the corner of his eye he saw Lloyd Kelso come in. He slid out of his seat and glided effortlessly over to him. He had to act before Lloyd got snatched up by someone wanting to include him in a game.

Toshi's English was quite good, considering he'd picked it up on his own. It's true that his livelihood depended on it. Lloyd didn't see Toshi coming. "Hi, Lloyd. How are you? Bob's not with you?"

Well, Lloyd's mind was somewhere else. He was playing *South Pacific*, the musical, in his head. It helped him get some distance from what he called his latest bout of "fatigue." He'd seen the show on Broadway just a few months before going into the army. Toshi's question jolted him just when he was seeing in his mind the scene where the Tonkinese woman Liat is alone with Lieutenant Joseph Cable for the first time. Suddenly Lloyd was face to face with a skinny Asian guy with shiny, oiled hair. He quickly replayed the question he'd heard coming out of Toshi's mouth and then answered from far away, "No, Bob's not with me."

Toshi tried to be funny, mocking the way Bob talked. "Make new friends, huh? Go beyond ourselves. Every day's new—don't let it slip away! What we're experiencing is amazing! So many opportunities—I can't tell you!"

Lloyd needed a beer and he put one foot in the direction of the bar. Toshi cautiously waylaid him, placing his hand lightly on Lloyd's arm. He flashed a quick, fake smile, and his tone turned imitation-polite. "Please, I have something to ask you."

With the attack on his younger brother Noboru, Toshi Nakano realized he was vulnerable. He'd always been aware that any of his black market competitors would be happy to put him out of business. He took care to avoid places where he might be trapped. He habitually eyed wherever he was for escape routes. In case he had to run he was sure he could outrun most hoodlums. But because he was practically untouchable, his enemy might attack his brother as a way of sending a message to him to get out of the black market. That was one possible interpretation of what happened on the train.

Concerning the talk quietly spreading that pointed to Akiyama as the one who'd attacked his brother, Toshi felt the Ainu man incapable of it. Toshi had never seen him in town after dark and didn't believe anyone who said they had. "On these freezing nights? Past his bedtime, with nothing to do? That feeble, insane creature?" Toshi scoffed inside.

When Bob Fernandez had been at Tsuru Lanes two nights before, Toshi had conversed with him. As a result of something said, Toshi had been looking to run into Lloyd as soon as he came to Shimizu again.

Something had happened between Bob and Toshi. As far as Bob Fernandez was concerned, Toshi was a bantam jerk looking to get something from anyone he encountered.

When a bowling game ended two nights earlier—a game in which Toshi filled out a team—Bob felt like bullying the smartly dressed young Japanese of not-so-mysterious means. Bob could get sadistic when he got drunk.

Toshi's team had lost, in no small part because Toshi didn't know how to bowl.

"Your team stank," Bob said with a big grin. "And my team had me with my sore hand. You're a good sport, though, huh? I'm going to buy you a few drinks. Do you know any American drinking games? No? I'm going to teach you one."

The game went on for almost an hour, the two men taking turns pitching pennies in the other's glass.

"You just got a penny in my glass, dope," Bob said in a slapping tone. "Okay, go again."

Toshi bounced a penny toward the empty glass, and he missed.

Bob took his turn, bouncing his penny. It didn't go in either. On the fourth round of tries Bob got a penny in the glass and Toshi had to drink. Bob took his "reward" turn. It didn't go in.

After Toshi had drunk four glasses of beer to Bob's one, Bob smirked, "You need it, man. You've been twitching. Beer takes the edge off, doesn't it?"

As the game continued, Toshi loosened his florid tie and unbuttoned the top button of his shirt. He got better at their game or just luckier. In a few minutes the score stood at five drinks for Bob and seven drinks for Toshi. Bob wanted to drink the little punk under the table so he could watch him pass out. But it looked like that might not happen and it rattled him. He wanted to get under Toshi's skin.

"What's been eating you?" Bob didn't know Toshi's brother had been attacked. "You haven't been rooking so good rately, hophead."

Toshi didn't respond. "Go ahead, you can tell me, faggot."

Toshi pretended to not understand Bob's jabs. "Do you owe too much money? Got a health problem? Some kind of disease?"

The room swayed slightly. Bob's mind was filling with hatred for the twerp sitting across from him.

The alcohol had loosened Toshi's tongue as well. Otherwise he might not have said what he said, at least not to a G.I. "My little brother was attacked, you know?"

"No, I didn't know that, goofball." Bob's voice swung like a whip.

Toshi continued, "He was coming back from work five nights ago—it was Thursday. He fell asleep on the train when it parked at Chitose. He was all alone. Somebody went into the train and tried to kill him."

"Oh," Bob said, lackadaisically. The room tilted to the left for a second and tilted back. Then it sunk into him that the victim of the attack that Ryuichi Gibo mentioned was related to Toshi. No surprise there. It occurred to him that here was a new way to badger Toshi.

"Well, I did hear something about that," he leered.

"Really? From who?"

"Ryuichi Gibo, at Bar Tomy."

"What did he say?"

"I don't know. He just mentioned it."

"When?"

"Oh, a couple of nights ago."

"There are people that want to kill me. But they can't." Toshi was full of himself. "I'm smart and they can't catch me. I always know where they are. They couldn't get me, so they went after my brother. Yep. They want to drive me out of business."

"You believe that, you vely smart nip?"

Toshi nodded. He paused, thought for a moment and then said, "What happened in Shimizu Thursday night? You were here. It was really cold that night."

Bob did not know Toshi's motive for asking the question.

Caught off guard, he answered without thinking, "Not much. It was pretty dead."

"Oh," Toshi said, poker faced. "You must have seen something."

"No, I didn't." Bob thought for a second and then was suspicious. "Hey, how'd you know I was in Shimizu last Thursday?"

"I didn't. You just told me."

Bob was outraged that Toshi tricked him. Bob struggled to not show his anger. Damn, the clever Jap! he thought. "Anyway, the rail station is not Shimizu," he said, trying to regain his position as the guy on top.

"Oh," sighed Toshi, hoping for more information.

The short silence that followed the sigh suggested that Toshi was superior to him.

To counter that, Bob dangled this: "It was crummy outside. I mean, the weather. I was with Lloyd. I was drunk. I hardly remember anything, though I hurt my hand somehow, had to punch somebody hard, I guess."

Toshi became more alert instantly. "Who was there besides Lloyd?"

"There was some garbage around, some of your people. It's all fuzzy to me."

Bob knew he had Toshi now. He said slyly, gloating, "We left Mommy Eri's… and Lloyd said he saw a fellow who looked like a drifter—no, a hunter, standing there in the distance with a hockey stick in his hand. I couldn't see the guy. I thought, wow, it's freezing and what the hell's going on with Lloyd? But then maybe your guys jumped us because the next thing I knew, Lloyd and I were down on the ground and my fist was hurting. Neither Lloyd or me were able to get up for a while."

Toshi's eyes filled with fire and curiosity.

"Well," resumed Bob, "We weren't near the train station. It wasn't where we were headed."

Bob saw the interest and agitation sweep across Toshi's

face and it pleased him.

But then Bob shut up because he saw he had Toshi on tenterhooks.

Toshi knew Bob was messing around with him, that it had to do with his catching up in the game of *pennies*—the name of the drinking game they'd been playing. What a wicked boy, he thought.

Questions swirled in Toshi's mind: *Was the hunter that Lloyd saw, Akiyama? Had Toshi's enemies, on their way to harm Noboru, jumped the two G.I.s? Why would Japanese hoodlums attack American G.I.s? That would be stupid to do. Did they hurt Akiyama, too? Akiyama was known to deal in valuable, illegal furs. Was this…?* The whole thing was a jumble.

Toshi got up from the table. "Game's over. I don't want to drink anymore."

He lurched his thin body away from where he was. Bob had had his fun. He'd been a devious flash bulb that had triggered distress in him.

The fact was Toshi had never been close to his younger brother, since he'd always been absorbed in himself. Yet the whole thing was, someone could be sending him a sign. "I need to talk to Lloyd," he muttered decisively to himself. He needed to find out more about what happened to them that night.

Toshi had done business with Shigeru Akiyama a few times. The filthy Ainu brought him pelts from *kuroten* (sable) he'd trapped. The deal worked out well for both sides. Toshi would pay Akiyama a low price for the fur and Akiyama could cash in despite the ban on Ainu being allowed to trap, fish or hunt. Eventually the sable would fetch high prices at the end of its black market journey.

Toshi didn't want to get close to the investigation of the attack on his brother. The last thing he wanted was contact with the police. When they'd briefly questioned him concerning the attack, Toshi worried, how much do they know about my business? Are they looking to arrest me?

The only thing Toshi believed of what Bob said was that he'd been with Lloyd and they'd been at Bar Eden on the night his brother's throat got slit. The thing to do was to question Lloyd.

As Toshi gently pressed Lloyd's arm, preventing him from heading over to order a beer at the bar, which was less than fifteen feet away, he recognized that Lloyd was taken up with other thoughts and needed to be handled carefully. Better hold with questions until I give him some background, he thought.

He told Lloyd, "Bob was here the day before yesterday. We bowled together. I don't know if you know, but something strange happened on Thursday night. My brother was injured in a train at the station. I wasn't involved. Don't think I'm trying to pull you into something. Please."

Toshi continued at a fast pace, "Bob said you and him went drinking at Bar Eden."

"Oh, yeah?" Lloyd responded without caring—nobody likes being pestered.

Lloyd remembered that Bob had bragged earlier in the day in the barracks that he'd gotten "that scrawny ne'er-do-well Toshi" very drunk the night before.

"Can you tell me…"

Lloyd broke in, "Bar Eden isn't on my radar anymore. There are better places."

"I'm only interested in Thursday night. Were there people outside there or in town that you got in a fight with?"

"No," Lloyd said drily.

"I have a brother," Toshi declared. "He was attacked. Yep, it was so bad that he's in the hospital."

"I'm sorry for you and your family." Memories of Thursday night were coming back to Lloyd, and it wasn't a comfortable feeling.

"I just want to know what you saw that night when you were with Bob."

"Ask Bob."

"I did. He couldn't remember much. He was drunk."

"I was, too."

"But you must remember something. Bob told me that you saw a man standing out there in the freezing cold doing nothing."

"Don't believe everything Bob tells you."

"I don't. That's why I'm asking you."

"I'm not feeling well, okay?" Lloyd's pulse had increased.

"So, Bob's lying to me. I'd just like to know what you saw."

"I didn't see anything. Look, I don't want to talk to you anymore."

"Come on. You saw something. What are you trying to hide?"

"I said I don't want to talk to you!" Lloyd's throat tightened. He put his left hand to his shirt collar, he massaged the lower part of his neck. He could feel his palms sweating.

Toshi entreated once more, and it was as comforting as hearing a baby bawl. "Look, I'm just trying to figure out what happened to my brother."

"Brother, aren't we all?" Lloyd said.

That took Toshi by surprise. He didn't know what to make of it. It shut him up for a moment. But Lloyd was growing anxious and felt he might panic again. He looked to his left and right, to see if he could get away from Toshi. But then what he dreaded happened: his gums started bleeding from the stress. (Back home in New York, later, a doctor would prescribe vitamin D—a deficiency of it was causing the condition.)

Toshi persisted. "There was someone you saw standing in the distance. Was he a hunter? Or something else? Were there guys who came along and tried to beat you up?"

Lloyd swallowed the blood frothing from his gums so no one could see it. He wanted to get away from Toshi, but he glanced, and a new group had just come in, crowding the bar area. He didn't see a spot there where he could escape to. If

Lloyd were a snake, he would have hissed at him.

Instead, Lloyd burst out, "I don't care about your brother!" He strained to reign himself in, trying a half-smile to implore Toshi to leave him alone, but his teeth were already red. Then the blood coated his lips.

For a moment, Lloyd's tense vocal cords relaxed enough for him to be rather impolite to Toshi, a guy who didn't know when to shut up or leave someone alone.

Lloyd uttered the words, "Now you can see the truth I'm hiding." He opened his mouth wide so Toshi could see the blood.

Toshi's alcohol and speed-addled mind spun into another dimension. He tore out of the bowling alley, shocked at what he saw. It made him picture a bleeding slit in Noboru's neck. It was the first time he'd thought of his younger brother in a couple of days.

Later, as he made his way home on foot, his stomach churned. He vomited on the side of the street, Naka no Hashi Dori, after getting a few blocks past the bar district.

CHAPTER 8

It frightened Kiriko that people blamed Akiyama (and yes, there was much hatred in their voices) for the attack on Noboru. She was scared that if the owner of The Swan found out she was Akiyama's natural daughter he would withdraw his offer of work.

The previous night she didn't let onto Satomi that she felt as though her world was falling apart. She even thought she might have to run away—she could escape to Sapporo, with its streetcars, its bustle, its population of almost one million, and be anonymous there.

She needed to do something now, almost anything, to distract herself from her thoughts. Maybe there was something she could do to not only distract herself, but to be useful to others, as well.

She'd had glimpses of her father, from a distance, once or twice a year, in Chitose's local business district, which abutted Shimizu. Akiyama would be going about his errands, keeping to himself. She would just happen to see him. (Normally she wasn't in the area much—her school wasn't there, and most of the shopping was done near Aunt Satomi's.) Whenever she caught sight of him, she did not think he recognized, or even saw her.

He'd never been asked to Aunt Satomi's house, and he never attempted to go there. She hadn't spoken to him since she'd lived with him. Her adopted parents intimated—and it was said around town—that he was mentally ill.

A warm breeze was dispersing the town's smoke as

61

Kiriko pedaled her bike up a street that paralleled Chitose River. After crossing a bridge, she turned left onto a cart trail running alongside the riverbank heading upstream. Soon the center of Chitose was behind her. A patch of meadow was on her right, away from the river. In it sat a towering, wide, quick blooming *kobushi*—a Japanese magnolia. What a sight. It would only last a few days. The tree's white blossoms, when seen together, formed a huge blotch of vegetable snow. The splendid display was all the more breathtaking because the deciduous trees in the vicinity were still leafless and darkened by pollutants in the air.

Kiriko took the sight as a good omen.

A few hundred yards after that, the trail turned away from the river and became muddy. She had to walk her bicycle through the grass next to it.

An American plane coming from Camp Chitose whirred loudly and climbed in the sky above her.

The cart path let out into a new street in a new ward— Katsuragi—that was under construction. The hard surface was dry, and she got on her bike again. There were slabs and slabs of concrete—a hundred brand new cheap homes would be the result. Workmen pounded away, the echoes of their work mixed with sounds of circular saws, gasoline generators, bulldozers, and backhoes.

The new ward abruptly ended at a line made by the town planning office and Kiriko was soon on the shoulder of the road that went up to Lake Shikotsu. After a couple of minutes, she stopped riding and chose a maple tree to lean her bicycle against. The trail up to her father's cottage began nearby.

She'd only been on the rising footpath a minute when a *karasu,* a large crow, high up on a branch, squawked noisily at her. She walked the zigzagging path through the woods. At one sharp bend some creature rustled in the undergrowth. She had no idea what it was, and it jarred her: she hadn't spent much time in the wild as a teenager. Before she knew it a swarm of gnats converged on her, and she inhaled them. She stopped in her tracks. She cursed. What a miserable trail! This was no place for a girl. This was no place for *anyone!* She'd forgotten how hard this land was. As she spit out the insects, she noticed they'd even flown up her coat sleeves.

She started walking again, her eyes half open. Tears welled up. Wiping them away she found that insects had lodged themselves in the corners of her eyes.

Five minutes later she was in a part of the woods she'd dreaded when she'd lived with her parents. It was just as she remembered: death invaded life there. Huge, choking vines as thick as a baby's head twisted like snakes through ferns, dead leaves, and fallen wood. The vines crept gloomily along the forest floor, their color was bizarre: blackened brown, it looked as if they had survived a fire. These burned tentacles slithered up healthy trunks and threaded around sure, green limbs with the sole purpose of strangling any progeny. They were unstoppable.

As Kiriko got closer to the cottage the forest thinned out. Here was the wilderness where her father had been forced to settle, far from the river with its thriving fish and game.

An elm tree, perhaps fifteen years old, had an *inau* tied around its trunk. The *inau* must have been placed there by Akiyama before the onset of winter. Pieces of it had fallen away after the elements had torn into it. That it wasn't a fresh *inau* made Kiriko think her father hadn't been near the cottage for quite some time.

Akiyama's small house wasn't a traditional Ainu thatched roof home with a dirt floor. It had a sloping aluminum roof, and Kiriko saw it glinting now. He'd built the cottage himself twenty years before. Its walls were made of boards. It had windows on every side, and in addition to its large main room it had an adjacent bedroom and a kitchen toward the back. All the floors were of wood.

There never was any yard, only space cleared around the cottage, and some gravel spread out on the ground in front and back. On level land in the back there was land for a garden.

There was a window each on either side of the front door. She noticed that the earthquake had broken some of the windowpanes.

Kiriko slowed down as she neared the place. It wasn't that she was afraid, it was that she hadn't been there in such a long time. She dragged her feet across the gravel in front just to make sure anyone inside heard her coming. She shouted, "*Konnichiwa!*" (Hello!)

No response.

The glass of the window to the right of the front door had a hole in it. She stepped up to it and looked in. Soft, natural light brightened the main room and touched two of its corners. She peered in at the bare walls; in a corner to the left she saw three large cylindrical Ainu containers holding keepsakes and items used in rituals.

The bare planks of the floor were strewn with pieces of wood, a couple of *mushiro* floor mats in disarray, two coils of rope, a spool of wire, and hunting knives and a rolled-up canvas tarpaulin. No one was living there. Much was in disarray. She hadn't been sure what she was going to say to her father if she saw him there. Now she was relieved of that concern.

What she didn't know was that while her father might not be living there, he was still using his house to store equipment and food: the police found food laid up in two metal storage barrels buried nearby in the ground—dried salmon and seaweed, tins of mackerel, sun-dried and roasted Japanese dace, some rice, millet and bottles of *sake,* as well; and even a third barrel, which had a hasp on its lid with a combination lock—it contained fishing paraphernalia, wire, rope, knives, kindling and matches. Some of the gear was illegal for an Ainu to possess.

Kiriko could see that the earthquake had damaged the windows but the cottage itself appeared entirely livable. Why her father wasn't living there, she did not know.

Seeing no signs of anyone in the cottage didn't stop her from being drawn into it. On the contrary, she felt freer to go in.

The door was unlocked. It stuck at its bottom, but it gave with a few strong pulls. Once she yanked it open, daylight flooded the musty room.

Her move away to Chitose nearly blotted out memories of life here. What existed in her mind now were family member's shadows, moving; objects, fuzzy and without color, fading in and out; she heard the voices of her past family as muffled voices in a radio play that somehow was losing its sound.

In the main room she noticed a table she hadn't caught sight of when she'd surveyed the room while looking in from outside. The memory of Fumito standing on that same table, naked, rushed back to her. It wasn't an inchoate dream or recollection. It was lucid. His flesh was shiny; the room was chestnut colored. Fumito was just out of the bath. Kiriko could still see her mother holding him by the arms.

A life cut so short, she sighed, and didn't want to dwell on it.

She walked the few steps to her parents' bedroom. Some panes of the window in there were broken and an animal skin on the floor underneath it reeked of mold. Otherwise, there was nothing remarkable or anything she could remember about it. She turned back into the main room and walked over to glance through the broad open doorway that led to the kitchen where a frying pan lay on the floor, as if it had just fallen off a wall.

Suddenly a queen bumblebee crashed into the main room through the open door and careened into her face, smacking her on the cheek. Kiriko screamed. She wasn't stung. The furry ball zoomed around with insane curving lines and came back to her, colliding with her arm, again without stinging her. The bee was obsessed with smashing into things, racing from one place to another. At the same time, it seemed to be laying claim to the front door, and Kiriko, startled and scared, felt she wasn't going to be allowed to get out that way.

She ran into the kitchen, knowing it had a back door. She undid its lock, flung the door open and looked down because she remembered there'd once been a treacherous step there. With her body moving forward at full force and her head lowered, she slammed into a large, immobile object. The smell of the object was overpowering. It was of animals, dirty fur, dried blood, and human waste.

Kiriko instantly knew instantly what the rigid figure was. It was her father.

She screamed, turned, and dashed back through the house, the queen bumblebee bashing into her one last time. By the time she was on the gravel out front, tears were wetting her cheeks. She hurled herself onto the footpath away from there and raced toward town.

The police's only lead was Akiyama. Though all assumed he no longer lived in the cottage, the police thought he might visit it if he was still alive. A twenty-four-hour stakeout was deemed excessive, what with the cold nights and the temperature hovering just above freezing. However, at this time of the year sixteen hours of light was available. So, two shifts a day, eight hours per man, with the first cop arriving at 3:30 a.m. and the second leaving at 7:30 p.m., were set up. Sheriff Deputy Hidekichi Iwate replaced Deputy Shigesuke Kobayashi, at 11:30 a.m. This was ninety minutes before Kiriko climbed the trail to reach her father's cottage.

When Deputy Iwate came up the trail, he encountered even more insects than Kiriko later would. "What ate insects?" he thought. Little birds. But he saw no small birds. What he did hear—and it startled him—was a big *karasu*. He didn't see it. Apparently it took off from its perch on a lower branch near him to reach a higher one. It flapped its broad, heavy wings and the loud sound of them went through

Iwate's body like thunder before the bird released a couple of obscene caws.

At half past eleven, after Kobayashi whispered to Iwate that there was nothing to report, the latter watched silently as his partner slipped his knapsack on and crept over to the trail to go back to town.

He sighed. It would be cold in the shade, and he'd have to stand up from time to time to catch the warm rays of the sun.

Before sitting cross-legged in the middle of a clump of evergreen bushes, Iwate laid out the contents of his knapsack. There were two aluminum canteens of water, *onigiri* (flavored rice balls) wrapped in wax paper, a police service revolver, and a knife. In those days, walkie-talkies were cumbersome and expensive; police didn't use them. Even if they would have had them, the terrain and the distances would have ruled out their use.

A cluster of pine branches hid Iwate from view. When he wanted, he could pull them to one side to observe anyone coming toward the cottage. The trail was the only practical means of reaching the property. It would be dangerous to attempt to approach the cottage from any other side, where the slope was steep, and footfalls could set off a mudslide. The police thought it unlikely Akiyama would ever try to go up that way.

Hidekichi Iwate saw and heard nothing unusual during the first half hour of his watch. His mind drifted to thoughts of his family: his wife, whom he'd courted for four years; his one-year-old daughter who was born the year after they married. Both he and his wife grew up in Chitose; he'd been a policeman for six years. His wife was pregnant again. They were hoping for a boy this time.

He pulled the cluster of branches aside as he did every five minutes and looked over at the cottage. His mind turned to thoughts of Akiyama and quickly meandered into ill will against the Ainu man's troublesome, filthy race. What an affliction they were on Hokkaido. He would be glad when the last of them were gone. Here he was wasting valuable time having to deal with their kind.

Thoughts then came to him of the unpleasant stretch of woods he would now have to pass through every day until they found Akiyama. It was that jumbled section of vegetation where charred vines drooped from forks in tree trunks and plunged into the ground only to reemerge a few yards later to grab hold of yet another wholesome tree. One of the grotesqueries there reminded him of gallows: it was impossible not to notice a blackened brown "rope"—a vine that no longer had any place to grow to and had just ended mid-air—slung over an outstretched dead limb.

An hour into his watch he got hungry. He unwrapped the various *onigiri* from their wax paper. He thought he heard a field mouse—or was it a tiny squirrel—as it made little swishes, crawling through dead leaves and pallid nest-like clumps of last year's grasses.

What a wonderful cook his wife was! The rice balls she made were delicious. She'd prepared six kinds: pickled *kombu* (kelp), *umeboshi* (sour pickled plum), salted salmon, *katsuobushi* (dried, fermented and smoked tuna), and *tarako* (cod fish roe) and lastly, his favorite, *ikura* (salmon roe).

As Deputy Iwate sat there calmly chewing in peace, a heavy rock smashed the back of his skull, rendering him instantly unconscious. To make sure Iwate would die, the assailant, clothed in animal skins and having arrived from downwind, pushed him on his back, allowing him to face the sky. The flesh of his neck was then torn; the jugular vein bled out all his life force.

CHAPTER 9

A small, elevated wasteland on the banks of Chitose River—just south of the railway bridge that crossed it—was a kind of unofficial city park. The land had been denuded of trees during the war for firewood; brush and small trees struggled to grow back. At a corner of the barren land, at the farthest extreme from the river, a small Shinto shrine soberly rested on a small terrace among young, planted *haimatsu* (Japanese stone pines). Perhaps it was a prayer for vegetation to return.

The park wasn't exactly on a cliff; the land was a gentle hump. Because the terrain favored a southeast view, the mornings could be sunny. There was a small level spot which was the favored hangout of Chitose's muscle builders. The ground was sandy and entirely treeless there. This was the men's "Muscle Beach." American G.I.s didn't know the place existed.

It was 9 a.m., the sky cloudless, the sun's rays strong. The men brought barbells, dumbbells, weights, and benches. There were a dozen or so dedicated bodybuilders in Chitose but almost twice that number came to hang out, smoke, and sell *shabu* and steroids.

"They've got to find Akiyama—that's the thing! Don't make excuses for him and don't blame the Americans," said the brawniest weightlifter of the bunch, sitting on the edge of his workout bench, in loose trousers, stretching his arms. A flannel baseball shirt covered his big chest, and he wore an insulated undershirt beneath it.

"I'm not making excuses," protested a guy with high

cheekbones, wearing a work shirt and a homemade sable vest. He stood ready to spot for the muscle man when he began pressing barbells. It didn't look like that was going to happen right away—the conversion was too heated.

"Akiyama is nowhere to be seen for days, a cop goes to his house and the cop vanishes," the barrel-chested man barked.

"Who told you that?"

"Everybody knows except you." The big guy was pretty sure who was responsible for the attack on Noboru and Iwate's disappearance.

"I agree, it *could* be him," the guy with high cheekbones said, meaning Akiyama. "But right now, all they've got is circumstantial evidence. Not that I care one bit for an Ainu."

"Yeah, well, don't care too much. It might cause you to tip over because of your big head," the weightlifter said, breaking into a grin.

Listening into the conversation was a man close by wearing a fringed cowhide jacket. The coat was something out of the Wild West. If he'd had a gun and a holster, he could have been a pioneer on the Oregon Trail. Instead, his right hand pushed a dumbbell up in the air. He said nothing. He only concentrated on his exercise.

"American soldiers are involved if you ask me," said a lanky fellow with a raspy voice standing nearby, whose exertions consisted of smoking cigarettes.

"We didn't ask you," grunted the voice of the weightlifter as he lay down on the bench ready to take hold of the barbells.

As the men recreated in the crisp morning, they could take in, if so inclined, a wholesome view of Chitose River flowing northeast; both banks of it were elevated, then the land tapered down a mile farther away, settling into the sprawling Ishikari Plain.

An hour into the men's spirited interactions, Sheriff Danjuro Fujita paid a surprise visit. Middle-aged but still youthful in appearance, wearing a thick wool coat that covered his suit, Fujita was clearly on business, even though it was a holiday. He asked everyone to stop what they were doing: he had something to say.

He was known to many in the crowd, but not personally. A dozen men fell into a semi-circle around him while another ten or so hung back from getting close. They weren't always strictly on the right side of the law, but they listened—at a safe distance.

Fujita said the police had been up at Akiyama's cottage since early morning. A policeman who'd been on stakeout duty had vanished there. As Sheriff Fujita continued to address the crowd, Toshi Nakano approached slowly. He'd noticed the men were gathered around a man, but he couldn't see who that man was. Toshi was in a clean navy-blue suit that went well with his spiffy brown loafers, which were spotted with mud from the trek to Muscle Beach. He flitted around in back on the fringe of the crowd until he saw that the man who was speaking was Danjuro Fujita. Toshi had slept ninety minutes the night before; his face was pale, and his hands trembled. Seeing the sheriff, he knew he'd better stay out of his line of sight.

"We know Akiyama is alive," explained Fujita to the crowd, "because a reliable source saw him up there, and we believe that was after Officer Iwate's disappearance.

What he didn't explain was that Kiriko had told Aunt Satomi of her visit to her father's house the previous night, and that Kenshin Wada phoned the Sheriff's office to report Kiriko's sighting of her father.

It had vexed Aunt Satomi that Kiriko had waited a few hours before mentioning she'd seen Akiyama. The only way she found out was by questioning Kiriko—clearly, something was affecting her deeply. Satomi always steered away from talk about Kiriko's life before she was adopted. Kiriko never brought up this period of her childhood; Satomi wanted her to have her privacy. (Kiriko didn't know it, but

Satomi was prepared to talk to her about it if she ever wanted to.) At first Kiriko didn't want to say she'd been at Akiyama's cottage. She was afraid Satomi and Uncle Kenshin would scold her for it.

The high cheek-boned man asked Fujita, "Did the reliable source see Officer Iwate up there?"

Fujita replied, "No." Fujita paused intentionally, and then continued, "Deputy Iwate relieved Deputy Kobayashi at 11:30 a.m. It was some time after that the reliable source saw Akiyama."

"It's safe to go up there?" asked the guy wearing a fringed cowhide jacket.

"We'd like as many of you as possible to help us. That way, no one will be alone."

The looks on the men's faces showed that they regarded Fujita to be a sensible and methodical fellow.

Fujita continued smoothly, "You're all able-bodied men. Now that we've established that Akiyama is alive and in the area he's to be brought in for questioning. You'll go with our deputies and search the broad area around his cottage for him and for Deputy Iwate."

To a man, everyone in the semi-circle directly around Fujita said they would join in the search. Half of the men beyond the semi-circle were silent and stared at their feet. They weren't going to take part. It wasn't that they were cowards or idlers—they just didn't want to get close to the police.

Fujita was pleased with the response and said, "Good, we'll meet at the police station at twelve noon and depart from there. We'll have about seven hours of light."

Toshi stayed out of the way as Fujita left the scene with three volunteers who were immediately at his side asking all sorts of questions, most of which Fujita calmly said he wasn't authorized to answer.

With the policeman gone, the men who'd been exercising went back to pack up their training equipment. Toshi managed to dodge being seen by Fujita, which was an accomplishment, considering that his clothing was loud and quite unrelated to the setting.

Toshi glided over to spot where there were a couple of benches and a stack of weights. He knew the guys weren't going to ask to buy *shabu* or steroids—the police had just been there. He asked them, "So I heard right? The cops want you to go with them and look for Akiyama at his place?"

The brawny man in the baseball shirt was attending to his barbells on a stand, taking them apart. He didn't bother to look at Toshi, who went on:

"There's an American soldier named Lloyd—Lloyd Kelso. We should be going after *him*. Akiyama's a loser. He couldn't kill anybody. He couldn't kill a cop."

A stocky guy as short as Toshi but with much broader shoulders snapped at him:

"What are you talking about? Didn't you hear what Fujita said: Iwate disappeared up at Akiyama's place and Akiyama was seen there. This has nothing to do with some American named Lloyd."

"Don't be so sure!" Toshi retorted.

The guy with high cheekbones shouted at Toshi, "You're nuts."

"You haven't seen blood come out of his mouth like I have," Toshi said.

Continuing to disassemble his weight equipment, the barrel-chested guy bellowed. "What are you babbling about?" He liked Toshi no more than Bob Fernandez did, though he'd never met Bob and never would.

"He's a creature…" Toshi began to explain but was cut off by the guy with the fringed cowhide jacket who was smirking.

"Oh, he's a creature, is he?" he wisecracked. He was now helping another weightlifter put some weights in a box.

Toshi raved, "Blood. Yep, he likes blood. He'll take your blood. He'll bite you for your blood. That he wants. Your blood…"

Mr. High Cheekbones interrupted, mocking him, "Do you realize how many times you just said, 'blood'?" Then he added as an afterthought, "You've got the shakes."

The lanky guy with the raspy voice took the cigarette out of his mouth and placidly advised Toshi to calm down and take less *shabu* in the morning.

Toshi didn't relent. "Yep, that's the way it is for creatures like him. They want blood, they can't live without your blood…"

At that moment, a dumbbell flexer who had decided to get in some more exercise before leaving, put down his weight, stepped forward and gave Toshi a push that sent him reeling. "Get out of here, pretty boy!"

Once he'd gotten his footing back, Toshi snapped, "Leave me alone!" He was petulant, hurt and looked like he was going to leap at the guy.

Color seemed to come to the cheekbones of the guy in the sable vest when he said to Toshi, "You're a mess. You wouldn't want somebody around here to punch you in the nose and get blood on your suit. Go home and get some sleep. Otherwise, no matter what you put into your system, you're not going to make it to the bowling alley tonight."

The strongest guy at Muscle Beach—the barrel-chested one—had withdrawn from the conversation. Perhaps his mind was on the search party he'd be joining. He left it to the others to childishly banter with Toshi. After a little more of their back and forth, he heard one of his comrades say, "Step right up, young man! I'll give you a bloody nose. There'll be blood and more blood. Didn't your mother ever tell you that?" Then he heard the men snorting and guffawing.

Toshi wanted to spit at them but thought better of it.

How they laughed! To Toshi, high on drugs, it was deafening.

His person ridiculed under the bright sky, he turned his back on the men, spinning around, finding himself facing the mountains to the west. He spotted Mount Tarumae there, an unusual natural sight near the horizon. The distance is far, but the day was clear. He saw the mountain—an active volcano—venting its steam and poisonous gases. Inside himself, he, too, fumed.

CHAPTER 10

His discovery of the stranger hiding under low hanging boughs of trees near his cottage showed that the dangers were multiplying. What was odd was that the stranger was a man, not a spirit.

After examining the man's belongings near his body, Akiyama found a revolver. It appeared this man was hunting him. Why? And with a revolver? What could this mean? Was his intent, like that of the evil spirits on his trail, to annihilate him? Who was this Japanese man who dressed like any man in any town in Hokkaido?

Akiyama must leave as soon as possible. But first he needed to move the corpse, separate himself and his home from it.

It strained him to carry the body away. It put him in a nervous state.

Afterward, he went through his supplies buried in the ground—he did this rather than take the time to pray for a cleansing of the spot where the man had lain—where he had died, where the land had been disrupted.

Then a girl-ghost invaded his cottage—presenting itself in the image of his daughter, Kiriko. How traumatizing this was! After the ghost ran away, he went out to the cluster of branches and recited supplications, pleading for the removal of the impurities there—the girl-ghost had come to upbraid him for not having done that before.

Akiyama then put a few necessary supplies in a sack and hastened away.

He stopped to rest a quarter hour after he'd left his place; he sat with his back up against the trunk of a thick gingko tree.

He passed out. He remained unconscious for several hours. When he came to, the sky was almost dark.

He was not certain where to go. Old habits told him it was best to go into town and find shelter there—this time furtively. He prayed to various animal spirits, right on the spot, asking them to make him invisible. He slung his heavy sack on his back.

Reaching Chitose, smoke hung in the dense air, but it was less slippery underfoot than the last time he'd been there. Colorful streamers, banners and flags hung from homes and businesses indicating that this day was the eve of Golden Week. He moved faultlessly and, if he detected someone near, he hid himself on the sides of buildings where he couldn't be seen.

He saw a schoolhouse and, knowing it would be empty for some days, knew it'd be a safe place to take refuge. Entering from the back door, which was unlocked, he found himself in a corridor. There were classrooms on both sides of him. He went into one of them and on the floor in the front, under the blackboard, he placed his belongings.

He would be undisturbed in the room for days—if he needed that much time. Just enough light came in from a streetlight for him to see the primary school's diminutive desks and chairs in neat rows for the young pupils. In the front of the room, where the teacher would stand and speak, he laid down layers of furs and clothing. He would sleep on top of them. He prayed that those hunting him would not find him here.

He did not realize he'd curled himself up and fallen asleep on top of the clothing and furs when a light came on in the cold classroom. A switch hadn't turned it on. The light was just there, in all its brightness. He could see out the windows it was the middle of the night.

He threw his head back in surprise and rubbed his eyes when he came fully to his senses and saw that, sitting in the elfin seats with desktops, were various wild animals—but they were not in their usual proportions—each one was approximately the same size as the other. It was also surprising they were already in mid-conversation. They took no notice of Akiyama as they chattered.

The first words he understood were spoken by a huge rat that was sitting with his long tail laying limp on the floor behind the back of his petite chair. His pitch was not as high as Akiyama might have expected. "Well, it's been confirmed, if you ask me," the rat said in response to something that went before.

"We didn't ask you, but it's confirmed because there's proof," croaked an enormous frog sitting two desks away. "Humans are hunting him; it's not just spirits."

Then a snake, a dark blue-green *aodaisho,* curled up in a nearby chair, far greater than its usual size, commented: "It serves him right for accosting that woman, the owner of Bar Eden. What did he hope to gain from that?"

Akiyama was so flummoxed that he wouldn't have been able to respond if any of the creatures had noticed him and had asked him directly. The reason why he set out to frighten Mommy Eri was that he'd observed during his rambles in town that Kiriko was working for her. (Through the years he'd seen Kiriko in town, always without her knowing it.) He didn't want his daughter working in a place that American soldiers frequented, because Americans were among the combatants that Fumito was forced to fight in the war. Fumito's spirit, seeking a resting place in Chitose, if reaching out to Kiriko for help in doing so, would immediately fly away once he found his sister was tainted by fraternizing with American army soldiers—he had fiercely battled them in war. Chitose, at all costs, must be made safe for his son to come back to.

A white-tailed eagle sitting at a desk in front of the snake turned around and said to it, echoing Akiyama's thoughts, "What he had to gain was the knowledge that Chitose would be safe so his son's spirit could return."

The snake hissed back, extending its head at the eagle. It didn't like the bird to answer or upstage it; that the eagle was one of its natural predators didn't help. It sneered at the eagle, "He doesn't know it, but maybe his daughter once was a pupil here."

The eagle, not wishing to get embroiled in an argument with the snake, rose from its chair and hopped across the room to take an empty seat far enough away from the reptile to avoid being physically lashed out at.

Yes, it was incredibly odd that each of the animals fit comfortably in their seats and at their desktops, their sizes completely lacking the spatial proportions that they had to each other in Nature.

A raccoon-faced *tanuki* offered advice to the last two. "Eagles and snakes of similar sizes ought not to fight. There may not be a clear winner; one may be older than another, and before one of you falls down, I can eat you both."

An adult deer chimed in, muttering to the *tanuki,* "Well, I can eat you." The deer was no larger than a fawn and sat peacefully at its desk. For a moment Akiyama's mind abandoned his body and merged into the peaceful being of the deer—although it was bizarre that it was saying it could eat the *tanuki* when it was the other way around. Akiyama felt deer legs under him. They were like short stilts. They were folded under his abdomen and at the rear. Akiyama shook his head once with a forceful nod to bring himself out of the form of the deer; somehow he returned to himself in no time.

A ridiculously large squirrel, sitting three rows down in the center, added its voice to the banter. "And I can eat you. I can eat you. I drink less water than you!" it squealed.

A plump brown owl was sitting in the front row, facing Akiyama. The bright light bothered it. Its eyes were shut. I might be dozing.

But Akiyama's eyes were wide open in shock.

The *tanuki* turned a black furry cheek to Akiyama. It was the first time any of the animals spoke to him. He wasn't against animals talking to him. He regularly called upon such spirits. Yet...

The *tanuki* explained, sounding like the smartest pupil in the class:

"Not to upset you, we know you prayed to him, but... there's no wolf here. We all know what happened to the wolf."

This comment shot gloom into Akiyama, even though intense light surrounded him.

He needed to save himself from this gloom. The consequences of it consuming him were grave, even fatal. This crazy squabbling and babbling of animals sitting like school children made him want to sob deep sobs—he felt inexplicably vulnerable and at the same time he felt great empathy toward the creatures who were subjected to bullying and affronts.

The large snake hissed once more, but this time addressing Akiyama as well as all the animals: "The teacher's not here. He's an expert on the color green and has gone to bed."

In a confidential but stately tone the *tanuki* said, "It won't surprise you that the teacher is a bear. The bear has finished hibernating but still it must sleep when tired. We have to be cautious, with humans here at this hour."

"I know," answered Akiyama for the first time.

What an oppressive situation. He felt he was the one who'd shrunk in size, that the animals hadn't grown larger. But then he realized that made no sense—because the classroom hadn't changed size and no squirrel, for example, is as large as a *tanuki*.

A crow, a black *karasu*, which hadn't been heard until now, announced in a repulsive voice, "Humans think they're making things better for themselves. All they're doing is increasing their numbers..." It paused when Akiyama shuddered and then went on, "...At our expense. And furthermore, those humans who are the victors... they live to have many choices—if they don't kill themselves first."

Akiyama solemnly nodded "yes" to himself upon hearing this.

After this, the white-tailed eagle peered across the room from where it now sat. In response to what the crow had just said, it proclaimed, "I see it every day from high, just as you."

The crow barked, "The natural world gets punched in the nose..."

Akiyama heard his own voice, but it did not come out from his mouth. Instead it came out from the mouth of the eagle and finished the sentence: "by the Japanese."

His voice fazed none of the animals.

But Akiyama was. To hear his voice come from any of the animals unnerved him. He uttered in the calmest voice he could muster, "Please excuse me. I did not wish to interrupt." He believed the room to be possessed by wicked spirits, or at least those which were demented. He didn't know, and couldn't know, that some Tai societies of Southeast Asia believed that the day the animals got together and chatted among themselves signaled the coming of the end of the world—first, drought would strike, then the Great Deluge would follow.

He began packing his things so he could leave the room. His back was turned so he didn't know which animal said, "You'll have one or more followers—offspring—to replace Fumito." He didn't know what the creature meant and muttered to himself, "I cannot have another son. My wife is dead."

Almost done with his packing, he heard the rat speak behind his back. It was not exactly speaking, though. It was more like rat singsong. "Look at your weathered ha-ands. They're wrinkled and gray-ay!" sang its squeaky festive voice. Akiyama didn't have to be looking at it to think: this rodent is a fine one to talk—its body has sharp big whiskers that are ancient looking.

The rat continued with its mocking song, "Your hands have done the ordinary things—predictable stu-uff—a lot of work—in the course of staying ali-ive—and now you aspire to be a warrior serving the Great Wol-uf!"

Akiyama felt more than one pang of anger. To be made fun of by a rat… what an insult.

A mountain hare whose heart was beating nervously, whose nose was twitching and sniffing—and who was of course, at least five times his normal size, spoke up. He'd never spoken until that point. His voice filled with pity, he knew he would be dreamed of by Akiyama when the poor man finally fell asleep. It said, "I come from the burrow to help… the distress in you."

Akiyama then left the room with his things, moving across the corridor into another classroom. It was pitch black and quiet; he sensed no spirits there. He arranged a bed for himself on the floor and passed out, sleeping the whole night through, though at times busy with nightmares. But he did have one pleasant dream, and it was of a mountain hare.

CHAPTER 11

The engine of the Sikorsky S-51 helicopter sputtered out. After a moment, with its blades still whirling, a sturdy officer with his cap in his hand stepped out of the "taxi." Keeping his head lowered as he walked, U.S. Army Captain Gideon Forsberg, in a padded army-issue winter coat, arched his eyebrows and kept one eye on the ground and the other on the horizon. He leaned his body forward, stepping firmly against gusts of air. His thick dark brown hair, cut short, seemed not to move in the kicked-up atmosphere.

This was his third day on Hokkaido. He'd been in the army for eight and a half years, since joining as a seventeen-year-old. He was from Minnesota's Iron Range.

Once he was clear of the landing area, he scanned the surroundings. A one o'clock sun shined over the flat terrain fanning out around him. So, this was Chitose, he thought. His nose smelled the town itself, just north of where he stood. He shifted his gray eyes to the west. Visibility was good: snow powdered mountain tops, a few miles distant; the mountains' cone shapes instantly discernable, their volcanic origins obvious.

He felt an odd attraction to the idea of volcanos. Maybe this feeling was connected to a primitive awe of fire. He said to himself, "Strange landscape here."

With the noise from the chopper's rotors dying, a humorless sergeant was there on the spot, ready to take him to the building which would be under his command.

Military Police Headquarters was all neat brick, built in

the western style. It was a holdover from Japanese Army days.

In an office that was two doors up the corridor from where Gideon Forsberg's would be, Master Sergeant Pete Velchoffsky, a thirty-four-year-old career sergeant read down a column of evaluation scores on a sheet of mimeographed paper. Velchoffsky conducted the workaday business of the 545th Military Police Company, Chitose's MP unit, which included the hiring of new MPs. This was uppermost on the master sergeant's mind at the moment—he needed to add two dozen new part-time MPs to the unit.

The sergeant's door was open. When he heard a man slow his step near the threshold of his door, he stood up from behind his desk. One person he knew it would not be was Captain Gideon Forsberg. Choppers from U.S. 1st Cavalry Division Headquarters at Camp Crawford in Sapporo ran on time and on schedule. The captain would arrive in ten minutes. As always, Velchoffsky had scheduled his appointments tightly.

It was Private Lloyd Kelso who halted in the sergeant's doorway, stood rigid, raised his right arm and saluted him. The sergeant, who had short, bristly black hair and a neck and chin darkened by a five o'clock shadow, looked Kelso straight in the eyes and saluted back. Lloyd thought that with a name like Velchoffsky he would be meeting a man with paler skin. The sergeant's almost Mediterranean complexion surprised him.

"Come in, private," Velchoffsky said, quickly dropping his salute. He motioned to Lloyd to take a seat in a folding chair that faced his desk.

The sergeant settled back down in his swivel chair, adding curtly, "Good afternoon." He lowered his head to glance at a sheet of paper in the folder on his desk that would remind him of the name of the soldier in front of him.

"Thank you, sir," Lloyd said from his chair, too loudly. This was to cover up his nervousness. His motivation for becoming an MP was entirely self-serving.

Velchoffsky raised his eyes and launched in: "Chitose is a major lifeline to the United Nations and American forces in Korea. Many soldiers' lives depend on what we do here. Just so you know, I don't hire beaten-down soldiers who are desperate to get out of the army as soon as possible."

On hearing this, Lloyd suppressed a nervous swallow.

Most soldiers who sought assignments as part-time MPs weren't acting out of any personal interest in law enforcement. Rather, joining the police unit would normally shorten their service by anywhere from three to eight weeks. Draftees could understand an offer like that. The master sergeant was familiar with any fake enthusiasm a soldier might show for the job.

He studied Kelso and didn't break his gaze as he further declared, "I'm here to weed out the type of man who's only out for himself. Is that clear?"

"Yes, sir," Kelso said without blinking. Naturally the reason Lloyd was seeking an MP assignment—though it added an extra ten hours onto a man's workweek—was that it could get him discharged from the army quicker.

Velchoffsky picked up a few papers from Lloyd's service record folder and dispassionately spread his fingers underneath them. "Your superiors have paid you compliments, your test scores are sufficient, you're a hard worker, you pitch in when a hand's needed, you appear to ask the right questions if questions need to be asked, etcetera, etcetera." The sergeant set the papers down. "All that's fine." He continued methodically, "You don't have any experience in law enforcement. We'll give you the skills you need if we take you on."

Lloyd sat at attention, awaiting the master sergeant's next words. They came quickly.

"Do you believe you're physically and mentally fit for the job, private?"

"I do, sir." There was no other response to that question.

"I've been told you're friends with Private Fernandez," the unsmiling sergeant said noncommittally. He wasn't expecting a response and did not get one.

"I'm sure you know I've already interviewed him."

"Yes, sir."

Velchoffsky had disciplined himself to not let trivial details slow his momentum. None of the applicants had experience in police work; combat and its trauma had scarred not a few of them. If too many candidates were crossed off the list, he'd be left with no personnel. He was aware that Lloyd had seen heavy action in Korea, and men like him never went to see an army psychologist for fear it could delay their exit from the army.

Even at this point in the interview the sergeant knew he'd hire Lloyd. He'd already made up his mind about Bob Fernandez. It was a good idea, when possible, to take on men who were close buddies. It made their days less tedious, fostered good morale—the young guys were overworked, away from home, and didn't choose to be where they were.

"You know from our packet of information what the job entails: keeping order, enforcing the law. However, what must be emphasized about Chitose is that though it may seem peaceful, security threats abound. You're aware of that. All soldiers here are."

Hokkaido, only a couple hundred miles from the Russian Far East, now the Soviet Far East, had been of great geopolitical significance to world powers since the mid-19th century. Communism was just an island away. It did not please the U.S. that the mayor of Sapporo belonged to the Socialist Party.

Where there were communists and socialists, there was infiltration by Moscow. Information was gathered surreptitiously. Buildings were bugged. If you turned a dial on an AM radio you could get broadcasts, in Japanese and English, originating from Russia. A soldier who was not right in the head might start working for the Soviets; there could be sabotage.

For one moment, the sergeant conjured up the hell of Korea.

"We're at war. I don't have to tell *you* that." He added, almost sounding like he was finishing the interview, "You'll be told a lot more if selected."

It wasn't much of an interview—it was more like a pre-orientation.

"You know what we expect of you. Now it's your chance to ask me additional questions.

But a heartbeat passed, and it wasn't Kelso's turn to talk after all.

"But I'll save you the trouble," the sergeant said, ignoring the minor fuss he was causing. "Here's your question to me: 'Sir, what's the toughest part of the job?'"

Velchoffsky's manner struck Kelso as unkind. But presumably the sergeant had a lot of interviews to do. It seemed he'd rather be working on something else.

The sergeant answered his own question, "It's not the use of force—that will happen—on occasion. No, the toughest part of the job is when you personally know the man who's the cause of the trouble, or who's being the *spy*." Velchoffsky raised his eyebrows during the last part of his sentence. "If you don't know the offender, that's best. You always have to put your individual thoughts and feelings to one side and do your duty, just like with any job in the army."

Velchoffsky kept his gruff exterior but spoke softer. "I don't want to daunt you. It's your turn to speak. I'd like to hear *you* talk now."

This was the part of the interview where Velchoffsky engaged the man in loose conversation, while keeping him under his thumb. He proceeded onward, raising his own voice in volume as spoke, "I want to hear the sound of your voice, private—to see if there's any authority in it. Because you'll have authority even when you're dealing with those above your rank—authority which you don't have now." He pretended to briefly glance down at Lloyd's file. It was theater, but how was Lloyd to know. The sergeant softened again, slightly: "I notice that you come from New York state. How was it there?"

Lloyd spoke, not moving a muscle below his neck, "Small town, two thousand people. Good school, lots of countryside, good place to grow up. Good place to get away from because it's rather small, sir." He was impressed with himself that his words flowed out and were loud.

"All good, then, huh? Now you're expanding your horizons, aren't you?"

"Yes, sir," Lloyd said, without blinking.

"We try to have that happen," the master sergeant said in a more relaxed manner. He reached into another paper folder on his desk and Lloyd didn't see what he took out of it because his eyes were locked straight ahead. He didn't want to do anything that would make him fail the interview.

"Have a look at this photograph," Velchoffsky said as he pushed it to the edge of his desk toward Lloyd.

Lloyd shifted his eyes to the desk.

"We have a new commanding officer, Captain Gideon Forsberg. He's arriving today. It'll do you no harm to know who he is if you pass him."

The sergeant took the photograph back once Lloyd had had a look at it.

He then asked Kelso in a gruff voice, "Do you believe you're up to the job?"

"I do, sir. Thank you for interviewing me, sir!"

"You're welcome. We'll let you know by tomorrow if you'll be going to Camp Crawford for training."

Soon after entering the main corridor from the master sergeant's office, Kelso veered to his right, stopped, and saluted. He nearly stumbled into a captain—he saw that right away from the two-bar insignia on the officer's collar—and his sergeant escort. The officer seemed to be the unaffected type. He was apparently deep in thought. He did not acknowledge Kelso's salute and wasn't speaking to the staff sergeant accompanying him.

Kelso recognized him from the photograph that Velchoffsky had just shown him: Captain Forsberg.

Speaking of the devil, he thought to himself

Having shown Forsberg to Velchoffsky's office door, the sergeant alongside him turned away discreetly and vanished up the hall. Velchoffsky heard the footsteps and set down the pen he'd had in his hand. He quickly rose from his desk to salute Forsberg who stood in the middle of his doorway.

"Master Sergeant Velchoffsky." Forsberg spoke crisply and courteously, returned the sergeant's salute, then relaxed his arm and lowered it. The sergeant was older and more experienced than he. All reports testified he was top notch at his job.

"A pleasure to meet you, Captain Forsberg, sir," the sergeant responded to his new boss, dropping his salute with a respectful terseness. "Welcome to Camp Chitose."

Moving from the doorway, Forsberg took one step into the office. Though not small, it wasn't a comfortable place for visitors to be: file cabinets, a coat tree, a coat rack, cabinets, tables under windows with folders spread out on them, emphasizing that the master sergeant had his own bear den which none should enter unless there was important business with the bear. All the chairs except for Velchoffsky's were folding ones.

Indicating he was only going to be there momentarily, Forsberg said, "Thank you. A pleasure to meet you, sir. I understand that my office is two doors down from here."

"Yes. Lieutenant Nichols's is between yours and mine. I'll show you down there, if you like, sir."

"We'll be meeting in, what," Forsberg paused to glance at the clock on the north wall of the sergeant's office, "Ten minutes?"

"Yeah, in the conference room. I'll stop by your office and take you there, if you like."

"Good. Thank you."

"I'll take you to your new office now."

"Sounds good."

Sergeant Velchoffsky got up from his chair and led Captain Forsberg down the corridor to his office.

A dozen men were at the staff meeting in the conference room. The captain was acquainted on paper with those at the table—he'd been shown copies of their service records at the provost marshal's office at Camp Crawford. Likewise, everyone in the room had already been introduced to Forsberg on paper, in a memo that had circulated a week before. What remained, of course, was to rub eyeballs.

First Lieutenant Todd Nichols was about the same age as Forsberg and at five feet eleven, as tall as him. There the similarities ended. Nichols was relaxed, well-mannered, and people liked him. On his desk, among his official papers, lay a paperback of the thriller, *The Thirty-Nine Steps*. One got the impression he was not a "lifer," and that eventually he'd leave the military to go into management in corporate America— or maybe not. Maybe he'd accept an executive job at a non-profit organization like the YMCA or Boy's Town.

Nichols began the meeting. After the introductions around the table were completed, he passed the baton, as it were, and Forsberg informed all present that he'd read through the recent program status reports and looked forward to ensuring a smooth upsizing of the unit. He gave the impression he didn't feel there was much to talk about at that moment, since he'd read up on all matters of importance. He surprised everyone by proceeding to what was the conclusion to what he had to say: he pointed out the continuing need for conscientious dedication to their work, prudent intra-unit communications, and vigilance regarding security threats of all kinds.

After his speech, except for Lieutenant Nichols, Sergeant Velchoffsky and Forsberg, those present left to go back to their jobs. Five minutes had elapsed—this included Nichols' shows of respect and a few civil pleasantries.

There was no specific agenda for the second half of the meeting. It was set up to be a preliminary discussion addressing the division of labor now that Forsberg had arrived. Velchoffsky's duties and responsibilities wouldn't change. But what about First Lieutenant Todd Nichols? He had been the chief executive officer; it appeared that leadership figured there would be too much for him to do alone and that was why Forsberg was brought in as the new MP commander.

While ten thousand new troops (those soldiers would be living in tents on wooden platforms in Chitose II) were due next month, and would be busy training every day, it appeared to Nichols and Velchoffsky—though they respectfully refrained from discussion of it—that Forsberg had arrived too early to be useful. Besides that, they wondered—and again, they used no words to state it precisely—if he was truly necessary at all because Nichols and Velchoffsky were a very good double act. They believed they could easily handle the scaling up of the unit, and that assigning more second lieutenants was all that was needed, not another layer of administration above them. Nichols felt the new arrangement was fraught with potential infighting; it might even slow admin down—he took Forsberg's arrival as an unofficial demotion. He even wondered if he'd done something to provoke army provost Tyler's (Major Milton Tyler was the head of all MP operations in Hokkaido) disfavor.

Now that the three men were alone together, Forsberg sensed that it pained Velchoffsky to move from being Nichols' NCO assistant to being his. He sensed that Velchoffsky's first impression of him was that he wasn't of the same caliber as Nichols. (True, Velchoffsky knew from reading Forsberg's service record that he'd advanced in rank much faster than usual, starting with a battlefield promotion near the end of World War II's Italian Campaign. He wasn't keen to be under the administration of a lucky young man who was eight years his junior.)

Forsberg also noticed that Nichols' previously animated face was now passive.

Forsberg knew he was being regarded as an intruder. He saw that he must address their discomfort. He told them he'd heard and read superlative things about them, that, for the moment, nothing would change. He said he'd just finished commanding an MP unit in Korea, had not taken any leave, had been feeling run down in the past few days, and planned to take a few days to study more reports, as well as maps of the bases and the area in general. There should be no rush to integrate him into the administrative hierarchy.

Relief spread over the faces of Nichols and Velchoffsky. Forsberg flashed a quick smile after he saw his effect on them.

While Nichols and Velchoffsky each was curious why Forsberg wasn't still in Korea, this wasn't a proper question to ask, nor did they discuss the question among themselves. As for Forsberg's finessing himself into some R & R, there were many instances of officers below the rank of lieutenant colonel, who were new to their assignments and didn't immediately plunge in. There were mental adjustments to be made to the job and the new locale.

Forsberg's manner signaled that further discussion between the three of them would come later.

Velchoffsky appended to the final moments of their little conference the remark that he was assigning Private First Class Stan Shuck to take Forsberg around Chitose II. This time of the day wasn't the most favorable time to show him Chitose I—there were many vehicles on the roads and the layout of the camp didn't differ much from other army installations. On the other hand, this was a good time to look over Chitose II, since only construction personnel were there.

The two camps were four miles apart; a busy public road

connected them. Chitose II, despite a marked rise at its main gate, was mostly flat once inside. Huge sections of the camp were left wooded, to be used in training exercises. The base, twice the acreage of Chitose I, had been carved out of semi-wilderness; construction had already moved into the interiors of the new buildings during the winter.

The afternoon sun was low enough for shadows to form. With few men in sight, the camp looked like a park on a cool spring day, though some smokey air from town was headed in its direction.

Private Shuck drove Forsberg first past empty lots for trucks, artillery and heavy equipment. The private wore glasses. He seemed unaccountably nervous. They next passed storage depots; after that, barracks, which were, of course, Quonset huts, those ubiquitous semi-cylindrical buildings with corrugated steel exteriors. Shuck then took the captain to the new building where a C2I office at Chitose II would be. The new place was all but finished, the door was open; carpenters worked in the cold. It was colder inside than out. Shuck was a man with a pencil thin mustache and of slight build. He tried not to shiver.

Next, he drove Forsberg over a road that predated the camp; the captain noticed some foundations which likely had belonged to a collection of small farm buildings that had been torn down. The ruins gave a temporary home to a dump that consisted of lumber scraps, shipping pallets and spools that'd held thick cables. The road curved. The private pointed out the quartermaster's facilities. Not far from there, surprisingly, was a thin canal, about five yards across. It wasn't maintained. It flowed in and out of an undeveloped part of the camp no one seemed to be too concerned about. Sensing the day would soon turn colder, Forsberg felt the urge to have the sun shine against his face. He asked Shuck to stop. Shuck's dutiful answer to the spur-of-the-moment request was, "Where?"

Forsberg gestured imprecisely and said, "Anywhere

here."

The section of land around them seemed to have been used as farmers' fields for a long time. One building in ruins had been an old icehouse. What was left of the structure were thick rock walls imbedded into the earth. Forsberg had grown up with icehouses in Minnesota. He supposed that the canal was used to float slabs of ice out of storage.

While they were stopped there, Shuck took out a map of the base and spread it on the hood of the jeep. Doing his best to control the shaking in his hand, he pointed out on the map several places they hadn't driven by yet. One large area contained platforms for tents. Nearby were mess halls (more Quonset huts), a snack bar (a Quonset, too) and basketball courts. Forsberg wasn't really looking at the map, even though he pretended to let his eyes fall on it from time to time. His attention was elsewhere. Something that Shuck couldn't see was distracting him. Shuck displayed his knowledge, pointing, speaking without being asked.

"Captain, there's where the stockade is," he rambled on. "Nobody thinks we'll ever have twenty-eight men in there at the same time, but since there's plenty of land in these parts it was decided to build big. Um, we'll go there next, sir."

"We don't need to go in. Let's just drive by," Forsberg grunted. Something was preoccupying the captain. He made his eyes fasten on the map and locate a spot on it. Shuck could think of nothing more to say. There was silence. The private grew nervous as the silence lengthened and Forsberg's eyes continued to focus on the same spot on the map. Shuck wondered what was going through the captain's mind.

Forsberg's eyes were on a small circular symbol on the map that indicated the location of a nuclear fallout shelter. It was off to one side of the base, but maybe future construction would make it more central.

He felt his palms moisten. He didn't feel dizzy—no, the opposite: strength surged within him. He thought back to a time during the last days in the Apennine Mountains in Italy, toward the end of World War II. To have these physical sensations here and now was strange. His senses sharpened; this struck him with foreboding. He took a deep breath before he spoke: "Drive me to the fallout shelter."

It wasn't Private First Class Shuck's place to ask why. The captain's request was a surprise. This Forsberg was an odd bird, he thought to himself. Well, so much for Shuck's planned route. He rolled up the map and put a hand in his coat's flap pocket to find a place for it there. As he did this, a small white box spun out of it.

Forsberg heard the box of Benzedrine pills hit the ground. The sound was louder to him than it would normally be. He looked down to Shuck's feet where the box was. Shuck saw him look.

So, the private took pep pills. He could be prosecuted for it. So could at least a few hundred other G.I.s in Chitose.

What a welcome incident. Now Forsberg had something on Shuck. He could call on him for favors.

He said softly to Shuck, "Judy Garland." There was no need to say anything more. Everybody knew the famous Hollywood star had problems with pills. Shuck's eyes blinked nervously. He got the message: the captain knew. He looked at Forsberg's quiet face and understood he was to pick up the box, put it in his pocket and no more would be said.

They arrived on the west side of the underground shelter where some trees had been left standing. After getting out of the jeep, the captain wondered aloud, "Why put a fallout shelter so far to the edge of camp?"

"This is for the soldiers in the tents. There are basements in the buildings in the center of the post that'll be used as shelters, too." As Shuck spoke, Forsberg felt an animal muscularity growing within him.

His sense of smell spiked. There was an uncommon odor in the air. Nervous excitement gripped his limbs. In his mind—a feeling of dread.

What was in this area? He could hear finer than normal. Much finer. This wasn't good. He wanted it to go away.

They'd taken only a few steps in the direction of the shelter. He heard his own footsteps—they were too loud—but he wasn't walking in a noisy manner. He stopped walking.

Turning awkwardly to Shuck who was following a few paces behind, he said, "I've seen enough. We're going back to Chitose I, now." There was a puzzled look on the private's face. Forsberg knew he ought to explain, "Something I ate. My stomach's acting up."

"Oh," Shuck said, dully.

"Take me to my quarters. I'll rest there for a short while and call you when I feel better so we can come back."

When Shuck pulled into the small lot next to the 20-by-48-foot Quonset that housed Forsberg and three other officers at Chitose I, he pointed to a nearby jeep and said, "Oh, there's your new jeep. The keys are in the ignition."

Forsberg nodded his head in acknowledgment and said, "Private, tell your sergeant you are to remain at the police station for my call. We've got a few more hours of daylight left."

Less than a five-minute walk from the back of Akiyama's house, the land plunges to an elevation closer to that of the fields and streets along Chitose River. The steep ravine, covered with thin trees, saplings, brush, and grass, stretched at a sixty-degree angle. At this time of year, the ground was wet and the new growth on the face of the slope was attached to a thin layer of soil that had an underbelly of clay. Uninformed climbers could easily cause a landslide. To search the slope by using binoculars from the brow of the hill was no solution. A group from the search party had to make a sweep there, personally.

Nothing had turned up after four hours of searching. The men—police and firemen, members of the local Rotary Club and volunteers from Muscle Beach—had spread out and scoured the area within a half mile radius of Akiyama's house. That was after exploring both sides of the path that led up the steadily rising terrain. They'd bushwhacked, brambles and tree parts poking them, insects swarming around them, aiming for their eyes. They'd toiled in groups of three, for safety.

Since there was no sign or clue regarding the whereabouts of Akiyama or Iwate, Sheriff Fujita had no other choice but to order a search of the one area that remained.

The delicate task fell to two sheriff deputies and Daichi Ito, a thirty-five-year-old businessman, Rotary Club member and fitness buff. Ito had some mountaineering experience. What was required was that a man be lowered to the fragile ground, one end of a rope tied around his waist and the other to a sturdy tree on safe ground on the top of the hill. Binoculars could be used in the process, but it was imperative that the gradient was inspected closely.

The men took turns at cautiously descending and ascending. A number of times their feet slid, their ropes went taut, and they needed to be pulled back up. It was scary work. Sheriff Fujita let the rest of the men in the search party go back down to Chitose if they wished. A few stayed to watch the progress of the operation.

In the first two hours, the men saw no trace of human activity on the slope. They beat back their exhaustion and struggled on. A policeman couldn't simply vanish into thin air.

It was Deputy Shohei Hashimoto's turn. He was on section of the slope, to the extreme right side of his comrades above. His body ached all over. After bringing his binoculars up to him to get a closer look at something unusual he thought he'd seen in a tangle of dwarf pines, he yelled, "I think I see something!"

The sheriff, who was watching the three men's actions, felt his heart beat faster. This was welcome news, possibly—

but it made him very anxious.

Hashimoto peered through his binoculars, adjusting the lens, zooming in, verifying his initial impression. It was awful: the dead body of his fellow cop, Iwate, lay there. He recognized the clothes. The body had been stopped in a downward roll by the wild shrubs. "It's Deputy Iwate!" he yelled, in shock. Hashimoto let his binoculars fall; they dangled in front of his chest. After his strong voice carried upward, the other sheriff's officer, Tetsuya Sugai, strained to get a glimpse of the body with his binoculars.

From the crest of the hill Sheriff Fujita shouted, "Is he alive?"

"No," Hashimoto thundered back.

Fujita turned to Deputy Sugai and Daichi Ito and told them to grab the rope and help bring Hashimoto up. Then he called down to Hashimoto: "We're pulling you up."

Everyone there knew it would be a challenge to retrieve Iwate's body.

In the last hour the temperature had dropped enough for them to see their breath. The sky, too, was dimming. The discovery that Iwate was dead weighed down their spirits.

"Iwate's body will be recovered tomorrow." Fujita's voice was somber. He knew he was probably wrong—he'd seen the weather forecast—it was for heavy rain.

In any case, he knew he'd have to contact Camp Chitose for help. Climbing up or repelling down the steep hill covered by such topsoil was out of the question. A helicopter would be needed.

The remaining men of the search party gathered up whatever equipment they'd brought with them and the whole group proceeded back to town, understanding the hunt for Akiyama was now completely in the hands of the police.

Back at the station in Chitose, the sheriff asked Deputy Hashimoto to draw a sketch of the hillside, indicating where the body lay.

CHAPTER 12

Once back in his quarters, the strange sensations that Forsberg felt at the fallout shelter dissipated. After a half hour of thinking over the situation he knew what he had to do next. The sole telephone in his Quonset was in the common room, at the rear of the building.

Private Shuck was surprised to receive Forsberg's call so soon. But then again, the captain was an odd guy.

"Private First Class Shuck?"

"Yes, sir."

"Captain Forsberg, here. Is there anyone in your office that could hear this phone call?"

"Not at the moment."

"Good." He paused for a moment to impress upon Shuck that he was very serious. He then said gruffly, "Look, the tour is over for today. Now… I need a favor from you. You're never to mention I asked you for it, you got that?"

Shuck recognized that the captain had him under his thumb. If didn't do as he was asked, Forsberg could officially report his drug use and life would get difficult.

"Yes, sir," he replied.

"So this favor never happened, did it?"

"No, sir."

"In the future, if the evidence shows it did, the most you could ever say is that you don't remember, right?"

"Correct, sir."

The thought flashed through Shuck's mind: well, it's not so bad he's asking me for this—it means he trusts me.

"Now, relax and find a piece of paper. You're going to make a list."

Forsberg waited for Shuck to find some paper.

"Sir, I'm ready now," he said, his hands shaking from the amphetamine.

"I want you to get me a chain. Like the size of a chain for a porch swing or kid's swing. Nothing thinner or heavier than that. I'll need twelve feet of it."

"Okay."

The private wrote on his paper: "Swing set chain, 12 feet."

Forsberg waited a few seconds, then said, "Roll it in a coil. …And I want a tarp, also. It needs to be about twice the size of the hood of a jeep. It shouldn't be thick. It can be the wall of a tent, if you want, but if you get it from one, you'll have to cut it to size.

Shuck jotted on the paper.

Forsberg continued. "Get me the sturdiest tent stake you can find that I can pound in with a hammer—and get me a hammer, a regular one.

He gave Shuck time to write and went on, "I need a flashlight and a combat knife—make sure the sheath for it has a belt loop."

The captain paused for Shuck to stay with his instructions. Then he said, "Get me one set of leg irons and a pair of handcuffs."

Shuck's eyebrow automatically went up when he heard the last two items. Forsberg paused for him to write them down, then said, "That's it."

Forsberg waited long enough to know that the private had finished writing his list.

"Don't get anything from the Quartermaster's—at least not the front door. You don't sign for any of the stuff—you just take it. Nobody knows you take it. …You know what equipment's in the police building. When you go out to find the rest of the stuff, don't be seen. If anybody does see you, walk away with nothing. You're a cop, you look around, you patrol, it's your assignment." Bring the things to my quarters as soon as you have all of them. I'll hear you when your jeep pulls in."

Stan Shuck said, "Yes, sir, right away, sir, and hung up the phone. He muttered, "Strange."

Lots of equipment and supplies sat out in the open at Chitose I. Since there were more jobs than there were soldiers and everybody was in a hurry to get a job done, there wasn't enough time to stow everything. Plus, when so much stuff is out in the open, you can grab it quicker.

He arrived at Forsberg's quarters with the scavenged items in less than an hour. Hearing him outside, Forsberg came out, coatless, but with a pistol in the holster on his hips, and ordered, "Put the things in my jeep, please."

"Yes, sir. Everything you wanted except for the tarp and the chain is in a duffel bag."

"Good."

As the private took the things from his jeep and transferred them into Forsberg's, the captain enquired, "Did anybody see you?"

"Probably a few guys, but nobody from the police station."

"Did they say anything to you?"

"No, everybody was busy. They didn't care. It wasn't theirs."

Forsberg paused, to make sure that his words could be understood as a threat. "I hope what you say is true."

Once Stan had put the duffel, the tarp and coil of chain in Forsberg's vehicle, the captain dismissed him, saying, "Now, get moving, right away."

Before climbing into his jeep, he glanced at the twelve-foot chain. It would do.

He arrived at the fallout shelter in Chitose II and parked behind some trees. He looked over at the sunken structure through the jeep's window and he felt his temperature rise.

His hearing and sense of smell got sharper. He took off his coat, laid it on the passenger seat. He threw his hat there, too.

He stood eyeing the walls of the fallout shelter. He had no choice. He had to be there. Fate was pushing at his heels. He must go inside. He wasn't sure what he'd find, but he had his suspicions. He'd made what preparations he could. His adrenaline surged.

He grabbed all the things Shuck got for him from the back of the jeep and armed himself—he put the handcuffs in his back trouser pocket, the sheathed knife on his belt, the coil of chain over his left shoulder. His pistol was loaded.

There was enough codeine in his system. He hoped to remain a man. If he remained human, he'd be able to use his pistol and the knife. That would be an advantage. He switched on the flashlight.

He pushed one of the doors to the shelter. It opened quietly. A wide, descending ramp was in front of him. He walked down it slowly, keeping the beam of his light on the ground, not knowing the degree of its slope.

His nose hurt. The scent was even stronger. The only sound he heard was the sound of his own beating heart.

The ramp ended. The floor was level now. The place was like an empty underground parking garage.

He lifted his flashlight. No need to divide the darkness into sections and search. His nose told him where to shine the beam. He did not know how powerful his opponent was. The light drew attention to where he was. He had the strange feeling he was there to defend his territory. It was an animal feeling.

His light found an indeterminate mass lying on the ground fifteen yards away, near a wall. He needed to confront it. But how to lessen the danger?

He crept slowly in its direction. He wanted to take the coil of chain from his shoulder—it was a burdensome nuisance, distracting him from what he needed to smell, hear and see. His body needed to be unencumbered, agile. He would slip it off in an instant, at the first sign he did not need it right away. When only five yards separated him and the human-size mound, he could see it was motionless. But with his heightened senses he could hear it breathing. It was a lump of ragged cloth, animal hide, fur and hair.

It was hiding there—that much was clear. Could it smell him, sense him? Yes, he thought it probably did. Thinking this made his adrenaline surge more.

It wasn't making a move for him. But he couldn't let it hide there. He couldn't let it rest undisturbed.

He thought for a few moments, the sound of his heart almost swallowing the space around him. He would attempt to make it understand he would do it no harm.

He slipped off the coil of chain from his shoulder and placed it carefully on the floor. He bent down to it and put his flashlight on top of it. He let its beam illuminate the space between them.

He gently shushed "shh," as if he were quieting a child. He whispered to it again as he got closer. A cramp jolted through his body, momentarily halting him. When it was over, he had movement again. However, his muscles were charged with gripping, abnormal strength. It was such a difference in physical power that he shook his head once, as if to re-calibrate his sense of balance.

Suddenly the mysterious heap in front of him thrust itself up from the floor and growled. Forsberg had no idea what he was looking at. It was a form between of man and beast. He stopped in his tracks.

Instantly, his skin toughened. He felt thick hair spring up on his back.

The next moment the being stepped one of its feet back; it was preparing to throw itself at him. The beam of the flashlight caught the creature's eyes. They glistened. Forsberg gaped at the the eyes and the area below it: its nose and chin jutted out, almost in one piece. Its face was entirely covered with fur. It opened its mouth to make another sound: its teeth were animal sharp.

Forsberg stopped thinking.

He and the creature flung themselves at each other. The moment they touched they began to grapple. Neither wanted to kill the other at first; they did not use their mouths. Each wanted to prevail, to dominate. With all his might Forsberg tried to push the creature back down to where it had been lying.

He was unsuccessful. He freed himself from the creature's grasp and retreated, positioning himself three yards away. He exposed his now sharp teeth, and he snarled.

The creature did the same, in return.

The pain of his own teeth pressing on both sides of his face made him feel like he would go crazy at any moment. Oh, no, he thought. He did not want to further transform.

There was something he had; something he always had; somehow, someday, somewhere, he thought, it might be useful. It was an inexplicable feeling, but he'd learned not to discount such feelings. That's why he kept the thing so close to him.

He tore the two top buttons off his shirt and reached down his chest. He grabbed a neck chain, next to his military dog tags, and pulled it over his head.

On the chain was a bronze medallion. It had the image of a wolf's head on it; it was among the things he'd pilfered when he and his company swept through Bavaria in 1945 and took war booty.

The captain did not want them to fight. Why fight? What was there to fight about?

There was something about the creature that made him pity it.

Forsberg's held out the *Wolfsmedaillon,* dangling it, letting it swing like a pendulum, allowing its shiny surface to catch the light. He hoped somehow he could communicate that they were of the same kind—that he shared in the horror that tortured them both.

But the medallion didn't seem to attract the creature. Instead, it scanned Forsberg, its eyes focused on his neck, which was now more available since he'd torn off his two buttons.

Forsberg had tried. It didn't work. He let the medallion drop from his fist to the floor.

He managed, remarkably, to hold back his own impulse to leap. But more changes occurred in him. Soon he knew speech had left him. Only wolf sounds would come from his throat. A growl, and then more growls sounded loudly in him as he gnashed his lengthened teeth. His eyes, once gray, turned yellowish orange; the whites of his eyes, pink.

At the same time, across from him, the tendons of the creature strained to keep up with the changes in its bones. There would be a more vicious clash now.

There was a momentary pause before either leaped at the other. During this tiny lull Forsberg's eyes penetrated the creature's body. He thought he would see sinews and blood vessels—no, he only saw *old age*.

The creature was past the midpoint of its life. This would limit its capacity to strike. This didn't guarantee, however, Forsberg's success. He believed the being would fight to the finish. Forsberg couldn't let that happen.

He leapt first.

It was a snarling rumble; with saliva dripping and struggles to get tight holds. Each had a different intention— Forsberg wanted to subdue; the creature aimed to sink its teeth in and kill.

The captain's strategy was more complicated. He had to keep it alive. He forced it to fight hard, wanting to wear it out. He was advantaged by his strength; it continued to well up from deep within him.

On the floor of the shelter they gnashed, pawed, rolled, and twisted.

A minute into their melee, their bodies swung into the beam of Forsberg's flashlight at a certain angle—there, the beam illuminated the top of Forsberg's head. This caught the creature's eye.

Its reaction to what it saw was unexpected. Almost immediately the frenzy between the two stopped. The creature pressed its body away from Forsberg and unentwined itself.

Forsberg sensed it wasn't backing off to get distance for a powerful spring at him. He was mystified. Why had it stopped? What was it thinking?

It moved away because it saw something that Forsberg couldn't: the captain's hair had turned white.

Positioning itself at a safe distance from Forsberg, the creature, this changed form of Akiyama, panted. It could not stand as humans stand. After a moment its exhaustion forced it to settle its limbs down languidly to the ground. It tucked it limbs underneath it and gazed at Forsberg's head.

Through the creature spread gladness and veneration. This was the Great Wolf! Akiyama didn't know that the Great Wolf would have a *white* coat. But it was here—before his eyes! He was in the presence of his people's primogenitor. It had come up from the underworld to punish and repair this world! Akiyama thought: I am alive. The gods have not forsaken me. I cease any thoughts about myself. I surrender. I shall only serve.

Forsberg moved farther away from where the creature lay. He was relieved at the outcome of their fight. He was in awe of the mysterious creature.

He couldn't believe his eyes. The idea of it—though he'd suspected, because of the smell and his body's reactions, that possibly he'd stumbled on something like this—it was so much to take in... he still wasn't mentally prepared for it... he never thought too much about what it would be like to meet some thing like him. It frightened him...

All this would take time to sink in. He was in the presence of... this is a... *werewolf!*

CHAPTER 13

He'd been on a long and torturous road. Suddenly there was a new, radically different turn. Expect the unexpected—he should always be thinking that.

What is it about this place? he thought. He was resting on his side now, on the fallout shelter's floor, his muscle spasms abating. Was I sent here for a reason? I arrived in Japan only a few days ago; already I've met one. Are there more of these werewolves here, in Chitose? What would it be like, a group of them?

The creature lay peacefully in front of him at a small distance.

Forsberg continued to think: but rather than being sent here, was I *drawn* here? I do not know. I don't know how this works—all I know is my body deals with the power *The Rule* has over it.

He hurt all over his head. The changes that had come to it were reversing. Its human features were coming back.

The situation has altered now, he thought. What am I to do? I want to communicate with it. Certainly, I've never been able to talk to anyone about my lycanthropy. Maybe this place will be home for me. How will this affect me?

The creature stared at him.

I must not become overwhelmed. I must not let this disorient me. I will re-orient myself to this new *era*. I still don't see a big picture of any kind. I still can only take the world step by step.

Forsberg studied the werewolf's body. Its nose was

rewrought, so, too, its jaw—cartilage and bones had bent and shaped themselves into features that he knew, at times, he himself possessed.

He thought: what was it feeling that caused it to stop fighting? Can I communicate with it if its human features return?

That would be unlikely. I don't speak Japanese.

Forsberg felt the powerful strength in his limbs subsiding. It was a relief to him. After resting a minute on the floor— with the creature at rest, in front of his eyes, too—he thought: I will do nothing to provoke it in any way—but all the same, I must move.

Soon, all animal features left Forsberg, but his white hair remained.

He thought: I need to fashion a plan out of all this. I don't know how it found its way here, but I'm sure it needs help to leave. This creature is old. I may have wounded it. I need to take care of it, or at least get it out of this place safely.

There were the things he had with him in the fallout shelter, and the items he had in his jeep.

He needed to move fast. It must not be found by anyone.

Though at first he thought he wanted to communicate with it, he understood that above all, it should be taken to a safe place.

But where was a safe place? Did it have kin? If it did, did it have a place among them, or had they banished it?

It was still daylight. Forsberg would have to be patient until the cover of darkness could allow him to complete any plan.

The creature was still staring. The captain heard its breathing grow weaker. This alarmed him. It had clearly been weakened—at least for a while.

The Akiyama werewolf imagined that the White Wolf might give it instructions. But Akiyama was hearing none. Instead, Akiyama watched as the White Wolf went over to the *Wolfsmedaillon* neck chain, bent, picked it up, and slipped it around its neck. The White Wolf then walked over to the coil of chain and picked that up.

All sights and all smells suggested to Forsberg the creature would not fight him again. He didn't want it to follow him out of the shelter. No, the creature should never risk being discovered.

He didn't know what state of mind the creature was in. He did not want it to wander away once he was gone.

He approached the aged creature thoughtfully. It didn't flinch as he got near. He then slipped the chain around its body—there was no resistance from the creature. Forsberg did not want it to be able to shift from its spot on the floor.

He took out the set of handcuffs. The creature did not have wrists. Forsberg used the handcuffs like padlocks, passing their semi-circular metal halves through links in the chain, then locking them.

Akiyama was docile the whole time. He didn't believe he was being shackled. He saw this as part of the process to prepare him for his service to the Great Wolf.

Forsberg left some of furs as a rug for the creature to rest on. He gathered the rest of the skins and cloth the creature had used as garments, bundled them, was able to tie them.

He picked up his flashlight and left the shelter.

He returned a minute later, with the tarp in his hand. He unfolded it and wrapped it around the werewolf's body. The creature must stay hidden, neatly, while he was gone.

All the while Akiyama made no sound.

Forsberg went away.

Akiyama would wait patiently in the darkness for instructions for doing battle at the side of the Great Wolf.

While he waited, he dozed off.

Outside the shelter, the late afternoon sunlight shone on the jeep. Forsberg stuffed the creature's clothing in a duffel bag. He climbed into the driver's seat. Instinctively he glanced up to the rear-view mirror.

What he saw was… His hair had turned white!

What? How did *that* happen? It had never happened before.

He told himself: you must continue to concentrate.

He paused for another moment, then made a movement that came to him without thinking: he reached over to his right, swept up his olive drab army cap there, and put it on.

Back in his quarters Forsberg took out a folder of orientation materials and examined local road maps and maps of the regions surrounding Chitose. He thought the best idea was to move the werewolf as far away from the camp as he could get him—he just didn't know, but since it was hiding, it was probably running away from something; he could protect it by taking it away to a distant place.

The captain's eyes fell on the spot of the map that showed the Ishikari River Plain. The flat expanse extended thirty-five miles, beginning at Chitose's east side. It ended when it met another range of volcanic mountains. He saw only a few scattered, remote settlements were there. Set the werewolf down in the foothills of those mountains on the opposite side of the plain, he thought. The creature needs to live— even though my plan cannot guarantee that—my desire to communicate with it is impractical—sometime later I can try that.

After he returned to the fallout shelter his chest and arms felt leaner but monstrously strong. Strange. At this time of day—after sunset—the codeine in his system usually made him drowsy. Suddenly he was on edge. He was even fearful his plan would be ruined.

He got out of the jeep, flashlight in hand, and opened the door to the shelter. Inhaling the strong odor there made the hair thicken all over his back. He walked down the ramp.

There were no signs of anything unusual in the empty, cavernous space. He shined his flashlight over to where he last left the creature. From the distance he could see it was still swaddled in the tarp, perhaps sleeping. But it was too quiet to not be worried about. For a moment a pang of fear struck him: he'd injured the creature and it had died! But then another thought crossed his mind: its strength had come back, it had changed its mind, had wriggled free, was hiding under the tarp and would engage him again in a fight.

As he neared the quiet mass with the flashlight pointed straight at it, there was a rustling under the tarp. He didn't know whether he should be relieved it was alive or scared that it was.

Under its cover, the creature struggled to rise. Suddenly the tarp slid away, and the chains were at its feet.

Forsberg beheld an unimaginable spectacle. If his scalp could've reacted with the same intensity as his brain did now, his hair would've turned white a second time.

In front of him a *wolf* stood on all fours. Yes, a wolf. Its tawny coat gave way to darker hues; it was bristly black on top. Its amber eyes seemed almost feline. The end of its snout was coal-like. The animal seemed to hesitate for a moment, then with all its might…

It howled. Its howl was loud and lasted so long it made Forsberg nervous—it reverberated throughout the entire underground structure.

The wolf did not advance on Forsberg; nothing in its demeanor was threatening.

Forsberg gazed at the creature's complete transformation and gasped in astonishment, *extraordinary!*

The being is unequivocally of Nature now, he thought. This is something that will never happen to me.

This second thought struck him to the quick with sadness.

There was silence. Forsberg had to make the next move. Wolves have a pack leader, the alpha wolf, he thought. If I want this animal to follow me, I must show I'm strong enough to dominate it, but that there's no impulse in me to do it mortal harm.

However, nothing of the sort was necessary.

The wolf sat down on its hindquarters. Forsberg peered into its eyes and thought he read submission there.

He was right. The wolf, at the age it was, could not and would not seek to lead. It could only follow.

There was the chain and handcuffs to pick up off the floor, as well as the tarp and furry mat it has rested on. He gathered those and took one step toward the exit of the structure. He turned his head and motioned with a nod for the animal to follow behind him.

To the captain's pleasure, it did—slowly though, seeming to be amble with fatigue, pain and age.

Like so many parts of the interior of Hokkaido, the Ishikari Plain had been primeval land, with only a tiny Ainu population before the Japanese settlers arrived. The fertile plain now supported vegetable and grain fields, dairy farms, and orchards. There was just enough moonlight for Forsberg to make out the cone-shaped peaks that formed the horizon beyond his destination. There were no towns or villages along the way, only small clusters of houses and buildings at crossroads and the roads were invariably straight. While enroute he saw barns and buildings made of aluminum, as well as old wooden houses covered with shingles, with roofs steep enough to let the winter snow slide off. The area reminded him of his native Minnesota's sparsely populated prairie lands—it didn't look particularly Japanese.

The wolf, wrapped in the tarp in the back of the jeep, was quiet and calm.

Forty-five minutes after leaving Chitose the terrain rose markedly. The farmers' field and pastures, just driven by, gave way to woods. Forsberg noticed a man-made water ditch running parallel to one side of the highway now. It was for run-off from the higher ground they were headed for. Five minutes later the highway narrowed and became a simpler road which climbed the foothill. There was no evidence of human habitations anymore. The woods grew thicker.

During the next ten minutes he passed small mountain roads issuing from both sides of the main road. Finally, he chose one of the small roads, turning onto its dirt and gravel surface and slowing the jeep down. Bumps and ruts jiggled the vehicle—this was a logging road, evidently. He wouldn't have to go much farther. He was satisfied with the area around him.

He pulled the jeep onto a flat niche that had a tall standing rock nearby. He got out to look the spot over. Cold air pressed down from the slope above. Would there be a frost? He didn't want to place the wolf's life in danger.

The sound of cascading water pleased him. There would be water for the wolf. He hoped there'd be pockets of warmth in the dense forestland.

Glancing at the ground he saw ivy pushing up from the soil, and new creeping shoots of pachysandra, as well. He also noticed broad, green aconite leaves. Good, he thought to himself: aconite grows in Japan, too. His jaw tightened.

He pulled the front seat of the jeep forward and removed the tarp over the wolf with care. He lifted it from its litter in the back of the jeep, and guided it through the door space, setting it gently down. The animal struggled onto its legs.

Here is where it belongs, Forsberg thought. The wolf would have to fend for itself, and that might not be easy, since it was old. But it now had a place—a natural, proper place—there are no proper places for werewolves.

Forsberg felt his lungs smoothly taking in the frigid mountain air. He was still in profound wonder at what had happened over the past hours. Though at times he experienced strength and power that other humans could not access, he also felt more damned than anyone else. Gideon Forsberg would remain a closed-off phenomenon, susceptible to violent transformations.

But *this* other creature…it was freed from damnation, from creating new nightmares for others. It had ascended to heaven.

The captain felt the spirit of the wolf all around him.

CHAPTER 14

People in town awoke to heavy rains. Many turned on their radios. The continuing story (the events themselves had ended) of the recent May Day protests in Tokyo by Japanese communists. It was old news, but radio in Japan was government-owned and news about protests which turned into riots helped to unify the Japanese nation in outrage. What the people would never learn from their radio sets was that Hidekichi Iwate, a local sheriff deputy, had gone missing in the hills outside town, and the three men who'd concentrated on the slope behind Akiyama's cottage had found his body and he'd been murdered.

Rain with little break was predicted for the next two days.

This meant police work in the field would necessarily have to pause.

Mommy Eri

The noise from the rain beating on the roof of her prefabricated house drowned out the ticking of her recently repaired clock. As she anxiously smoked her first cigarette of the day, after waking to music on the radio, she was seized by the fear that Akiyama would take advantage of the bad weather, and use it as a cloak, and come into town and kill somebody. After all, nobody knew where he was. It meant he could be anywhere. He could be outside at her front door even right now.

After her cigarette, she got out of bed and turned on the

115

heater in the sitting room. That was the room where she'd received visitors in the past—customers, actually. It was when her husband was alive. She wasn't going to spend time in the room. On a day like today it was damp and depressing. She put the heat on low to save money.

Not long after the Americans took over Camp Chitose, Eri and her husband Hachemon started a brothel. Prostitution was still legal and soon Mommy was attached in front of her first name. Their house could accommodate only one customer at a time. (They were on the upper story. Another couple lived downstairs.) While a young man was being entertained, Mommy Eri would withdraw to the kitchen in the back with another girl—she always had two on hand so the soldier could have a choice. Once the soldier was "accepted" into the home, Hachemon would take a brief trip to a billiards club where he could continue the process of smoking and drinking himself to death.

But the cause of his early demise was most likely resentment. He had to endure being around Americans who had sex with amenable young women who were off limits to him. He hadn't thought about that part when they started the business.

Eri's husband had died in the depths of winter, fifteen months ago. Hachemon Maeda was fifty-seven years old, although from the way he looked and moved, people thought he was closer to seventy-five.

With Hachemon gone, Mommy Eri closed the brothel. It would be difficult to run by herself: sometimes a G.I. was drunk or unruly and it had been Hachemon's job to see him out the door. There was some money left after Hachemon died and Eri made the transition to opening a bar.

She had nobody to protect her, and a maniacal killer was still at large. She had the couple living downstairs. They were old and hard of hearing, and she made believe they were a kind of effective insulation against the outside world. She went into the kitchen to boil water for tea.

She figured she knew almost as much as the police did, courtesy of her connections in town. She knew about yesterday's search party. Shigeru Akiyama had attacked Noboru Nakano and had done the same to Hidekichi Iwate. She was sure of it. Everyone was in danger until he was caught.

Eri lit a fresh new cigarette. Golden Week meant she could close Bar Eden for at least six days without anyone asking questions. She felt she needed some time to come up with a new angle that'd draw servicemen to the bar. She needed a gimmick or she'd need to close it down. Then she thought: maybe I should just go back to what had made so much money before—but it makes me think twice because Hachemon's not around. Look at the trouble I got into doing it by myself, with the bar, with hiring Kiriko, being followed by Akiyama…

Her brain hadn't fully woken up. It was better not to try to think so much, though she'd be in trouble if she didn't make the right decision!

Noboru Nakano

He lay in bed listening to the storm outside. Rain was hitting the house slantwise. It sounded like hard peas. He'd left the hospital the day before. A few days ago it was the annual holiday, *"Midori no hi,* "Boy's Day." His parents especially fussed over him this year. What strange experience being the center of attention.

Noboru always looked up to his old brother for being a tough guy. Noboru was the younger brother who felt weaker, inferior. He blindly adored Toshi with whom he had little contact. Now, since the attack—which he looked at as a sort of an initiation into manhood—he hoped that Toshi would be proud of him. If only the attack would prove to have been carried out by gangsters. To be attacked while he was asleep by a dirty Ainu—even if he was Kiriko's father—there was no honor in that.

He missed the friends he'd made working in Muroran and was looking forward to getting back to work so he could help support the family. But nobody was telling him when he would be allowed to go back.

Later in the afternoon he often wanted to smile at his mother and father when they were attending him, bringing him food, drink and presents. But the bandage around his neck would have made smiling excruciating.

Toshi

He'd worn a crisp, bleached white underpants and undershirt, as well as a red polyester fleece jacket to bed. He awakened to his ears ringing, just as they had been for so long. At some point in the day or night (he didn't know when. There was only one window in the front, with its shade pulled, and no windows anywhere else in the apartment) he decided he should sleep—so he downed five cups of whisky to counteract the *shabu*.

He wanted to live somewhere else than in this primitive, bare-bones apartment. The building was rotting, its wood smelled. However, the owner did not pry. If he moved to a better place, it was likely that wouldn't be the case.

It came to him: what did I do yesterday? Oh, that's right, it was raining hard. It was supposed to rain all day. After I stayed in and paced and fretted for hours, I made myself go to bed. This must be the next day. It's still raining. Is it morning, afternoon, or night?

There's no point in going out in cold, wet weather like this. Nobody goes out in it. You're forced to stay home and smoke and listen to the radio.

He was hungry. He needed to get up, boil water, and eat some noodles. How stupid to have to eat!

He remembered what he had been thinking before going to sleep yesterday: there's no proof that Akiyama did anything. And… Ha! Now, the Sheriff's Office has a real job on its hands! They're not going to solve the crime. They've got the whole thing wrong.

He remembered how nervous he felt yesterday, why he had to knock himself out so he could sleep: the police need to shoot Lloyd Kelso! He drinks blood. He drank the blood of my brother, and he showed it to me, he admitted it. His mouth was all red! He would have killed me if I hadn't run out of the bowling alley. No one has any idea what the Americans are up to. They think just because their bodies are bigger than ours and they beat us with their bombs, they can drink our blood and finish us off without the world noticing. They can't hide Hiroshima and Nagasaki, but they can hide Kelso!

They wouldn't find Akiyama—he knew that for sure—because Lloyd had killed him—the police are so stupid to point their finger at Akiyama! Lloyd set the whole thing up. Then he went to Ainu's cottage and killed Iwate to strengthen the set-up, to put a cherry on top of the cake, as the Americans say.

Thoughts like that gave Toshi a case of the jitters again. Maybe he'd gotten too much sleep. He was too refreshed, too full of energy. What could he do with all of it?

Anyway, he went to the hot plate, boiled water in a saucepan and made ramen.

He sat down crossed-legged on a mat, placing the bowl of hot noodle soup on the short table in front of him. Rather than lounging while eating, his mental perturbations caused him to split his mind in two: one half saw to it that he slurped at the noodles in the bowl without choking on them, the other half stared at the bare wall directly in front of him. On that wall appeared something like speck, a speck on the horizon that, while gradually getting closer, could finally be identified as a ship traveling on water. Instead of a ship though, growing in size on that wall, were one scene after another from a samurai movie he'd seen two months ago, *Araki Mataemon: Gatekeeper of the Duel Locksmith*. Many of the fighting scenes took place on ancient dirt roads, outside small dwellings, in a *light* rain.

He thought to himself: I liked that movie. The rain is heavy now. But the rain had to be light in the film, or you couldn't clearly see the stars and the characters they were playing.

In his mind he played back scenes of the master samurai leading his minions in swordfights. He saw a dagger go into the enemy's chest, an archer killing a swordsman who rushed toward him…

The other night, in the bowling alley, Bob Fernandez had humiliated him with that drinking game. Toshi would get vengeance. Bob's life wasn't worth anything. The world wouldn't miss him. Like in so many samurai movies he enjoyed, Toshi would get a thug to do Bob in. Also, he would find somebody—the same thug, if he worked out—to either kill Lloyd, or to hurt him badly enough so the army would send him packing, back to America. Kelso was a vampire who attacked his brother—and killed the cop Iwate and Shigeru Akiyama. (This was not to say he cared about Akiyama—he didn't. He only cared about one person—he, himself—it was he who was threatened by having a vampire on the prowl.)

Aunt Satomi

These events happening in Chitose—they only made things worse for the Ainu. The townspeople were, for good reason, scared. Not at all confident that what was going on would soon be over, she was afraid for them—and afraid *with* them.

There was no keeping the truth from anyone. Most people had already known or suspected she was part Ainu. Now they would associate her closely with Akiyama, whom she was never on familiar terms with. She was strong, but this meant from here on out her life was forever changed. She would be regarded with suspicion. She'd be on the defensive.

She worried about her husband. Certainly he would be treated differently from now on. Although he wasn't Ainu, there might be some people at his job that would make life unbearable there.

She pitied Kiriko and didn't know what to say to her. Kiriko was a good girl, her early childhood tough. She'd assimilated, though she had no close friends. Getting a job for tough for an Ainu. Though Kiriko's job as a bar hostess was a menial one, it was her first, and it allowed her to practice English—a key to success in Japan. Satomi didn't doubt Kiriko would be able to take care of herself if for some reason she was unable to find a suitable husband.

Of course she couldn't know at that moment she'd revisit these thoughts and feelings in less than twenty-four hours, because of what would happen to Kiriko that night.

Kiriko

At times the rain lashed at the rain gutters—sounds that seemed to be coming from a disturbing world far away: a world of anger.

Again, Kiriko confronted the image of her father at his cottage two days before. She feared him. She feared his being caught. She was terrified of what they'd do to him if they caught him. He was an ill man. Somebody would act as he had only if they were deranged.

But she was also scared he wouldn't be caught and the people of Chitose would live in fear for a long time…infinity spread out in her mind.

That night, as usual, Aunt Satomi and Uncle Kenshin went to bed at ten o'clock. Kiriko was already in her bedroom asleep and didn't hear them.

At two o'clock in the morning, first Satomi, and then Kenshin, were gradually awoken by a sustained, shrill, piercing sound. It was too high to be an electronic alarm of some sort. It was like being able to hear a dog whistle that you weren't supposed to hear. The sound, which they'd never heard anything like before, would last for three or four minutes, then break off for a short time, then begin once more. It was so unusual, loud and startling that it caused them to sit up in bed, wide-awake. In the darkness, the couple felt each other's bodies. Each felt the visceral reaction the other was having. Kenshin reached over and turned on an electric lamp. Where was the sound coming from?

It was coming from inside their house. The more they listened, the more they realized it wasn't a sound from an electronic device. Kenshin asked, while his heart raced, "What is it?"

Satomi quietly, tentatively, responded. "I don't know."

It was some odd, high-pitched vocalization, something beyond a scream—there wasn't a word for what they were hearing. Because it was so loud the neighbors might have been able to hear it—if the rain hadn't been striking the puddles outside so hard.

It was coming from Kiriko's bedroom.

"It has to be Kiriko," Satomi whispered, frightened.

They didn't know what to do; they were stupefied.

But then, as the minutes of noise continued to pass, they realized they needed to do something. The sounds might not end anytime soon.

"I'll go with you," Kenshin said, with no attempt to speak softly. "You go into her and see what's the matter. I'll stand behind you. I don't want to be in the way."

They got up and put on their robes. The blood-curdling high-tone persisted. Kenshin was amazed that a person could produce such a sound. Satomi got a flashlight from a kitchen drawer. She didn't want to turn a light on in Kiriko's room. It might frighten the girl—and her.

Kenshin slid the bedroom door open for his wife. When Satomi entered the room she found Kiriko sitting upright, cross-legged on her bedding, no more disheveled than any sleeping person; she was catatonic, looking like what Satomi imaged a sleepwalker would look like. They couldn't wake her up. She was in a hypnotic state. She didn't notice Satomi and Kenshin were in her room.

This had never happened before.

"Kiriko, it's me," her adopted mother said gently, but it had no effect on the girl. She followed with, "Why are you doing this? Can you stop? It must be hurting you. It's very loud."

This was to no avail. Kenshin stood behind his wife, letting her minister to the girl. The sounds would end when Kiriko's energy waned and start again when she got it back. Satomi decided not to touch Kiriko, for fear something violent—though she knew Kiriko wasn't a violent person—would happen.

Aunt Satomi motioned to her husband she was going to leave Kiriko's bedside. The couple slid the door half shut and went into the living room. When Kenshin could see his wife's eyes, they were full of panic.

He said tiredly, "We should call a doctor. It doesn't look like it's going to stop."

"I know." Satomi said, holding back tears. "It's… shocking."

"I'll go call now," Kenshin said, hiding his being annoyed.

Just as he picked up the phone receiver to make the call, Kiriko's latest nightmarish squeal stopped. Kenshin put down the phone without dialing the number. He went over to his wife and said, "Let's wait a few minutes. If it doesn't begin again, we'll talk to a doctor in the morning."

Kiriko went back to sleep, seemingly unaffected by the episode.

The couple went back to bed but couldn't sleep the rest of the night. They lay there, half-stunned, thinking how creepy the situation appeared to them, how mysterious it sounded, and how it suggested Kiriko might have a psychiatric problem. Aunt Satomi was disconsolate with worry.

In the morning she asked Kiriko if she knew what had

happened several hours ago in the middle of the night. Kiriko answered, "No, what?"

"You were screaming in your sleep."

"Was I?" Kiriko asked incredulously. "I'm sorry. I hope I didn't wake you both up."

"You don't remember?"

"No," the girl said innocently.

"Well, it was unexpected. If it happens again, we should tell a doctor."

Sheriff Danjuro Fujita

Two very wet days for Chitose, the Ishikari Plain, the southeastern Hokkaido coast, the inland to towns of Muroran, Noboribetsu, Shiraoi, Tomakomai! That meant important clues and tracks, if any, could get washed away. Dutiful, young Iwate had been a cop in good standing. He didn't take bribes or poke his nose into the black market—and as far as the sheriff knew, neither did anyone else on the force.

The sheriff sat in his office and doubted the black ceramic phone on his desk would ring with someone on the line providing him with useful information concerning the Akiyama case. A wider search will have to take place. But what kind of wider search? The surrounding area has small cities, but outside them the districts are rural; then there are the wilderness areas that go on for miles. Truthfully, a thorough search was impractical. Hokkaido is an immense island where an Ainu can disappear and quite possibly never be found. The unacceptable must be accepted.

There'd been no reliable sightings of Akiyama. People will become angry with the police if they cannot find him soon. They often feel let down by the authorities and this will be yet another time. Golden Week is supposed to be a period of commemoration. It's always a quiet time, a family holiday. It's quiet now, but it's not calm. Violence has come to Chitose and the adults who know what is going on live in fear.

The Ghost of Sheriff Deputy Hidekichi Iwate

The ghost of Hidekichi Iwate could see through the rain, even when it was pouring down hard. His corpse was caught in a backstop of bushes. It was swollen. It was being bathed, fully clothed. The wind blew the bushes next to his clothes. The bushes tugged on their roots, loosening the soaked earth. A mudslide could be unleashed with the slightest contact.

"So this is my earthly end? My end came in spring—the time for renewal, not death—and in addition to that, I was still young! A double insult. My family is fatherless now. The longer my body stays here, the more time I have to think of my revenge. There'll be other corpses after mine. I demand it."

Chitose River

Where once salmon swam and spawned
And sedge and moss and soft *igura* rushes lorded
  the shore,
Their thin green branches cleanly yawning upward…

This month of May, this month of May,
The sewage drains straight into the river.
This month of May, month of May,
The algae burns and dissolves and sinks.

On the floor of the creek, crud-crusted stones,
Dust-dingy cinnamon, the color is drab.
Coal burns for electricity
Hokkaido's factories screech and jab.

This month of May, snowmelt can't wash it away.
Neither can the rain.
The buds on the ash trees and adder
Look more like large black aphids.
This month of May, month of May…

CHAPTER 15

He was too exhausted the previous night to do it. Now he faced the mirror above the cold water basin soullessly. He was not lucid because of all that happened yesterday, and the lack of sound sleep that followed it.

It was 6:45 a.m. He'd never shaved his head before. His hair was already short. First, he took scissors and cut off as much as he could. Then he lathered his head with shaving cream and shaved off what remained of the white hair.

What he saw in the mirror now was not entirely normal, but on the other hand there were soldiers in the army whose hair was cut so short they looked bald from a distance.

He'd cover his head from now on with hats—in the army, you have little choice of them. Hopefully his hear would grow back brown.

The mirror reflected much of the narrow living space behind him. His eight-by-fourteen-foot room, with its single bed, dresser, wardrobe, small desk with shelves above it, and straight back wooden chair, was identical to what the three other officers had in their quarters in the shared Quonset.

Rinsing the remaining lather off his shaved head, he thought of the locked box in the bottom drawer of his dresser where he stored plastic vials of codeine pills. The box was camouflaged with folded undershirts on top. There was almost no chance a soldier would go through his room, and his quarters would never be subject to routine inspection. But he wasn't going to take any chances. He did not want the drug discovered. It must always be there, ready in whatever quantity he needed.

Once fully dressed, he slipped a vinyl poncho over his wool overcoat, put a foldable cloth khaki garrison cap on his head, and went out into the cold rain. He drove his jeep the short distance to the police station. Pulling himself out of the vehicle, he made a dash for the entrance of the red brick building, his boots grinding loose wet gravel underfoot.

Once through the front door, Forsberg acknowledged the salute from the soldier at the front desk and then paused briefly while the soldier swung up the flap door for the captain—it was one of those wooden counter slabs that was flush with the front desk's countertop—you had to flip it up and enter through the space to get inside the station. Once in, Forsberg went down the corridor, passing a couple of closed doors.

Velchoffsky's office door was open. He was putting a page into a loose-leaf notebook. It was the list of those soldiers being sent to Camp Crawford for MP training. The sergeant had completed all the interviews.

"Morning, sir," Velchoffsky said, seeing out of the corner of his eye half of Forsberg as he hastened past. Without looking up from his desk he said, "It's wet out there."

Forsberg quietly opened the heavy wooden door to his office and vanished inside.

Seeing Forsberg conjured a thought in Velchoffsky: true, the army was in the process of expansion, but maybe there was another reason for Major Tyler to assign him to Chitose. It could be he was an undercover investigator. As commander of the 545th, Forsberg took his orders from the provost marshal's office at Camp Crawford. Couriers (many helicopters went back and forth between the camps daily) delivered sensitive information. If Forsberg were undercover, what he was he looking for? Who was under suspicion?

It was the height of the Red Scare and a period filled with espionage. Julius and Ethel Rosenberg were awaiting execution after being found guilty of spying for the Soviet Union twelve months before. Julius Rosenberg had been an electrical engineer in the Army Signal Corps in New Jersey. While Camp Chitose had no labs or research facilities, supplying the war in Korea meant many top secret operations were underway. Add to that the local political landscape. Hokkaido, like the rest of Japan, had a Socialist Party. The Americans didn't dare ban it—that would fly in the face of democratizing the conquered country. There was no doubt the Soviets had infiltrated the Socialist Party of Japan. Operatives were around, eyeing American installations for weaknesses in security. There was a military intelligence unit at Chitose, but the purpose of having Forsberg undercover would be that he was separate from it—even military intelligence itself, at present, could be infiltrated.

Velchoffsky shook his head back and forth tersely, as if to help eject such thoughts from his mind. It wasted time to conjecture. The day was just starting. He had a lot to do, as always.

Forsberg settled into his swivel chair in his office. An hour passed. Lieutenant Nichols came to get his signature, but it also was an attempt to get better acquainted with the captain. After Nichols' knock on the door Forsberg called out for him to come in. The captain pretended to be going through some paperwork. The room was still not fully put together.

With Forsberg's arrival, Nichols technically ceased to be the final authorizing official of the unit. From now on the captain would have to sign off on various requests, orders, and reports. The lieutenant had an Operational Needs Statement request in his hand. Forsberg had him sit down in the hard chair facing his desk and gestured phlegmatically to him to give him the paperwork. Nichols duly handed it to him, along with a pen he'd brought with him.

When Forsberg glanced at the subject heading of the request and saw it concerned military working dogs needed from the training center at Camp Crawford, his face tightened. He didn't immediately put the pen that Nichols handed him to paper. Nichols thought it was odd that Forsberg didn't sign right away. As the captain was hesitating, the lieutenant's hazel eyes drifted to the top of Forsberg's forehead. Something was different there, he thought. The cap on Forsberg's head was... no, it wasn't his cap. Did Forsberg shave his head? Possibly. That seemed strange for an officer who was not old.

Forsberg signed the papers.

Nichols then tried to engage him in light conversation, with, "I hear that in Germany you were surrounded by refugees, and in Korea, as well. Quite a change, being assigned here. Not a refugee in sight. Probably a welcome change, sir?"

Forsberg answered evasively, "The world continues to change. You and I have to change with it." He wasn't interested in establishing rapport with this man. He believed the lieutenant's statements and question had nothing to do with refugees, but rather he was simply prying—like policemen should. He supposed Nichols was wondering whether he'd requested a transfer or had been given one.

The sharp looking and sharp thinking lieutenant didn't let the vaguely philosophical and oddly tangential response deter him. He remarked, "I haven't changed much since I was a kid, people tell me."

Forsberg let the remark go nowhere. He eased himself against the back of his chair.

Nichols pressed on. "I guess they told you at Camp Crawford that Chitose has quite some history to it. It was in old Building 5 here that plans for the attack on Pearl Harbor were drawn up."

"Yeah, they told me that," the captain said, adjusting himself again to get comfortable, reacting to mention of one of the greatest sneak attacks in history like he'd just been told somebody had dropped an egg salad sandwich on the floor in a cafeteria far away.

Nichols knew it was time to stop. He wasn't going to get anywhere. He should leave.

Rising from his chair, with a "good-bye" ring in his voice he said, "Well, you've arrived at a good time. Spring this far north comes late and fast. It'll be summer before you know it.

With that, he turned away from the captain and went to the door, closing it softly behind him.

On this first morning in his office the only thing Forsberg could think about was the creature (and the sequence of events that followed after he'd met it). He'd never encountered a werewolf before—it had to be that "werewolf" was the right name for it. Previously, he foresaw no way to be freed from the horrors of his own changes. The will to unprovoked aggression, to destruction was ingrained in him. But what he saw yesterday—he never would have thought that a werewolf could completely change to a wolf. At least now he saw a new possibility... it was something so different—and something so clean.

He'd worked out a concept that was useful for him to survive, at least mentally. He gave it a name: The Rule. The idea of The Rule helped him cope with what he was, and with the mysteries beyond his comprehension.

Now, The Rule had introduced a new part of itself to him. That his military assignment should take him here, to Chitose, where he would straight away encounter a being not unlike himself was staggering—but then again, The Rule was sometimes like that.

For a few moments, he became excessively aware of the cap on his naked head. It was perched there, snug, a foreign object, dead. It was helping to hold his brain together. He did not want his brain exposed to the air.

Then it occurred to him, and not for the first time: I need to know more about *this area*. Is there something special about here? Encountering the creature was either a choice or a monumental coincidence. A coincidence made to happen by The Rule?

Then he thought about his own survival. It was essential that he take codeine daily. Here in Chitose, he would have a new doctor. His medical records indicated he was still under treatment for pain and discomfort because of a blunt injury to his spleen and large intestine in 1945—seven years ago, during the Italian campaign. This dull red-purple organ had been removed, but he, like thirty percent of people, had a second one, a smaller "accessory spleen." His second one hadn't been damaged. So, his immune system wasn't affected—but nerves in the area were—this made it too painful for him to have sex.

When his internal injuries healed, the real reason he continued to take codeine (a drug derived from opium, which is one of the earliest medicines used by humans) was because it curbed his lycanthropy. It was by chance that he discovered the peculiar effectiveness of opioids against the transformations. How bizarre that syrup from the humble poppy plant, used commonly to suppress a cough, could be used successfully to arrest a condition of much graver dimensions.

With each new army transfer—a dozen up to now—he would need to see a new doctor. They'd be reluctant at first to prescribe large doses of codeine sulfate when he asked them, but then he would tell them to read his medical records carefully and see the notes that previous doctors made concerning his condition. The notes always remarked on his need for, but high tolerance of, the drug, and reported that he showed no debilitations or loss of workdays due to taking so much of the medication. A new doctor, after reading what had been indicated, would always yield, and continue with the treatment.

But Forsberg did indeed feel the side effects of his drug. Now, with it flowing through his veins, his office warm as toast, and the tip-tapping of rain beating outside, he felt drowsy and disassociated from the day.

He'd requested an electric coffee percolator for the office. Now, at the side of the room, a Farberware pot on a small table finished sputtering. He got up, poured himself a cup of black coffee.

He set it down on his desk, sat down, and waited.

While he waited for it to cool, he thought about… coffee. Yes, coffee… for human beings. But he, despite his present outward appearance, and the fact that he drank coffee … he could never live among his fellow men as one of them! It was pie-in-the-sky to believe there was a human niche for him to live in—or on the other hand, a niche for him among nature's animals.

He was left to think of that being who changed into a wolf before his eyes, while his mind repeated: it had been a werewolf yesterday but was a wolf today—such a thing will never happen to me. And no protector will appear on the scene, as he had, to guide that wolf to a forest.

If only his destiny would be the same as the creature's!

Could he do anything to help make this happen to him?

No. As far as he knew, it was on The Rule that was in control.

He brought the cup to his lips and swallowed another codeine pill. For some reason he felt he needed more of it today.

An unusually heightened sense of smell assailed him, and he didn't know why. His olfactory sense was so acute he could smell the cologne on Velchoffsky, even though an interior concrete wall eighteen inches thick separated his office from the sergeant's.

He drank his coffee, which stank of burned soil. His mind flitted over to the volcanic mountains he'd seen to the west when he took the chopper from Camp Crawford to Chitose. He'd never seen ones like them, blasted cone shapes, the daylight doing nothing to brighten their spookiness. Upon landing, he thought it was those baleful peaks that were somehow causing the throbbing he felt in his chest and temples. But no, now he believed it was the energy of the creature reaching out to him.

At 10:30 a.m. he went to the officers' mess hall for lunch. Lunch began then. He wanted to avoid people. Thankfully no other diners were there. Lunch smelled strong. There was something unnatural, something artificial about it. He ate quickly and returned to his office.

He settled back into his chair again, taking comfort in knowing Velchoffsky and Nichols were keen on running the MP unit themselves.

He spent the next two hours sitting behind his desk daydreaming. The codeine was having its desired, mollifying effect. At one point in the swamp of it he thought: Was there someone in the army who The Rule controlled, who was responsible for transferring me from Korea to Chitose?

It could also be that that his assignment to Chitose involved something like a gravitational pull, a phenomenon that is strange and inexplicable to human consciousness—as is, for example, the phenomenon of the homing instinct in dogs.

He thought about the possibility that he'd been inserted into this new environment because there was a plan for him. But that seemed to him delusional, bordering on the religious. The feeling he was in a place that would nourish him, give him energy, provide him with a community of like beings and rebirth him—this was quite a fantasy, he decided.

The afternoon drag started. At one point his foggy mind was struck by a memory from when he was in high school. He was in a classroom. The English teacher was speaking about mythology and legends and their influence.

There was one story the teacher told the class about… Forsberg couldn't imagine how a culture could come up with it. It had to do with the beginning of humanity. As the legend went, the gods created humans but their size was double our present size. It was because two humans were stuck together as one—they were joined at their backs. There were three kinds of these first humans: one kind that was male on one side and female on the other; another that was male on both sides; and the other that was female on both sides. Because these humans didn't show enough reverence to the gods, Zeus split each of the three types of humans in half. This meant humans from then on must search for their other half, they're pursuing wholeness. If Forsberg remembered correctly, the legend continued with Zeus warning that if the split humans still weren't sufficiently reverent to the gods, they'd be split once more in half. He'd had never heard such a bizarre legend in his life.

Now he thought he had some insight into it. He thought he'd been split by The Rule, that today's humans had thumbed their noses at the natural order, and he was one of those punished. He was thinking now that he had found his other half in the werewolf that turned into a wolf.

But this was a crazy idea. He was full of them.

During his daydreaming Nichols interrupted him once. The lieutenant had him rubber stamp another official document. Sometime after that Forsberg rose from his chair, put on his poncho, and left his office with a book, smaller than a normal paperback.

He couldn't avoid passing Velchoffsky's office which was on the way out of the building. The master sergeant's door was open. He was there, at his desk, masses of paperwork diminishing his humanity. He was a muscular man with his physical strength wasted at this desk job. Forsberg stuck his head in the door and announced he was retiring to his quarters for the rest of the day. He casually waved a Japanese phrasebook—standard military issue—suggesting he was going to study it as part of easing himself slowly into his job.

Glancing up at the captain for a moment, Pete Velchoffsky now realized he'd shaved his head. Well, he'd seen stranger things than that in the army. "Have a good afternoon, sir," he said flatly, and went back to work.

CHAPTER 16

By the next day the army base was water-logged; fat clouds that hardly moved hovered over all of Chitose. The hum of aircraft overhead merged with the steady metallic drumming of the downpour on the corrugated roofs of the Quonset huts. It was almost one o'clock now and most of the junior officers were back at their desks.

But four officers lingered at tables in the officers' mess. The building was windowless. There was a degree of privacy to the place.

A pimple-faced waiter, a Private First Class with effeminate gestures he couldn't seem to control, was trying to look busy, trying not to listen to snatches of conversation after he'd just finished clearing tables. He was the opposite of a guy with hairy arms and tattoos who would slop food on a tin tray in a mess hall where soldiers, just finished with basic training, would eat.

Major Timothy Beaumont had striking rust-colored hair and friendly gray eyes. His parents with their young children had emigrated to the United States in the 1930s, seeking a better life, at least economically speaking. He was a grandson of the famous French general Victor Cordonnier. He was also one of a half dozen Americans in Hokkaido whose French was impeccable. From time to time when international delegations visited Sapporo, the U.S. government asked linguistic favors from him. (He also had some experience in assisting when there were exchanges of information between the U.S. and the French military in

Colonial Vietnam, where the French were fighting their own battle against communism.)

Beaumont was the executive officer of C2I (Command, Control & Intelligence) in Chitose, and since much of the work was in Intelligence, he was restricted in what he could say. Yet, he didn't let this hamper him from engaging in small talk.

Captain Jake Torrington, the head of the Civilian-Military Co-operation unit (called "CIMIC"), sat across from him at a table for two at the side of the officers' mess, the farthest away from the kitchen you could get. Both were slowly working their way through spaghetti and Spam, with Kaiser rolls on the side. They sipped Coke with the meal and mincemeat pie was on the menu for dessert. There was something about Captain Torrington's smile and conciliary face that invited trust in him.

The only others dining in the officers' mess were Major Anthony Seidelman, head of Finance, an alcoholic, and Major Alan Washburn, an excessive drinker with a lusterless complexion as well, who ran Personnel. Both were well on their way to going to seed. The waiter stood at attention near the entrance to the kitchen. One of the waiter's eyes was always on the two men, ready to serve them in case they should beckon. Seidelman and Washburn were in the center of the room. They could raise their voices if they wanted to, and it wouldn't bother anyone. They'd nodded perfunctorily to Major Beaumont and Captain Torrington when the two had come in. They were just finishing dessert and would be gone soon.

Tim Beaumont was more than pleased to be able to talk to Jake out of earshot of the two older officers and the waiter—it was a necessity.

Jake Torrington was flattered that the elder Beaumont liked him. Around the base Beaumont was respected for his earnestness and one couldn't help being attracted to him— he was charming and had many connections in the army and beyond. All Jake knew was that Timothy had done secret work in France and Germany and he'd spend time on the battlefield during the war there; he spoke the languages of both of those countries. He'd been part of the Allied Military Government in post-war Germany. It was a mystery to him why someone of his stature would be at a comparatively sedate post like Chitose. Beaumont couldn't freely associate as some of the other officers could—sure, he dined at the officers' mess, attended all the events, played golf, handball—he was your handsome officer opponent, or partner, depending on the game. People knew enough to watch out what questions they asked him; he had a high security clearance. The first time Jake had ever spoken at length with the major was nine months ago.

Beaumont liked Jake; the captain had the air of a by-the-book commander but in reality he was flexible, even creative; he decided he was a man whom he could also trust with secrets and it wouldn't be necessary to put him through any formal security checks. And what Timothy Beaumont was about to talk about wasn't something to be written down.

Major Beaumont said matter-of-factly, "Okay. Now that the waiter isn't going to pester us for a while, we can get down to business." Torrington thought he saw a severe look steal across Tim's face.

The major felt the best tack to take was to be circumlocutory—wasn't it best to grease the skids for a while, before insisting to a rational man that he needed to reorganize his mind?

"It's one of the new arrivals I need to talk to you about: Captain Gideon Forsberg. A little bit of history: drafted to serve in World War Two, he stayed on afterward—wasn't interested in being demobbed—no interest in going home. He'd learned some German—actually he grew up speaking Norwegian in Minnesota, so German wasn't such a stretch for him."

He took a sip from his Coke. "The army put him to work

as a microfilmer. He had some knowledge of photography—
as a kid he'd indulged in the hobby, had his own darkroom.
He was in a unit that moved around microfilming Third
Reich documents."

These records needed to be preserved; there wasn't a lack
of small-but-significant anti-Allies actions by members of the
populace. Many people—not just former Nazis—would
have liked official records to go missing.

"During that time, officers in Germany and Austria got
to know him better. With the higher-ups on his side, he
returned stateside, to Fort Riley, Kansas, and did well enough
to graduate from OCS." Beaumont spoke evenly, avoiding
condescension. The program at Officer Candidate School at
Riley was the crash-course training school that enabled an
enlisted soldier to become an army officer. It couldn't match
the education a nascent officer got at a four-year university
in tandem with traditional, slower, officer training.

Beaumont continued, "But when he graduated in late
1947, the army certainly didn't need second lieutenants for
the infantry."

In 1947 the Army was drawing its numbers down. There
were no battlefields, only the Allies' occupation of Germany
and Austria, and the American occupation of Japan.

"So Forsberg was trained to work in the military police,
and was sent back there. He remained there until last year,
when he was assigned to command an MP unit at a garrison
in Korea."

Torrington listened respectfully. His shallowed-lined
forehead showed no emotion. He had a gentle upturned
nose. He was a man you could be honest with; he'd hear you
out; not betray your confidence.

"Then there were two promotions, in the military police
in Germany—quick by all standards, and especially quick in
peacetime," the major reported dryly. The major raised his
eyebrows, "Promoted to first lieutenant and then to captain."

In the military it was possible to be rapidly promoted, but

these were nearly always "battlefield promotions."

The major continued, "What is also interesting about Forsberg's career in the army is its paper trail. There isn't much to it. It's… intentionally superficial. I'll tell you why, soon." Beaumont drew out the story leisurely—he had to do it that way.

The major then nodded at Torrington, urging him to speak, to add something. Torrington searched his mind and said, "Forsberg's work is top secret? He's working in espionage, maybe."

Beaumont replied somberly. "That's what people who get his file in their hands are meant to think."

How much more do I need to tell him before I get to the point? Beaumont asked himself. He took a bite out of his Kaiser roll, chewed it, and had a sip of Coke. Torrington wound some spaghetti around his fork. There wasn't anything for Jake to say. Beaumont had set up their meeting. It was he who was going to do the talking.

"Yes, those in Chitose who have access to his service record will suspect its brevity is due to his real work being highly classified. His file forces you to imagine what might be between the lines. The first thing that comes to mind is, of course, espionage. His work in Korea is also not well described. Being a captain in a military police unit gives you cover—there's not a lot you have to say about an officer in that position. Which brings us to Chitose—I mean, which brings *him* to Chitose. We don't really need him here, you know. Or we do need him—wink, wink—there's always that way out. If you accept it on the level, he's here because Chitose's expanding and the MP unit's going to get a lot bigger. I'll tell you: in reality, he didn't make decisions of any consequence in the unit in Korea. He was there as commander in name only."

By his tone of voice Torrington could sense that Beaumont had arrived at the end of his preparatory remarks.

Torrington took a sip of Coke and Beaumont continued,

"Let's just go along with the idea that being assigned MP unit commander was just cover."

Torrington remarked, "So what you're saying is he was in military intelligence in Germany and Austria, and he's remained with them ever since?"

"Yes, and a few army brass know what he's up to—but most don't."

Beaumont paused. His face darkened. He changed the subject. The change seemed out of the blue.

"Let me say that we're at war, Jake, and unconventional warfare is part of it."

His voice halted. Torrington knew he had more to say and waited for him to continue.

"Unconventional war, Jake," the major repeated himself to let the idea sink in. He then sounded nervous or hesitant—Torrington couldn't tell which. "Ah… here's what Forsberg's working on. He's not routing out communist sympathizers in the American Army."

One part of Beaumont felt he hadn't taken enough time to prepare Torrington for what he was about to say. He was uncharacteristically slow in his manner. He put both his hands on the table, and they lay there.

"I'm sorry to digress, but I have to. I promise I'll get back to my main point." After taking a breath, he continued, "There were things I heard when I was getting a haircut the other day. You know that partition between the officers' barber shop and the rest of the room where the boys get their haircut?"

"Sure."

"You can hear everything on the other side of it."

The major's hand traveled over to where his fork was resting on his plate. He picked up the fork and shifted its position slightly and put it right back down on his plate. He was simply collecting his thoughts during that moment.

Then recounted the confrontation he'd overheard as he sat in his chair on the officers' side, while he was getting his haircut.

A sergeant named Ted Fontana, who'd recently arrived in Chitose as head mechanic at the motor pool, was in one of the barber chairs on the other side. Private Second Class Brian Yoder was going to take Fontana's place after he was done, and a third soldier was waiting for his haircut as well.

Fontana hadn't been in Korea. But Brian Yoder, a dark-haired native of North Carolina, had. The third solider— Beaumont didn't catch his name—had also been there. The Korean veterans were criticizing Fontana for acting as an expert in things he didn't know anything about. When the major started listening in, it appeared Brian was satisfied he'd scored a point against Fontana. Yoder said, "So you agree that dropping the bombs ended the war?"

The head mechanic hesitated and then said reluctantly, "Yeah." He had to admit there was some truth to what Yoder had said. The head mechanic hedged, "By a few days less."

"So what's the gripe, then?" Brian demanded. "Hundreds of thousands of American soldiers are alive because of those bombs."

They were talking about Hiroshima and Nagasaki. The head mechanic had an East Coast urban accent, it sounded like from one of the Boston neighborhoods.

Fontana felt like he'd conceded too much. "Maybe those G.I.s wouldn't have died had there been a ground invasion instead of the A-bomb. We'll never know," he said.

"Oh, thousands and thousands would have died," retorted Private Yoder. "You don't know anything about combat. It's just a fact that because of the A-bombs, we didn't need to invade."

The head mechanic took another tack. "The two bombs weren't dropped on military installations. They were dropped on women and children. We burned them to ashes in a second. We poisoned everyone with radiation. The survivors are still dropping like flies. They're dying ugly deaths. You talk about combat. That's not combat. It's murder. It's against the Geneva Convention—terrorizing and liquidating innocent people. Plus, on a different level, we're interfering with the universe: the bomb changes matter. We change solid into liquid into vapor into boom."

When Major Beaumont heard the word "boom" he sat up in his chair and the barber silently repositioned his scissors to follow the major's move. People, especially in Japan, argued over the decision to drop the bombs, but Fontana's choice of words about the radical way the bombs worked caught his attention.

Ted Fontana pressed on. "Our country's going to have to live with this for eternity." He didn't back down: "Have you *visited* Nagasaki or Hiroshima?"

Fontana knew he was being severe with Yoder. He softened his voice and said to him in a conciliatory fashion, almost pleading, "We didn't need to kill civilians."

"That's easy to say." The soldier with no name butted in. "Were you here in Japan on the front lines, with the Japanese army trying to murder you?"

"Ted," Yoder explained to Fontana, "you understand that we'd been bombing the Japanese like crazy *before* the atomic bombs. We torched a hundred thousand civilians in Tokyo in their paper houses. So, I don't see a big difference."

"Well, we're torching a hundred thousand civilians in Korea," Sergeant Fontana said.

"Hold on there," Brian countered, offended.

Fontana pressed on. "It's worse in Korea than it was in Japan."

"Fontana, how would you know?" asked the soldier with no name.

"Oh, I know. You'll see. The public will finally find out. There were a million civilians killed in Japan. It'll be two million in Korea. And the Koreans never attacked us."

"They did," snapped Brian.

"We got no Pearl Harbor from the Koreans."

"I don't even know why you're in the military," Brian

said, exasperated.

Nobody responded to that. They knew you got drafted. You couldn't just send your regrets to the Army, saying you were otherwise engaged.

"If there were more voices like mine in the service, the world would be a safer place," Fontana said, his comment sounding pompous.

"You really believe that?" The soldier with no name couldn't believe what he just heard.

Ted Fontana shot back, "If everybody were like you and Brian, we'd have bombed Russia with an A-bomb already and we wouldn't be sitting here on our asses talking right now. We'd be vaporized, along with the whole world. You've heard about the Concerned Scientists so-called Doomsday Clock? You where the hands of it are set right now? Three minutes to midnight, midnight meaning complete annihilation of the human species....I know there's no way the carpet bombing of Korea is going to stop, but at least we're not setting off another A-bomb."

"Bet you just love Russia," Brian said to Fontana, kind of egging him on. He was basically accusing him of being sympathetic to communism… in other words, to the Devil.

Brian was obviously deeply angered because he was a corporal, and the man he was snarling at was a sergeant—so, technically, Fontana outranked him, though Brian wasn't under his command.

But Yoder didn't have time to regret letting the words pop out like that. He was young. That was that. He came out of the Korean bloodbath alive—he was even wounded once, and sent straight back in after recovering—and for that, they gave him mosquito wings—a raise in rank to private second class.

Timothy Beaumont finished his story; Torrington listened and chewed his food. Beaumont asked, "You see my emphasis, right? We understand that Fontana has a right to his opinion. But people like him can get seduced into working for the Russians. It's hard for military counterintelligence to root out those who go over to the other side unless they're able to get quite physically close to them."

Torrington was confused. He said, "I thought you said Forsberg is not rooting out communist sympathizers among us."

"Yes, I did say that. My point is rather something different, but still related. It has to do with us being at war— more than a Cold War, as some people try to call it—with Russia."

"I understand," Torrington said deferentially, but not understanding.

"I just happened to be on the other side of the partition, able to hear those enlisted men. Normally, I don't come into much contact with them."

Beaumont was almost rambling…"Just note that Gideon Forsberg's rank—it's too high. There would be too many questions raised if he, in the role of an administrator, tried to personally access information on men so he could investigate them. Certainly, he's not of a low enough rank to mix with folks like a Fontana. Maybe he would oversee an investigation from headquarters at Camp Crawford or even down-country in Japan? Yes, but not here—here in Chitose, if he tried to do that, he would be seen to be in the way, delving into matters that aren't part of his assignment. So, you see, it doesn't make sense that he's here to investigate in some close-up way."

"Yes, I understand that." Torrington thought: the major can't help repeating himself. It's odd. He sounds fallible; he's normally not that way.

Majors Seidelman and Washburn, having finished their dessert, sipped from flasks of liquor in their coat jacket pockets, and got up from their table. They waved goodbye to Beaumont and Torrington and left the executive canteen.

By now, Torrington had finished his meal. Beaumont had

barely touched his. Torrington thought about signaling to the waiter for his dessert.

After the front door snapped shut behind the two majors, a few thoughts went through Jake's mind: I enjoy Timothy Beaumont's company. I'm attracted to him, in a brainy way. But I've never seen him like this before. We're sitting here and he's talking in circles. I'm sure he doesn't want me here so he could waste my time. I think he's been afraid to say something to me because the two other majors have been around.

Yes, Beaumont had been uncomfortable they were there.

He drew in his breath and spoke. "This will sound odd, but Forsberg doesn't gather intelligence. He's a *piece* of intelligence himself."

Jake couldn't conceive of what Tim meant; he kept quiet.

"The real story is… look, I'm telling you only. You… need to know because there's nobody else in Chitose that I trust as much as you. You'll do the right thing if you find yourself the last man left standing."

Torrington thought: what's that supposed to mean?

Beaumont quickly chimed, "I mean, if you find yourself the only man left who happens to know the truth."

Not knowing what to say, he said, "Okay."

"No one's going to suspect you're in the know. There's nothing to trace back to you. You'll be safe. I've thought it over. I don't believe it's going to be a burden that'll endanger your life."

The suggestion of peril did not sit well with Torrington. He was not a weak man, but wasn't the type who sought relief from boredom by joining the army and taking risks.

Beaumont wasn't finished. "Please have confidence in me, Jake."

Torrington sat there and took that in. He didn't know what they were talking about, so what could he say?

Beaumont continued, "Later today or tomorrow, as chief of Civil-Military Cooperation, you're going to hear about some acts of violence that occurred in town. What I'm saying will help you to separate that out from some issues of our own that we have."

Again, the unit commander of CIMIC couldn't image what Timothy Beaumont was talking about. He looked down at his plate, his head cocked to his left as if to ward off an oncoming blow. Perhaps he'd been in the army too long; he knew something was about to fly at him.

Beaumont spoke calmly, "You need to know that Forsberg is a werewolf."

Had any food been in Jake's mouth, he would have automatically spit it out, out of surprise and disbelief. So this is what Timothy has been working up to? Did Torrington actually hear the word "werewolf"? Beaumont is the quintessence of stability, of rationality. His actions on post are always well thought out. He's an analytical and insightful guy. There's a reason why he's the head of C2I. He's a consummate professional. Measured, restrained, fair. Someday he'll likely be a base commander. But he says something like this to me?!

Beaumont saw the expression on Jake's face and said softly, "And it's not a joke, unfortunately."

Jake thought he heard some defensiveness in his tone. He said respectfully, "I'm sorry, Tim, but could you repeat what you said just before 'And it's not a joke.'? I just want to make sure I heard correctly."

"Forsberg is… a werewolf. Look, he's been transferred here and there since we found out. We're not sure what to do with him. But we're trying to keep things safe."

"So I heard you correctly." Torrington was at a loss for what more to say.

"Jake, at first flush, I know you think what I'm saying is crazy. I thought the same thing the first time I heard it."

"So, you're serious… huh?" Torrington asked, his head swimming in confusion and disbelief.

"Yes, I am."

"But, um… there's one thing… I don't believe in werewolves."

"Neither did I."

Beaumont counted to five slowly in his mind, letting the silence between the two men just be.

Then he spoke once more, this time with no hesitation. "I know how you feel. But if I told you eight years ago we had a bomb smaller much smaller than a car, that could flatten a city of half a million people, would you have believed me?"

There was a pause. Torrington answered, "No."

"Jake, there's only so much we can know. Millions of things live in the world. We let them buzz in the background. We don't have the sensory capabilities to perceive most of them. Things are out there, and we're not experts. Just think of the ocean floor, for example. Do we know it in its depths? No, we can't get there. Yes, we're trying to, and we will someday. …So maybe that's a bad example, because we know the ocean has a floor."

Torrington said, "Yeah, there's nothing debatable about that. Science is exploring it."

Beaumont had another idea. "Well, let me try this, then. "Do you think a scientist can predict with any precision the exact break up of a drop of rainwater after it splashes against the surface tile on the ground?

"No, it would probably splash a different way every time—so I get your point with that example."

"Yes, it's the concept of *turbulence*. So, what if I use that concept?

"Fine," Jake said. He didn't mean to be disrespectful, and his words weren't taken to be such.

"So I've at least reached you intuitively with my second example."

"Yes."

"But Jake, … scientists don't concern themselves with turbulence. Did you know that? It's too complicated. So they turn away from it. They'll never be able to predict its outcome. What's the point of investigating random motion? It can't be put into equations—the equations won't repeat themselves the next time the water splashes."

Beaumont took a breath to continue, "So I'm asking you to have an open mind."

"All right."

"Um... Forsberg became a werewolf sometime in '45. The army in Europe found out in early 1946. It's been kept under wraps since then. As you can imagine, it's been hard."

If it was true that Forsberg was a werewolf, Jake thought Beaumont's last comment was an understatement.

Beaumont tried to think what might be going through Torrington's mind. He asked, "You may wonder what it was that turned him into a werewolf."

"I suppose I might," Jake said hesitantly, still not a believer in the concept.

"We don't know," Beaumont said forthrightly.

"Okay," Jake said, accepting the response, though it was all so... preposterous.

"I'll tell you that we can't bring a team of scientists in on this—not yet. It has to stay secret."

The question was forming in Jake's mind: just how long has Beaumont been involved in this? He felt it wasn't the time to ask him, though—partly because asking him the question might demonstrate to him that he believed in werewolves.

Jake did, however, ask, without appearing to sound aggressive, "Why is Captain Forsberg being allowed to live among us? Shouldn't he be put in a detention space?"

"You're thinking like an army man—*detention space.* Though, honestly, what else is an army man—I'm not insulting our kind—supposed to think in a case like this? That's one of the problems, isn't it?"

"I'm not sure I know what you mean?" Jake said.

The major said bluntly, "It's true he kills people. There

have been corpses. That's how we were able to figure it out in the first place."

"Then why let him stay on the loose?" Torrington exclaimed, letting go of some of his reserve.

"He's not on the loose. He's with Nichols and Velchoffsky. They're an able team. They could deal with him better than most if he gets out of hand. But there's more than that. He has his condition under control with drugs."

Torrington spoke, ignoring Beaumont's last remark. "What does he do at night? If he's a werewolf, he goes out and kills people."

"No, that part is under control, we believe."

"You believe?"

"Yes, that's what we believe. We're watching over him."

"Isn't it hard to watch over him?"

"Well, yes, and no. We do wish we had more latitude. For example, we wish we could log his comings and goings out the front gate of the post. But if we asked for that, we'd raise suspicions, and awareness of our efforts might get back to Forsberg. But as I said, he takes drugs to control his condition. It's not like he changes into a werewolf at every full moon. It's not like that at all." Beaumont paused and thought for a moment; he emphasized again, "His condition is under control as best as it can be."

"Wouldn't somebody think it's lethal to have him around? He could turn somebody else into a werewolf."

"We don't think he can do that. He's showed no signs of it. Look, an army lives with danger. It has soldiers, and these soldiers are, when on duty, never completely safe—for example, guns abound. As for his being a risk to civilians, there's little risk if he's on post most of the time."

"Most of the time?"

"We do our best."

"Jesus, why is he being allowed to go free?"

Beaumont gestured to Torrington to keep his voice down, and then explained to him, "He's not free—I emphasize that. He knows what happens to him and he struggles against it. We don't talk to him about it, but we know, we observe him."

"Does he know you know?"

"No."

"Has he ever approached the army and reported what's wrong with him?"

"No, he wouldn't do that," Beaumont said, looking straight at Torrington. "Go ahead, in your mind, lay out the challenges of his situation. Try to see it from his point of view. He'd last a few days and then he'd be dead."

Torrington thought for a while. All he could think in his mind was, "wow."

"Well, listen…" he paused and continued to speak in a volume that could not be heard by anyone more than fifteen feet away. "The right people who were up to the job know the score. They even sent him to OCS to become an officer."

Torrington reined in his exasperation—or at least tried.

This was so far away from the simple lunch with Major Beaumont he envisioned he was going to have today. It was wise, he thought, to focus on logical questions that the situation prompted. Yes, he would pose reasonable questions, even though they were fantastical at the same time. "Why on earth did they want him to become an officer?"

"It's a good way to hide him. Look, we both know that from time to time the army reassigns people who they haven't found the right slot for. They don't want to put an end to Forsberg. He may be useful as a weapon against the Russians."

"They really think that?" The mental image of a comic book monster came to Torrington.

"Why wouldn't they? All options are on the table when you're dealing with the Reds. I'm sure you remember Stalin wanted to occupy Hokkaido after we were the ones who defeated the Japanese."

Torrington changed tack. "You say I'm the only one

besides you in Chitose who knows about Forsberg. Why not inform Colonel Brewster?"

"There's no reason he needs to know at this time.

"Okay," Torrington said apprehensively.

Beaumont was defensive. "Look, we're operating on the idea that this is a man-made disaster—we're trying to manage it."

"I don't know what that means," Jake responded a little too quickly to be polite.

It was clear by the look on the major's face that he wasn't about to explain.

Torrington continued, "You want me to know in case I wind up being the last man left here that knows. But you've also said you don't think he's a danger to us."

Beaumont tried not to sound too defensive. "Well, what I meant was if the Russians were to drop a bomb and I was killed—and you were the only one left here who knew."

The pimple-faced waiter came over to the two men and cleared their plates. "Can I get you gentlemen anything else?" he queried. "Kitchen's about to close."

"No dessert for me, thanks," Beaumont said, tugging his trousers at the knees, readying himself to leave. The waiter looked at Torrington. The captain had decided dessert was out of the question now. He said, "Me neither, thanks."

The waiter turned on his heels and walked away. The two officers got to their feet. Beaumont's purpose had been achieved: he'd brought Torrington into the loop.

The major pushed his chair in and said softly, "Jake, there are unexplainable things in the world. Think about chicken pox—common chicken pox. We know a virus causes it. But we don't where viruses come from—they could come from outer space—really, I'm not kidding, we don't know."

He held out his hand in a gesture to guide Jake away from the table and continued, softly, "Chitose's an out of the way place—one of the safer places in the world for him. It's got a low-density population." He peered into Torrington's eyes as if to ask, can you appreciate what we're doing?

Beaumont led Jake away from the dining table and they strode to the door.

While rain dashed against the sides of the military police headquarters building, heat inside continued to pour out of the clanking, steam-filled radiators. Gideon Forsberg sat in his office, cap on head, door closed. He was in the same condition as he was the previous day. With his door closed he didn't have to pretend to sort through papers, read, review documents—he didn't have to keep up an appearance of being busy.

A 3:30 p.m., just before he was getting ready to leave, Lieutenant Nichols knocked on his door.

The Chitose Sheriff's Office needed help retrieving a body on hazardous terrain. It had a rough map, hand-drawn. It showed where the body lay.

The sheriff had telephoned Velchoffsky who provisionally agreed to Fujita's request for the U.S. Army favor, saying he had to get the O.K. from his unit commander after clearing it with Nichols. The job was routine and would require a helicopter, its pilot and two men. Fujita said he would send over the map with the location of the corpse, along with a detailed topographic survey.

Nichols needed Forsberg's signature for the short mission.

Forsberg swung around in his swivel chair when he heard the knock. "Come in."

"I hope I didn't catch you at a bad time, sir." Lieutenant Nichols had strong blue eyes; his uniform looked sharp on him today. He took two steps into the office.

Forsberg made no reply.

"The Japanese sheriff is asking for assistance. It entails army personnel and equipment. They're trying to get to a spot where the body of one of their deputies is. The corpse has been there since before the rain started a couple of days ago."

"Really?" Forsberg, half-exclaimed, his face coming alive. "What do you propose to do?"

"We'll send over an eggbeater to get it," Nichols said, intentionally using slang to show Forsberg he didn't want to be treated as an aloof administrator. "One pilot, one MP, and one muscular soldier. The body's on a slippery hill. There's danger of a mudslide there. So the chopper hovers over and a cable with a solider on it is lowered from it. The soldier grabs the body and the hoist brings them up into the aircraft."

"Good," Forsberg said with sureness. "I'll be part of it."

"Well, actually," he said hesitantly, "You don't need to be. That's not why I'm here. I'd like your signature for the mission."

Nichols tried but could not hide the surprise on his face.

"No, no," Forsberg said. I'd like to take part in the mission itself."

"All right, sir." Nichols did not know what else to say.

Forsberg knew he had to explain straight away. "I'll take responsibility for getting the body up to the chopper. I'll go down, on the cable."

"Excuse me, sir. You don't need to involve yourself. It's okay." Nichols had no idea what Forsberg was thinking. He also thought it was rather odd that the captain wanted to get involved because he hadn't anticipated the captain doing anything for the next week.

Forsberg replied, "I know I don't need to. But I want to. Someone has to take responsibility."

"We do take responsibility. We just need to sign for it."

But it was fruitless to try to overrule the captain.

He said, "We should have an MP with authority on board, because the chopper's going into an area under Japanese jurisdiction. Might as well be me. A chopper's a valuable piece of equipment. We need to know where our equipment is at all times."

Before departing at 7 a.m. the army helicopter pilot, studying the drawing made by Deputy Hashimoto—as well as a Japanese topographic map—jokingly remarked that on a hill like that, after a couple of days of rain, dead bodies had been known to seek out a change of scenery. (By that he meant a dead body could slide down a hill.)

The task was uncomplicated. There was the pilot, an MP operating the winch, and Forsberg, who was wearing a helmet to hide his bare head.

The S-51 chopper flew along the ridge behind Akiyama's house and they spotted the bloated cadaver against some bushes, its skin washed clean by the rain. The pilot hovered in position, cautiously eyeing the incline, keeping his chopper's blades away from it.

The winch operator hit the switch and lowered the cable down, with Forsberg riding at its end.

Once he got near the body, Forsberg saw a grotesque brownish-pink recess where the policeman's nose and skin had been torn off; it extended to the top of his right cheek. A small, flap of flesh—Iwate's lower lip—curved away from his teeth. The wet hair on the back of Iwate's head covered a gash on it.

The captain attached a paratrooper's harness around the corpse; he hooked that harness to the cable he was on. He signaled to the winch operator to hoist them up.

Gideon wasn't originally supposed to descend to get the body. But once in the chopper and in the air, he insisted on changing jobs with the other MP, ordering him to operate the winch. The MP sergeant thought: what a fussy and impetuous officer.

CHAPTER 17

Danjuro Fujita, in his stocking feet, stood in front of the paper screen door with a tray in his hand. He spoke softly.

His mother whispered back, "Come in."

Carefully sliding the door and stepping into the cozy bedroom whose broadest wall displayed a *kakejiku* (a hanging scroll) with grass blade-like calligraphy on it, he glanced down at her. Her face was pale. She lay on a futon under a flower-embroidered quilt.

Fujita knelt on the tatami mat and tucked his legs underneath him. Her elbow wasn't far away. Hisano Fujita stretched her hand out toward her son, and he grasped it gently.

"I don't feel well," she said. It was a common utterance of hers.

"I've brought you some tea."

She sat up and took the small porcelain cup from his left hand without thanking him.

She sipped it and said tersely, "It's cold in here. And clammy."

"It's been raining quite a lot."

Danjuro had spoken to his mother little during the last two days. Usually when he looked in on her she was asleep. When he was out at work, she would rise and fix herself simple meals.

At last she was awake when he was home. Mrs. Fujita looked her son up and down. As if from out of nowhere, she said:

"You're not the same person as before. You've changed."

This was a favorite remark of hers. She inserted it into a conversation; obsession drove her to it; she was oblivious to it being a lie.

"I don't know why you say that," he said, turning his head away as he said it quickly, softly—he knew it was pointless to challenge her remark. She added it for spice, it seemed; she wanted to lead their conversation.

She took a sip of tea and then continued.

"Ever since the war…" She was going on one of her favorite tangents. "The Japanese have changed. Everybody's changed."

"Except you." He smiled.

"Everything's about money now." She managed to infuse her stony face with drama and foreboding.

This was another favorite complaint of hers. She wasn't completely awake yet.

"That's not always true." Danjuro shifted his weight to his other side. "Chitose is not as bad off as most other towns in Japan, mother."

The sheriff was right: Chitose was a world apart. Hokkaido, with its great reserves of fresh water and vast, jagged coastlines teaming with wildlife, was vastly different from Japan. Economically and politically, too, it was the most stable part of the country.

Hisano Fujita wasn't in the mood to hear that Chitose was in better shape than the rest of Japan.

She was a petite woman, her color fading with age, who oscillated between having bright, energy-filled days and many more days filled with depression. She lived on the ground floor of their modest two-story clapboard house. Her son spent long hours at the Sheriff's Office, coming home to find her asleep before trudging upstairs to his room. Fujita tried to convince her to have the house torn down and replaced but his mother would have none of it.

Danjuro knew if he allowed her to vent, she'd calm down

and begin to consider the world outside herself. She was of a generation that clung to old, questionable habits, yet sometimes she had insights that were valuable to him as a policeman. There were times where she could find the foe where he, better natured than her, thought he had a friend.

The rambling conversation with his mother had to drag on for a while yet.

"It's damp in here. I don't hear any rain. I've been aching so much I haven't felt like going to the window to see if more rain is coming."

"Oh, it's definitely going to rain again…"

His mother interrupted him, and her remark was unexpected. "The rain is good for spring planting."

Her son took up from where he left off. "Barometric pressure will continue to be low through tomorrow. You should turn on the radio. I'm only repeating what the radio said."

"I haven't listened to the radio today."

"Yes, I can tell," he said, not sure she was telling the truth. Desperate for attention, she was frequently play-acting. Her husband had had to deal with this and now it was his turn.

"You know, mother, it's Golden Week." The son wanted his mother to know, if not the day, at least what time of year it was.

"Constitution Days is tomorrow," she responded, adding, "Don't you think I know what today's date is?"

Danjuro's father had died of pneumonia in the winter of 1944. His father had always been attentive to his wife, but it was never enough. Danjuro got along well with him, never rebelled, and respected his father for his even-handedness and business acumen. Danjuro viewed the interaction between his parents with alarm. For him, a woman with a disposition like his mother's would be an unbearable marriage partner. But how could his father have known? They married young; there was no lengthy courtship.

Danjuro was forty now and still unmarried. It was

because of when he was born. By twenty, he was in the Japanese Imperial Army on his way to a bureaucratic post in Korea, and from there to Manchuria and then Singapore. That gave him no chance to find a Japanese bride. Eventually he was taken prisoner by a group of Australian soldiers. At the end of the war he was thirty-eight years old; his father had died and his mother felt sorry for herself. History had taken its course. It was too late for him to get married. He settled into his job at the Sheriff's Office. He could fairly easily shoulder the responsibilities. He liked his work mostly, and especially liked not traveling. His job sometimes even fascinated him.

Danjuro said, "It's a pity about the rain. There were some gorgeous *kobushi* trees in full bloom." He was wistful. "All the blossoms are strewn over the ground now. A bit like snow." The way Nature had challenged Chitose's filthy scene-stealing air and won gladdened him.

Observations like the one about the *kobushi* would've only interested Hisano Fujita if she'd made them herself. That her son had voiced them—this she received with indifference.

Danjuro continued, but darkening, said, "But I must say, something awful and unexpected has happened in Chitose. We've lost one of our deputies."

There was a short silence.

"You've lost him?" she asked, with no emotion. "Do you mean he's far away... what do you mean?"

"He's dead. He was killed. He was killed because he was a cop."

"Oh, I know what you're talking about."

"You do?"

"Yes, I listened to the radio yesterday. I also remember you telling me that Shigeru Akiyama was being sought for questioning."

"Well, he's the man who killed Hidekichi Iwate." He added ruefully, "We can't find him. Although people have seen him."

"Of course they have." She spoke like an authority of some kind.

"If they see him and don't contact us quickly, he slips through our fingers," Danjuro said. Almost reluctantly he ventured, a touch afraid his mother would say he wasn't a good cop, "We don't know where he is. The weather is raw. Nothing can proceed quickly. But he doesn't have any friends that we know of."

"Then how will he ever be found?" His mother's voice had defiance in it.

"He may never be found. We hope he'll be spotted again, somewhere, soon." His voice dropped at the end of the sentence. As far as leads were concerned, he and the police were empty handed.

"Who saw him last?"

"His daughter. She's not usually in touch with him. She was adopted years ago. But she got it into her head, I suppose, to try to help us. Since she saw him, there's been no trace of him. Except that there's the body of Iwate."

"Are you sure he killed Mr. Iwate?"

"Iwate was watching Akiyama's house. The last time Akiyama was seen was at his house just after Iwate's murder." Danjuro sounded certain that Akiyama had killed Iwate. "Most of the town has heard the news by now. Understandably, they're terrified."

"Someone so difficult to find, he must be a demon," his mother explained.

"Well, many townspeople believe he's not human," he responded, placating his mother. He had no interest in the old superstitions.

His mother kept on her track. "A mountain demon who chooses when to be seen and when not to be seen. That's the way these things are."

"Why do you say mountain demon?" Danjuro tried to avoid making his question sound like he thought his mother's statements were outrageous.

"Because his name is Akiyama and the human form he takes is that of an Ainu man." *Akiyama* means "autumn mountain" in Japanese. Years before, Ainu families were assigned Japanese surnames so the authorities could monitor them.

"I don't think he's a mountain demon, mother."

"But he has vanished. You know very well that mountain demons can fly." She spoke as if what she was saying was as logical as algebra.

"I don't know very well that mountain demons can fly. I don't believe in such things," Sheriff Fujita said softly.

"He undoubtedly has become one." She reformulated her idea. "Or rather, he's possessed by one."

"Which is it," asked Danjuro, "Is he a mountain demon or is he a human who is possessed?"

Making distinctions like that was apparently no longer on his mother's mind. She added pessimistically, "He's always been one. It's evil magic, possibly even serpent magic. It can spread."

Danjuro maintained his rational manner. "Regardless of all that, he has murdered a man and brings hardship to the young Iwate family, and to Chitose."

"Keep an eye on all the major crossroads. At one of them he'll be meeting with his friends," his mother warned.

"His friends?"

"His fellow demons." She paused for a breath. "If he leaves Chitose, don't think he's gone for good. Don't sigh with relief. He'll still be here because his witchcraft has overtaken a person who didn't adequately defend him- or herself against him. His malevolent acts will continue." He thought: it's always odd listening to my mother hold forth like an expert on such things. Nevertheless, Danjuro sat patiently because he could tell she was far from saying everything she wanted to say.

"You're certain there's more than one of him?" he inquired.

"You can count on it. Do you think these spirits act completely alone? They cannot." She almost chuckled.

"I will relay what you say to my fellow policemen." His mother was oblivious to the note of sarcasm in his voice.

"It will be difficult to get hold of him if he has taken a different shape!" she further warned.

She sipped three times at her tea. The sound of her sipping was rather loud.

During the two days of rain there were multiple sightings of Akiyama. He was spotted under a bridge, or standing at the side of this road or hurrying down that street. The police couldn't check on every report, but they knew enough to know that these sightings were imaginary and that Akiyama was likely away from Chitose.

In some people's homes a bowl would fall off a table. This would be attributed to the spirit of Akiyama prowling about. This same thing went for someone slipping on a staircase or someone else cutting herself in the kitchen: Akiyama caused it. Stories circulated where people worked or gathered, and they only frightened people more.

Finished with her tea, his mother set the cup down next to her and perked up, "Also, keep an eye on the river—where last year's tall grasses have fallen. Spirits hide there."

"Mother, we are looking for a man."

"Yes, it will be hard for the police to look for a spirit hiding in dead grasses. There's no one among them who's experienced in these matters."

"Yes, mother."

There was a pause. Danjuro was thinking that his mother was almost through, but she said, "I never liked moving here."

With those words Hisano wasn't only complaining, she was expressing a deep regret.

"I know," he said.

"It was only because of your father's job."

"I know," Danjuro said again.

So now they were slipping back into repetitive territory where there wasn't anything to be gained. He'd heard it a thousand times before: "We would've been better off staying in Kobe." Kobe is near Osaka, in central Japan.

"You wouldn't have changed had we not moved here," she said, neglecting to bring the war into the matter.

Well, any meaningful talk has ended, he sighed to himself.

His mother intended to go one last round. "Anywhere outside Chitose is dangerous." She said this as if it was the first time she'd ever mentioned it. But it'd always had been on her mind.

Why? Because when the Japanese settled the area, the native name for Chitose was *Shikot*. In Japanese, this sounded like "dead bones." So the name of the town was changed to *Chitose* which means in Japanese, "One Thousand Years" or "City of One Thousand Years." Curiously, the name of the lake (Shikotsu) remained unchanged. The whole area beyond on the town, with its creepy Ainu names, still spooked a lot of Japanese. His mother, like many others, considered only the *town* to be safe—with its name, its size, its police force, and the adjacent military installation.

"Well, you're out of harm's way in this room," said Danjuro, as he snatched the empty porcelain teacup where it lay by his mother's bed.

CHAPTER 18

Many hours had passed since Iwate's corpse had been retrieved. Forsberg lay in bed in an opioid twilight unable to fall asleep—he'd increased his dosage of codeine sulfate threefold. This was the first time since discovering the effects of codeine on him more than six years ago that one full-blown episode of the dreaded changes had quickly followed on the heels of another. What could he do but put as much codeine into his system as he could bear?

A week passed. He took so much codeine that he had little appetite.

He put on his uniform and went to his office. He sat in the chair behind his desk. He did almost nothing. Almost nothing was required of him. Unneeded, but needing to show up, he arrived every morning, closed the door to the outside world, and was idle. He decorated his desktop and shelves with operations manuals, open dossiers, notebooks and orientation materials—to give the impression, if someone were to come in, that he was functioning. If Nichols or Velchoffsky wanted something from him, they just picked up their phones and called—they didn't bother coming in.

During nights, in his quarters, intrusive scenes assailed him as he endured opioid "twilight sleep". He kept telling himself they were storms he could wait out, that by simply lying there in bed, sufficiently drugged, he was, despite all things, repelling the forces that wanted to overtake him.

When a day came again, his head swirled in a heavy daze. There was no stasis. All was flux. Day and night he had to endure visions and cruel, harassing memories that appeared in his mind's eye.

Forsberg's Battlefield Promotion

Oh, no. Not that place, that Italian mountain hamlet toward the end of the war, home to some fifty people who were now scattered, in hiding. Late April. Afternoon.

Smoke from explosions fouled the air. Mud and stones were everywhere. Clouds and mountain peaks meant that huge shadows were cast on the corners of buildings, over uneven ridges, gullies, and trenches. Mortar shells from the Allied Armies whizzed in the distance, their artillery having gotten a jump on the German cannons, pushing them to retreat. But there were Nazi soldiers separated from their detachments left behind.

There was a yard for chickens behind a weather-worn home, made of stones. All of it was on an incline. There was a battered shed in the yard. It was probably an outhouse.

Corporal Forsberg's squad leader, Sergeant Harold Anspach, was pointing his M1 Thompson submachine gun in the direction of the shed. The three other members of his fire team—Chet Rohr, Matty Torres and Chuck Klein—had been killed in the last ten minutes. The man behind the shed was the sniper who'd done it.

The sun was just past the meridian and smoke still hung from napalm fires in the not-so-distant hills. Anspach yelled, "Come out from behind there!" and then *"Komm raus! Jetzt!"*

A grimy but tough young German soldier momentarily stuck his head out from behind the shed to look at the American shouting at him. Then he ducked back behind. He cried out, *"Nicht schiessen!"*

The German had no support from any in his unit. His comrades had retreated or American soldiers had killed them as they swept through the hamlet.

Forsberg's company of a hundred soldiers had several German speakers in it, which is why it was part of the first wave of infantry sent to break through the Nazi defenses that Hitler named "The Gothic Line." The rugged terrain with rocky crags and a few crude tracks was still pocketed with remnants of the occupiers who had crazily decided to fight to the death. If they could be taken alive, they'd be interrogated in hopes of gaining useful information.

Forsberg never liked Anspach. He was cocky, proud of his language skills, the same age as he was—he lorded his talents over the men in the unit who couldn't speak German, insinuating how brilliant he was. He'd been made a sergeant and squad leader because he was fluent in the language the Nazis spoke. Not only was he arrogant, he was aggressive. Maybe he never got along with his father or his uncles, and by battling the Germans he was battling the males in his family.

Anspach shouted again in the direction of the shed. He said in German, "So, what are you thinking about back there? Come out with your hands up."

Forsberg knew the German didn't stand a chance. Why take a soldier prisoner who just killed your buddies? Why be burdened guarding him? If the commanders of 3rd Platoon, First Lieutenant Russell Otis and platoon sergeant Fred Stolar had been present, they would answer, "We take them prisoner because we get intelligence from them that will save our own skins." But those two were still lying wounded where they had been shot, waiting for medics to arrive.

So there stood Anspach with his Tommy gun in a muddy, stinking yard. Considering their position, Forsberg knew that no one else could see him, Anspach and the German. Sergeant Anspach didn't say anything to him about the two of them acting together to capture the soldier. Instead, he proceeded to taunt the soldier and brag in German for what seemed an eternity. Forsberg was impatient. He felt the undulating, murderous hills pressing in, forcing him to act. He never got more than five hours of sleep at night. He was sick of hauling munitions, of cold rations, icy winds, improvised shelters, days of rain, trench foot. He wanted it to end. He wanted to get some place that was warm, dry, and not steep. It didn't seem like Anspach was going to stop. He was enjoying himself too much.

Forsberg raised his M-1 Garand semi-automatic rifle and fired three bullets into Anspach's chest. He wasn't thinking. He just snapped.

Then he picked up Anspach's weapon and fired all the bullets it had in its magazine at the rundown outhouse. There were more than a dozen; they went through the thin wood of the shed and enough of them struck the German solider to kill him. He didn't die a painful death. Like many Nazi soldiers (and Hitler himself), he'd been taking morphine and methamphetamine. He died quickly, heavily anesthetized, without his mind ever grasping what was happening.

Eighteen men—half of Forsberg's platoon—were lost in the assault on that hamlet. Forsberg was later decorated for bravery.

In addition, he was promoted to sergeant and became the squad leader, replacing the fallen Harold Anspach.

Childhood, at Home

It was out of focus when Forsberg first brought it to his mind. He had the feeling it was symbolic—that there was much more to it than just pure visual images. If he continued to turn the images around in his mind, he'd finally comprehend the true meaning of what he was seeing. The pressure to get at the meaning of the scene—that is what it was—caused him great anxiety.

The lines on his mother's forehead were creased with complaints. She'd just had a fight with her mother in the late morning of a holiday week when Forsberg's grandmother and his parents were all there. It wasn't clear what the holiday was. That part didn't matter—it was merely a plausible setting in which his mother and grandmother could be together. At the root of the fight was a struggle for power between the two women. Forsberg's father appeared to be caught in the middle of it. He'd withdrawn into the next room to stay out of the field of fire. Something he'd done— he'd left his toolbox out in the open—his grandmother thought this was dangerous—one of the children might grab a tool and hurt themselves. Forsberg's mother seemed to be telling grandma that even though she was right she should've spoken directly to her, rather than to her husband. Speaking to her husband about the toolbox was as rude and intrusive as asking him about the monthly mortgage. His father was overworked and didn't need advice from his mother-in-law. She was getting too familiar with him, too close. His mother's words were like acid.

Then that scene evaporated into air. It was replaced by his mother standing in that low-ceilinged living room in their old house. An aura formed around her and with it came this image: a game of straws was in progress.

The fingers of a hand grasped the bunch of straws in its fist. Now it was someone's turn to draw a straw and hope he or she didn't get the short stick. This anguished Forsberg intensely—he felt he'd been coerced into playing a game he wanted no part of. He didn't understand why the dream was built the way it was.

He wanted it to end. There was no way this nightmare could end happily. Of its meaning, he could only reflect that his mother had done nothing to him, in any way, that contributed to his ruin.

A Wolf Looks at Primitive Humans

A wolf prowled on a precipice overlooking the caves below. It watched a group of men at the opening of a cave that opened to the sea. Somewhere in the cave's dark interior women with children worked and played. They were dressed in animal pelts and footwear made of fish skins. From the opening of the cave to the sea below were bare rocks. Pools of seawater along the rocky coast were deep enough to have two-feet-long fish swimming in them.

The assessment of the wolf: there's not anything there now that arouses me to act.

Forsberg, too, saw the scene; he looked closer and saw the people were hairier than humans he knew, with bigger heads, and they stooped. The sounds from them were strange. It seemed their throats were permanently sore, making them incapable of uttering words.

The bright moonlight showed small mountains pointing out of the ground, on islands some four or five miles from shore.

A small boat filled with six prehistoric human men using oars came nearer and nearer to the caves. The hairy beings on shore let out yells and screams to frighten the intruders away. They sounded like monkeys and hyenas. The wolf observed the humans in the boat; they could speak; they shouted words and shook spears to frighten the cave inhabitants. The cave dwellers threw rocks at them.

The hairy men beneath where the wolf was standing felt danger. They needed to drive them away. They assumed the invaders had come from the gloomy mountains across the water.

They successfully warded off the boat.

Again, the assessment of the wolf: at present, I am not moved to act.

Whenever there was no fog or mist and the cave dwellers could see the small islands and the mountains, they were careful not to stare at them—they didn't want to invite evil spirits from those places to attack them. They created talismans to deter the boatmen from coming back. They prayed to the gods, begged them to sink the islands into the sea. They did not know that they themselves were also on land that was an island.

The wolf looked into the waters below the cave. Two silvery fish next to each other barely moved. They didn't want to be noticed by the cave dwellers.

Though the cave people had settled in a place where they could live in material ease. Yet the existence of those foreigners who came in the boats tormented them—plus, sometimes there were high tides and waves of water coming close—too close—to the entrance of the cave sometimes.

When the sea level was frightening—which happened certain years—they sacrificed—they killed a member of their family—an offering to the gods, praying that the water would go down. They didn't want to be forced to leave their cave.

Forsberg did not see the cave dwellers as noble savages. There are no noble savages.

Eating Dog Meat

Forsberg, newly arrived in Korea, sat in a restaurant in Busan, the city in the south of that country, temporarily serving as its capital. Some young junior officers had chosen the restaurant. It had a good reputation, they said, and they did the ordering. The food that Forsberg saw on other diners' tables looked unappealing. Furthermore, the restaurant had a smell that made him nervous and stirred uncomfortable sensations in him. First Lieutenant Stu Backus told Forsberg that Korean food was an acquired taste, but he should be initiated, and would get used to it in time.

While Forsberg took a swig of Japanese lager as they waited for their food, Backus went on a spiel, "Unfortunately we are always too busy with defending Korea to get out and know the people and understand their culture. I'm sure they look at us like we're uncouth heathens from outer space. You know, Koreans have the most sensible writing system in the world. Their culture's been steeped in Confucianism and Buddhism for over a thousand years." During the bloviating discourse, the captain noticed that another lieutenant, Charlie Bisik (often called "Charlie Beeswax" behind his back), was gawking at him and had a smirk on his face.

A couple of dishes arrived. One was a meat dish, the other a kind of vegetable that Forsberg didn't recognize. There would be other dishes arriving once they were fully prepared.

The men began eating.

Backus continued to dominate the conversation, saying that Koreans were known for their "dark" taste in food. The men around the table cast side glances at Forsberg and seemed to be holding back talking. Forsberg didn't notice they were suppressing guffaws. Forsberg told Backus he didn't think Korean food was for him, that it looked undercooked and he didn't like cooked vegetables served cold, as Korean vegetables often were.

"Well, it's exotic, we have to say," retorted Backus.

Then another captain at the table, Larry Claflin, grinned and spoke, "You know, Gideon, I swear one platter we had once tasted a whole lot like Basset Hound."

Forsberg found the idea repulsive. The smells in the restaurant were making him nauseous, making his body tense up. He was just fast enough to slide away from the table. Grabbing a handkerchief from his trouser pocket, he had just enough time to get it to his mouth and vomit into it.

Those at the table pretended not to notice. The captain had successfully held off any outright retching. He made like he'd just trapped a violent sneeze in time. But they knew. (Unsurprisingly, vomiting is far more common in army life than in civilian life—think of combat tension, food poisoning, bad water.)

Claflin continued in his deadpan manner, "Korean food has its unique delicacies. Their approach to food here wouldn't always be approved of in America."

To continue to "entertain" Forsberg while they were eating and waiting for the rest of the food to arrive, Lieutenant Backus proceeded to recall a recent, particularly gruesome, experience in the field. He was part of a unit that had liberated a POW camp. Half of those taken to the camp died in the three months they were incarcerated there. "I saw piles of bodies," he said. "They were stacked like cordwood." He went on about the filth and the snow, and how "the

North Koreans and Chinese hate our guts" so they don't feed their prisoners or give them medicine.

In wartime you hear such stories when you're at a table eating. Still, it seemed to Forsberg that this was a twisted and surly group of officers.

The rest of the food arrived. Lieutenant Backus again emphasized that Korean food could be strong tasting, that it was best to wash it down with beer.

Forsberg could smell the "aroma" coming from one of the new hot platters. It smelled like dog.

He rose from his chair carefully. As he left the table, with whatever composure he could maintain, he heard roars of laughter coming from the junior officers as he headed to the door of the restaurant. He could discern comments like, "Aren't you man enough?" through the noise behind him.

If only they knew.

"No," he wanted to tell them. "I'm not a man, I'm a werewolf, and by doing something like this you're playing with your lives."

A month later Forsberg had one of his "episodes" and Charlie Bisik met a grisly end. Forsberg would rather it had been Backus who got eviscerated, but things weren't personal when he was in that state.

Outside Modena, Italy

The Po River Plain, flat and broad like the Ishikari Plain, was green with spring. American soldiers, their vehicles, their armaments filled the roads. The plain stretched out around them in all directions. In twelve days, the Nazi forces in Italy would surrender to the Allies.

The crowded truck that Forsberg had been riding in with a dozen other soldiers and equipment stopped at a beat-up shop at the side of the road for a five-minute break. The shop was a single small building. In it, tobacco, soda and candy were sold but there were only empty shelves now. The place was once a filling station. There was one pump out in front, but there hadn't been any gasoline for many months.

The soldiers were all out of the truck. They'd unscrewed the tops of their canteens. Looking to fill them with safe drinking water.

A short, wrinkled, balding crone with what was left of her white hair stuffed into a faded dark headscarf was sitting on an upturned crate under a tattered awning. She was blind in her right eye and had a black patch over it. She wasn't the owner of the shop, but the shop owner let her sit outside for whole days.

The sun had come out and the woman was letting it warm her leathery skin. As a light breeze blew, she watched the army trucks barrel past the establishment. It was three days after the fateful afternoon in the Apennine mountains. He was already feeling sick, and not just sick from the physical blow to his body.

Somehow he'd been pulled into the old woman's unappealing but magnetic field. She was speaking to him, still had her front teeth and a few more that showed when she smiled oddly. She spoke broken English (and it appeared she was able to communicate, in an elementary fashion, in several languages); however, in Forsberg's opiate recollection, her English was almost perfect. "We all suffer. You suffer now, and you'll suffer much more, I see that. You have a sickness most people, thankfully, will never have. As God gave me life, I must provide you with words that have been provided to me. God uses me as he wishes."

"The war shows us men's greatest sins. Men kill and are wicked beyond what we can imagine. Accept Jesus Christ as your Savior: that is the start in the fight against evil conversions. There's no point in fearing the end of the world—it's going to happen, but while life here goes on, we are condemned—if we don't give our souls to God. You'll have trouble standing on two legs. You're a changed man."

"I came here to get some water." Forsberg said, dismissing her words.

"I can give you a Bible to read; that's what I'd normally do, but it's in Italian and you won't understand." She smiled, "But I do have a deck of Tarot cards. You need directions. I know you do."

Some Christian, he thought.

She took out the stack of miniature pictures from within the folds of her cloak.

He should have walked away from her.

She asked him, "Did you say Tolè, with its thirteen fountains of natural springs, each with a name?"

He said, "I don't know what you're talking about."

She glanced around with her one eye for a surface to place the cards on, to begin reading them. There was an upturned bucket near her.

But then Forsberg's commanding officer, who by this time was Second Lieutenant Eddie Frabosa, shouted. He said they were going to move on now.

When the crone saw what was happening, she cried out huskily, *"Il bocca al lupo!"*

As they were leaving Forsberg asked Frabosa, "Did you understand what that woman said?"

Eddie smiled. "She wished us good luck. But Italians are superstitious. They don't want to jinx a situation, so they say the opposite. She said, 'Into the wolf's mouth!'"

In the Mountains Across the Ishikari Plain

Protected against the cold by its bulky gray fur, the old wolf that was once human moved slowly among the thin trees, evergreens of all sizes, birches glowing white and older, taller, thick-trunked brown trees. Some of the trees had breaks in their bark, slits where tiny branches would sprout. A squirrel jumped between branches in a group of pine trees. A wide-eyed rabbit lingered in a patch of grass. The wolf flinched its ears from side to side. A deer was some two hundred yards away, quietly grazing on buds. It could be smelled and heard. The wolf sensed all the warm bodies around him.

Animals don't transform nature, they *are* nature, Forsberg thought, esteeming them.

Humans have consciousness. They have done good with it, have done much evil with it, too. They have created machines. The swath of destruction they've cut across the world is monumental. Animals don't see death coming. They instinctually avoid pain. They experience desire. They know what to ignore. Animals' experience of "here" and "there" is spatial and connected to their habitat. It is only temporal when they're dreaming. But since their consciousness isn't advanced, they don't have the ability to remember their dreams, let alone learn from them. They lack the ability to go crazy the way Gideon Forsberg does. He knows he is insane now.

A German Mortar Shell Hits a Barn

Blown back on his heels and hurled to the ground, his backpack cushioned his fall. The tug to his head under his helmet and the impact on his ears... momentary silence.

Numbness. Were his feet gone? His collarbone, what of it, he wondered? A flurry of debris, wood splinters and small stones. On his back for only five seconds, Forsberg rolled to the side and forced his eyes to squint, though powdery dirt rained down through the smoke—he had to do it, to prove he was still alive.

A few seconds went by before he got up on his knees. The weight of the gear on his back felt like another man was clutching him. He wriggled out of his pack. You can't patrol if you can't walk.

Sound returned to the barn, tufts of grass were growing at its side, wildflowers among them displayed their colors gaily—that was incongruous. It was macabre because this was a blood-letting battleground. He heard a man wail and cry "Medic!" They were fighting building to building, in the village of Tolè, Italy, in the northern Apennine Mountains.

Amid the rubble of fallen walls of a barn made of red bricks, one wall was still intact—it had been built into the side of a slope. The roof of the barn was gone now, the sky was open, dark to see because of the smoke and the granular sediment lifted by the blast.

He was still on his knees. It was after the death of Sergeant Anspach, during the last gasp of the Nazi army, before soldiers of the Allied armies barreled to the Po River and hastened the war in Italy to its end.

At any moment bullets, grenades, another shell might hit.

He'd caught and tortured small creatures when he was a boy. His behavior of that kind didn't last long. He discovered his power as a human and how so many living things were at his mercy. He was ashamed of what he'd done. He wasn't ashamed he'd killed Harold Anspach, only angry with himself for having to carry the burden of such a secret for the rest of his life.

Of all things, at that instant there was a wolf pup standing between him and the brick wall. It gaped at Forsberg as dark, sandy mist expanded in what was left of the structure, and mortar fire, gunfire, and near and far away explosions clattered and thudded.

The pup was separated from its pack, it was lost, it was in shock.

It was a great danger to be there. Gideon wanted it out of the barn.

He yelled at it to "git." It just gazed at him, dopey, immobile, unresponsive. It was a startlingly cute animal. He gazed at it. Blue eyes, a light brown coat and a gray tail. Forsberg changed his mind. It wasn't cute—it was the embodiment of Beauty.

It was intolerable to him it could be destroyed in the games men played.

He bellowed at it once more to get out, to run. The pup stood inert, showing no reaction to an encounter with a human.

He scooped a handful of gritty dirt and threw it at the pup, but it just blinked its eyes.

Forsberg got to his feet and moved toward the animal.

Without thinking about what he was about to do he advanced on the immobile pup and screamed, "Stop looking at me so stupidly! Move!"

Frustrated, he kicked it sharply in its jaw. He just wanted to drive it away.

Then it happened. A large, female wolf leapt from a dark space near the top of the blown apart barn wall. She came flying at Forsberg, over the wall of brick, in an unstable angle, slamming into his abdomen with its muscular hind. Forsberg was just barely able to stay on his feet. Her hind feet touched and rebounded from the ground. Her muzzle lunged for his jugular vein while he swayed, off balance. He twisted around, avoiding being bitten in the neck. Her mouth instead grazed his helmet strap and her teeth reached his collarbone, tearing into the soft flesh there. Then he threw all his weight against her and knocked her off him.

The wolf pup's mother was defending her young.

Forsberg reached to his belt for his knife to continue defending himself. There was no need. The mother wolf was already moving toward her pup. She quickly snatched it in her jaws and scurried away.

Blood oozed from Forsberg's clavicle wound. It soaked his shirt and jacket. He could feel it wasn't a deep wound. His lower abdomen, though—it felt like an anvil had hit it.

He dragged his backpack off the ground and stumbled out of the barn.

He got outside. The world spun around him. "Medic!" he yelled. He passed out, dropped to the ground.

He never recovered. Two months passed before he realized the she-wolf's bite changed his life forever.

Somebody Has to Know

It haunted him that somebody in the army *must know*

about his condition. He always tried not to think about this too much because it would drive him crazy.

Years ago, what happened in the library at Officer Candidate School at Fort Riley, Kansas, was just too strange to believe it was happening by chance.

On several occasions when he went there to study, he would pass by a table and see on it an aging leatherbound copy of *The Poetical Works of John Keats*. It was as if someone was trying to direct his attention to it because the book was there quite often. (Some people think the holdings of libraries in armed forces colleges consist of books only concerning military matters; nothing could be further from the truth; classics, such as Keats, are always there.) Sometimes the book was open. When it wasn't open, it had a bookmark in it. When it was open, it was opened to "Ode on Melancholy." What was curious was Forsberg didn't always study in the same spot in the library. If he studied elsewhere in the library, the same book would sometimes be there, nearby on another table. It was as if someone or something was trying to communicate to him, to send him a secret message.

After seeing the book many times, he finally stopped and glanced at it.

The title of the poem was high on the page. Then he read the lines below it.

> *"No, no, go not to Lethe, neither twist*
> *Wolf's-bane, tight-rooted, for its poisonous wine;*
> *Nor suffer thy pale forehead to be kiss'd..."*

The first two words of the second line were underlined in pencil—the words, "Wolf's-bane."

Another day after that Forsberg saw the book once again but it wasn't open. Instead, it was bookmarked. He opened the book at the bookmark and there it was: "Ode on Melancholy,"—with the words "Wolf's-bane" underlined.

At that time he didn't know what wolf's bane was. It seemed whoever or whatever was trying to reach him wanted to tell him about it. His curiosity was piqued because "wolf" was part of the phrase.

He found some information in library books about wolf's bane—also referred to as aconite, when wishing to use a more scientific term. It was a deadly poison, and yes, if you were "melancholy" enough, you might try to take your own life by ingesting it.

Indeed, his condition sometimes depressed him nearly to a breaking point.

Somebody had to know what was wrong with him—it couldn't be a coincidence he was finding this. What was he being told? That this was a way out of his condition? He believed that for a short time, until fortuitously, he discovered among the few books on botany that the library possessed, a copy of Rohde's book on medicinal herbs published in 1922, *The Old English Herbals*. In that book, the beneficial uses of small quantities of wolf's bane were explained.

Strange… and helpful.

Murder in a Chitose Lane

There were straight lines everywhere. This neighborhood was the result of city planning. Forsberg could see to the far end of the street. There was a door there, a garage door. Because of the time of day, some things were easily visible, others were buried in shadow.

Forsberg's vision was not right. It was not reliable in the nearly dusk atmosphere. Maybe there actually wasn't a garage door where he thought he saw one—instead, there were just shapes that reminded him of such a thing.

This neighborhood was unfamiliar to him. To his right side were houses, on his left side, across the street, more houses. There was a boy in the street. Though there was a breeze, and it was chilly, the breeze couldn't be felt because at the same time that he was outside, he was also inside—

inside something like a huge hangar for dozens of planes.

He shuddered and sizes changed. The hangar became a large terrarium, the size of the inside of a theater. The roof of the theater was partially open, so part of the roof was just clear sky.

There was a smell of doom in the air even though doom doesn't have a specific smell.

The seven-year-old boy with a skinned knee (Forsberg smelled the wet dirt in the wound) was playing alone in the middle of the deserted street—only deserted because families were inside their homes eating dinner. There was no herd of children to protect the boy, no other children given permission to play with him. While this was in front of a home, the home's boundaries extended out into the space past where the physical walls of the house ended.

Forsberg felt the changes taking over.

The street—just a neighborhood lane in a working-class residential ward in Chitose—and the air around it, beat like a heart. The ball bounced on the dirt ground; the thumping heartbeat drowned out its sound. Forsberg couldn't stop his body from changing. The boy smelled of youth and vital movement.

Sometimes the boy would pause the bouncing of the ball and go over to a small drainage grate in the street and kick loose dirt down it. It was pointless. It was all part of a child playing.

Forsberg was in a street parallel to the big road—the one just outside that perimeter fence enclosing Camp Chitose I. The housing development in this ward was built the previous year with the support of the American occupied forces. The development was called the Heiwa Residences. *Heiwa* means "peace" in Japanese.

Suddenly, Forsberg's left field of vision was blocked. In an instant, hair sprang up on his back. No, Forsberg thought. The muscles against his bones strained. His tongue lengthened. The boy became a gesticulating, jumping, enchanted doll to him.

But the boy wasn't a doll. The monster saw into the boy. It saw meat. The meat of prey.

The ball bounced and dribbled away when the monster leaped at him.

First, the boy's vocal cords were severed so he couldn't make a sound. As the boy was gored, his clothes were soaked in red. Pieces of tissue and muscle took wing.

Afterward, the werewolf dragged the core of the body away, off to the side of the lane, leaving it on a tiny lawn in front of one of the houses. No one heard anything. The ball remained at the other side of the lane.

The monster scurried away, found somewhere to hide until its beast-like form left it.

CHAPTER 19

Arriving back at the base, Forsberg skimmed by rows of Quonset huts in his jeep on a dimly lit road. The air on base smelled of spring grasses and petroleum. He'd spent the day, and the previous one, wrapped in dreams and visions but now he was in better condition. He didn't know why or how his mind had cleared, but he knew he wasn't dreaming now, knew this was real, knew exactly where he was.

He passed a gravel parking lot full of snowplows detached from the trucks that used them to clear the snow from the base's roads. The ploughs lay with their shadows in the dim light. Everything around them was either dark or desaturated in color, just as it should be at this time of evening.

The flesh covering his facial bones was tight. His face ached. He had only a little strength in his arms. His legs felt limp. But his body had changed back just in a few short minutes after that attack on the boy. Here he was, so quickly after the attack, back at Chitose I.

It was amazing that he could remember the boy and the scene, the frenzied breathing, his body rushing, a stunned child, the small boy's blood and guts. Usually, he remembered almost nothing. He didn't, however, remember why it was he went over to the boy's neighborhood; he had no recollection of driving there.

Did anyone see him?

If no one did, he had enough of his wits about him to think of how the news of the boy's death would play out tomorrow. With simplicity and certainty, people in town would think that Akiyama did it. The Sheriff's Office would continue their search for the Ainu man. Fear would be ratcheted up in town.

And law enforcement authorities would find nothing.

He pulled his jeep into the lot at the officers' compound. He was relieved to find no one in the corridor after he opened the Quonset's front door.

He mused to himself as he put his key into his door's lock: having people believe that Akiyama was a mortal threat, that he was nearby and could strike again—this was a belief that must be stopped. Something needed to be done even though Akiyama's corpse couldn't be produced.

He still had Akiyama's clothing. There must be a way he could use it to suggest that the Ainu had just died, right after he supposedly killed the little boy.

He turned the key to the lock on his door and went into his room.

As he did after most transformations, Forsberg swallowed a handful of mineral pills—magnesium, calcium, potassium with a glass of heavily salted water. It always almost made him retch. Then he drank a glass of water with bicarbonate of soda mixed in. These "home-remedies" were ones he learned by reading a book on werewolves, at Fort Riley.

After he downed the bicarbonate he stopped right where he was and it hit him like a flash: he had Akiyama's furs, his skins—*and these held scent.*

"No, no!" he murmured to himself and closed his eyes. The realization came over him: that's why the codeine wasn't working: I've had the smell of Akiyama in my quarters and it's what's made me constantly sick—that's what made me transform tonight and kill that boy!

He opened his eyes and shook his head, resigned.

He hadn't given much thought to disposing the clothing. Could it have been unconscious sentimentality that played a part in his holding on to it? That would be unusual. He didn't think he had any sentimentality left. What a horrendous mistake!

He breathed in deeply a few times. Unbelievable that it never occurred to me, he thought.

The bare outlines of a plan came immediately to him: use the clothes to stage Akiyama's death. Make it look like an accident or suicide, do it some place where it would be impossible to recover his body. He thought: the sea—there were stretches of beach and wilderness at the Pacific Ocean less than fifteen miles away. But no, he reasoned, the body could wash in. Anyway, he had little experience with the sea.

He thought about rural land. Find deep holes. Find a well. But he wasn't familiar with the area. All he knew was the terrain climbed from Chitose River, climbed to the mountains.

He stepped over to one of the cabinets in his room and took out all the maps he had. He examined them for anything that might give him an idea of exactly where he might materialize his plan.

Going through all the maps and any information he could find, he decided he had only one choice. It was Lake Shikotsu, the second deepest lake in Japan. It was accessible by a public park at its southern shore. The park and an adjoining private small business provided services such as rental rowboats, rods, bait, and tackle.

Once he had the plan in mind, the exhaustion hit him. He didn't even turn off the lights. He turned and swung his body onto his bed, keeping his boots on and passed out.

The captain opened his eyes after six hours of uninterrupted sleep. He was still spent from the attack on the boy—he was satiated by it, too—so though he'd be handling Akiyama's clothing, it wasn't going to have the effect it'd had on him—at least not right now. He must act fast.

It was an hour before sunrise. Once outside the base and finished with the streets that took him cross town, he steered his jeep onto the road that follows Chitose River up to its source: Lake Shikotzu.

Upon arriving at the park his eyes had to adjust to the early morning mist.

All year long the crater lake never froze over because of its great depth. He discerned an unpaved parking lot large enough to accommodate fifty cars. The lot was devoid of any vehicles. A group of three houses was across the road from the parking lot, further away from shore. They were unoccupied. With no one anywhere in sight, he parked.

Between the jeep and the shore, he spotted a cottage that served as an administrative office. It had been on the map. The area was as Forsberg hoped it would be—deserted. The park was still closed for the season. The temperature at this elevation was just above freezing. The wilderness around him brought to mind the Kabetogama State Forest in his home state of Minnesota. He would have known this wasn't much like Minnesota if he had been able to see the active volcano at Mount Tarumae just four miles away.

He walked closer to the lake over hardened loamy soil with an army duffel bag in his arms. He reached the spot where more than a dozen overturned rental rowboats lay, twenty yards in from the shore.

The ground everywhere was hard. Good. He'd leave no tracks. He turned one of the wooden rowboats right side up and slid it over the ground to the shoreline. The boat didn't belong there, and he knew it would attract attention. He took the skins and furs that had covered Akiyama out of the duffel and put them into the boat. Looking over the scene he felt there was a good chance investigators would conjecture that Akiyama had taken the boat out into the lake, jumped out of it, and that the boat had floated back to shore without him— all to save himself from being taken alive.

It was the best plan he could think of, though the distance between Chitose and the lake was considerable. The boy was murdered just over nine hours ago. That meant Akiyama would have around eight hours to get by foot from Chitose to this place. A man would need all those hours at least—it could be done, at a brisk pace, knowing exactly where to walk.

The scene was cold and serene. Some of the fog would lift soon. Turning away from the rowboat, and with the shore at his back, he felt a sense of relief and tried not to blame himself for holding onto the clothes for so long. He took a worn path that led to the parking lot. It passed between trees, still leafless.

He looked down to make sure he wasn't leaving any tracks. The path, not lately traveled much, was strewn with small sticks and decomposing leaves from the previous year. Just before lifting his head up, a few steps later he saw to his left side a thin patch of vegetation. In it were some aconite plants, not yet green.

"I'll have some of that," he said to himself, and he stopped in his tracks. While he hoped he'd never have to use any of it, it was still a good idea to have some. He drew his army knife from its sheath. He bent down and scooped up some brown leaves to insulate his hands from contact with the plant. He stayed bent down and dug out a couple of plants by their roots. He speared the roots with his knife and placed them on the dead leaves and wrapped leaves around them. He took out a handkerchief and tied it around the leaves. He held the small bundle in his hand carefully as he began walking again.

Using aconite was a method of last resort. All parts of the plant are toxic. If it doesn't kill right off the bat, it heavily reduces lycanthropic transformations, Forsberg found. It could even prevent them. Forsberg wasn't aware of it, but Ainu hunters used wolf's bane—they tipped their hunting arrows with aconite paste and it paralyzed their prey, rendering the prey unable to breathe. They used it on arrows shot from the bows, as well as on arrows rigged in the booby traps they laid in the forest.

Forsberg didn't meet a soul on his way to and from Lake

Shikotsu. He was fortunate. Just moments after he reached town, a couple of empty logging trucks and a man on his motorbike headed up that one and only road to the lake.

At 6 a.m., Isao "Tori" Shirata, the park's custodian, arrived on his motorbike and parked at the side of the one-room wooden building that was the office for the park at Lake Shikotsu. He opened the office, lit the fire in the wood stove, then went on his routine early morning inspection of the premises. Within a minute he spotted the rowboat alone at the shore and went over to it. He found shaggy furs and worn animal hides in it. He didn't know what to make of them.

Tori's mind was feeble. A few loutish boys in Chitose made fun of him behind his back, giving him the nickname "Tori" because he was short, and his chest protruded when he walked. *(Tori* is Japanese for "bird.") His mental handicap and his odd gait were a result of injuries and deprivations he suffered while serving in the Japanese army. The boys even said he left huge bird tracks behind him when he walked.

As Tori Shirata was discovering the strange pile of abandoned clothing, an American station wagon, Major Christopher de Graff's 1950 Ford Country Squire, climbed the road from Chitose to the lake. Private First Class Ricky Travers was behind the wheel, his eyes focused straight in front of him. The major had loaned him the giant (by Japanese standards) car for the day with the proviso that he bring it back before sundown. His window was cracked open to let some cold air in to help him stay alert. The incoming wind had no effect on his buzz cut hair.

Ricky was a terrifically hard worker under de Graff in the Logistics Office—a battalion always struggling to keep up with ordering materiel, receiving it, arranging where it would appear and at what time. Plus, it had a near-overwhelming task to allocate troops on base. De Graff had taken a shine to Ricky—the young Texan who worked had an upbeat manner that none of the other clerks in the office matched.

Bob and Lloyd worked tirelessly in the sprawling Logistics Office, too, but they weren't as genial as Ricky was.

Bob Fernandez sat next to the window on the spacious seat. Brian Yoder sat in the middle, between Bob and Ricky. Lloyd was in back, stretched out and sleeping on the long seat there.

Fernandez had a hot thermos bottle at his side; his cup of coffee sloshed around when the road got bumpy. He jabbered away, pumped up on caffeine. "The Japs in Hokkaido aren't as desperate as the ones in Honshu." (Honshu is Japan's main island, with twenty times the population of Hokkaido). "Just look at all they've got around here."

He gestured with his head to the wooded lands on both sides of the road.

"What do you mean?" Yoder frowned, not exactly understanding the point Bob was trying to make.

"They have plenty of natural resources around here, that's what I'm saying."

"You can't eat trees," Yoder said.

"Did I ever say they could? Did I tell you they could make rice out of trees?"

"No."

"Well, then that's that."

"What's what?"

Ricky's complexion brightened a shade because he thought Bob was going to get into a verbal fight with Brian.

Bob continued to follow his own train of thought, ignoring what Brian just said to him. "They don't make rice out of trees, but rice is sold on the black market to dodge rationing coupons. So how do Japs get money to buy on the black market? They help themselves to some natural resources and sell them to get money. Hokkaido people can do that. The rest of Japan can't. We're in the land of milk and honey, that's what I'm saying. Or at least *they* are, compared to Japs in other places."

"Not all Hokkaido people have it so good," Ricky snorted.

"Keep your eyes on the road, Tex," Bob shot back, playfully. Ricky was a good sport, Bob knew he could get away with teasing him if it was in the spirit of fun.

He kept jabbering, and with apparently nothing else to yak about, he launched into monologue about the black market in Korea versus the black market in Japan and how soldiers did people favors by buying goods at the BX and re-selling them to the locals, despite the locals raising the original price after they got their hands on the American goods and squeezing money out of their own countrymen.

Brian Yoder interrupted the monologue at its two-minute mark, feeling like ribbing Bob now, "Why buy from Americans? I like the Japanese." He pointed to the trees their station wagon was flying by. "They're so resourceful. They'll go into the woods and come back with a vacuum cleaner they built out of stones and branches."

Bob, peeved at being interrupted, retorted, "You're not funny. That makes no sense. After you leave the service, that's what you'll be doing: selling vacuum cleaners door to door. That's all you're qualified to do."

Brian just laughed. Ricky, gripping the wheel of the car in his fleshy hands, laughed too.

Ricky felt like razzing Bob—just like so many people who knew Bob, such a thing never was far from their minds—after all, he had it coming. Travers was happy that Yoder was sitting between them because he knew what he was going to say next might wind Bob up and then who knew if matters might go beyond the verbal.

"Hey, Bob," Ricky asked in a sly, humorous voice, "I've lost track of how things were going with you and that Japanese girl Kiriko. I haven't heard you say anything about her lately. Are you hiding something from us?"

"She's not at her job anymore," Bob snapped back, not wanting to talk about it.

Ah, what a pleasure it was to needle Bob!

Brian saw what Ricky was doing and piled on. "You told me she changed her job—I wonder why." His manner of speaking suggested Bob had pestered her so much that she'd quit the bar to get away from him.

Bob didn't turn toward the men to reply. Instead, he stared out his window at the passing woods outside and growled, "You better watch it, you guys!"

The two soldiers suppressed their amusement.

"You know something, I've never seen her," Travers continued drily, and staying attentive to the road. I hope she's not imaginary. But if she's real, I wonder if she's my type."

"Drop it, Travers." Bob said, hotly.

Ricky Travers, with no expression at all to his voice said, "You're right. It's way too early in the day to be talking about this kind of stuff." Boy,was he delighted that Brian was between them! Easy to bring things up, and easy to let them go.

As for Brian, he sat there thinking. Bob doesn't know when he's being teased.

 It was impossible for Fernandez to let Ricky have the last word. Staring again out his window at the trees he said, "There are Japanese people from Hokkaido who can squeeze enough money out of these woods to buy a vacuum cleaner… that is, after a few trades and swaps, they can!"

Kelso had wanted to get as much sleep as he could. He was successful in his endeavor; never once did he wake up during the ride.

Now their boots scuffed along the forest path to the Army's fishing camp. They had maps, a compass, lunches, water-filled canteens, cigarettes, beer, and old jam jars full of earthworms in their backpacks. This was their last day off for a while.

Lloyd walked behind the group and half-wished he hadn't come along. He wasn't feeling well. He didn't trust the woods anymore. Korea had ruined them for him. Gunfire could start at any time you were in them. Might as well say that Korea had ruined Nature for him. Before the war, Nature was fine by him, it was relaxing. You could go swimming and walking and thinking and dreaming. Now it was full of malevolence; quicker than you blinked, you could die.

So, now they were going to catch small, swimming creatures and butcher and eat them? They should just be left alone.

Why was Lloyd in such a foul mood? He'd had too much to drink the night before—plus, he had a secret that ailed him: he too was smitten by Kiriko.

It was depressing that she'd vanished and no one knew where she was. Lloyd didn't have a girl back home like Bob— Bob himself let that little fact slip when he was drunk one late night. Lloyd thought morally it was shady and shabby… Bob chasing a Japanese girl, while at the same time having an American girl staying loyal to him at home in California.

It was dishonorable, if you thought about it—it made him think of American soldiers and POWs in Korea who were struggling mentally to survive—only a girl back home waiting sustained many of them.

Yes, he saw a disrespect for life in Bob. True, he was probably blowing things out of proportion—that was pretty easy to do. At least he, Lloyd, wasn't deceiving anybody. And all in all, he was grateful and felt damn lucky to be alive, with no shrapnel in his body and no amputations.

Before they reached the cabin, a brown jay the size of a pigeon launched itself from a tree branch and zinged over their heads. It flew low enough that the men ducked. Brian Yoder cried out in warning, "Wild pitch!" The soldiers laughed and the jay vanished between the trees.

When the laughter finished, Bob tried to follow up with a joke of his own. He mimicked a golfer, placed one hand on each side of his mouth and yelled, "Fore!"

Nobody laughed.

Bob moved fast to stop the rejection of his joke from

lingering. "Did you see the tail on that bird?"

No one responded, but all of them had seen its grotesquely long tail.

The four soldiers had a full day off before military police training started at Camp Crawford in Sapporo the next day. Aside from when the bird flew by, they didn't talk anymore for—the change in temperature put them off it. They walked in silence for the next five minutes until they got to the fishing camp. It was a mile and a half downstream from where Chitose River begins at a narrow outflow of Lake Shikotsu. The fishing camp was situated on a man-made pond called Horomon Reservoir. (It sounded big but wasn't.) There were always *nijimasu* (rainbow trout)—they were stocked—in it. The place, a gem that was the result of the uppermost dam on Chitose River, had been taken over by the U.S. Army from the Japanese after the war.

The small administration office at the park on Lake Shikotsu proper didn't have electricity or a telephone. To talk to the rest of the world you needed to switch on a battery-operated two-way radio. In this way Isao Shirata contacted the Sheriff's Office in Chitose. The cop on the other end asked him questions and told him not to touch anything near where the garments were found; someone would come up to investigate; it would probably be in an hour. Mr. Shirata, who lived in Chitose, knew the search was on for Akiyama, but he didn't connect the clothes in the boat with him.

Even for those who hadn't heard about the murder of the boy the night before—and that was most people—the previous night had not been easy. There still was no sign of Akiyama. Now the town woke up to the news on the radio that a boy by the name of Keitaro Fukuda had been brutally murdered. Naturally, everyone suspected Akiyama. That didn't need to be mentioned. The seven-year-old had been playing out in front of his house. The sun had just set. There were no witnesses. No one heard anything.

The Sheriff's Office knew about the murder by eight p.m. Fujita conducted a couple of searches through town and he kept his men on patrol for the rest of the night. They found no clues and nothing unusual happened overnight.

Fujita was in his office by seven a.m. The news had just come in from Lake Shikotsu. He was desperate for a break in the case and possibly this news would provide him with one. Hides and pelts? Yes, they could turn out to belong to Akiyama. Within minutes Fujita was out of his office. He and a deputy headed up to the lake.

When they arrived at Lake Shikotsu, Mr. Shirata led the way to the upturned rowboat. Sheriff Fujita was aware of the man's unwanted nickname and observed that the man's way of moving did remind him of a bird. While questioning him, Fujita discovered he was lucky that Shirata happened to be at the park that day. During late spring, the disabled man only worked from seven a.m. to one p.m. on Wednesdays, Saturdays and Sundays.

Fujita's interest was piqued the instant he saw the furry garments. He examined them with care, passing his hands delicately across them and inside them. He held one of the sewn animal skins up in the sunlight—daylight was increasing by the minute. All the clothing was rustic, improvised. There was neither mass production nor a woman's touch in them.

He and his deputy scanned the scene around them. There was the lake, the chilly hardened surfaces of land around it, and tens of thousands of trees. This is vast, they thought, looking for clues beyond the shore and the parking lot would be like searching for a needle in a haystack.

They gathered the clothing and took it back to their car. The deputy suggested that Akiyama could have jumped into the deep waters to take his own life. Fujita just nodded, only communicating to his subordinate that he'd heard him, not that he agreed with his assertion. They spent an hour walking around the immediate area, found no clues and drove back down to Chitose.

There was no forensics expert who worked at the Sheriff's Office. Fujita laid out the garments on a table in a room the Sheriff's Office used for staff meetings, interrogations and lunch breaks. One by one he brought all those on staff into the room and asked each of them, "If you have ever seen Akiyama, have you seen him wearing clothes like this?"

For those who'd seen Akiyama, the answer was usually yes.

The lack of more clues was deeply frustrating. The prospect that the investigation would be locked in a stalemate—at least until another crime occurred—impelled Fujita to drive back up to the lakeshore one more time. They would arrive there at two-thirty. At least it would be a lot brighter and warmer at that hour.

He took a different deputy with him this time—a new set of eyes. Yet they found nothing, got in their car and took the road back down to Chitose.

A mile or so from the park, a Country Squire station wagon, at a safe distance away, pulled out in front of them from a side road. Fujita knew the road led to the fishing camp. Fujita told his deputy, who was driving, to accelerate and stop the Americans. There was nothing to lose by asking them if they'd seen anything while in the area.

The deputy switched the siren on. Once Private Travers heard it, he slowed and pulled over to the side of the road.

"Excuse me for bothering you," Sheriff Fujita said politely. "I assume you were at the fishing camp."

"Yes, we were, sir," responded Ricky politely.

"When did you arrive in the area?"

"About 7:30 this morning."

"Did you see anything usual at that time?"

"If you mean anything suspicious—uh, no," Ricky said. Ricky looked to the others in the station wagon, who nodded also that they hadn't seen anything out of the ordinary.

"Thank you." Fujita bowed his head slightly to the men. "How'd the fishing go?"

"Not bad," Ricky said. "Enough trout for an…." He wanted to say "army," but thought it would sound too odd. Instead he said, "Enough trout for an R.C", which was slang from where he came from, for "Roman Catholic."

"I see," Fujita smiled, not understanding. He went back to his car. Both cars got back on the road to Chitose, with the Sheriff's vehicle in the lead.

Once back at his office Fujita telephoned Sergeant Velchoffsky to inform him that he'd stopped some servicemen in their car as they were leaving the fishing camp near Lake Shikotsu. It was a routine stop. He was looking for information, and they had done nothing to cause him to pull them over.

Velchoffsky asked politely if it had anything to do with the investigation into Iwate's death. It did, Fujita replied. There was silence on the line before Fujita spoke again. He said he didn't know if Velchoffsky had heard the news yet, but that there'd been another murder: a young boy had been attacked in front of his house. It was on the other side of the road from Chitose I, just a block away from the post's main gate.

"Now, that's pretty close to home," Velchoffsky wanted to say out loud, but didn't. Instead he asked, "You're still looking for the Ainu man?"

"Yes," Fujita said just above a whisper. "But we found a fur coat and animal hide clothing at Lake Shikotsu and we think they belong to him."

"Congratulations on finding *something.*"

"Thank you. There have been so few clues."

"What do you think your find means?"

"It's easy to think he went there and killed himself. It's one of the things the lake is known for."

"What?"

"Suicide."

194

"Strange."

"Eastern cultures have a different attitude toward it than the West. Take kamikaze pilots for example."

"Hm," Velchoffsky assented into the phone, words failing him.

"Actually, we're going to release the news that the clothing was found and that we believe Akiyama is dead. He had to hike quickly to get up there after the murder, but a man can be fast when he knows the law is after him."

"What was wrong with the man? Do you know?

"We think it was mental illness."

"But you don't have anybody to prove he's dead."

"Correct, Sergeant Velchoffsky. But everybody in town is frightened out of their wits. As usual, they stayed home during Golden Week, and that's good. But now Golden Week is over. This constant being on edge can't go on. We're emphasizing that he committed one crime too many in Chitose and that he'll never come back."

"You know, sheriff, if there's anything we can do…" the master sergeant said, his voice trailing off.

"I don't think there's anything but thank you."

"We'll keep an eye out." Velchoffsky tried to sound helpful.

Immediately after speaking with Sheriff Fujita, Velchoffsky, following protocol, informed both Captain Forsberg and Lieutenant Nichols of their conversation. Forsberg was glad to hear that the Japanese were, for the time being, promoting the actions, and the conclusion, that his plan had suggested.

A dirt yard behind the military police station sheltered the guard dogs. New dogs were being brought to the kennel as operations expanded. An M38 truck had been sent down from Camp Crawford that afternoon at 4 p.m. with a new German shepherd and his handler, Corporal Jimmy Chen.

Forsberg was just leaving his office for the day. As he

walked out the front door of the police station to go to his jeep and his quarters, Corporal Chen bounded out of his covered four-by-four parked in the parking lot, and called the German shepherd, Troy, out from his place in the back of the truck.

Troy jumped down onto the gravel of the lot and the corporal gave him a friendly tap on the top of his head and fastened a leash on him.

Jimmy had been instructed to take the path on the left side of the police building and put the dog in a holding kennel in the yard out back, and report to Velchoffsky.

Forsberg had just stepped into the small parking lot when Troy whipped around after catching his scent.

The captain always did his best to keep his distance from such dogs. It was difficult and trying.

The German shepherd growled and then snarled when he caught sight of the captain's eyes. Forsberg was ten feet away and the dog, with its eyes knife-like, lunged at him, though the distance was too far for him to strike successfully. Troy's weight against the leash nearly threw Corporal Chen to the ground. The corporal was astonished at the dog's behavior. He and it had bonded; Troy never would do anything that his master hadn't commanded him to do.

He'd had never seen anything like this before from Troy. Before he knew it, the dog was crouching on its hind legs, ready to spring again at the distant captain. It made no sense to him. When a dog attacks, it's judged the space around it, and it knows the vulnerable spots on the animal it must bite. Furthermore, this was a uniformed captain in the U.S. Army. The dog would know that.

Troy barked, showed his teeth, and then growled deeply as Jimmy struggled to restrain him. The dog jumped. Jimmy yelled, "Heel!" The dog lurched toward Forsberg with a torrent of strength while Jimmy's feet dragged the ground, and he vigorously clutched the leash. The captain thought for an instant that the dog might reach him and bite him. He roared at the dog with a hideous snarl and he widened his eyes to threaten it. Jimmy fought to keep hanging on. He didn't see Forsberg's face but heard the growl and thought: what a strange sound to hear coming out of a man.

Troy's handler yelled at him, "Down!" But Troy was gaining ground and getting closer to Forsberg who stood in place and made no attempt to hurry away.

Just then a shot rang out. The driver of the truck who'd driven Jimmy and Troy down to Chitose from Camp Crawford fired it. The bullet hit the dog's spine, killing it instantly.

Forsberg said to Corporal Chen, to console him, "I'm sorry for you. Dogs sometimes go AWOL, too." Forsberg walked slowly away to go to his jeep.

The driver of the truck, a private by the name of Archie Rudd, apologized to Jimmy, plaintively repeating a couple of times that he'd had no other choice. Jimmy let the leash he was holding fall to the ground. Stunned, he didn't know what else to do but go into the police station and report to Velchoffsky.

CHAPTER 20

It went around town that after the young boy was murdered, Akiyama fled to Lake Shikotsu and killed himself—though his body hadn't been found yet. That he took his own life far away from town was looked upon as a blessing.

Most people in Chitose believed this, though there were some skeptics.

It was the last day of the holiday week. A few shops were open. "Naomi's Dressmaking and Alterations Shop" in Shimizu was one of them. There were young women whose livelihood depended on looking their best for the Americans, no matter what the day was on the Japanese calendar.

Naomi Takamura's shop was in Shimizu, between a tiny bar and a drugstore. It was contained all in one room. Three clothes racks, a screen behind where you could change clothes, a table with a sewing machine on it, and behind that, a chair for Naomi—somehow all these fit in the room.

A young Japanese woman who went by the Western name Sally was there picking up a dress the seamstress had sewn for her. The two women had exchanged only a few words when there was a knock at the door. Toshi pulled the door open, let himself in, dropped his chin down in a quick bow, and said good evening as he closed the door behind him. His nose was running. He wore a sheepskin coat. He ignored his shivering.

Naomi, a forty-year-old, medium-sized Japanese war widow was not pleased to see him; his abrupt entrance stopped the women from talking.

Toshi behaved as though Sally was not there. She was an affected girl, putting on haughtiness and daintiness which disgusted him. She didn't act like most Japanese girls: subservient, feigning a shortness of breath, eager to please, self-effacing. He regarded her as a traitor, selling her body to the Americans.

He'd come in to pick up his sports coat. He'd put a hole in one of the elbows when he'd slipped on some ice and Naomi had sewn matching oval patches on each sleeve.

He said to Naomi, "The Americans can't deny it's one of them now," the pitch of his voice rising with foolish excitement. So much for people in Chitose refraining from speaking of murder for the rest of the day.

It was clear to the two women that he was high.

They also thought it was strange that Toshi was bringing the Americans into a matter that was entirely Japanese.

Naomi would take care of business with him right away to get him out of the shop as quickly as possible.

But Sally said airily to Naomi, "I'll be late for work if I don't go now." She was one of Mommy Eri's new hires and an American G.I. would be waiting for her when she arrived at Mommy Eri's nearby. Sally opened a small pale blue suitcase she'd been carrying at her side. Naomi took Sally's new dress off the rack and carefully folded it and placed it, and a receipt, in the young woman's case. Closing it, Sally smiled curtly and bowed in thanks and in goodbye. She slipped out the shop's door, closing it delicately.

Then Toshi exclaimed, "You know what I'm talking about. Everybody should know what I'm talking about."

Naomi answered, "It'll be fifty yen, please," refusing to be engaged in conversation. She went over to the clothes rack and took his newly mended jacket from it. She gently swung the jacket side to either side to show off her handiwork on its elbows. Seeing the patches, Toshi's eyes lit up. He thought they were quite smart.

She held up the jacket for him to try on. This was

something she knew she had to do. He couldn't be just whisked away without ritual and ceremony. He quickly shucked off his sheepskin coat. Once the mended jacket was on him, he glanced at himself in the mirror that was on the back of the door to the shop. He broke into a grin. He looked like a student from a well-to-do family, not a thug. All at once, thoughts of Americans and the murder of the boy vanished from his mind. With Naomi's aid, he wriggled the sheepskin coat on, over the jacket. He drew a crisp fifty yen note out of his wallet and slapped it on the table next to Naomi's sewing machine. He was a happy man—at least for ten seconds. He thanked the seamstress briskly and bobbed his chin down once as a bow. Once out of the shop, he turned left, in the direction of Tsuru Lanes.

Cigarette smoke permeated the lobby and the noisy bar area of the bowling alley. The haze was thinner on the bowling concourse and petered out down the bowling lanes. Each lane had its two teams playing against each other. The men gathered around the scorekeeper's desk or sat on benches waiting their turns. Automatic pinsetter machinery swept away pins with a muffled garble of wood against wood.

Loud men laughed at inexperienced and drunk players when their balls spun into the gutters. The few guys who knew how to keep score sat like whiz kids at the little scoring tables, smoothly sliding out of their chairs when it was their turn to step onto the lane.

Training exercises were over, and the base was packed with soldiers. Bob Fernandez, Lloyd Kelso, Ricky Travers, and Brian Yoder were among them. They had a few beers in their barracks before they rode the liberty bus into town. They were drunk before they got to Tsuru.

Toshi had arrived an hour earlier and asked other G.I.s about Bob and Lloyd. He'd been told that they'd spent the day up at the Army's fishing camp.

For Toshi, the fact that Akiyama's clothes were found nowhere near Akiyama's house proved that Akiyama had nothing to do with Iwate's demise. Lloyd, on the other hand, was in the area where Akiyama's clothes turned up, linking him to the murder and making him Suspect Number One. He was probably the man who had attacked his brother, too. The image of Lloyd's blood seeping over his gums haunted Toshi.

Even dressed in his newly patched sport coat, Toshi's pallid face and jittery movements made anyone who gave him a good look think he was a ticking time bomb. The dapper young man hung around the concourse pretending to be interested in what was going on in the twelve lanes of bowling.

He directed his attention from time to time toward the bar. There! There they were. They'd come in, slipped in when he hadn't been looking in that direction. He tried to relax and put on a show of walking over to them nonchalantly as they waited in line for beer. Smiling at Bob and Lloyd, feigning conviviality, he addressed Kelso. But it wasn't that simple to conceal his hostility.

"The cops are looking for Akiyama," Toshi raised his voice to be heard over the noise. "They've got the wrong idea. He's dead. He didn't kill anybody. He's old and weak. You know my brother was attacked and they've tried to pin that on Akiyama, too. You think nobody's going to do anything?" Toshi continued, "that you're just going to be able to continue to kill when you feel like it? You're not going to get away with it."

It was so usual to hear Toshi saying outrageous things. Bob heard the words directed at Lloyd and looked at Toshi like a mosquito he was ready to swat.

Lloyd looked down at Toshi's loafers and thought: what an oddball.

Bob said, deadpan, "The *shabu's* got hold of your mind, man. You should lay off it."

Toshi boomed to the two of them, "Lloyd and you, Bob, are always around when somebody gets attacked or killed!

You've just proved it today by being at Lake Shikotsu when they found Akiyama's clothes after Lloyd killed him."

"I don't follow, Toshi," Bob said. "I've been with Lloyd the whole time you say he did whatever he was supposed to have done and we weren't exactly where you think we were."

"Lloyd has done these things and you're his… what's the word?... *accomplice.*"

"That's enough, Toshi. You're getting on my nerves." Fernandez struggled to restrain himself and found himself peering into the young Japanese's face. "If the police are looking for Akiyama, they've got their reasons. I don't think you should be talking to us. We're not interested in what you're saying. You're not a friend."

"You're right, I'm not your friend," Toshi said acidly, and finished with, "You're in this together, the both of you."

Then he turned on his heels and strolled back over to the concourse, continuing his pantomime of being interested in what was happening at the different lanes.

"What's the world going to do with Toshi?" Bob said to Lloyd, jesting

"Maybe he'll drop dead from a heart attack. All those pills!"

Bob snorted, "We're not interested,"

They ordered their beers and waited.

Toshi only stayed on the concourse a minute. He seemed to be weighing matters in his mind. He decided something. He slipped out the bowling alley's front door.

Once they got their beers, the boys went over to where Brian Yoder was bowling with a team. They watched the game and talked about what they'd heard about night life in Sapporo.

After the game ended, a player dropped out and Brian asked Bob and Lloyd if they wanted to join in. Lloyd jumped at the chance. He was trying to push the encounter with Toshi out of his mind.

Bob was alone at the bar when Toshi reappeared.

"You're back?" Bob sneered, his body tensing. "I ought to punch you out, you sniveling punk." One thing about Bob: he never felt danger could befall him in Chitose. When he was drunk, he and his kind acted as if they were gods, not humans, in Japan.

Toshi thought to himself, I'm glad he's going to get it. But then he said to Bob, "I only came back to say I'm sorry. I didn't mean to say that Lloyd's a killer."

"Well, what about me?" Bob frowned.

"I just didn't mean it, okay?"

"Well, no need to bother Lloyd to say you're sorry. We don't want to talk to you, got it?"

"Bob, you're an ambitious guy. Me, too. With lots of ambition, sometimes I get excited—too much. Like, look at this place. If I'm seeing right, I see a bowling alley. A sports place. People are supposed to *enjoy* sports."

If Bob had not been inebriated, he would've just walked away. Instead, he said back to Toshi, "You're not a good bowler."

"True. It's the enjoyment of the sport, though, that matters." Toshi smiled. He continued, unpredictably, "Your philosophy of experiencing new things—that's my philosophy, too—or at least what I want it to be. You see, I want to be rich." Toshi waited for Fernandez to respond.

Fernandez almost didn't. But then he retorted: "It's hard work getting rich unless you're born that way."

The conversation lulled. Metal frames swept bowling pins to the floor clattering. After a while Toshi started in again, "It's funny that you say, 'born that way'. You know, I said Akiyama's weak. He's old. He can't carry out violent acts. But you should also know, he's the father of the Ainu girl, Kiriko."

Toshi made his remarks with a sly smile. He'd heard Bob going on about Kiriko a couple of times in the past.

Bob's ears pricked up. Toshi next said. "Yep, she's born of his blood. She's a good kid. So I'm saying her father can't be bad if the daughter is so good."

Toshi then pretended to pull away, saying "Yep, Akiyama... He's an Ainu and he's being blamed wrongly—by who, I don't know." Then he pounced. "Bob, I have something else to tell you about Kiriko."

"What?" Bob drawled, pretending that this new turn in the conversation had no effect on him.

"She was adopted by a Japanese family when she was seven years old. I grew up in the house next to her. She was a playmate of my younger brother, the boy who was assaulted in the train."

"You're lying." Bob was interested but tried not to let on he was. He was doing his best to stand up straight. It had been a day of many beers.

"Ask her if I'm lying."

"How am I supposed to do that?"

"She's out back, by the river."

"No, really?" Bob was genuinely surprised. "Why would she be there?"

"There's a wharf out there. People walk out on it to watch the river flow and look up at the stars."

"She wouldn't be out there alone!" His mind rushed to make sense of the new information. He hadn't heard there was a wharf out there before. He wouldn't have believed it if he'd been sober.

"She's sad about what's going on in Chitose. She's ashamed of who she is. Everybody says the killer's her father. She had a new hostess job, but she lost it. She's so beside herself she might take her own life. She's wandering around in the cold tonight. I was just out back by the river, looking at the stars, and I found her sitting there, on the dock. I talked to her. I'm sort of like her older brother, you know. I told her not to worry—that people don't think badly about her, that some people really like her. I know you like her. I think you should go out there and tell her that you like her. Tell her everything will be all right."

Such extensive news of Kiriko and the news of her being nearby was music to Bob's ears.

"You could take her dancing. That would cheer her up."

Bob had taught himself a phrase in Japanese from a book sold to thousands of G.I.s in Japan every year: "What we have is real and special." He hoped to use it one day with Kiriko.

Bob Fernandez left, weaving heavily, and headed out back.

Getting Bob to go out back, in Toshi's mind, partially restored his honor. He wanted respect, and now he would get it. No more would there be any rowdy, brotherly voices sticking up for Bob; there would be no games, no drinking or music.

CHAPTER 21

He thought of The Rule—he didn't want to, but he couldn't get it out his mind.

The Rule is hunger. It's also aggression, with no explanations, no apologies.

The Rule is Nature's presence and pain.

Nature eats to breathe—and breathes to eat again.

Another will eat you to breathe and survive. Don't get distracted. Don't let any sense be disengaged. You need all of them. The Rule means balance, balance to survive.

Forsberg then thought: I'm driving myself crazy now.

There are dogs, he thought more. *Panting* dogs. They're dependent on a master. From their master they get food to survive. Dogs are separated from Nature, attached to Man. They've lost their integrity.

Then he thought, why am I thinking "lost their integrity?" There are healthy dependencies in nature. Not all parasites kill their hosts. Dogs give companionship and affection.

After arriving back at his quarters he'd showered to wash off the smell of an animal—this time, Troy, the army German shepherd. He then put on a fresh new set of clean clothes.

He lay down on his bed now, not taking them off. He would try to nap.

He kept his shoes on. It was a wise precaution to avoid being barefoot. You don't want to be barefoot—it places you in a physical state closer to that which an animal lives in.

As he lay there to try to sleep, he thought: I don't *live* his body, I'm *caught in* it. But the Rule is that you *are* your body.

Thus, I fail The Rule.

He drifted off to sleep—or rather a nightmare.

Market Square Nightmare

While assigned in 1945 to his microfilming unit that moved around Germany, Forsberg was temporarily loaned out for two weeks to a displaced persons (DP) camp. Instead of microfilming, his brief job there was photographing new arrivals.

The medieval German marketplace: stone pavement, stone walls. The din of the crowd; they're assembled to witness my execution; they wear piles of clothes, some of which turn into medieval-style clothing.

The morning sun has risen from being a low glow near the horizon. The air is cold and brittle.

"You're no Kidler!" People spit and jeer at me. I have no idea what they mean.

Everything around me is gritty and grubby. I'm grimy and bloody. The crowd's dirty. The animals are encrusted.

Pavlenko's organized this. He knows livestock. He knows meat. He's got the horses.

I could have turned him in, but since he'd been their slave, I thought it was okay for him to get something out of the Germans. (Pavlenko was kidnapped, in Ukraine, by the Nazis when he was a teenager; he was brought to work as an apprentice in a butcher shop in Germany for the entirety of the war.)

The smells of the new DPs nauseate me. My job's easy (just take simple identification photos) but hard to do because the constant arrivals stink of excrement. They're sick with dysentery. Blood flows out of their bowels. They have lice. I can see their festering wounds. All sorts of diseases have broken out on their skin.

We don't treat them as prisoners. We treat them as unfortunates.

Pavlenko's healthy. He's a swimmer. He lives in town. He comes to the camp to help translate. He helps sniff out Nazis who are posing as DPs. I happened to mention the smells to him, and he gave me nose plugs—he uses them when swimming. It saved me from turning into a raging animal.

He was nice to me before I found out he slaughters cattle illegally, butchers them, ships them, gets high prices for them in bigger German cities. They have a whole network. I let him be.

He doesn't like me. It's because he knows I know.

Ropes are tied to my arms and legs. He's attached the ropes to horses. The horses will try to pull me apart. If they don't succeed, Pavlenko will butcher me while I'm spread out.

How can he know what I am? There's nobody to tell him. Maybe he doesn't know—he only hates me because I'm onto his black market business.

He sees my taut body glistening with sweat. He crows to the crowd, "Hallo, let me get to work, I'll be cutting his balls off now!" He laughs that my body's stretched so much but is not being torn apart. It doesn't surprise him—he knows anatomy well.

He has his thugs clear the salivating, snarling dogs away from me. The thugs say to them, "Not yet, not yet, wait and you'll all get a piece!" Then they thrash the dogs to within an inch of their lives.

The crowd roars. It applauds him. It's made up of German provincials. They think he's scum but that's beside the point.

I am naked now. He cuts off my sac and detaches my penis. He makes deep cuts at my joints. He slices me down the front of my chest. He shouts at the horses to tug again. He yells to the crowd, "His head, his head will be the very last. But we've got a way to go before that. We have his entrails and organs to deal with!"

It wasn't the first time he'd had this nightmare.

He shook himself from it. He was still horribly frightened.

He rose from the bed, took off his clothes, showered again (somehow, Troy's scent was still there). He put on yet another fresh shirt and pants.

"Ansbach" was the name of the town where the DP camp was.

Ansbach. How could it not remind him of the American sergeant, Harold Anspach, who he'd shot in the mountains of Italy?

He pushed the window in his quarters open. A cool breeze came in. He spread his nostrils, drawing the air in and down to his teeth. The muscles in his stomach pinched. Veins in his neck and chest pushed against his skin. When he swallowed, there was a harsh feeling from the roof of his mouth to the bottom of his lungs. His throat was dry.

Was he still smelling Troy's smell? He doused himself with cologne. Now he stank of cologne.

He sat down in a chair, lowered his chin and let his head roll to one side, thinking he might drift off to sleep in that position.

His body twitched. It didn't work.

Moment by moment he felt energy inside himself increase. It tore at his insides.

He had a sense of foreboding like that experienced by those with epilepsy before a grand mal seizure. He'd stumbled on that subject once when reading in the library. He felt he knew this kind of anxiety. It gnawed at him now, churned within him. The scene of Troy lunging at him played in his mind, over and over again, in slow motion. Troy, such a powerful dog with such piercing eyes—slowed down, he was even scarier.

Sitting in his chair, he endured wave after wave of the German shepherd lunging at him; the visualizations smelled: a heavy, reeking dog smell.

A voice in his head seemed to come from far away,

though from deep inside him. It told him he must get miles away from this Troy; he could get away from the dog by leaving his room and getting in his jeep. The voice said, "Flee from your quarters, leave the army base, *at once.*"

He understood if he was going to leave in the mental condition he was in right now, others must not see him.

He got out of his chair and began to gather things. It was dusk now. He put a flashlight, a towel, another set of clothes and a knit cap into a duffel bag. He had little time. He needed to hold onto his human form for as long as he could.

Suddenly he was hit by a massive throe of fatigue. It made him sit down. He caught his breath.

It was going to be tough, he thought.

A numbness enveloped him. It seemed as if it was descending from the ceiling, but the ceiling itself appeared to be dissolving.

It was terrible and weird. His mind, or his brain, or what was in his head, rose from the top of his neck and ascended through the numb shroud to take its place where the ceiling had been.

This contrary motion upward, through the numbness, was confusing and couldn't be stopped.

Now his mind was looking down on him. His mind could see that his forehead was raised and gazing in the direction of where the ceiling had been. The eyes in his head were staring up at his mind.

At the same time, items in his room were releasing their individual smells. These smells thickened to become strong, flowing odors—smells of hair, clothing, fresh leaves, dog-smell, canvas bag-smell and mud. The smells were irritating.

He felt as if he was under a hellish spell. He wanted it broken.

It could not be broken. It got worse. Time became an element of it. A feeling of nostalgia came over him. He started to reminisce—yes, *reminisce*—about what had only taken place a minute ago. He saw himself throwing the flashlight, the towel, the set of clothes and the knit cap into the duffel bag.

This was the lead-up to a metamorphosis that would bring violence to whatever crossed his path. He knew he had to fight, with all the power he could muster, *right now,* to beat back the condition threatening to overtake him.

His mind watched from above with a sickened feeling.

His mind saw his body get up from his chair. It saw him go to the closet and take out the package of aconite root he'd gathered from the soil near Lake Shikotsu. His mind watched as his body got a pair of gloves out of a drawer, went to the sink, put on the gloves, unwrapped the package and rapidly cut the aconite root into small pieces with a jackknife. He saw he hadn't let any of the root touch his skin. The aconite had a powerful psychological effect on him. Just his proximity to it was enough to send a jolt through his system and give him hope that he had time to fend off the unwanted transformations.

With the gloves on, he grabbed an empty coffee mug and his shaving brush—this would be a homemade mortar and pestle. The opposite end of the shaving brush served as a pestle; he crushed the aconite pieces against the side of the mug to make a paste. The paste could kill him. But it was the only thing that could possibly shock him out of changing into a werewolf.

His mind watched his gloved hands fit a small plastic bag (a used empty bag that had had a loaf of sliced bread in it—these bags were used and reused everywhere on base) over the mug of aconite paste.

It was now time to find cold water—not a glass of cold water, or a bucket of it. He needed to find a large body of moving water—a pond, a river, a lake, the sea.

An image of Chitose River came to him. Could he get there in time? It was at least fifteen minutes away. He remembered he'd seen a few docks there, jutting out from the shore. If he could get to one of them, tether himself there, let the flowing waters wash the poisonous aconite paste off him… maybe he had a chance.

Somehow he escaped his room unseen. He got in his jeep, and it took him past the front gate where he felt the hair on his back growing and his face wanting to contort.

It was the only place to park without being seen. But he was on the other side of the river from the docks—there was a bridge he needed to walk across. There was no one on it. He hurried over it.

At this side of the river, sure, there were docks. But the river's edge was clotted with mud and vegetation—and old pieces of timber from buildings knocked down by the army, which were too close to the river's shore and unhygienic threats to the construction of the bar district.

He made his way stealthily down the shoreline, over the debris, in the murky air, carrying the cup of aconite paste enclosed by its plastic bag. The place was deserted. No one had any reason to be there.

In the gelatinous dimness, small lights glowed, emanating from the other side of the buildings. (The rears of the buildings backed toward the river and its muddy shores.) The lights were from Shimizu's tiny bars. In the near distance, blurry light from the bowling alley illuminated the shore.

A dock was ahead. It protruded from ground that gently descended into the water. This small pier stretched almost ten yards out into the river; a timber frame supported the rough boards that fitted together to make its surface.

Muffled noise came from the bowling alley. It came from the crashing of bowling pins when they were ploughed to the floor to allow for a new set of ten pins to be set for the next bowler.

He got to the dock and rested against it. His hands shook as they took the cup of deadly aconite paste from the plastic bag he was carrying.

He stuffed the duffel in a crevice formed by crossed timbers on the underside of the dock.

Before entering the cold water, he removed his clothes, threw them in and let them drift away downstream. He smeared the aconite paste all over his body, quickly got into the water and clung to one of the wooden piles of the pier. The swirling water would rinse the fast-acting poison off him but not before it sent shock waves through his body. This would prevent his body from becoming so wracked that his organs would fail.

Drastic measures, but they would stop the transformation. He gripped the timber of the dock harder to steady himself.

All the toxin was washed off him in less than five minutes. The only thing he could feel was the pounding of his heartbeat.

Bob Fernandez, teetering, walked into the space between Tsuru Lanes and the building next to it. The alcohol in his blood warmed him, protecting him from the frigid air. He stopped and urinated. After finishing, he tucked himself up and stumbled farther along behind the buildings, where he made out what looked to be a fishing dock up ahead. But there was no sign of Kiriko.

He stood at the edge of a large space, of weeds, stone, and rubbish. A husky Japanese guy he didn't know materialized out of the shadows and stopped him, asking if he wanted to buy *shabu*. He was so drunk he wasn't surprised, and told the guy no. Seiichi Suzuki, the man who was accosting him, stood with his back to the river. Things happened quickly. Seiichi slugged Bob in the gut. He doubled up, falling to the ground. Seiichi slammed his foot on his ribs to uncurl him, then he lowered himself forcefully on the American, placing his knee on Bob's chest to crush it. He gripped Bob's head with his right hand while his left bashed his jaw on the ground.

This ambush was making good the promise Toshi made to himself to payback Fernandez for humiliating him, by getting him so drunk three nights before, and insulting him while doing it.

But Seiichi and Bob were not alone.

In the chilly flow of the river, Forsberg jerked his head this way and that to determine what kind of motor control he had in his upper body. But the torso didn't belong to Gideon Forsberg anymore—his muscles had reshaped, there were re-growths of cartilage. His body had been forced into the dreaded form he'd struggled against. Now *he* was no longer; he was an *it*. The aconite remedy had failed. Awful changes had claimed a body that once had been human.

Enough light seeped in from the space between the buildings for the creature to see Seiichi crouching in wait. This human presence drew the creature out of its aquatic hiding spot. The creature dragged itself onto land, reptile-like.

With its heightened sense of smell it could smell Seiichi, though he wasn't close by. The Japanese man, alone, was apparently waiting anxiously for somebody else to appear. It seemed he might want to attack an enemy.

Wild, intense energy surged through the creature's body. Its eyes locked onto Seiichi's dark shape. The creature's intent was to strike. And it would strike—it must—at the man's uppermost part.

But then Bob Fernandez appeared. The creature saw clearly: the G.I. entered the gap between the buildings. Seiichi saw Bob and lurched forward. He swung into Bob with his right arm. He sent the American sideways, slamming him into a wall.

Bob slid down from the wall and onto the ground. Seiichi bent over and grabbed him violently. Bob was conscious and tried to swing back at Seiichi, but he had no room to first pull his arm back to make an effective thrust. Seiichi smashed his right fist into Bob's left eye.

Then the two men's figures merged into one shadow. The creature, while flooded with adrenaline, stopped in its tracks and watched. One struggling side of the clumpy shadow combined with the other. The resulting Goyaesque mass then rapidly changed shapes—or rather its outline did—with the punches, the twistings, the bucklings.

The creature could look on no longer. It launched itself in their direction. The creature landed on the blob of two men in the cold narrow space.

The creature distinguished between the two men by smell. The drunk American was weaker, an easy target. Vomit smelling of beer spilled from his throat. The werewolf bit into him first, biting him adroitly in the jugular vein. Blood spurted out in a burst. Bob's body had no time to react, his hand did not raise to cover the area of his wound.

The creature then rammed its hulking body against Seiichi. Its jaws tore into the Japanese man's face. Ruddy yellow vomit came up from the man's innards and out from his throat, too. The creature slid its teeth down and mutilated Seiichi's dripping chin, then gnawed at his neck until Seiichi's body joined Bob's on the ground.

Though Bob was dead, the werewolf pivoted and jammed its left front paw into Bob's body with the force of the butt end of an ax. It cracked the boy's ribs.

The mutilations were not over. The monster turned to Seiichi and slammed its wolfen foot on his face, crushing this eyes and nose into his head.

But this wasn't enough. The creature's jaws tore again and again into both men's faces, rendering them unrecognizable as human beings; it spit out bits of flesh and muscle. It tore into the men's clothing, making them blood-washed rags. In a frenzy, the creature bit off Bob's right hand.

Panting, the creature turned away. It caught the smell of the river and jerked itself away from the bodies.

It spied the dock.

It scurried to it in an uneven lope. It reached the water, waded into it. It sprang into the deepening part. It swam, heaved forward. It would cross the river, for it knew it was on the other side of the river where Forsberg had parked his jeep.

Once on the other side of the river, it set its legs under its body. Currents of harsh electricity still flowed within it; however, the farther the creature got from the destruction, the less strong they were.

It reached the opposite shore. In the stiff cold air, it advanced with heaviness on the slope from the water, struggling to bring itself into a fully upright position.

The slope met ground of dirt that had been leveled. Moving upon the new ground, further distancing itself from the river, it reached the small patchwork of streets.

At first it saw no one. It was a residential area; few would be expected to be out at that time.

However, not after more than a dozen steps on the unpaved street, it saw a young woman approaching. She was still a block away and oblivious to any other living presence than her own.

The creature knew it must take cover right away.

It saw an empty shadow at the side of a nearby house. It glued one eye on the young woman's movements to be aware if she changed direction, possibly signaling that she knew it was present.

She kept on coming. The creature lurched over to its chosen shadow by the house. Still, she apparently saw nothing. It hid noiselessly.

When she crossed into the creature's direct line of vision, the creature instinctively propelled itself toward her. It toppled her violently, like a breathing lump of clay. Like Noboru Nakano, she never knew the moment of attack or what struck her. No sound came from her; the impact could have killed the petite girl. Once down on the ground, the creature raised a hand—not a paw—to maul her.

The changes had partially reversed.

It had flung against her, had knocked her down, but the young woman's cheap perfume was so irritating to smell that it slowed the creature's movements. The creature recoiled from the woman's body, the fragrance on it hurt almost like the sting of a hornet.

It did not maul her. The creature needed to get away from the unbearable smell.

There were no streetlights in this section of town. There was no light from Shimizu here—pools of darkness everywhere, though.

The creature smelled a clump of evergreen bushes in space in a tiny empty lot.

It would flee to that dark spot and get its bearings there.

It lay in the bushes, quivering, feeling the earth's magnetic field with its animal senses. Then it almost inexplicably became mostly human again.

A quarter of an hour had passed. Forsberg's left field of vision was damaged, at least at that moment. But he knew what to do. He'd experienced it before.

He got on his feet and knew where his jeep was parked. To walk normally, to lift his feet that way, felt strange. At first it was difficult but then it came back to him naturally.

His left field of vision was still not functioning but in other ways he was gaining equilibrium—for one, he was thinking like a human. He found his jeep, opened its door and extended his best functioning hand to grab a clean set of clothes that lay on the passenger seat. Once in the clean clothes he slid onto the driver's seat. It was only a short distance to the post, an easy drive—but it would require carefulness because of his impaired vision.

He started the engine. Exhaustion bored down on him.

Upon arriving at Camp Chitose's front gate he had the feeling that the sentry was an imposter—it was just some guy picked off the street, put into an army uniform—or it was an American actor faking his way through an important role in a foreign country with strident dishonesty while the film was rolling. Forsberg knew strange thoughts like these would ramble through his mind for another couple of hours. This was common after a transformation.

The sentry acted as if he recognized him, waved him on, and Forsberg listlessly sped the vehicle up and entered the base. He felt no emotion. There was no guilt. There was no sadness. There was nothing except what he saw in front of him.

He got to his Quonset and parked his jeep. Once through the front door, the only door, to the officers' compound—a rather grand term for a modified Quonset for captains and second lieutenants—Forsberg, cap on his head and clutching a duffel bag in his hand, started down the hall to his quarters. He noticed his sight was no longer impaired.

To get to his room he needed to pass two other officers' rooms on his left and right. Tonight, the door on the left— the door to Second Lieutenant Terry Leventis's room—was open, the light was on, and it was easy to see inside. Leventis wore steel rimmed glasses, his hair was thinning and receding even though he was the same age as Forsberg. He was soft-spoken man with a triangular face, an open man, the opposite of conspiratorial. Forsberg desperately wanted to avoid contact with anyone. He kept his head down and grasped his duffel tightly.

As he tried to walk naturally, he glimpsed a few *Field and Stream* monthlies lying on the coffee table that Leventis had put near his door. It reminded him of the way magazines are spread on a table in a waiting room at a doctor's office. He noticed a magazine on top of a small pile. It had a colorful image of an African lion soaring through space, about to swoop down on a zebra and tear it to pieces. The caption read, "The Truth About Safari."

Out of a florescent-lighted tunnel to and from nowhere the smooth sound of Lieutenant Leventis' voice resonated, "Good evening, sir."

Damn! Leventis was home—oh, no!

"Good evening, sir," Forsberg responded mechanically, not raising his head to look at the lieutenant.

"So, we finally have the pleasure to meet. I'm Second

Lieutenant Terry Leventis."

Forsberg knew this would turn into a sort of friendly interrogation if he didn't nip it in the bud right away. He tilted his head upward, but not far enough to look Leventis in the eye. "I'm sorry but I'm tired."

"I understand. Just happy to say hello, sir."

The lieutenant had twelve men in his platoon. They were loaned out to majors for office work, but technically they were still under his command. Some of them—Bob Fernandez, Lloyd Kelso, Ricky Travers, Brian Yoder—had volunteered for military police duty.

Leventis clearly wasn't sleepy enough to go to bed. Maybe he was an insomniac. That wouldn't be good. Leventis let it slip almost cheerfully, "Four of my men are joining your unit part-time. They go to Camp Crawford tomorrow. I told Velchoffsky to let me know if they make any trouble."

"Okay," Forsberg muttered.

He realized Forsberg was in no mood to chat. Furthermore, the captain was two ranks above him. The second lieutenant settled on just three words to get off the hook with Forsberg, "Good night, Captain, sir."

Once back in his room Forsberg let his duffel bag drop to the floor. He'd had his wilding and was spent. Take some codeine, he told himself.

He did. He slowly drank a fifth of vodka to stop his mind from racing and deaden his nerves. Though he had little energy, he still needed to wind down. He got out a deck of cards. He played solitaire. It was hard shuffling the cards; it was hard positioning them on the table.

Inside the bowling alley, Lloyd had been wondering what happened to Bob. He was absorbed with his bowling team, though.

Toshi had joined one of the teams. When neither man returned to the lanes, he assumed Seiichi had successfully made the attack and had run off to establish an alibi somewhere. He drank a couple of whiskies to celebrate; he was high enough and drunk enough to overlook the idea that Seiichi could've come back once the deed was done and claim he'd never left the building.

They'd never discussed what Seiichi was supposed to do after he beat up Bob, or if they had, Toshi didn't remember.

The lights dimmed in the bowling alley for five seconds, a warning that it was 10:30 p.m. and curfew was approaching.

Lloyd caught the bus back to the barracks and looked for his friend. Did Bob stay out past curfew? Maybe he got involved with a girl.

To Toshi, curfew time meant his business was over for the night. He could go home, listen to the radio, while away time until the drug that was keeping him awake lost its effectiveness.

The next morning, after Velchoffsky had seen to it that the men had boarded the bus that would transit them to Camp Crawford for training, the sergeant told the men he had an announcement to make. He informed them that Bob had been in an accident. Velchoffsky hesitated when a couple of soldiers asked him if he could provide more details. So Velchoffsky corrected himself and said that Bob had died, that more details would be forthcoming.

CHAPTER 22

It was like being back in high school, sitting in a classroom with the teacher at the front.

The instructor, a second lieutenant, lectured them on the mission and duties of the military police.

This was the first day at Camp Crawford MP training.

Lloyd found it nearly impossible to pay attention. The spring day out the window was luminous. If he hadn't been shaken up by Bob's death, he would've reveled in the familiarity of the *type* of day it was. From what he could see from glimpses through the classroom window, the weather reminded him of this time of year in New York State where he grew up.

Camp Crawford had been carved out of sparsely inhabited Ainu land, developed by the Japanese—with the help of American agriculturists—in the late 1890s. Even though some of the buildings looked like they were part of an American college campus—this was institutional architecture of the period, clearly—the handsome sturdy brick buildings were built to house business operations for a large Japanese state-run dairy. (The initial cattle stock even came from the U.S.)

The manicured great lawns of Crawford had been cow pastures.

During the war, the property was taken over by the Japanese Imperial Army. It had escaped being bombed during the war. There was no strategic advantage to attacking Hokkaido. The focus was on points south where most

Japanese lived.

As the spring weather dazzled outside, Lloyd could only think about Bob. Sure, Fernandez came on strong. What a character he was. Bob's words rang out in his mind: "We're twenty, twenty-one, twenty-two years old... We race like horses—and fight like dogs when we need to—but only when we need to—otherwise if we fight when it isn't right, we're stupid and we're missing out on amazing opportunities that The New has for us!"

One thing you learned in the infantry, in battle: there's never time in the army to mourn.

All day long he couldn't eat. All day long all he wanted to do was get loaded and forget about Bob and death.

The notes he took in class were a mess. His instructors' words mostly sailed over his head. After the day of classes ended, he went out with Ricky Travers, Yoder and his other classmates.

The process of getting drunk started with two shots of straight vodka. No, he didn't care where it would lead him. He didn't care if it made him sick as hell in a few hours. His friend was dead, that was all. And he wasn't even killed on a battlefield. Combat infantry badge, bronze service stars, United Nations service medal—big deal—he was dead and gone. When Lloyd arrived in peaceful Hokkaido, he thought the days of losing friends was over.

Being around the other G.I.s didn't help. Many in the group knew Bob, and with varying degrees either liked him or didn't care that much for him.

But everybody wondered exactly what had happened.

For some odd reason he recalled that Bob grew up in a family that followed Christian Science; he wondered how that church handled funerals... he didn't know a thing about that religion. Bob always dodged conversations about it and you didn't know what he actually believed.

Lloyd played back some of the previous night in his mind. Bob was in the bowling alley being his usual self. He got drunk. He probably said something provocative, like he often did, except when he was moody and it was constitutionally hard for him to talk. Yes, Fernandez liked to be center stage. Lloyd always figured it was because deep down inside his buddy couldn't bear boredom.

The walls of the bar they went to near Camp Crawford that night were covered with wallpaper. *That* was different from Chitose; it seemed so American. Indeed, the owner of the bar knew that papering the walls would help lend the place a homey feel to the Americans.

In Lloyd's present condition it only made him homesick.

It's not that he felt the United States was perfect and that being back there would solve everything. Like many of his generation, he thought there was too much bullshit involved in getting a job and paying the bills. He thought the rich called the shots. He thought females were hard nuts to crack.

Lloyd felt his vision wavering—though he didn't wear glasses, nor did he need them.

After a few beers in the bar, the guys there were distorted-looking. Some were too short to be in the army and he wondered how they got in. Well, the army needed men—it needed cannon fodder. Some of the soldiers in the bar had stubby arms—how they could pull themselves up from the ground mystified him. Others had arms that were too long—like frogs' legs. It didn't make sense to him—they were laughable, and they should be in a cartoon, dying in pursuit of the roadrunner, like Wiley E. Coyote, and then springing back to life in the next scene.

There were two rooms in the bar full of wisecracking, noisy, drinking G.I.s Their voices hurt his ears. He caught scraps of what they were saying to one another. They seemed to be saying anything that came into their heads.

If he truly wanted to be honest with himself, he felt it was all bullshit. It had no meaning. They were a bunch of fools. Misshaped fools who were sleepwalking or dead.

Lloyd lit a cigarette, realizing that there was something

wrong with *him,* not them. He hoped the smoke would settle his mind. Though some men were only an arm's length from him, he refused to let his eyes meet theirs.

He should've stayed back in the barracks at Camp Crawford but there was no way he could. He had to get out.

The bar was interesting in that there were captains and lieutenants in it—not just lower ranking enlisted men. It meant you had to be better behaved than you normally might have to be in other places.

Ricky Travers and the other two guys he went fishing with yesterday were mingling, drinks in their hands, but he didn't say much to them. Their arms and faces suffered from distortions. Bob's death didn't stun them as much as it did him. They thought he might've gotten very drunk and fallen from a bridge and drowned in the river.

There was a wooden set of stairs against one wall of one of the rooms in the bar. Lloyd couldn't figure out what it was there for. A minute later, the paper-paneled door slid open at the top of the stairs and a Japanese girl emerged with an empty tray in her hand. She came down the stairs and began picking up empty beer glasses to bus them out into the backroom to be washed.

My God, the Japanese girl is Kiriko, Lloyd inwardly exclaimed.

Her hair was neatly folded at the back and held by a lacquered hairpin and clip. She wore a royal blue rayon dress that fit her body unassumingly. The skirt length of the dress—many inches below the knee—indicated it was old and not up with the current fashion. Modesty was the norm in Japan; to wear a dress like that signaled the girl's modesty, as well as her meager income. The dress wasn't displeasing to Lloyd—on the contrary, it looked fine. Its cute, rounded, but spread collar at the front was buttoned neatly. She even had on a dainty silk-flower (white rose, green stem, and leaves) corsage over her left breast.

The girl's head happened to turn in his direction and her

eyes met Lloyd's. Lloyd was dumbstruck. He thought how sweet and poignant she looked in her past-fashion blue dress. She looked at him with frankness. Her eyebrows signaled sorrow. Then she swiftly averted her gaze and glancing to her side, found a path through the men standing in the bar with glasses in their hands and she was gone.

He was astonished she was working in this bar. What an incredible coincidence. He wanted to follow her into the other room to look at her again, to see if she would recognize him, but the crowd of soldiers was thick, and he didn't have the energy to break through it.

He overheard Brian Yoder chatting with a soldier that he, Lloyd, didn't know. The soldier was eyeing another G.I., telling Brian he was surprised they gave him a liberty pass and was being allowed in the bar.

The soldier telling the story was named Andy. He was a Camp Crawford soldier. Andy continued with his story as he held a half-filled beer mug in his hand. "One night three weeks ago I was here. Me and the Crawford guys and some new recruits. That guy was one of the new recruits, his first time here. Apparently, he'd been stationed near Tokyo. He said Sapporo was "way better than Tokyo.""

Andy gave Brian a weird smile. He asked, "Do you know what happened?"

Yoder said, "No. You tell me."

"He was drunk off his ass." You know what he did? He whipped out his cock and jerked off in front of everybody."

"Jesus!" Yoder exclaimed.

"Yeah, it was something. He's probably seeing a shrink on base and they're giving him a second chance to behave himself. Look, there's people talking to him."

"You see such shit in the army," Yoder said acidly.

Lloyd was sorry he'd heard the conversation. It made him think again about all the bullshit involved in living.

The noise level of the bar was hard to bear. Lloyd started to sweat. He thought to himself, what a bad bunch of humans we are. Sad and bad and I just want to get the hell out.

In a small group of soldiers, he heard Ricky Travers shout aggressively, "Don't argue with me! Cool off. We all know what you're going through." He couldn't make out who it was that Ricky was yelling at. It could have been someone who wouldn't shut up about how sad it was that Bob wasn't around.

The next thing he knew, he himself was baring his teeth and snarling, "Leave me alone. I'm not the problem."

People in the bar ignored Lloyd's outburst. They let his friends try to quiet him down. However, one of the class instructors from that day's military police training had kept his eye on Lloyd. He was Second Lieutenant Eddie Kobayashi. Kobayashi walked up to Lloyd calmly. He was a taut, fit Japanese American, five-feet-seven tall, with penetrating eyes. He was a black belt; he taught self-defense and karate at Crawford. With his strength and swiftness, he could've downed Lloyd in a flash. When he was within a foot from him, he asked, "Do you need a cigarette?"

Both the intrusion and the question surprised Lloyd. He didn't recognize Kobayashi from class today. He didn't know what to say. He paused vacantly then blurted out, "What is your cigarette going to do? Bullshit me?"

Eddie ignored the question and said, "If you'd like one, it's yours." He paused amiably, and almost by magic there was a pack of Lucky Strikes in his hand with one cigarette sticking out of it for him to grab. "Take it."

Lloyd swatted Eddie's hand away and the pack of cigarettes landed on the ground. "Where's Kiriko?" he muttered.

Eddie said, "I don't know what you're talking about, private."

"Don't be stupid," Lloyd snarled.

Kobayashi was a junior officer with a calm disposition. Being called stupid by a drunk buck private was something he could handle.

Brian Yoder squirmed. He was standing less than a yard away. He was embarrassed for Lloyd.

Eddie bent and picked up the pack of smokes. Then he measured his words carefully, "Listen, Lloyd, I know it's been a tough day for you. I know about your buddy. You've had a lot to drink. You should think of going back to your barracks."

"Don't defy me," Lloyd shouted at Eddie.

Yoder cringed watching their exchange continue.

The lieutenant did what would seem to most to be the most counter-intuitive thing to do. He walked away from Lloyd—instead of issuing him an order or laying a hand on him. A small group of soldiers were five yards away. He went and mingled with them; he got the group talking again; the men had heard Lloyd and they'd stopped conversing among themselves.

All the same, Kobayashi kept Lloyd in his field of vision.

A minute passed, during which Ricky, with Brian by his side, approached Lloyd and calmly suggested they all go back to their rooms together.

Any of those paying attention to the three of them could hear Lloyd shout, "No, I won't!" Anger rose in him, and he reddened. He added, "You've got a lot of nerve, moron!"

Then Lloyd did something nobody expected because he wasn't the type. He threw his hands at Ricky's chest and shoved him hard. Ricky fell back but stayed on his feet. Ricky shouted back at him, "Do that again and I'll smack you, Lloyd!"

Now it was Brian Yoder's turn to quiet Ricky down. Yoder said, "Don't hit him. Never hit a fellow soldier when you've all been drinking. There's no point in it. It'll only get both of you arrested."

In a move that made him look like a caricature of a martial arts fighter, Lloyd widened his stance by snapping his feet far apart. He clenched both hands into fists. He dropped his hips and shoulders, lowered his chin, and stared ahead with his eyes.

Brian turned to Lloyd and shouted, "That's exactly what you shouldn't be doing. What's gotten into you?"

Lloyd shouted back, "Don't tell me anything. I'll kill you!"

When people heard, "I'll kill you" they stopped purposefully ignoring him and the two G.I.s beside him. Their conversations trailed off. Eyeing a young man drunk out of his mind, they knew he wouldn't be able to kill anybody. They felt sorry for him. He'd snapped. It was quite sad.

No one was armed except Sergeant Dave Markewicz who had a blunt-nosed automatic in his MP's holster that hung under the jacket of his plainclothes (this was always the case when he patrolled bars in Sapporo at night). His eyes had been following Lloyd since he'd heard the troubled young man's voice ring out, and weighted, from afar, the exchange with Lieutenant Kobayashi some few moments ago.

Now that the men's voices had trailed off, was possible to hear "Blue Tango" playing on the bar's little radio.

Sergeant Markewicz adroitly left the group of soldiers he'd been talking with. Unnoticed by Lloyd, he started his approach from behind.

As "Blue Tango" was serenading the air, the Japanese girl of nineteen in a royal blue dress came through a doorway that connected the two rooms of the establishment. There was an aura of nostalgia about her.

The girl was not Kiriko. Her name was Mihoko Takeda. She had a tray of empty beer mugs in her hands. She wondered why the voices in the room had died down. She saw Markewicz approaching Lloyd and halted.

Lloyd's eyes found their way to her. He gazed at her face, thinking of Kiriko.

Lloyd's head swayed once. But he still kept his boxer's stance.

Suddenly Dave Markewicz threw his arms under Lloyd's

and clasped his chest. As he pressed his sturdy bulk against Lloyd and held him firmly, he whispered in his ear that he was going to escort him out of the bar and take him back to Crawford; that he had a gun and would use it if he had to. Lloyd instinctively squirmed against him only for a second and then he went limp.

Lloyd muttered, "I… I…" Looking at his face you could see that reality was dawning on him. It was harsh and deeply embarrassing.

He groaned, "I've gone too far."

Hearing that, Markewicz loosened his grip and pried himself away from the poor guy. He nodded to Lloyd, and Lloyd, who just a half-minute before had been ready to take on all comers, walked ahead of him sheepishly, to exit the bar.

The military police office at Camp Crawford wrote a report before 9 a.m. the next morning; it was sent to Camp Chitose. Though disciplinary action—such as a misdemeanor charge—wasn't planned, there would be administrative action. They weren't going to let Lloyd become a part-time MP. Among the signatures for the paperwork, Captain Forsberg's was needed.

The only thing that Toshi had on the walls of his apartment was a piece of rice paper roughly the size of a standard letter page. He'd taped it on the wall. The Japanese character for the word "peace" was painted on it in black ink. One day an old man had been selling a few examples of his calligraphy on the street, as souvenirs, to passing servicemen. No one was buying any of the old man's works; Toshi took pity on him a paid him a whole dollar—for which the old man thrusted "peace" into his hands. His landlady didn't want him to put anything on the walls of his flat because she didn't want any holes in the walls. But who could argue with "peace" being taped above the table where he ate.

During the day, Toshi usually hid himself away from the

world, staying in bed, or when the effects of crystal meth were plaguing him, pacing the floor.

As Lloyd Kelso was attending his first day of classes at Camp Crawford, Toshi was at home, pacing the floor in his stocking feet, his brain buzzing. He was up the whole night. His ears wouldn't stop ringing.

At just before nine, a driver of a motorized rickshaw—a bicycle fitted with a small motor, with its frame elongated so that a cab for two passengers could be drawn behind—climbed the creaky wooden steps of Toshi's outdoor staircase to his flat and banged on Toshi's door. The driver went by the English name "Johnny." He'd grown up with Toshi. He'd stayed friends with Toshi, though Toshi could care less about him. He was a scrawny guy with thin arms and a boney face. He figured that Toshi hadn't heard the news. He was right—Toshi hadn't.

Toshi yelled at the closed door, "Don't knock so loud! You want to bust my eardrums!"

"It's me, Johnny. There's some news. It's not going to be on the radio."

Toshi went over to his door and unlocked it. He didn't have on his jacket, tie and his penny loafers but he still looked natty for it being just nine in the morning.

Toshi sighed after opening the door and seeing Johnny. "You can tell me standing right there. No need to take your boots off."

Johnny then blurted out, "It happened last night in Chitose. Seiichi Suzuki was attacked and he's dead."

Toshi had assumed Seiichi had wandered off quietly after doing the job. He was shocked to hear he was dead. "Are you sure?" he questioned.

"Yes."

"Where?"

"Back of the bowling alley."

Johnny then said that not only had Seiichi been killed, but a G.I., as well.

Toshi thought: Well, the G.I. must have been Bob. He told Johnny, "Oh, um, I'm sorry to hear this. I knew Seiichi, but he and I haven't had much contact lately. Thanks for letting me know."

"I thought you'd like to know because I thought you knew him pretty well."

"No, I didn't, I don't know what gives you that idea," Toshi said tautly.

He then thanked him for stopping by and giving him the news. He could see Johnny was wondering why he was so neatly dressed; Toshi said he hadn't gone to bed the night before and was still up. With a quick movement he grasped the doorknob firmly but at the same time bowed a shallow bow a few times toward Johnny and repeated, "Thank you, thank you." It was a signal for him to leave. He did.

Toshi wasn't concerned about Seiichi—not any more than he had been about his kid brother when he was attacked.

What concerned him was that his Japanese enemies in the black market were threatening *him*. They had a hoodlum or two that killed Seiichi and Bob—they were sending Toshi a message: they wanted him to cease involvement in any black market and drug deals.

Bob Fernandez was killed alongside Seiichi—this meant the hoodlums didn't want witnesses, so Bob had to be killed.

Just before Toshi started pacing again, his eyes fell on the full-length mirror in his apartment. The *shabu* he took the night before still wasn't wearing off.

A young man looking just like him—but wearing different clothes—a cardigan sweater and dark blue woolen slacks—appeared in the mirror.

Toshi approached the mirror. He stood there, staring. His sense of balance was off. Colors were changing.

Yes, it looked like him. But he didn't feel it was.

Then the reflection spoke, "It's not hoodlums who did the killing, it's Akiyama."

Though the reflection speaking to him scared him, he

muttered automatically, "But Akiyama's old. He's a weakling."

"But he's strong now. Because he's possessed by Lloyd."

Possessed by Lloyd? Toshi ought to take seriously the conversation he was having with this Japanese guy who looked just like him.

He asked the reflection, "So how did it happen that I was inside the bowling alley with Lloyd while he was outside killing Seiichi and Bob?"

"Well, Akiyama did the killing. But Lloyd directed it."

There was another point to raise. Toshi's mind was quick. He asserted, "But Bob is dead, and Bob was Lloyd's friend."

"Lloyd wanted Bob dead," the voice in the mirror said.

"Why?"

"He was jealous of him. Bob could catch people's attention. Lloyd couldn't. Bob used his big mouth to attract people's attention. He wouldn't let Lloyd be noticed."

"So Lloyd took action."

"Yes. Bob needed to be eliminated so that Lloyd could be Lloyd. Also, Lloyd hates people, all people. He doesn't like the Japanese. Most people will blame Akiyama for the deaths. And they're scared they may be the next victims. Yes, they may be the next to be killed. Not by Akiyama, but by Lloyd."

Toshi remembered the time in the bowling alley when Lloyd didn't want to be around him and he'd opened his mouth and there was blood all over his teeth, and Lloyd had said, "Now you can see the truth I'm hiding."

Ah, so, Toshi thought. "Lloyd was telling me then."

The figure in the mirror sounded expansive, "He doesn't like you. Instead of having Bob beaten up, you should have had Lloyd killed. He hates you more that Bob ever did."

"I had to get Bob, because he was a bastard to me."

The reflection told him next, as if speaking out of the blue, "If you don't get some sleep, you won't be effective against Lloyd. You need to drink whisky right now. That will help you sleep."

Toshi looked away from the mirror and glanced over to a bottle of whisky he had on a shelf. When he looked back at the mirror his strange reflection wasn't there anymore.

He went over to the bottle, grabbed it, opened it, and poured the liquid in a glass. After adding some water, he took a sip. If he wasn't careful, it would make him vomit.

Two hours passed as he drank the diluted whiskey, sitting cross-legged on the floor. Twice he lost consciousness for fifteen minutes and came to, still sitting where he was.

Hallucinations like the guy in the mirror had never happened to Toshi before, though he'd heard about others having them.

Finally he got four and a half hours of sleep. When he woke up he knew he'd have to go outside and see what effect Seiichi's death was having on everybody. The one way of getting the best and latest news was to go to Tsuru Lanes that evening and listen to what was being said.

So, he thought—he took in a big breath of air and let it out before searching for a fresh cigarette in the apartment— his eyes narrowed—I will go to the bowling alley at six.

That evening it was quiet at the Wada residence. Kiriko slept through the whole night and not once did her voice emit the dreadful high-pitched sound. Her aunt and uncle hoped that what had happened the previous night was never going to happen again. If it did, she'd have to be taken to a doctor.

CHAPTER 23

At 11 a.m. the next day Sergeant Velchoffsky came into Forsberg's office and handed him a report written at Camp Crawford only two hours before. It recommended the orders for Private Lloyd Kelso to train at Camp Crawford be rescinded; it meant he wouldn't be a part-time MP in Chitose.

Velchoffsky expected Forsberg would sign off on the papers immediately.

Forsberg took the paperwork in his hands, tilted back in his swivel chair, and read through it. He grew more and more interested as some details were gone into. Kelso, the report said, was mourning the death of his friend, Bob Fernandez, also from Chitose I, and he got excessively drunk and belligerent after the first day of instruction in the classroom. Apparently, he'd fallen in love with a girl who worked as a bar hostess in Chitose—one of things noted in the report was that he'd wailed the name, "Kiriko" in the bar where he was drunk and his conduct violated army code.

"I'm not going to approve this order," Forsberg said. "Keep the young private on." "It's best to put the incident behind us." Velchoffsky was surprised by what he considered to be a display of wisdom from Forsberg when the captain continued with, "Army life is something he never asked for. If he committed a crime, it was one with no victims but himself. He'll straighten out. Let him complete the eight-day course. Then we'll go from there and see if he can do the job well."

Forsberg thought to himself: I want this kid on my side.

I don't know him yet, but he's likely to feel grateful for what I'm doing for him.

"Let the commander of MP training at Crawford know that we'll be arranging a telephone call between me and Private Kelso. I wish to offer him my official condolences for the loss of his buddy."

Velchoffsky hadn't expected to hear this from Forsberg. Phone call? A captain reaching down the ranks and offering a private he does not know his condolences when it wasn't even combat?

Forsberg continued to the master sergeant, "I know what it's like to lose a buddy. I don't want that boy falling apart and being of no use to the army."

Regarding the first part of what he said, Forsberg was lying. He'd never lost a close buddy because he'd never had one. He was also unaware of how sensitive Lloyd was, and how much combat in Korea had affected him.

The sergeant inwardly shrugged and made a mental note to himself that he'd avoid, at least for the first two months on the job, putting Kelso in a position where the young man would be taking the lead in any significant way.

During his law enforcement career Danjuro Fujita had come to form certain ideas about those who carry out crimes. It was less common for older men to commit them, especially for the first time. Criminality and violence are phenomena that start when one is young, he believed. When older men commit crimes, they do so out of emotion, or they can be acting as part of a group or a gang. But Akiyama didn't belong to a gang. On the contrary, he'd always kept to himself, a solitary man of strong moods, prone to unpredictable attacks of furor. Still, it was hard for Fujita to see how, late in life, he could be transformed into a murderer.

If his emotions caused him to act, who or what triggered them? It was true that Akiyama began living another life after the earthquake struck. What happened at that time? What would make him murder people indiscriminately? There had to be a reason. Something vague, like "pure insanity" couldn't explain it. Not at his age.

The sheriff stood outside his mother's room. She told him he could slide the door open, and when he did, he found her reading a book. He entered and knelt next to her futon.

"Mother, there's a reason why we lie down at night. It relaxes our body and mind so that we may more easily fall asleep. If it's lunchtime, as it is now, and we are in fairly good health we should not stay in bed. We should get up, make tea, eat, do things—no matter how small or devoid of meaning they are."

"I don't feel well enough to get up," she frowned.

"You understand you're merely extending your illness. Your lying there only induces more lethargy."

His mother didn't respond.

"Do you want the doctor to come?"

"No."

"Are you afraid of something?"

"What makes you say that?"

"Because of things happening in Chitose."

His mother lay the book she was reading down by her side.

"No, the quietness of Golden Week has been having an effect on me. There are so few sounds coming from the streets, only the noise of the Americans… and the rain."

The sheriff gave up trying to rouse his mother from bed.

"I didn't think things could get any worse than they were. I've never seen anything like this in my life. I try to think as Akiyama might be thinking—it could help guide me to where he is. We found some of his clothing at Lake Shikotsu and now there have been more killings. Nothing makes sense."

"Well, he doesn't need his clothes anymore because he's changed shape," his mother retorted.

"I'm looking for explanations that are psychological. Akiyama was living his life. His life changed after the earthquake. I'm aware that many believe things happen in the world because of the gods but I must put that approach to one side if I'm going to get anywhere. I'm thinking, what caused him to start killing? Did someone or something anger him? He's not acting as part of group. He's acting as an individual."

"He's acting as part of a group," she said flatly.

"What, as an Ainu?"

"No, they're not strong. They have no power."

"So what group is he part of?"

"Demons."

"No, no, not again," Danjuro let himself laugh at his mother.

"The demons that came with the earthquake."

"It's staggering to know you believe that." Fujita pressed on, trying to maintain a logical argument. "What does he have to gain from killing people? The only answer can be is that he's acting upon his emotions; he's alone and angry. But what made him start? What makes him continue? If I can figure out his motive, I believe I can find him."

"He's not acting alone," his mother said firmly.

"All right, so he's with a band of demons. Is that going to help me find him? We are not aware of any enemies he has in town. Certainly he may consider all Japanese as his enemy. It could be to my disadvantage to pay no attention to that."

"Son, you're right on that point."

"Yes, but you could be saying that because it's automatic for you to demonize the Ainu."

"If you're looking for my thoughts on the matter, I've given them to you."

"I'm at an impasse."

"So you should consider what I've said," she insisted.

"There's nothing scientific about what you say."

"Why does something have to be scientific?"

"Scientifically speaking, I know you're my mother. That is actually important to me."

"It's convenient to connect things with science for people like you."

"I wouldn't be so critical about science. Science explains diseases and it's with science that we stand a chance of curing them."

"But war is a disease and so is murder. Diseases come and go."

"The first part of what you say is not scientific. The second part of what you say is scientific but it's a passive observation that requires no action. Science at its best leads to taking actions, *expert* ones."

"A plague is upon Chitose. It will pass. We need to stay out of its way."

"We need to stay in bed," Fujita responded, sarcastically. "Why not?"

"No, something has to be done," he said, seriously. No conversations filled with myth and legend, please, Fujita told himself, ruefully.

Usually he tried to stay away from bringing up his work when he talked with his mother. Yet sometimes he vented his frustrations. He thought: These are the first murders I've experienced as sheriff. It's my job to do something. People want answers and I don't have any. There are false sightings (I think they're false, but not everyone agrees) of Akiyama everywhere. When crime of this magnitude occurs, it's no longer so easy to be head of the Sheriff's Office. There's more to deal with than you ever imagined. Things go every which way. Instead of having the feeling you're protecting the community, you feel it's impossible to do it.

His mother proffered, "The answer is to get the demon before he sheds his clothes."

"Demon? What exactly do demons wear for clothes?"

The old lady turned away from her son without answering him and picked her book up again.

The book was, unsurprisingly, an old edition of ghost stories.

CHAPTER 24

The loudest sounds came from the sky—American planes and helicopters. Helicopter trips between Chitose and other military installations were, for officers and NCOs of higher rank, the backbone of the army's air "taxi service;" the traffic in the low skies continued until a lull in the forenoon. Like most everyone in Chitose, Forsberg automatically tuned out the morning noise.

He arrived at his office at 6:30 a.m. sharp. He removed his overcoat and hung it on a clothes tree. His office was still bare. A pitcher of water was next to a percolator on a tray; he poured water into it from a jug nearby. He put coffee grounds into the strainer and switched on the percolator.

Before sitting down behind his desk, he walked back and forth between the percolator and a window, which looked out on another building, just twenty yards away. (It was one of many of Chitose I's non-descript buildings used for storage.) In his office, only three file cabinets, partially filled, and documents and copies of documents on a shelving on a wall opposite the window suggested that his work had something to do with administration.

He'd scheduled a phone call with Private Lloyd Kelso for 6:45 a.m. that morning.

He paced softly back and forth, knowing he needed to focus. He was wide awake, but the codeine in his system was exerting its muffling effects, despite the pot of coffee he brewed in his Quonset's kitchenette and drank.

On his desk were two reports. One was of Kelso's

behavior at the bar in Sapporo. The other was of the murders and mutilations of Bob Fernandez and a young Japanese man by the name of Seiichi Suzuki.

What he hoped to get out of Lloyd was new information about Akiyama, since there was a connection between Lloyd and Kiriko and it was now known the girl had been born to Akiyama. Possibly, something that Lloyd would say could tell Forsberg more about the mysterious Ainu man.

When one werewolf meets another for the only time in its life, the werewolves are going to have questions about each other.

Fifteen minutes before Lloyd was to report to MP class that morning at Camp Crawford, he was connected to Forsberg by phone.

Lloyd was in a cluttered office that was the domain of the staff sergeant who handed him the phone.

"Private Kelso, I extend to you my condolences concerning the loss of your friend, Private Robert Fernandez," Forsberg said crisply. "I don't have to tell you that Private Fernandez was well liked here in Chitose and many servicemen will miss him."

"Yes, sir. Thank you, sir," Lloyd said timidly.

"I understand the pressures that come with being a conscript. I also understand the reactions that our minds have to death. I also understand the affect that excess alcohol has on a person." The captain waited for Lloyd's response and was pleased with the one he got.

"Yes, sir. I won't contest any charges brought against me."

Lloyd said this despite being told he wasn't specifically going to be charged for his wrongdoing—he was only going to be taken out of MP school.

"There will be no charges, private," the captain said evenly. We understand your grief. "Incidentally, Fernandez's next of kin have been notified that he lost his life off-post, that he was murdered, that there was a fight with a Japanese man, who also was a murder victim."

What could this mean, Kelso thought. This was the first time he'd heard the details. Fernandez, murdered? How could that have happened? He thought Bob had had a drunken accident, that he'd fallen into the river and drowned.

Lloyd felt like he'd been socked in the gut.

Forsberg continued, "I'm telling you—his buddy—these particulars because you were close to him and you deserve the truth. However, we'd appreciate it if you kept this information to yourself. Your buddy died in a fight to the finish. It was hand-to-hand, bloody—there was a knife involved—he stood up for himself. But he didn't make it. The investigation is in its early stages. There was at least a third man involved, if not a fourth. That's why I'd like to ask you what you know about a girl named Kiriko Wada."

The mention of Kiriko's name stunned Lloyd. He was almost in tears having just heard that Bob was murdered; now Kiriko was brought into it.

Forsberg went on, "Kiriko, we know, works as a bar hostess in town. The report on my desk says you mentioned her several times last night. The Chitose Sheriff's Office has informed us she's the daughter of a man wanted for murder, one Shigeru Akiyama… but she's had little contact with him for many years, they say, because she was adopted by relatives." He paused to let the information sink into Lloyd, then continued, "Is there anything you can tell me about this girl?

Lloyd couldn't believe he was talking to Captain Forsberg about Kiriko. He stammered, "At least a dozen times when I've been in Shimizu, I've seen her. Yes, she's a hostess. I took a liking to her. That's why I mentioned her."

"Did you know her well?"

"No."

"Did she like you in return?"

"I don't know, sir."

Forsberg was disappointed. It looked like Lloyd wasn't

going to have any useful information for him. "Hearsay was included in the report on Fernandez's death. There was talk of his activities in Shimizu, what he said and did there. Apparently he'd taken a liking to Kiriko, as well. She seems to be a pretty popular girl. Did you and Fernandez fight over her?"

Kelso's heart skipped a beat. "No sir, Private Fernandez never knew I liked her. I never told him. He would have never known, so there would have been nothing to fight about."

Kelso was sweating. He couldn't believe he was taking about such things over the telephone. Though telephones were common, they were used sparingly, and important business was never conducted over the phone. He'd never spoken to a captain, nor any officer, on the phone before. In addition to that, he'd rarely ever had a phone conversation with anybody that had lasted over three minutes. (At the three-minute mark, there was a large step up in the cost of the call.)

Forsberg questioned more. "Would you say that you and Fernandez got along extremely well?"

"Yes, sir."

Did Robert Fernandez ever mention anything about her father, her natural father, that is, the Ainu named Shigeru Akiyama?

"No, sir."

"Do you know anything about this Akiyama, Private Kelso?"

"The only thing I know sir, is people in town think he has gone crazy, that he's in hiding, outside town, and that he comes into town some nights and kills innocent people."

"Is there any one man who told you this? Is it an American or a Japanese? Can you give me his or her name?"

"I don't think it's just one person saying it, sir. Many Japanese are. You hear it when you go into town." Lloyd consciously avoided saying he got any information from

Toshi Nakano, because he didn't want to be associated with Toshi, who sold *shabu* to the troops.

Forsberg looked down at one of the reports on his desk and asked, "Is there a person named Toshi Nakano, who frequents Tsuru Lanes, who talks about the wanted man, Akiyama, and insists he isn't responsible for the recent assaults and murders?"

Lloyd's mouth dropped, though Forsberg didn't see it because he was reading.

Forsberg didn't give Lloyd time to answer. "The reports mention that you and other G.I.s fraternize with Toshi, that he sometimes joins your bowling teams. Perhaps you know that he sells amphetamines and is active buying and selling other items on the black market in town."

"Yes, I know, sir," Lloyd said, recognizing it was stupid to feign ignorance. He then answered Forsberg's previous question. "Toshi's different from most people in town. You're right. He doesn't believe the Ainu man is the murderer."

"Then who is?"

"He says the man's too old and weak."

"Who does he think is killing people in Chitose?"

Lloyd couldn't tell the captain that Toshi had suspected that he, Lloyd, was the one who'd been committing the murders. It was just too crazy; it also would falsely implicate him in the murders. It would bring confusion to the investigation. It would waste time.

He said to the captain, "Toshi's theory of who the murderer is changes week to week. Nobody takes him seriously. He's always high on drugs."

The captain said abruptly, "All right, private, that will do. One thing you'll learn in training is to be wary of unreliable witnesses." He continued unexpectedly, "Finish your training at Crawford. Sergeant Velchoffsky thought you shouldn't remain with us, but I understand your grief and I overruled him to keep you on. We'll see you back here in a week. When you're back, impress Velchoffsky with what maturity and professionalism you can muster. You are dismissed. Goodbye."

After hanging up his phone, Forsberg poured himself a cup of freshly percolated coffee.

How convenient it was that the blame for the murders of Fernandez and the Japanese thug was being put on the missing Ainu man.

CHAPTER 25

Captain Jake Torrington put his signature on some routine paperwork, then left his office at CIMIC.

It was a five-minute walk to Chitose I's parade ground. He'd be there at 10 a.m.

The sun glared on the empty area that was the size of two football fields. While a quiet May breeze drew away the dampness, a dozen Japanese robins had lighted there; they searched out worms and insects in the grass.

When not being used, the place was big enough to make you feel removed from the workaday world of the post.

The two officers would be able to speak without being heard.

Major Timothy Beaumont was there, on a street that flanked the parade ground. With a friendly hand, he gestured which way he would like them to walk. He and Torrington walked toward the grandstand.

"There's an early preliminary report," Beaumont said as they walked shoulder to shoulder. "It wasn't sent to you. You'll get one later, when the investigation is further along."

Beaumont was talking about reports from the military police office. They were rarely sent to CIMIC; they were sent to the relevant officials in other MP units and up the chain of command to provost marshal Major Tyler at Camp Crawford and sometimes, when appropriate, sent to the unit commander of Command, Control & Intelligence—which meant Beaumont.

To any onlooker, the two officers seemed to be having a

friendly chat while taking a break, walking in the pleasant spring weather.

The report that Beaumont wanted Torrington to know about had to do with the newly opened investigation into the murders of Private Robert Fernandez and a Japanese man named Suzuki. Beaumont told Torrington, "The bodies of the two victims were mutilated. The Japanese victim was a known ne'er do well."

The major continued, "The preliminary investigation notes that Private Fernandez had a barroom enemy named Toshi Nakano, who possibly had arranged for Suzuki, who was a bigger guy than he, to beat up Private Fernandez—to square accounts, as it were. It's thought that Fernandez was lured outside—and once he got there he was murdered, along with Suzuki. The murders were not premeditated. They were unforeseen.

Major Beaumont continued, "I suspect Captain Forsberg was overcome by his lycanthropy, that he attacked Fernandez and the Japanese thug. Possibly the two were just in the wrong place at the wrong time. Also there was a young Japanese woman who survived a brutal attack a short time afterward. She remembers nothing of the attack. Her mind's blocked it out. I suggest she was attacked when Forsberg was making his getaway— because she was assaulted in an area that's between where the double murder took place and the front gate of Chitose I."

At that moment the major and the captain were nearing the grandstand and grass was on their boots.

Beaumont continued, "I want to tell you about some things that happened in Germany. All brutal attacks are not the same. Some have common characteristics—the level of brutality is similar, and one suspect's proximity to the different attacks lead us think there are connections…"

They reached a bench near the grandstand. Beaumont gestured for Torrington to take a seat.

The two men sat on the bench as clouds moved west to

east, the Pacific Ocean drawing them in its direction. The sky stayed bright—it was going to be a glorious spring day.

Yet the major had to tell Torrington more than he wanted to know.

A Young Woman Returning Home
after Practicing the Piano

While the surviving Germans were breathing in the last warm days of summer before steeling themselves for another long winter of shortages ahead, she'd moved from the Eastern Sector to the Western one. She was lucky to get herself a room and a job in the city. The job was as a secretary. Directly after her work she would go to the Stauch family's house. She didn't live there. It was just that they had a piano. The Stauchs let her practice on it. She'd taken piano lessons as a child for six years. She couldn't afford a piano of her own. It was a boon for her to find the Stauchs after posting that notice which asked members of the public where she might find one to play for an hour a day.

If not for the piano, life would be unbearably drab.

Now autumn was coming to an end and snow had already fallen twice.

There was a metal door, at street level, that once opened, revealed a ladder. One had to climb down the simple metal ladder to reach the cellar floor. Excess merchandise for the small dry goods shop above were stored in the cellar. There was a tiny padlock on the door. It could easily be broken by someone who was determined to break it.

The air was humid, misty and cold. Light glowed from a three-quarter moon; a streetlight glowed dimly, such lights being spaced far apart from one another. The district was still being reconstructed. The area had been bombed and half of it had survived.

It was a comfort for the Stauchs to have her and her music in their home. They lived in anguish over their son who had been drafted into the war. He was missing—either dead, imprisoned in Russia, or he'd run off to start a new family in another country. It was hard to believe that last possibility, since he already had a wife and two children whom he'd by accounts had loved, whom the Stauchs were financially supporting now.

It was a fifteen-minute walk from the Stauch residence to the young woman's room. It was generally safe in the area at night, even when there was limited visibility on nights such as this.

The creature had taken refuge in the basement below the dry goods store, snapping the lock off with its teeth, throwing the door open, and then trundling down the ladder.

As the young woman walked along the street, she noticed ahead of her that a cellar door was open. She didn't think it was strange. Some people worked at odd hours; to rebuild Germany was a gigantic undertaking, with the end still not in sight.

As she got closer to the open door, though, it did seem strange that whoever was in the cellar was down there with no light. But she kept on her way, advancing.

The creature below was contorted in pain. After the changes it had been through the last half hour, it felt as though its body would burst. Its inner vision had been overtaken by throbbing colors which blinded it. It was nearly immobilized, so it looked for refuge and found it.

So it writhed below, not being able to proceed, wracked with stinging agony.

But the woman changed that. Despite whirling in the middle of its storm, the creature sensed a human being coming in its direction.

Her footsteps, now being heard, made the werewolf attend to something other than its own agony.

It scampered up the ladder to the sidewalk, collecting within it all its power.

It couldn't see her. It could only sense her. It thrust itself at her, slamming into her head-on.

The Stauch family had known her only for a short while, and as the creature had dragged the young woman's distended body some distance along the street before letting it go, they shuddered not only at her unbelievably gruesome murder, but at the length of time it took for the Fates to permit her body to come to rest.

When this attack occurred, Forsberg was stationed at an army base nearby.

A Man with a Glass Vial in his Pocket

Early spring, after rain, under black skies, a swollen, sallow middle-aged man walked along the sidewalk. He was alone. He crossed his arms upon his chest, over his coat, helping to keep the warmth in.

There wasn't anything he could have done to come back from the city center earlier. There was so much work to do. He did not sleep well. He was a hypochondriac (but perhaps there was something legitimate behind his need for medications).

He kept his footsteps on the sidewalk soft. He didn't want to make sounds to attract other men. He did not like this street. He always worried something could go wrong here— thieves, he meant. Yet it was the only street to his house from the tram stop. He could feel some coins in his pocket rubbing against his house key and a vial of antiseptic in his pocket. He'd just bought it in a pharmacy—just to have it at home in case there was need of first aid. There was a slight scrapping sound as the metal in his pocket met the glass vial. He hoped that no one else could hear the sound.

He didn't have much farther to go. He eyed his surroundings—a maze of small old lanes, recovering from war damage, still unfinished, a desolate place with low light and only minimal contrast between that light and the dark.

He kept to the right-hand side of the street.

He saw no one at the four corners as he approached them. It sprang out from the unseeable side—the one at a right angle to him.

At that corner was a butcher's shop.

The werewolf was suddenly there from an unknown direction, more like a force than a being... or rather like a violent gust of wind that instantly coalesced into bloodthirsty monster. The creature slammed the man down on the ground so it could mangle him. But instead, its body teetered, and it wasn't fully in control of its limbs. So, it squashed him like a piece of fruit.

It bore down on the rind of the man while clipping off his head with enormous strength; it squeezed the rest of him down to his seeds. The man's clothing, the flaps of his skin—ejected the pulp of him. Blood spattered everywhere.

If the werewolf could have, it would have crushed every tiny seed of the man, shattering each into specks as small as grains of sand.

Glassblowers make glass vials and bottles when they heat grains of sand (which are their raw materials).

It's a fact that when this attack happened Forsberg was stationed at an army base nearby, as he later was, in a...

A Rural Area, Near a Base in Northern Bavaria

His experience of working in his noisy workroom for so long gave him the ability to sense the movements of people around him even if he couldn't hear them. He, Wilhelm Eisgeth, had sent his two workers away for the night. He remained in the sawmill, working late.

He was a brawny man. Working in a sawmill, you need to be.

It was evening; the electric lights inside were dim, except around the saw.

He sensed instantly that the figure coming behind him intended to do him harm.

As soon as he could, he pushed the large circular saw away from him. Its guard slid over it on its way to its back bracket. Out of the corner of his eye he believed he saw the unexpected figure behind him dart to his right.

He pivoted to look directly at the figure, and to defend himself. It shocked him to see what it was.

It wasn't a man. It was something like a beast. He'd lived through wars, had lived in the wild, but he'd never seen anything like this. Could such a thing exist?

Various tools and implements hung on hooks on the wooden walls of the workshop. Many of them were old, going back many generations. They go back to when there were no motorized saws, blades, lathes. There were also axes, hammers, mallets and other tools used for repairs and maintenance. They hung on hooks everywhere.

Wilhelm Eisgeth thought: I need a weapon.

The creature growled low in its throat when Wilhelm's eyes met its yellow beast eyes, and it stopped its advance momentarily. It had corded muscles not even fur could disguise.

He moved quickly away from the thing, jumping to the wall on which a large millwright's chisel hung from a hook.

When he jumped, the werewolf lunged in his direction, scattering sawdust into the air. The hefty sawyer, wearing heavy, hard boots, with a mighty kick, was able to repel the creature for just enough time to grab the millwright's chisel. The blade of it was three inches wide. It was a formidable weapon.

The creature sprung back at him as soon as it got its footing. Eisgeth was ready for it, thrusting the chisel into the shoulder blade of the thing.

The massive chisel hit the bone hard.

The werewolf was injured, but to what degree?

The creature backed off, in pain, hissing.

The sawyer knew he couldn't tear out of the sawmill and escape the thing. It would only hunt him down.

It had to be defeated here.

It charged at him again, this time with the aim to deprive him of his weapon.

The creature was successful. The chisel went from being in the sawyer's grasp to flying through the air, away from them.

With one of its limbs, the creature was able to grab hold of Wilhelm's leg. He was able to violently kick away the creature once more.

He needed a new weapon to defend himself with. He rushed over to a wall and took down a heavy-duty steel hammer.

But the creature followed him. It was at his back as soon as he felt the hammer in his hand.

It was almost too late. The creature's teeth went into the skin on his back, gouging him, but Wilhelm was able to twist himself away quick enough to land a blow with the hammer—on the same place of the creature's body where he struck it before.

In pain, the creature momentarily retreated once more. The sawyer knew the thing to do was to kill it—or at least injure it so it would relent and flee.

Wilhelm Eisgeth was a Herculean opponent. Humans rarely come as rugged and with as much physical power. His fear receded as adrenaline took over.

It was hand-to-claw combat—though the sawyer's vision went dim, and he knew he'd pass out if he didn't will his eyes to stay open.

At one point after being thrown to the ground yet again he staggered to his feet, and bleeding on the back, his cheeks, his ear, he knew it was time to try another way to strike at a weaker part of the werewolf's anatomy.

The idea was this: there was a handsaw nearby. The handsaw was old and had been taken apart. The handle was very hard, but the blade was worn and was going to be replaced. The saw lay in two parts on the table.

Eisgeth, struggling with bruised ribs, threw himself toward the table.

The werewolf followed him.

The sawyer snatched up the robust handle part of the handsaw and fit it into his fist. It was like wearing brass knuckles. He turned around and struck the monster, slamming his new weapon into its snout with the power of a circus strong man.

The blow sent intense pain through the sawyer's fingers, but piercing agony was the greater woe to the creature. It pulled back and howled.

While it writhed, Wilhelm went closer and slammed his heavy booted foot into the flesh between its two legs.

The violence was too great for it. It could stay in the battle no more. It raised itself from the floor, roared at Eisgeth, turned, and loped out of the workshop.

Wilhelm Eisgeth was one of the few who survived an attack like this in Germany.

Major Beaumont got up from the bench he and Captain Torrington had been sitting on.

Japanese robins continued to peck at their food in the grass of the parade ground. Beaumont looked away vaguely, to the sky. A half mile away helicopters and small planes were landing every five or ten minutes, just as they had been while he'd been speaking. Beaumont thought: at least these events in Chitose are taking place in warmer weather rather than in fall or winter.

Beaumont stood, but he didn't move away from the bench. Why was he still standing? Torrington thought: Tim probably sat in offices too long.

Anyway, the captain could tell Beaumont wasn't finished talking.

"What's curious about the assaults and killings in Chitose is some of them could remind you of attacks that Forsberg's carried out—but the fact is he hadn't arrived here yet.

Neither man spoke right away.

Then the major asked. "So, what do you think about all that I just told you?"

"You think I ought to know more about Forsberg's history but I'm still struggling to know why."

"Jake, you react with the local community. You should know what's *really* going on. The murders in back of the bowling alley, the assault on the young Japanese woman the same night, and add to that the murder of the young boy in the Heiwa district nearby here—for me, these point to Forsberg, not to anyone in the Japanese community.

"Have you considered arresting him?" Torrington asked, offering some kind of solution, or at least a possibility that crimes by one man might cease.

"No, we haven't thought to arrest him for now."

"Why not? It's violence and death."

"We have no proof he did it. What are we going to say, Captain Forsberg is a homicidal maniac that has to change into a werewolf before he does the killing?"

The major explained, cautioning him about the distinctions to be made, "The Japanese police are going to assume that all the recent assaults and murders have been carried out by the same man. I want you to know, because you're CIMIC, that *that* can't be true."

Without knowing, Torrington touched on a subject which had been discussed among a small group of people for the past five years. The captain asked, "If we know of one werewolf in the world, isn't it likely that there are more of them?"

"Anything is likely, the major said. "There are a number of conjectures, I suppose, huh?"

"Maybe there's a werewolf here in Chitose," Jake Torrington suggested.

"Maybe. It could be that it's under the control of the Communist Chinese, and they've brought it here to frighten people and disrupt our supply chain to Korea. Yes, we don't know if Russia has one werewolf or more…"

Jake could tell from the way he spoke that Beaumont had no interest in seeing the conversation go in that direction.

Beaumont added, "We don't know much about werewolves. It's extraordinary we know about them at all."

Torrington shifted the subject back to the immediate fate of Forsberg. "Do you have a plan about how to handle Captain Forsberg now that he's active?"

Beaumont nodded his head no, with frustration. "It's unusual for him to experience the changes here, and now. They've been mostly under control for years. Something's happened to him since he got here. I don't know what. There's going to be a meeting among those who are involved in this but for now…." Beaumont paused. It was obvious he was going to ask Torrington for something he wished he didn't have to. "I'd like you to move into the Quonset that he's in. We'll have you and one of the officers that's already there swap places."

Jake was shocked. "Is it safe for anybody to be in the officers' quarters with Forsberg?"

"Yes, I believe so. He hasn't been violent in the rooms he occupies. He always goes outside, traveling some distance from where he lives. Remember, he's trying to hide his condition."

Torrington fretted, "There could be a first time he stays *in* to be a wolfman."

"Well, that's never occurred before."

The captain saw the major wasn't going to budge on that point. But Jake had to voice his apprehensions. "It could be that a big mistake's being made to keep him alive."

"Others and I understand that."

There was a short pause while a helicopter noisily flew overhead. When he could be heard again, the major spoke, "We are hoping that Forsberg will, to put it in military terms, disarm."

This was no assurance in Beaumont's statement. Jake had a question that'd lodged itself in his mind, "Excuse me, Timothy, I know I probably shouldn't be asking, but who's 'we'?"

"I can't answer that now—soon, maybe," Beaumont said, and then shifted his eyes to peer into the depths of the sky.

Then he looked back to Jake and said, "By the way, the code name for this operation is Operation Grendel. Forsberg is himself referred to as Grendel sometimes."

It wasn't the brightness of the morning that made Torrington squint his eyes—rather, it was because he thought he'd heard the word Grendel somewhere else before—but not in the army. As his mind searched for an answer, Beaumont jumped in.

"You're thinking you know the word Grendel from somewhere, right?"

"Yeah."

"It's the name of a monster in English literature—in the story called *Beowulf*.

"Right…" The captain thought some more. "I read some of it in college first year English. The hero 'Beowulf' has got 'wulf' in his name… and Beowulf's the good guy."

Well, if you ever hear me say "Grendel," you'll know I'm referring to something different than the story."

"Except blood and guts were in the book, too."

"That's the point of the code name."

Torrington wondered how many higherups were in on Operation Grendel. It probably wouldn't be many because such an operation couldn't risk having Soviet spies discovering it. He thought of the capabilities of Intelligence during the last two years of the war against Hitler and the sacrifices that had been made. The Allies had broken Nazi codes and many times they knew the targets the Germans had their sights on. Yet the Allies had to allow some attacks to go forward—which meant U.S. military casualties—just so the Germans wouldn't know their radio messages had been intercepted. What an incredibly dangerous operation that consisted only of observation, risk, and death!

Beaumont spoke again. "Look, I know the 'secret weapon' concept of Grendel is fantastical and may not be workable. But my opinion is not the only opinion involved."

Torrington thought: What a mission to have! Observation. Allowing innocent people to be sacrificed so a secret could be kept. So the reason to transfer Forsberg to Chitose was for Beaumont to keep watch on him.

Torrington felt his heart sink. He said, "Just what exactly am I supposed to do when I'm in the same Quonset as Forsberg?"

"You're needed there to gather evidence. He might leave some useful evidence in the corridor or in the kitchenette at the rear of the Quonset."

"But you said you're hoping he's not going be active again."

"But if he does get active, we might know that much more about his precise coordinates. Is what I'm asking you dangerous? I think it's infinitely less dangerous than open-field combat."

Jake thought: Well, even comparing one danger to open-field combat is not a good thing. He didn't want to take on this extra duty. But it was the army. You have no choice.

He asked, "Can werewolves be shot and killed with regular bullets? Or do they have to be silver?"

He wasn't joking.

"After guns were invented, silver bullets came into the lore—but things are not going to work that way with Forsberg—not at all," Beaumont responded dryly.

CHAPTER 26

Kiriko wouldn't be home for supper. She'd trimmed her eyebrows to be less conspicuous, to help make her face look as Japanese as possible and went into town that afternoon. That morning she noticed something about her body she'd never noticed before. On the small of her back she discovered a downy patch of fine hair growing. I'm not an animal or a male, she thought. But girls shouldn't have hair there, no matter if its texture is light. To take her mind off it, herself, Akiyama her Wolf Clan father, and Chitose in general, she went to the movies.

The Orion was Chitose's smallest movie house. She steered clear of the biggest, the Chitose Cinema Theater, which was in Shimizu, where someone was more likely to see her.

She watched a double bill of two domestic films, both dramas. (There were few Japanese comedies being made; nobody wanted to make light of life and people wanted to commiserate with characters having tough times.)

Aunt Satomi heard her husband come in and leave his shoes, hat, and outer coat in the entryway. The weather had been pleasant all day, but Kenshin had put in an eleven-hour day at the department store and not seen much of it.

After they both said a quick "Good evening" to each other, Kenshin launched in, "Mr. Haneda and I have always been on good terms—or so I thought. Though he wasn't rude, he was... mechanical in his manner with me."

Normally, when Kenshin came home from work she'd always offer him a glass of whisky and soda. But she knew that was the wrong thing to do this evening.

Mr. Haneda was Kenshin Wada's boss at the department store. Kenshin had worked hard to be liked and respected there. He'd been made a junior manager, just under Haneda, four years ago.

Japanese men weren't so willing to communicate with their wives, especially about business matters, for fear it would make them look weak and not authoritative. It irked Kenshin that he heard himself speaking to his wife about trouble at his workplace.

In the past, his marriage to Satomi wasn't cause for vexation. There were some people who didn't realize she was partially Ainu, much less that she was a cousin to Shigeru Akiyama. In Japan, a marriage between a Japanese man and an Ainu woman wasn't taboo, though a Japanese woman marrying an Ainu man could stigmatize the woman.

Still, it might not always be smooth sailing marrying a woman of Satomi's mixed background, especially if dark, extenuating circumstances interfered.

Haneda, just like most people in town, had assigned the guilt for the murders to Akiyama. This meant he could blame Kenshin for marrying an Ainu and treat him in a disdainful manner.

Kenshin's tone remained solemn to his wife. "I looked at suitcases today in the store. We have two dozen different ones in stock. One should be bought for Kiriko."

Satomi glanced away from her husband. She wanted to sit down and cry. She could read what was on her husband's mind: soon Kiriko might find it uncomfortable to stay in Chitose. She, Satomi, ought to start thinking of relatives that Kiriko could be sent to in Sapporo because she could live anonymously there, get a job in a factory where they'd hardly take notice of her.

The idea of living without Kiriko so upset Satomi that she

mentally fled from such an idea and thought of the trellis next to her garden behind the house. The climbing hydrangea were still not climbing over the whole of it; at present she had long false bindweed—*kohirugao*—stems wrapping themselves around the lattices. She would get rid of the *kohirugao* if the hydrangea ever took off.

It was a small garden. It had to be. She didn't have much time to tend it. It had four slightly elevated flower beds, their soil held in by rectangular frames made from fitted planks. Like many things in Hokkaido, the Western influence was appreciable. Her garden wasn't much different than a small one you'd find in New England.

The daffodils had already bloomed, as had her few tulips. Her white peonies—which were Kiriko's favorite flower when she was younger—were large and bold now. The small azaleas and arctic poppies would be flourishing for some time. Next month the roses would open their petals.

In a few minutes Satomi and Kenshin sat down and ate dinner in silence.

After it was over, Kenshin remarked joylessly, "Mr. Komogata, whom I've always been compassionate toward because of his wife's health and their child's handicap, won't talk to me anymore."

People at work had been talking behind his back about him, his wife, and Kiriko ever since the policeman Iwate was murdered. After being treated rudely by Mr. Haneda today, Kenshin quickly looked back on the past week and remembered many interactions he'd had with his co-workers. Even Mr. Daiwa, the manager of men's wear, usually quite friendly, seemed to vanish every time Kenshin got within ten meters of him.

Satomi could have mentioned that some at her job were also treating her like an outcast.

There was nothing to say in response to her husband. She could have said she was sorry—certainly *that* would never console him—it would only make him feel unmanly and pathetic. It was best to be quiet. He needed to let time pass, slowly, softly, at home this evening, before he might take a drink—on second thought he wouldn't do that; he was feeling so down that that wouldn't help.

After dinner, until Kiriko came home, Satomi thought about her garden. In six weeks the daylilies would bloom, and then the irises…

Satomi hugged Kiriko when she arrived. She was especially warm to her. Kenshin said nothing after greeting her with the words *Konbanwa* (Good evening) and withdrew into the bedroom.

There, he thought: I have nothing to be ashamed of. But still, he felt shame. Man, his co-workers at the department store had truly scorned him.

Later, in the middle of the night, Kiriko made her high-pitched sounds again. There was no avoiding taking her to see a doctor anymore.

That sound had so unnerved Satomi that she'd contacted someone in the Ainu community, to ask what they thought about it.

She was told that an Ainu female shaman could be consulted. When the word "exorcism" came up in their conversation it disturbed her so much that she decided right away to abide by the Japanese way of addressing the problem. If Kenshin ever found out she'd gone to an Ainu to ask about Kiriko's condition, it could be the end of their marriage.

CHAPTER 27

Forsberg was in his quarters with his door shut. It was evening. Terry Leventis and Jake Torrington were having a conversation in the corridor outside. Something they were saying said made him prick up his ears. Several times they referred to an officers club off base, on land owned by an Ainu man named Kumakawa.

(During the past week, Jake Torrington had moved into the Quonset, replacing a first lieutenant named Rice—Forsberg did not suspect that the room change had anything to do with himself and Torrington watching out for him.)

Forsberg might have heard Kumakawa's name mentioned another time, elsewhere, but since there hadn't been any connection made between the guy and Ainu people, it wouldn't have caught his attention.

From what he understood, the place had first been a trading post/souvenir shop/snack bar on the road next to Chitose River before it came into town.

Forsberg found out that a few weeks after the establishment opened, Major Christopher de Graff's eyes fell on it while he was coming back from a Sunday drive to Lake Shikotsu last year in August.

The major pulled his station wagon into the lot next to the one-room building, parked, and went into the establishment to have a look.

The place immediately struck him as a location for an off-post officers club. There wasn't one in Chitose. Ah, to unwind in a roadhouse a little distance from work, a few miles out of town. In the back was the river. A pleasant setting.

One thing about de Graff: if he wanted something done and it was possible to do, he got it done. He ran Logistics. There was a quick mind behind his calm, rugged face. He was a brilliant delegator of assignments but if he felt he was the only one to get something done right, he stepped in and did it himself.

He'd chatted for less than five minutes with Tadao Kumakawa, the owner of the premises, which had a few racks of merchandise—snacks, bottles of soda pop, souvenirs of Japan, and small wood carvings made by Ainu men—when he proposed an unexpected idea.

Mr. Kumakawa's English was far from perfect, but de Graff, an imposing but affable six-footer with dark wavy hair cut short, managed to have him understand that he saw his establishment could be an ideal meeting place for American army officers who wished to have a club to themselves farther away from their jobs.

Kumakawa heard the charismatic major out. He wasn't against this surprise proposal, though he said he was planning to close in November and reopen after the snow melted in April.

De Graff responded to that quickly in his steady baritone, "We'll have to do something about that." (The forty-two-year-old officer could have been suggesting that he was going to keep the place shoveled all winter long so he and his fellows would have a place for themselves all year long.)

What de Graff did—and with the permission of the Ainu man—was to see to it that a large, roofed porch was built out back, attached to the one-room building. That way, the men would be able to drink and enjoy the view out back.

De Graff paid for the new construction.

They wound up knocking down the old one-room building. A new, larger one room building replaced it. A planked porch with sturdy walls and a roof were attached the new building. The property was kept plowed. (The place was unscathed by the recent earthquake.)

Given the history of the bad treatment by the Japanese, it might seem surprising that an Ainu could own property so close to Chitose. It was the first Ainu-owned plot of land on the road after leaving town and Katsuragi Ward. It informally signaled the start of the gentle fifteen-mile climb to Lake Shikotsu.

There'd been eighteen Ainu settlements up and down Chitose River as late as fifty years ago; somehow Kumakawa was able to hang onto his land. It's true that in the years before the U.S. occupation, he wouldn't have been permitted to open a shop on such a well-travelled road.

When Forsberg overheard that there was an *Ainu* on whose premises there was a private officers club, a jolt shot through him: here was a chance to meet someone who spoke English, who might know Akiyama!

The next day, after discretely asking where the officers club was, it intrigued him to learn it was just ten minutes away from the deadly slope behind Akiyama's cottage.

Forsberg went to Kumakawa's at 5 p.m. on a Wednesday. He figured that was a time when there'd be few officers there. He wanted to increase his chances of being able to talk to Kumakawa alone

He didn't wear a service cap with a brim. Instead he just had on a khaki garrison cap. It made him less imposing.

When he opened the front door to the club, the first thing he saw was Kumakawa, a forty-two-year-old man, neither too tall nor too short, with thick bones, a round face and neck beard that was cropped to be a couple inches in length, standing behind a small empty bar that had a cash register to the right of it. Mr. Kumakawa wore a dark Ainu tunic that was graced by fat curving lines of white fabric sewn into it. The inside of the building had a hunting camp feel to it.

He greeted Kumakawa, tilting his head quickly in a bowing motion. He quickly said he wanted to see if any of his friends were around before he ordered a drink. In a flash, Mr. Kumakawa was at the left of the bar, sliding the doors, opening them so Forsberg could go out back to the covered porch.

A couple of lieutenants were there. He didn't know them. They stood drinking at a high table, conversing. He greeted them for the sake of civility, and seeing no one else beside them, moved on, went back inside to the bar and its owner.

He was pleased he'd be able to talk to Kumakawa alone.

"A fine place you have here," Forsberg said depthlessly. "I'd like a bottle of Sapporo Lager, please."

He wasn't going to drink. He just needed it to seem that was the reason he was there.

Kumakawa carefully poured the cold beer out of the opened bottle into a glass.

Forsberg didn't want to come on strong. He didn't want to sound like a police detective. He took a sip of beer. After taking the glass away from his lips and setting it down on the counter of the bar, he said carefully, "I'm Captain Gideon Forsberg. It's my first time here. I work for the army military police. I'm not investigating the crimes in Chitose. That's the business of the Japanese police. Do you understand?

"Yes," Kumakawa replied, wondering why he brought the subject up.

Forsberg's eyes happened to drift over to the wall to his right. It was next to him and to Kumakawa. He hadn't noticed it when he first came in. On the wall hung a flat, crude object; one of the officers had created it—probably when he was in his quarters, drinking.

It was in the shape of a tombstone—yet it wasn't stone gray in color. The grain of the wood could be seen, though darkened by wood stain. This homemade work of art consisted of ten words in white, and at the bottom there was a painted image of Road Runner, the cartoon character. He was running through the desert, leaving a cloud of dust in his wake. The ten words in white paint above Road Runner were:

HEARD IT
>ALL
SEEN IT
>ALL.
DON'T CARE.
MEEP MEEP.

Forsberg, who had little feeling for art, thought to himself, how bizarre.

He turned his attention back to Kumakawa.

"I've been wondering about the fellow the police are looking for—Akiyama. My questions are completely unofficial. Do you happen to know him, if I may ask?"

There was a slight pause.

"He's older than me. Like everybody, I would see in him town."

Though there were gaps in Kumakawa's English, he made Forsberg understand that anyone who lived in the area couldn't completely avoid going into town at least a few times a year.

"So you didn't really know him well?"

"No."

"Did he stay with the old ways? Forsberg asked.

"I don't understand. What do you mean, 'stay with the old ways'?"

Forsberg himself wasn't sure what he meant, but he thought it had to do with being not modern Japanese and with Akiyama changing into a wolf. People at Camp Chitose likened the Ainu, when the subject came up at all, to American Indians back home in the States. But the Ainu didn't live on reservations and their population wasn't large. There also had been brief mention of them in the orientation materials that Forsberg received when he arrived in Hokkaido. The orientation materials had compared the Ainu to American Indians—you could see where the soldiers were getting their ideas from.

Forsberg wanted to know if there was anything in Ainu

culture that could be connected to werewolves, but he wasn't going to say it. You can't. One doesn't.

Kumakawa made Forsberg understand that Akiyama followed some of the old ways: he was a hunter and trapper; he lived surrounded by the wild.

Forsberg asked if there were many Ainu like Akiyama; Kumakawa answered opaquely, "The exact number is unknown."

The captain then asked Mr. Kumakawa what he thought about Akiyama's age and health. The Ainu club owner replied that Akiyama hadn't talked to many people in the last few years and it was thought that his mind was not sound.

None of that was news to Forsberg. He was starting to think he'd learn nothing from Kumakawa about Akiyama. He decided just to shoot the breeze with him.

"From what little I know, there are great differences between Ainu people and the Japanese."

"Yes, differences are big."

"You're not treated as Japanese people. You're treated as... not so well."

"True. The Ainu are not Japanese. That makes our lives hard."

"But you have a good situation here. You have this place."

"This is old Ainu land they did not manage to take."

"So other Ainu people are not so fortunate?"

"Correct."

"If I may say so, you're lucky, right?"

"Yes. But there are many kinds of Ainu. They're not all the same. Akiyama lives alone in the hills."

The Ainu man pointed in the direction of the wooded escarpment that began a hundred yards after you crossed the road away from the river. He continued, "There are Ainu who would live among themselves in groups of five or ten families. There are Ainu who live on the edge of town. Some Japanese are half Ainu or part Ainu—if they are, they generally keep quiet about it.

Forsberg said, "I'm glad for you that you've managed."

"Me, too."

Forsberg paused and took a sip of his beer, not at all interested in the taste of it. It gave him time to think of what to ask next. No suspicions for the last attacks in Chitose had fallen upon him. People blamed them on Akiyama. Whether he'd drowned himself in Lake Shikotsu was still debated. The Sheriff's Office's investigations weren't coming up with any new information. There were no more clues, no signs of Akiyama or his body anywhere.

Forsberg thought of a question. "Do you think that Akiyama kills people?

"Maybe. His head is sick," replied Kumakawa.

"Why do you think they're having so much trouble finding him?

Kumakawa made him understand that Akiyama knew the land, knew the forest, was an outdoorsman, that people who are looking for him spent most of their time indoors—so they lacked the skills to find him.

That sounded sensible to Forsberg. He was at a loss what to say next and could only come up with, "Are the woods in the area dangerous?"

The Ainu man thought for a moment and said, "Yes, there are bears in some places."

"How many places?"

"Enough of them."

Kumakawa let Forsberg understand that the forest was dangerous, and during winter you might freeze to death there.

Forsberg wasn't getting as far as he would have liked. He was running out of questions. "I'm just wondering," he said, "are there many wolves in the mountains in this area?"

Kumakawa smiled and said, "No, not unless you count Akiyama."

The answer shocked Forsberg. There, he'd stumbled on

something at last!

"What do you mean?" Forsberg asked. He didn't sound excited, but he was.

Kumakawa explained. "Well, he's not a real wolf. But he's from the Wolf Clan."

"So that makes you people say he's a wolf?"

"Yes, Ainu people talk like that sometimes."

"Are all Ainu people members of one clan or another?"

"Yeah, sure."

"If I may ask, what clan are you from?"

"The bear one."

"So do people call you a bear?"

"Well, yes, sometimes. My name is Kumakawa. For short, some people call me Kuma. *Kuma* means bear." Then he said with a wide grin, "But they know I'm a person, not a creature with four paws."

Forsberg was still trying to process this information when Mr. Kumakawa remarked,

"Each one of us is proud of our clan."

Forsberg tried quickly to think of another question. He asked, "Do you think Akiyama would feel close to wolves?"

"Yes, they're his family."

"If they're his family, would he try to run away to join them?"

"Well, it would be hard to find them."

"What do you mean?"

"It would be impossible."

Kumakawa said would be impossible insofar as there weren't any wolves left in Hokkaido since all of them were killed off when the Japanese government sponsored Japanese farmers to colonize Hokkaido and the extinction of wolves was deemed necessary to protect their livestock.

Forsberg flinched reflexively and told Kumakawa, "Much the same thing has happened in other parts of the world."

"Yes?" Kumakawa questioned, having theretofore thought only the Japanese could be so mean.

"In many places, in Europe and America, for example, people have the same reaction to wolves."

Forsberg thought: this chat is somewhat interesting, but I don't know of what use it is to me. He scoured his mind for any other questions that might give him more insight into Akiyama. Finally, he asked, "Are there many other Ainu people in Chitose who are from the Wolf Clan?"

"No—nobody that's full-blooded like him. Akiyama isn't originally from Chitose. He came here when he was young because there were all sorts of odd jobs between Eniwa, Chitose, Tomakomai and at the ocean. From what I know, most of the Wolf Clan Ainus live in the Saru River area. It's two hours away. It's across the Ishikari Plain."

This could not be a coincidence, Forsberg thought. He'd taken the wolf, Akiyama, to a forest that was his birthplace! The Rule—this was a manifestation of The Rule.

He thanked Kumakawa for answering his questions and left the officers club without saying goodbye to the two lieutenants out back, and without finishing his beer.

After the captain left, Kumakawa thought to himself how Forsberg's face looked slightly yellowish, in a sickly way.

Forsberg softly said to himself when he got out to the parking lot: "Strange. Akiyama could never have been bitten by a wolf like I was, because here there are no wolves. But on the other hand, he was born into the Wolf Clan." He shook his head in confusion and his ignorance stunned him. He was angry, too—he'd been foolishly hoping his meeting with Kumakawa might gift him with a revelation of some kind.

That night he tossed and turned and had codeine-affected dreams. At one point his body was an itching, throbbing eardrum listening, but straining to hear more, to know more. He was a slave to The Rule and he was fighting against it. He heard Ojibwe drums. (A few classmates in his school had Ojibwe blood in them and Leech Lake Reservation wasn't far from his boyhood home—they performed ceremonial dances at the reservation, and they invited Whites to come see them, as tourists.)

Then suddenly his body was made up of microscopic trees, with branches and the tiniest of twigs—curiously, there were no leaves. They all pulsed, sometimes pushing at each other. He felt he wasn't about to transform, but his body was nonetheless being assaulted. How long would he have to endure it?

Then he dreamed of Akiyama and wondered what the Ainu felt in *his* dreams, what he felt during his days, his nights… and his transformations.

He'd had such a tortured night that when he woke up the next day he thought of killing himself. But he'd never do that. The instinct for self-preservation was too strong in him.

CHAPTER 28

More fresh recruits arrived in Chitose; most were sent to Chitose II, for training on the large, rugged grounds there. Summer was arriving slowly, but in town there were frightened people who stayed in their houses as if it were still winter. No progress was being made with the investigations. Sheriff Danjuro Fujita felt the pressure.

At the end of a fine (weather-wise) day, after work, at home, he found himself reading a newspaper article in the national *Asahi Shimbun* about a new play that was premiering at Tokyo's chief kabuki theater. The article was a pleasant diversion until it described the plot of *"Kitsune to Fuefuki"*— the name of the drama which was based on a tale from an ancient anthology of stories known to educated Japanese people.

At the end of the story, the main character, Harukata, jumps from a small wooden boat into the deep waters of Lake Biwa to his suicide, intending that his body sink to the bottom and never be found.

When he jumps, he has the corpse of a young female fox in his arms. This fox had recently been alive, in human form—its mother had changed it into a living effigy of Harukata's late young wife, a beautiful musician. The mother fox, possessing supernatural powers, had done this out of gratitude—one day she was captured and was about to be killed, but Harukata intervened and saved her

The mother fox gave the gift of this replacement wife to Harukata—on the condition that he not have sex with it. But

272

he couldn't resist. One day he tried to make love to this flesh and blood effigy; it died immediately and reverted to the shape of a fox.

The plot of *"Kitsune to Fuefuki"* not surprisingly reminded Danjuro Fujita of the theory that Akiyama, to avoid capture, had killed himself by drowning in Lake Shikotsu.

The sheriff was inclined not to believe this theory. It would have to be proved.

But if the theory could be proven true it would be welcome. Almost any development would be welcome. Because of the present season, there were enough people now present at Lake Shikotsu. If any additional evidence washed up, they would be sure to see it. One can hope.

After reading the newspaper the bachelor sheriff fixed a meal for himself and his mother. Before going to bed he listened to the third movement of Beethoven's *Ninth Symphony* which played on the radio.

Toshi Nakano, like everyone else in Chitose, was impatient with the lack of progress in the investigations. He tortured himself daily with the idea that somehow, logically, he was the target for the next violent attack in Chitose. He also was upset that because of the attacks, the police seemed to be patrolling the streets more than normal. However, with more soldiers coming into the area, there were potentially more partners to trade with. Business hadn't slowed at all at Tsuru Lanes.

A song that was being played often by Japanese radio stations spooked him. One part of him told him the song was irrelevant to him. But the song, "Night Train of Tears," did disturb him. It sounded harmonically dreary, like so many Japanese pop songs. It was like a tango, but to a marching beat. It had a disturbing train whistle in it. It wasn't that it reminded him of the attack on his little brother in the train. It was something said in it that bothered him. He didn't like the way the male vocalist sang, *"Ashita ga ki ni naru namida no yogisha."* ("I'm worried about tomorrow.")

He didn't like the singer's style, the melody, and the words. The singer had nothing to worry about! He had a Number One hit record; he would make money for years on that song! On the other hand, he, Toshi, *might* have to worry about tomorrow, given his circumstances. Toshi thought: a lot of nerve that singer singing that *he's* got problems!

Though Chitose was hundreds of miles away from the action, there was no one at either Chitose I or Chitose II that wasn't following war events in Korea, more by reading the *The Stars and Stripes* than listening to the radio. The communists—be they Soviet, Chinese, or Korean –were not negotiating. The United Nations Forces—and this meant the United States military in no small way—waged a massive attack on the electricity-generating dam on Yalu River bordering Korea and China. The idea was to apply political pressure at the stalled truce negotiations at Panmunjom.

It didn't work, though North Korea lost electricity for two weeks and even China suffered almost an equally long blackout in its northeast. The dam, defended by the Soviet Air Force, not the Chinese, not the North Koreans, wasn't destroyed completely.

At Chitose the men talked about the Soviet Union's announcement that at the Summer Olympic Games in Helsinki, their athletes weren't going to stay in the Olympic Village. Instead, they were going to be bussed in from a nearby Soviet naval base every day and returned to the base every night. When at the games, they were "chaperoned" so none of them could defect to the West.

1952 was a year of an American presidential election, so the election candidates were constantly in the news.

The current president, the Democrat Harry Truman, had decided not to run for re-election. Dwight Eisenhower, army general and military hero, was the Republican candidate. He was favored to win over Adlai Stevenson, who was successfully branded as an egghead (he was in the habit of reading many books, and this meant he was out of touch with the people) by Republican strategists. Though there were differences in policies between the Democratic Party and the Republican Party, sometimes the parties weren't so far apart.

Stirring up the presidential race and politics in general, Senator Joseph McCarthy, a Republican, wanted there to be big differences between the parties. He wanted hard right-wing Republican rule—no power sharing with the Democrats. The Wisconsin politician spoke of the Democrats' "twenty years of treason," accusing them of being soft on, or even in league with, communists. The Gallup Poll showed support for him was at a meager fifteen percent—with sixty-seven percent having "no opinion" of him—and twenty-two percent of people having an unfavorable opinion of him. He cozied up to FBI director J. Edgar Hoover and created bogeymen and bogeywomen where oftentimes there weren't any. The newspapers granted him the attention he sought—it boosted their sales.

The U.S. military wasn't impressed. It was fighting real battles, not imaginary ones—and for much longer than the Wisconsin senator had been in power. Military brass saw McCarthy as someone injecting chaos into the organs of government that had tough, exacting work to do. The man was a grandstander, a dangerous neophyte, and many men in uniform in Chitose thanked God they were thousands of miles away in Washington.

While J. Edgar Hoover managed his partnership with Joseph McCarthy, he also declared that his FBI needed to hire and train more agents. He aimed to double his force from 3,500 to 7,000 agents. He needed more men, he said, to root out American communists who were agitators in the American labor movement or selling secrets to the Soviet Union.

Nichols and Velchoffsky, after reading an article about this in *The Star and Stripes,* bantered about eventually leaving the army in two or three years, no earlier, and going to work for the FBI. But they wanted to see some resolution in Korea, first. Plus, however bright the lure to move back stateside was, they didn't much like Hoover (he was a man who could not feel nuances, they thought).

The front pages of the papers covered the ongoing nationwide wide steel strike. 650,000 steel workers walked off the job. It took the whole month of June for them to go back to work.

There was news also of "explosion training" in the Nevada desert. Seven-thousand soldiers took part of exercises during which the government detonated four atomic bombs. The soldiers had to conduct tactical maneuvers; afterward, the army gave them psychological tests. The news outraged the head mechanic of Chitose I's motor pool, Sergeant Ted Fontana (the man who Major Beaumont had overheard talking while getting his hair cut in the post's barbershop). It was mindless to put men in unknown danger in a place where there was no enemy, where there was only a peaceful desert.

Stories in the news on a UFO sighting seemed to be everywhere on the back pages of the newspaper. Brian Yoder, who along with Bob Fernandez, Lloyd Kelso and Ricky Travers, had volunteered for part-time MP duty, lapped up those articles. The subject of UFO sightings displaced any interest he might have had in current politics—or baseball and sports for that matter. Corporal Yoder had inside information, he claimed, that UFOs were being taken seriously by the military and that the Air Force had a special unit for it; that the unit's chain of command was recently modified, and this emphasized just how much more they were getting involved, in earnest.

Notwithstanding that, it being summer, his buddies were following the baseball season in the U.S.

Teams' lineups from the previous year weren't much different. In a game between the Dodgers (the late Bob

Fernandez's team) and the Cincinnati Reds, the Dodgers whomped the Reds, 19 to 1. Lloyd's team, the Giants, played the Dodgers three times in May and beat them each time, and in June, too. If Bob had been around, boy, he would have been able to razz him.

But the baseball games didn't grip him the way they used to before Bob died.

Until he was stationed in Chitose, Lloyd might have flipped through *The New Yorker* when he saw it in a doctor's waiting room or someplace like that. That changed in Chitose when you had to make more of an effort to keep up with things going on back home.

"Wish You Were Here" was a musical he'd read about in the magazine. The characters were at a summer camp for adults. The stage set included a fully functional swimming pool filled with water.

He thought to himself: wow, they live in a world cut off from us who are fighting for their world to exist.

He felt sure that *those* people weren't plagued by quirky things coming into their heads like he'd been since Bob's death—like what Bob said their last day together up at the fishing camp, when Bob mentioned he didn't like eating fish.

Why didn't he like to eat fish? Because you have to eat them one by one. They're not like meat, where you take a chunk or slice out of the whole and eat it.

How was it that after somebody dies you remember the strangest, insignificant parts of conversations you had with them, and those parts stick in your mind...

There was something new to the U.S. Army's enlarged footprint in Chitose. While President Truman had ordered (using a directive, which bypassed Congress) in mid-1948 the desegregation of all branches of the armed forces, this was met with resistance by many who argued that until American society had embraced desegregation in day-to-day life, the military couldn't be expected to successfully integrate its ranks. Four years of discussion, evasion and delays ensued.

Some officers against desegregation were fired.

New ground was being broken—some. At the beginning of the year the University of Tennessee admitted its first Black student, and in April, Ralph Ellison's *Invisible Man* was published. More and more Black athletes were let into major league sports—one newcomer, pitcher Joe Black, was named 1952's Rookie of the Year and was the first Black pitcher to win a World Series game.

The army had seen Black units prove themselves to be skillful and brave; they'd served in combat for many years. In the Korean War, the Marines had increased the number of Black soldiers tenfold. Racial tension was generally absent. That quieted the nerves of military brass and counterweighed against opinions that integration, for years into the future, would fail.

The first of more than a thousand new Black summer recruits arrived at Chitose I and II. One evening in June, Major de Graff, who took it upon himself to feel out where some of the Black recruits—those not shipping out to Korea right away, that is—might best be accepted, was talking on the back porch of the officers club at Kumakawa's with First Lieutenant Nichols.

De Graff queried the lieutenant about integrating the military police.

Nichols responded to de Graff, "I would think it would have to be done slower there than with other units because I can foresee trouble with some White soldiers, rowdy or not, who refuse to acknowledge the authority of a Black man."

Chris de Graff countered that perhaps a Negro soldier should work for the military police in their office—it might turn out to be useful to have one on hand in the event of a dispute that had racial aspects to it—he might be able to help defuse any threat of group violence.

Mommy Eri closed Bar Eden down. With someone like Kiriko not working there, there was no way her establishment could survive. She couldn't find anyone to replace the girl. Chitose wasn't a large city.

Eri went back to the business where it was certain she could make money. This time she'd have to run it without her husband.

One sunny afternoon she went to the temple to pray for the business's success. On her way home she saw winged maple seeds dropping from their trees; she walked by a young woman who, it appeared, reflexively had sat down on an upturned wooden crate, and used it as a seat while she nursed her clinging infant. She took these as good omens—new life.

Bar Eden had above it a second floor. The owner of the building had never rented it out before because it got very cold. There was no fireplace, so it'd been used as a storage attic. In the past three weeks the owner cleared it out.

It was serviceable. She could make enough money in the next few months to buy heaters for when it got cold. Maybe she'd decide to move to another property.

There were four young women working for her now.

What used to be the space for Bar Eden was now the lounge where a soldier would wait before he met one of the young women upstairs in the two bedrooms.

Within a couple of weeks business was fine. It didn't hurt that there were more G.I.s than ever in town because Chitose II had opened.

This time around she felt more comfortable with the men. Running Bar Eden all alone had given her confidence—though maybe her dread of Akiyama and the fear he might come back to town and kill somebody also contributed to the change in her regarding the soldiers who were fit and ready to fight.

Kenshin didn't have to pressure Satomi to take Kiriko to the doctor. It was expected of her; she had to do all that she could to find out what was making Kiriko emit that high-pitched sound. Kiriko was, after all, *her* relation, not his. This was a big disruption to their family life and their family life

279

had already been profoundly shaken to its core.

Satomi took Kiriko to the doctor in Chitose, who then referred her to a specialist in Sapporo. They waited a week for the appointment. For the first six nights before the appointment Kiriko didn't make any of the strange sounds. Satomi was hoping Kiriko's frightening illness had passed. But on the night before their visit to Sapporo, the piercing sound happened again.

After examining her and asking her many questions, the specialist in Sapporo suspected Kiriko had a mild form of epilepsy. Her high-pitched sounds, which she couldn't control, were seizures, he said. He prescribed phenobarbital, to be taken daily. It was an anti-seizure medication, used for almost fifty years now, he said.

He didn't know, and certainly if he had known he wouldn't have told her, that more than a decade ago, a German family wrote Adolf Hitler, asking him if he might give permission to have their severely disabled son killed. Der Führer sent his own doctor to examine the five-month-old boy; the baby was given a lethal dose of phenobarbital. A week later, a group of psychiatrists was summoned to Hitler's chancellery. The doctors were ordered to start a clandestine euthanasia program. It commenced in 1940 at a clinic three hundred miles away from Berlin. Fifty intellectually disabled children were put to death by injecting them with large doses of the same drug the baby boy was given.

That clinic was in Ansbach, Germany.

Inside Chitose I, there were a half dozen interconnected small gently curving roads off to the side of the base's airstrips. For officers who had a few minutes of extra time, they sometimes took these small roads to enjoy a brief leisure drive.

Summer had built quite slowly out of spring. The air was soft today, with fresh reed smells. Forsberg was alone in his jeep. The few buildings he passed on the small roads had been decommissioned, were awaiting demolition, and new, bigger buildings in Chitose II had replaced them.

Wildflowers—flowers of the family that asters belong to—were everywhere in the ragged, open fields. The unkempt grasses lay on soil which just below, was clay. The land did not drain easily.

Forsberg had been part of a security inspection entourage on the grounds surrounding the system of runways that all planes coming into Chitose used. The rain showers of the last two days had stopped—at least, on base. Large puddles had formed in various places off the road.

The captain was trying to relax. There'd been no more murders—Chitose had been quiet in that respect for the last four weeks. His regimen of codeine was working well.

With the lack of buildings, the expansive dome of the sky seemed to all but speak to him with calming words. The vacant space around him seemed to liberate his mind; it flitted to the thought that just a few weeks ago man had, in an airplane, for the first time, landed at the North Pole.

After that thought passed, his eyes fastened on the show that appeared in front of him. A gauzy haze—a mixture of gray, light blue and white—was illuminated by the four o'clock sun behind him. It seemed like it was fifteen miles away, the rainbow that now pierced the awesome pearly sky.

The sight of the rainbow with its edges of precise color— aquamarine blue on its lower edge, fiery red on its upper— excited his visual sense; he took in all the land beneath the bow; he could see each green plantation on the Ishikari Plain, could see to the last of the hundreds of them, all the way to the horizon where they ended in sky.

It occurred to him that he was looking northeast, directly to where he'd taken Akiyama the Wolf for sanctuary.

The captain's hands swung the driver's wheel left instinctively.

But it was already too late. He hadn't seen the curve in the road ahead of him.

His jeep's left side slid into a muddy shoulder. The road and its shoulder were a couple of feet higher than the surrounding terrain—for drainage.

The jeep continued onward, slanted, and its right front tire slapped hard down on the grass which covered the loose soil, the rigid clay. The front wheels of the vehicle were turned in such a way that the jeep was destined for an erratic flip. While it flipped, it ejected the captain, throwing him into the air. He tumbled in that space three times before hitting the ground as the jeep raced ahead without him.

The right side of Forsberg's skull struck a flat, smooth stone twice the size of his head; he lost consciousness instantly, his head rested there. The lower part of his body— his thighs and below—splashed into an off-road puddle near the stone.

The gash was above his left temple. It bled on the stone and the ground. Below his waist the water settled and covered him. If his head had been there, he would have drowned.

Frogs in the vicinity had found the puddles soon after they formed. They laid their eggs in them. Now, young tadpoles darted here and there in the shallow puddle where Forsberg lay. Some brushed against his pant legs, his boots, his body.

The colors were somber: submerged olive drab, and black—black boots. With its glare, the lustrous sun in the southwest deadened the tone of his flesh that wasn't in water—it was wheaten; there was the incontestable liquid red of life on his forehead and hair. And there were those skittish, brown tadpoles an inch below the puddle's surface. If this little scene—with the man in earlier costume, of course— were transferred onto canvas with brush and oil paint by a competent artist in the Low Countries of Europe in the sixteenth century, it would have made for one fine allegorical painting close to the style of that time.

CHAPTER 29

An ambulance brought him to the infirmary at Chitose I.

Another junior officer had driven a jeep down the same road Forsberg had been on ten minutes previously—with the same leisurely objective in mind. He reported the accident.

Forsberg arrived bleeding and was unconscious. The blood came from a gash in his scalp, on the left front. Some had dried and matted. Looking closer, the doctor saw skull bone at the base of the wound. The captain's pulse was slow but strong.

After Nurse McGuinness dripped antiseptic from a glass dropper bottle and wiped away the excess reddish-brown liquid of it, Dr. Keith Tiller, the thirty-two-year-old chief physician on duty, shaved the area and cleaned it. The wound continued to bleed lightly; the nurse brought a new gauze pad to it and applied mild pressure, but not before the doctor probed beneath the scalp and found that Forsberg's skull hadn't been fractured. The doctor then closed the cut with a dozen stitches; he held the patient's head while McGuinness bandaged it.

Tiller pushed the captain's eyelids open and found the pupils were equal in size. He tested their reactivity to light using a flashlight. The response was sluggish, but nonetheless it was one. A positive sign. The skull was thick where the cut was. That thickness, and the brain's cerebrospinal fluid had protected the captain.

This is a concussion, Tiller surmised. At any moment Forsberg could regain consciousness. The patient would be watched for complications, and in the morning, routine X-rays would be taken to assess whether his cervical spine or his vertebrae had been injured. His breathing and blood pressure were normal; he wasn't in shock. Tiller found a few bruises on the captain's torso—these were minor injuries. In addition, he found the captain's left leg was broken—that would have to be set later, tomorrow, when it was safer to do it. Forsberg's leg and the bruises got ice packs.

For the next two hours it was important that his head not move. It was cradled in a soft pillow. A simple concussion is a bit like an ankle sprain: it responds to rest very well.

An unusual thing about Forsberg's infirmary admittance was that when Red Cross Nurse McGuinness first cleaned the dirt and blood off Forsberg's face, she found he had a thin layer of makeup on his face. She supposed he was wearing it to cover up the discolorations of his skin—with the makeup gone, there were small, odd areas of duskiness over his cheek bones. The rest of his face had an unhealthy pallor.

She didn't have to say anything to Dr. Tiller about the strangeness of it. She saw the jaw of his long face drop ever so slightly when he was looking him over after the initial clean up.

Seeing the captain's face in this state, one could understand why her arm pits were sweating—though she did have a natural propensity to over-perspire, even when circumstances didn't warrant it.

There were also discolorations on other parts of the patient's body. Tiller tried to think what skin condition it might be that would cause such variegated skin tones. He would check his medical encyclopedia.

McGuinness wasn't glad to see the back of the doctor's starched white coat when he left her alone, in charge of the patient. She nervously adjusted her nurse's cap, fidgeted with hairpins that coiffed her wavy hair. There was no reason for her fingers to travel up there. She was just stunned by

Forsberg's appearance.

Though the junior officer who'd found Forsberg at the accident site was from Operations, word quickly spread around the entire post. The news reached C2I and Major Beaumont within the hour. (When Nichols and Velchoffsky heard it, they kept their feelings each to themselves. Maybe he wouldn't be in his office for a while. This made things easier for them.)

Beaumont drove to the infirmary right away. He needed to know about Forsberg's condition but at the same time didn't want to give the impression that he was overly concerned.

He introduced himself to the doctor and said he happened to know Forsberg, that they they'd served in Germany together. He asked if Forsberg was going to be all right. Dr. Tiller said the next few hours usually showed the degree of severity of a concussion.

The major asked a few questions that had nothing to do with Forsberg. Tiller thought it strange he was being asked about the size of the staff and the current capabilities of the infirmary. The major also exclaimed, "Ah, tough luck for him!" Tiller thought to himself: I guess they're friends.

"I'd appreciate it if you'd call my office… keep me up to date, please, on his progress. Call, whatever time of day, leave a message."

"All right," Tiller said.

Beaumont didn't ask to see Forsberg. He knew it would show too close an interest in him. Plus, the doctor would likely say no, he couldn't.

The major was displeased that Gideon would be under medical care, that he'd have eyes close on him. Another concern of his was that tomorrow he was going to Camp Crawford for two days of intelligence briefing and conferences. (On the upcoming air raid on Pyongyang, monitoring the activities of the Japanese Socialist Party, continuing the deception plan regarding the British bomb, etc.) Well, if Forsberg's situation called for intervention while he was gone, there was Torrington, he could help…

Beaumont didn't tell Tiller that he'd be in Sapporo the next day and the day after. He left the infirmary saying, "Remember, don't hesitate to leave a message at my office— even tonight."

By 8 p.m., there'd been no incremental signs of him coming to; the captain still hadn't regained consciousness.

Concussions can be severe. A blow to the head with a loss of consciousness—if there's angular motion during impact, the condition can be very serious.

Also by 8 p.m., an odd look came over Forsberg's face. Instead of a peaceful expression—which many patients are favored with when they're unconscious—a *ghastly grin* had settled on him.

This unnerved Nurse McGuinness even more; her blouse at her underarms showed it.

Just after 9 p.m. Dr. Tiller, checking in on Forsberg, took stock and stated to McGuinness, "He's in a coma." He said there was no telling when he would regain consciousness. It could be some time.

The diagnosis of coma introduced a new set of protocols. Forsberg would be moved, gently, out of the emergency room and to a bed in the ward.

Tiller had an orderly call Beaumont's office and leave the message that Forsberg was in a coma and he was being moved into a private room.

Beaumont was still in his office, doing last-minute work. He didn't speak to the doctor personally—that would show too much interest.

How inconvenient, having to go to Sapporo tomorrow! He left orders to call him while he was away if any messages from the infirmary were left for him.

There were no other overnight patients in the infirmary. An attendant wheeled Forsberg to a room on the ground floor. (There was a floor upstairs, but it wasn't used.)

Forsberg's room had only one bed in it—a second one had been removed.

Once in the new room, Nurse McGuinness wheeled in the IV set. Dr. Tiller saw her wrists were sweating. He thought of her with concern—Forsberg's appearance was upsetting her.

After she swabbed an area on Forsberg's left arm and while avoiding having any of the sweat on her wrist drop onto the patient, the doctor himself took charge and slid the peripheral IV line into the captain's vein.

Too bad for Marcia McGuinness, he thought, though he had to admit Forsberg looked awful. He'd noticed that normally she held her emotions in check. She was well-organized kid from Scituate, Massachusetts (an Irish American enclave on the coast between Boston and Cape Cod). She was rather interesting: she spoke with a dark East Coast brogue that seemed to him, at least, to clash with her sandy blonde hair. Her father was disabled (a job injury, the doctor remembered from interviewing her when they first met). He was pleased she'd known something about nursing the sick before she ever went to nursing school.

After the IV line was in the captain, Dr. Tiller asked politely, "Would you please get the catheter and kit, Marcia."

Two seconds after the words were out of his mouth, she was out the door.

She came back with the catheter, its bag and a percutaneous kit. She had a thin ladies' handkerchief in her hand—she'd just wiped sweat from her hands.

Dr. Tiller took the catheter and its items from her. He cleaned the skin over the captain's abdomen with an antiseptic-soaked gauze pad. He thought: Yes I really have to admit, his is an unusual skin condition.

With his scalpel, he executed his incision as quickly as he started it.

Then the catheter was in. Now his bladder could drain.

If the room could have spoken, it would have said:

Wildness inside the body,
— fluctuations —
in the darkness.

As a matter of routine, an orderly had emptied the contents of Forsberg's trouser pockets. Again, as a matter of routine, the doctor had a look at them after he catharized him. He didn't find much: a money clip holding a few dollars, some coins, and a bottle of codeine tablets.

Tiller hadn't prescribed the codeine. This was the first time he'd seen Forsberg. Dr. Kalin's name (Kalin was another doctor at the infirmary) was on the prescription bottle's label. This meant Forsberg's medical record was on file in the cabinet. Good. Maybe his skin condition would be mentioned.

Tiller had an orderly locate the record.

Forsberg's file was a slight one. Tiller read that the codeine was prescribed for the chronic pain the captain had in his lower abdomen, in the area between his ribcage and his hip bone—a combat wound. It wouldn't be necessary to give him codeine now. As long as he was in his comatose state, pain wouldn't register in the body the way it does when one is conscious.

Three days passed.

Though the swelling in Forsberg's body went down and his left leg was set and put in a plaster cast (this was done the morning after his injury), the captain still had not regained consciousness. There were a few patches of black and blue from his injuries, but the disturbing thing was his inexplicable skin tones that ranged from ivory to brown to gray. (Tiller was still stymied in his attempt to find out what might be causing the discolorations.)

Major Beaumont stopped by on the third day when he knew Tiller would be on duty. He didn't mention he'd been out of town. He didn't ask to see Forsberg in his room because Tiller wasn't offering to take him there.

Tim Beaumont had to satisfy himself with the idea

Forsberg was incapacitated and was of no danger to anybody at the moment.

On Forsberg's fourth night, at 11 p.m., an hour before Nurse McGuinness's shift ended, she came to look in on him. She'd been checking him every twenty minutes.

It had been a warm, late July day. There was a window in the room and it was open. A beam of moonlight (it was nearly a full moon) streamed in.

When she saw him, it struck her that he'd slightly changed his position—at least it *seemed* to her he had. His head, she thought, as the very least, had shifted—it was turned to the right now. Also, the captain's uninjured right foot, which had been pointing straight up from under the sheet covering him, was now turned right. In addition to that, his right hand was curled into a fist—certainly, it hadn't been that way before.

She didn't know anything about the movements of a person when they're in a coma. She noted on his chart that his hand was now in a fist, and that quite likely he'd moved to his right.

She disliked being near Forsberg any longer than she had to (it'd had been tough to take his discolored, grinning face; she glanced at it only because she had to, and then swiftly turned her gaze away). As she wrote her comments down on his chart, the light in the room darkened—or at least it seemed to her it did. She glanced up at the window to see if clouds had occluded the moon. They had not. The moon was still there—a glowing button.

If the room could've voiced thoughts, it would have said:

> *The wound on the skull swiftly healed,*
> *the tongue grown longer*
> *(no one notices).*
> *In this body, what persistence!*
> *It squirms inside.*

She was glancing over the notes she'd just made on Forsberg's chart when she happened to look over to the patient.

His face seemed darker than it had been. His teeth seemed whiter. She felt his jeering grin like a punch to her neck.

She tried to reason herself to calmness. His face would be a little darker because the light had changed around it.

She felt her armpits release sweat.

Then it seemed to her that his bed swayed one time. Had it?

If the room had been able to, it would have said:

> *Power to rise,*
> *white tendons re-shaped,*
> *re-strung muscles*
> *must break the cage.*

But the captain with his leg in a solid white cast on his mattress was stationary. The metal bed frame did not sway. It was just that she'd felt a tiny bit of breeze come in through the window.

Her stomach was uneasy. Her armpits were wet. She hated being responsible for this man! She needed to get out of there right away.

She put his chart away.

Maybe she'd only imagined he'd changed position. (But there was his fist—that was indisputable!)

Could it be that she was just nervous and tired? But working at Chitose wasn't tiring. Her job was cushy; the only thing that would've made it even better was the kind of social life she'd have if she'd been assigned to Camp Crawford in Sapporo.

She left the room without closing the window.

Dr. Tiller was on duty. Good. He was the doctor in charge of Forsberg.

"Patients in a coma often don't move but some do," he said unworried, in his office. "Are you sure he did?"

She explained that Forsberg had turned to the right and

his right hand was in a fist.

Dr. Tiller told her to wait there and he'd go up and have a look for himself.

In a couple minutes he was back. "You're right," he agreed. "He's moved."

Thankfully, thought the nurse, the doctor had remembered what position Forsberg had been in. He added, "Yes, some comatose patients move. Some even curl into the fetal position."

She asked, "Does it meant he's regaining consciousness?"

"Not necessarily."

"Does it affect our rounds?"

"Yes. He's moved, so… his tongue could… there could be obstruction…" It pained Dr. Tiller to say it because he knew Forsberg's appearance shocked her and the other nurses.

"Somebody's going to have to be in this room at all times," the doctor said reluctantly.

McGuinness hung her head, pained.

He continued, "I'll call over to Chitose II and request that an additional nurse be sent over. If there's an emergency, we can't be short of staff.

Tiller thought so little of the shift of Forsberg's position in bed that he didn't call Beaumont's office and leave a message about it.

When Beaumont stopped in the next morning he was not pleased to find out the doctor hadn't called to tell him that Forsberg was being watched round the clock because his body had moved and there was a chance his tongue might interfere with his breathing.

Nurse McGuinness was again on the evening shift again that night. It had been another warm one; the room's window was open. The moon gleamed even brighter than the night before. She sat as far away as she could from the bed. She tried not to look at him. She just listened to his breathing.

In the infirmary at Chitose I, weeks would go by and she'd

realize she'd read every current magazine she could get her hands on. She read a novel or two every week, as well.

She belonged to the *Book-of-the-Month Club* and read *Reader's Digest.* That night she was reading *The Caine Mutiny.* It's set in the Pacific during World War II.

At one point she glanced over to Forsberg, if only to rest her eyes.

She thought she saw his left leg move.

That was odd because the left leg was broken, it was heavy, it was in a plaster cast. A pillow was underneath it.

Maybe it was her eyes, moving too quickly from the page to the captain in his bed.

She went back to reading. Lieutenant Commander Queeg, the new captain of the ship (named the *U.S.S. Caine),* is incompetent. His crew doesn't respect him. A lieutenant on board is keeping a secret log of the commander's behavior. He'll be sending it to Admiral Halsey, Commander of the Third Fleet.

She wasn't necessarily interested in military novels, but this was exciting. No wonder it was a best seller. She found she'd been reading straight for a half hour, so she raised her eyes to look over again at Forsberg.

His leg had moved off the pillow.

"What?" she exclaimed out loud, to herself.

She set the book down, got up and looked at his leg, being sure to avert her gaze from his face.

There were tiny cracks running down the cast.

She ran to the open doorway and yelled into the corridor, "Doctor!"

She looked up and down the hall to see who would appear. She waited. Nobody did. Where was the doctor?

She called out again, screaming almost, "Doctor!"

Thankfully Dr. Tiller was on duty tonight. Maybe he couldn't hear her in his office, but there was an orderly, a corporal—he'd be able to hear her yelling and would get him.

After her second yell she waited again. Almost a half a

minute passed. Forsberg wasn't supposed to be left alone.

She heard the footsteps of Corporal Roger Lumley, the orderly, before he turned a corner to come into her hallway.

"What's up?" he said, walking unperturbed in her direction.

"It's something the doctor needs to see," she adjusted her voice down to be quieter. It occurred to her she didn't know if one could raise their voice around a patient in a coma. Maybe loud sounds could be bad for them.

Lumley said, "Well, Dr. Tiller's at the officers' mess. He went to pick up a bagged lunch they fixed for him. He'll be back."

"No," the nurse groaned. "Couldn't he have sent you?"

"Yeah, the rules are that he should've. But it's eight minutes there and back. He believes in keeping fit—he's a doctor. He wanted to stretch his legs. He'll be back any second."

"Okay," McGuinness said despondently. "Please wait at the front door and bring him here the minute he gets back."

"What's wrong?"

"I don't know. It doesn't seem normal."

"Okay," he said and left.

McGuinness went back into the room and sat down in her chair. She couldn't read her book nor could she look at Forsberg. She stared at the floor.

A couple of minutes passed. Dr. Tiller arrived.

"Sorry," he said, excusing himself. "Something new?"

"Yes. He moved his left leg."

"How could he do that, it's in a cast?"

"I know."

"It takes a lot of strength to move a leg in a cast. Even when you're not in a coma."

"His eyes are shut. There's no sign he's conscious."

The doctor looked at Forsberg's left leg.

He said with disbelief, "The cast has cracks in it!"

"Yeah, that's what I wanted you to see."

"There wasn't anything unusual about the plaster when the cast was prepared?"

"No, it was fine."

He reached out and rapped the plaster cast with the knuckle of his index finger a few times.

He said, "This is hard plaster."

McGuinness waited in silence for what he would say next.

The face of the chief of Command, Control and Intelligence flashed in Dr. Tiller's mind He hadn't called Beaumont yesterday to tell him Forsberg's body had moved. He realized he needed to call him now, and tell him about the cast and the cracks, too.

Dr. Tiller told Nurse McGuinness to sit in her chair, that he had to go to his office and make a phone call. That he'd be back.

McGuinness sat back down, feeling terribly nervous.

It was late evening. Major Beaumont was likely in his quarters, asleep. There were no private telephones for officers in their quarters, at least for those officers below the rank of Lieutenant Colonel—this had to do with security concerns as well as the allocation of telecommunication resources.

Tiller would phone the military police and ask them to go the major's quarters and deliver a message. But first he'd call CI2 to see if by chance, the major was still at work.

McGuinness sat in her chair and stared intensely at the floor, trying to keep her mind off from Forsberg and her job.

The room would have moaned if it could have:

> *Ferocity without and within.*
> *Every fiber on fire.*
> *Lightning bolts, but not in the sky.*

She could have sworn she heard cracking sounds in the cast.

Her back damped with sweat. She screamed, "Aieh!"

Though he was in the front of the building, Tiller heard

her scream. He'd just gotten off the phone with Beaumont, who was still in his office. Beaumont said he'd be right over.

Tiller rushed to the room and found Nurse McGuinness shaking. She told him, "His cast is still breaking. I can hear it cracking. His leg has moved again."

"Let me take a look."

He looked at the fracture lines in the plaster cast. She could tell that he saw they were getting bigger.

"What are we going to do?" she asked.

"This is unusual. It's breaking apart. There has to be something wrong with the cast that we didn't know about. I didn't mix the plaster. Maybe the gypsum was off. Mistakes happen. By the way, Major Timothy Beaumont's coming over. He's a friend of Forsberg's." Tiller tried to calm her down, he said, "You don't have to stay with the patient. Go to the nurses' station. There's nothing you can do. Being here's only going to upset you. When Major Beaumont arrives, ask Lumley to show him here. I'll stay with the patient."

She left. Now Tiller examined the captain's right hand. Looking at the fist, he thought: the man appears to have great strength within him—but it's only his nerves causing that fist, not muscle.

He turned his back to Forsberg and stood there wondering. He hadn't treated comatose patients before. There was always something new to learn on the job. ...The nurse said she was hearing the cast crack? I'm not hearing anything right now.

Several minutes went by. There were no sounds from the plaster cast.

Major Beaumont, in a neat uniform but looking tired, arrived room, shown in by Corporal Lumley, who promptly left.

Beaumont looked at Forsberg and tried to suppress his shock. It was the first time he'd seen him since his accident. The grin and the discolorations on his face set against the white walls of infirmary and the doctor's white coat. He didn't say anything to the doctor.

"Something's wrong with the cast," the doctor said. He showed Beaumont the fracture lines on the hard cast. "And the fractures are getting wider. And, strangely, his leg has moved off the pillow that propped it up. It's scared the daylights out of Nurse McGuinness."

"Thanks for calling me. I'm glad I was still up." He hesitated, then added, "I thought about it today—his condition… there's more to consider…"

The doctor was about to talk, but Beaumont didn't let him.

Beaumont said he'd spoken with his staff and superior officers (this was a lie—he talked to no one); that he knew the upstairs floor of the infirmary wasn't being used. He told Tiller a room should be prepared, and Forsberg should be moved up there as soon as it was ready.

Tiller naturally asked why.

Forsberg had been privy to a great deal of top secret information, the major said. There was concern that when he came to, he might, in his foggy state of mind, his reveal sensitive information. He added, "I don't want to inconvenience you, but just as a precaution, I'm going to have a military policeman stand guard outside his room."

Tiller thought: the captain works for a police unit; not surprising that there are matters of national security."

But the doctor wasn't happy the upstairs would be opened. To have a comatose patient there, when it wasn't close to a nurse's station and the rest of the hospital staff? The least you could say was that the whole arrangement was inconvenient.

He told Beaumont Corporal Lumley would get the room ready.

Tiller and Beaumont left Forsberg. They passed by the nurses' station on the way to the front of the building. Tiller told Nurse McGuinness, "Please go back to the patient.

Thank you."

Beaumont was not out of the entrance door of the infirmary when a thought came to him. He moved away from the door and took Tiller aside, speaking to him in a hushed voice. "I assume you know Gideon was taking codeine for chronic pain."

"Yes," Tiller answered quietly. The doctor thought: well, the major seems to be somewhat close to his friend.

"Have you medicated him with codeine or any opiate?

"Why would I? He's unconscious. His body doesn't process pain the way it would if he were conscious."

"Do we know that for sure?"

"We doctors assume it."

"But you don't know for sure?"

"Since he's not, for example, screaming in pain, we don't think he's feeling any."

"How could he scream if he's unconscious?"

"Well, don't you see, major, this turns into a circular argument."

"I see how it could," Beaumont said drily.

The doctor continued, "Opiates slow down the body's vital processes. With an unconscious man, we want to keep those processes working as normally as possible."

"So we don't know about pain—and how his body might be reacting to it."

"Research hasn't found to what extent pain is registered in a comatose person," the doctor said insistently.

The major took a short breath and suppressed a yawn. "Well, if we don't know, let's consider what we do know. We know he's moved. We know, normally, he endures chronic pain and takes medication for it—daily. So I propose, since we don't know much more, that you put codeine sulfate into his IV—thirty milligrams every four hours. It's certainly one thing we can do in an effort to stop Nurse McGuinness from being frightened."

Tiller wanted to say it wasn't only the change of the

body's positions that scared her and the other nurses (and him, too), it was grin on the face and the discoloration of the skin. But it wasn't professional to admit such things. Anyway, their conversation had already been long enough.

Beaumont went out the door.

Tiller went to Corporal Lumley and told him that Forsberg was going to be moved upstairs, that he should open a room up and get it ready.

Lumley, surprised, said, "May I ask why?"

The doctor responded, "Apparently he knows many government secrets. There's the fear he might say something when he regains consciousness. He doesn't want him on the main floor."

"But what about his leg, and the cast?"

"We'll being taking care of that tomorrow. It's getting late."

Lumley asked, "So the nurses will have to care for him up there?"

"There'll be an MP guard, around the clock, so they won't be alone."

"An MP?" he asked, stumped.

"They don't want just anybody talking to him when he comes to, that's all."

In Forsberg's room, Nurse McGuinness felt bad she was leaving Nurse Mildred Castillano—next on duty—to be in the middle of such a weird situation. But never was she so glad her shift was ending.

A few minutes after Tiller told Roger to prepare the room upstairs, he was sitting quietly in his office. Suddenly he heard a scream ring out. It was Nurse McGuinness' voice.

Tiller rushed to Forsberg's room. Once he was there she exclaimed, "The cast—it's split open! Wide open!"

CHAPTER 30

Lloyd Kelso and most everybody he knew were still at Chitose I, though there were a hundred or so experienced sergeants and corporals from the older base sent four miles down the road to Chitose II.

Kelso got on with his work as a file clerk at Major de Graff's Logistics; he was learning far more about mobilization planning and military logistics than he ever wanted to. Though Lloyd thought of it as just job, the work at de Graff's office piqued Ricky Travers' interest—or maybe he was faking his absorption—it was hard to tell—it could be he was just a brown noser. Travers' dedication to Logistics of course pleased Major de Graff. He thought to himself: if I ever have a son, I wouldn't mind him being like Ricky.

Lloyd continued working part-time as an MP. The work cut into his spare time, but it kept him in motion, which was good for his body and mind. When Captain Forsberg landed in the hospital after his accident, it made no particular impression on him. It didn't seem to affect anybody, really.

But he didn't stop thinking about Kiriko.

She was nowhere to be found. She wasn't working in a bar. He never once ran into her on the street. If he asked about her, he always inquired discreetly. No one had any idea what became of her.

He thought of the name "Kiriko," and the name "Kelso." They both began with a "K" and ended with an "o." Yep. "KO." For him, she was a real knock-out, but in a completely different way than a movie star in a magazine or a showgirl on stage.

He still thought about Bob and thought that Toshi most certainly had something to do with his buddy's death. Not having Fernandez around made life at night a little less exciting, but it wasn't long before he made friends with a soldier new to Chitose—though he wasn't a drinking buddy like Bob was.

He began to look at Japan with a more serious eye—that is to say, he read more about Japanese people and their culture, and when he went into town on the liberty bus, he would come in a little earlier, before he met his pals for drinks, and walk around town and take in the surroundings.

He never again went off the rails like he did in the bar in Sapporo that first night after MP training. Though he did have his moods. He could get upset with the limited things for sale at the Base Exchange—though there wasn't anything he really wanted to buy except beer, cigarettes, or a magazine. He found he was getting upset sometimes with being in buildings with low ceilings. They made him feel hemmed in, were bad for his state of mind—as bad as somebody like the baleful Toshi whom he still saw, but refused to speak to, when they both happened to be present at the bowling alley at the same time.

Despite the irritations and usual gripes that any underling in the army has, Lloyd's mental state was better than it'd been since he'd been drafted. It being peaceful summer helped. It almost buried the summer of combat he'd had in Korea.

Nichols and Velchoffsky continued all their work from their offices at Chitose I, although the MP force at Chitose II was under them. The satellite office there was operational. They rarely needed to go there.

At the same time, African American draftees arrived in Japan and in Chitose. They were no longer part of segregated Negro units. They were integrated into units that were to consist of men of any color and any creed.

Majors and sergeant majors were tasked with assigning

Black soldiers to units and giving them jobs if they were not in training exercises for combat, being readied for deployment in Korea. In general, there was a quota system. The guiding statistic was ten percent—ten percent of the infantry, Black; ten percent of admin, Black, etc.

Because Korea was a raging battlefield, like most draftees, Black conscripts were destined for the infantry there. However, like all inductees, the army gave them I.Q. and aptitude tests; from time to time, high scores on one or more tests could set them on a path that would spare them the hazards of war.

Black recruits who tested high were flagged just as any conscript was. There was a guy from Harlem who had just arrived in Chitose after basic training in the States; Logistics was adhering to regulations when it "claimed" him, thereby holding him back from being shipped off to fight in Korea.

It was because of his typing speed. Thomas Delbert averaged 140 words per minute. The Logistics Battalion was the first to see his service record and it grabbed him. He was assigned to the typing pool in the Quartermaster Department, a unit that was one of the most hard-pressed of the four branches under Logistics. Massive amounts of paperwork were generated and copied there.

Normally, when giving Black recruits office work, the job required no extra security clearance. There might be some confidential information—nothing secret or top secret given to Private Delbert to type—and he would be so busy that they rightly figured it would go straight into his head and right back out again without him caring or taking notice. They were right.

He never had to work much at typing. The skill came naturally to him. He was a thin, tallish kid with a dark brown oval face and a wide nose. One thing he saw right away was that his new job was going to be a grind; it wasn't going to be different than being confined to a chair for eight hours a day in a civilian office.

He was the only Black man in the typing pool. Similarly, he was the only Black man in the Quartermaster Department; for a few weeks he was the only such one working in Logistics.

A few weeks before Forsberg's accident, Lloyd, with a ton of paperwork in hand that had to do with the exciting world of troop mobilizations, walked over to the typing pool to hand off marked-up files to the guys there. As a sergeant was taking the paperwork from him, Lloyd noticed the new Black recruit among the typists.

Soon after that, in the mess hall, Lloyd saw Thomas sitting alone. The large cafeteria was packed but there were empty spaces near Thomas. Why would anybody sit next to him? He was Black—nobody else was. There might not have been anybody there who knew him from work—and if they did, they already had their friends who they preferred to sit with. He was a stranger who couldn't help but stick out in the crowd. Lloyd was there in the mess hall and there was nowhere else to sit but by Private Delbert.

Coming from the area in New York State where he did, he'd never, in his whole life, had a conversation of any considerable length with a Black person before.

"Mind if I sit down?" Lloyd asked, tray in hand with an eight-ounce carton of milk, a plate of meat loaf, mashed potatoes, and watery green beans on it.

"Nope," Thomas Delbert said casually.

The minute he took a seat, Lloyd thought it would be ridiculous to be shy and sit there, across from Thomas and not say a word to him. Thomas wasn't going to be the first to speak up. Life among Caucasians meant many things to him, one of them being, don't speak unless you're spoken to.

"The food doesn't look good, as usual," Lloyd said, adding, "You'll find that Chitose is no different from anywhere else, I guess."

Thomas continued to eat and didn't say anything. He'd just been talked at, that was all. He hadn't specifically been asked a question. But then Lloyd asked him politely, "Where are you from?"

"New York," Delbert answered.

"I'm from New York, too. Where in New York are you from?"

"New York City."

"I'm from New York State—Central New York. The sticks. I've been to New York City. I've seen three Broadway shows. My parents took me to them. I saw you in the typing pool. What's your name?"

"Thomas Delbert."

"Mine's Lloyd Kelso. Nice to meet you."

"Nice to meet you."

Delbert remembered Kelso coming over to the typing pool.

It was awkward in the beginning, with Delbert being suspicious of why Kelso wanted to talk to him. In between mouthfuls of food the details came out that Private Delbert's father worked as a doorman at one of the apartment buildings that Columbia University owned; these were residences for professors and their families. His family lived not far away, north of 125th Street, in Harlem.

Lloyd felt they had something in common since his father and mother ran an inn (a small restaurant only, not with rooms for overnight stays), in Clinton, New York; Clinton was home to Hamilton College and visiting parents and alumnae were the inn's customers.

Colleges provided these two young men's families with income. That's what they had in common.

"Here we are, neither one of us in college. If we'd gone in, we wouldn't be sitting here. The thing is, I didn't want to go. There wasn't anything there I wanted to do," Lloyd said.

"Me neither. At least not yet."

There were three choices upon turning eighteen: enroll in college and thereby get a deferment, enlist in one of the armed forces, or be drafted into the regular army.

"Well, we've paid the price for not knowing what we wanted to do," Lloyd said without a chuckle.

"You're right about that," Thomas quipped, knowing he was lucky to be born to type so fast.

Lloyd tried to have at least one meal a day with Thomas. He'd always been interested in knowing more about New York City, and here was a guy who grew up there. The young Black man confirmed Lloyd's image of New York City as being a great, exciting place. Aha, Lloyd thought, my mother was a hundred percent right with her stories. (Lloyd's parents both were in their mid-thirties when they married and had him and his sister. His mother had "runaway" to Manhattan way back in 1916 with a female friend after graduating from high school in Clinton. They were eventually lured back to Central New York after they were sent made-up stories about the ill health of a favorite aunt.)

The New York that Thomas talked about was obviously different than the city his mother fled to thirty-five years before. But it still was New York.

Kelso was fascinated to hear that Delbert's father knew jazz musicians; that their family was around all sorts of city people, and also some former students who stayed friends with a Columbia professor who lived in the apartment building where his dad worked. (The ex-students befriended his dad and bombarded him with questions about which musicians were the ones to go to see in town.)

In 1952, New York State was still the state with the largest population in the U.S. People in the state took pride in being Number One. While Lloyd and Thomas came from opposite directions in the state, Lloyd, at least, thought of the two of them as fellow Americans, but even more so as fellow New Yorkers—of a sort, because there was that division between The City and Upstate.

Lloyd asked Thomas if he might like to join as a part-time MP. He could try to get him in. Maybe they could serve together as a pair. Thomas said he didn't know if they'd let a

Negro have such a job. But his job as a typist bored him and felt like he was tied to a machine.

Lloyd summoned up the courage to go into Velchoffsky's office and ask him if there was a possibility of hiring Delbert.

Velchoffsky heard him out, then spoke with Nichols. A little later, he interviewed Thomas Delbert. After the interview, Velchoffsky quickly made up his mind: yes, the young man from Harlem is hired part-time. He will be seen and not heard. He'll be at a typewriter for us, that is all.

This was the not outcome Thomas or Lloyd had had in mind. They'd gotten too far ahead of the practicalities of implementing racial integration in the military.

CHAPTER 31

The room upstairs was of a comfortable size. High above where the two beds normally were (but in this case there was only one) were two overhead light bulbs, bare, unshaded, on insulated cords that bent from the ceiling.

A counter and drawers stretched along the wall behind the bed. A desk lamp was on top of it. A modest window four feet up from the floor on the wall away from the bed faced southeast. The wall blocked the lower path of the sun or the moon. There were always a few hours before sunshine (or moonlight) came directly in.

As Corporal Lumley was finishing arranging the room so Captain Forsberg could be moved there, Beaumont was in the military police building ordering a 24-hour guard of the patient. (Velchoffsky was in his quarters asleep. The next morning, back in the office, he unhappily found his unit's resources were going to be stretched even more.)

That evening a more-than-half moon appeared velvety, dimmed slightly by smog coming from town.

Beaumont left the MP station and drove his jeep to C2I. A small graveyard shift of a half dozen men were at their desks. He went into his office, closed the door and made an overseas phone call. There was a twelve-hour time zone difference. Dr. Ilmar Holdinar answered the telephone; it was just past noon, his local time. The two men spoke sometimes in code and used the word Grendel.

By sunrise, Forsberg's cast was in pieces. Tiller came to work later that morning. A nurse had already cleared the plaster fragments away. All that remained was the gauze bandage that had been under the cast. Tiller cut the gauze bandage away from the leg.

He probed the patient's leg, touching where he'd set it. To his astonishment, his hands felt that there'd never been a break in the bone. How could it be? On the morning they X-rayed him, it clearly showed one. When Forsberg was first admitted, and Tiller examined him, his hands had felt it. Now it wasn't there.

He was confused. There was no broken bone—and this had nothing to do with a cast (the plaster of which was faulty) spontaneously falling apart.

"This is incomprehensible," he said to himself.

The unsightly grin was still on the captain's face, his skin was still frightfully discolored.

Tiller directed his attention to the scalp wound. It still was bandaged. Perhaps the bandage could be taken off now. With scissors, he cut part of the bandage, lifted it, and looked. It in the area that was shaved, dark hair was growing back. The wound was scabbed over. It was dry. He removed the bandage—or rather, he didn't have to—it slipped off on its own accord.

Now, how could he explain the matter of the cast to the infirmary staff? He would say it's wartime, that manufacturing processes are rushed, so this happens sometimes. To explain the non-broken bone? Again, it's wartime, the X-ray film was damaged during shipping.

The doctor thought: five nights have passed with him under my care; he's still in a coma, but his head wound has healed, he seems to be tolerating the codeine; it's time to run a nasogastric tube down through his nose so he gets liquid food—an I.V. can't sustain him.

Beaumont stopped in that evening and Dr. Tiller took him upstairs to see Forsberg.

Beaumont was satisfied with the room and the guard outside it. He saw the food tube in Forsberg's nose. The doctor said with the tube in, the captain would no longer have to be watched by a nurse twenty four hours a day. Beaumont was happy to see both Dr. Tiller and Nurse Guinness on duty. He thought: how fortunate it is that the manifestations come out on the evening shift when these two are there—it means fewer people get to see the worst up close.

What Beaumont didn't know was Marcia Guinness had asked the other nurses four days ago if they might swap a shift now and then with her, but they all of them said no.

During the first half of her shift, whenever Nurse McGuinness had looked in on Forsberg, she saw no change in his condition or appearance. However, at 8 p.m., she thought she saw something she should speak to Dr. Tiller about. She hoped she wasn't overreacting, but she didn't want to risk not reporting something she ought to.

When she went downstairs she found her timing was off again. The doctor was at the Officers' Mess.

"It's been a long day for him. He came to work early," Lumley said, defending the doctor.

Roger was in a swivel chair in a room where medical records and various supplies were stored. His feet were up on the one desk there. He was reading a paperback. Like many nights, there wasn't anything for him to do.

Though Tiller would be back soon, she urgently felt that someone else should look at Forsberg right at that moment. She needed to know if she was seeing something of concern.

She asked Corporal Lumley to go up to the room with her and have a look.

He gladly put down his book and went upstairs with her.

Once they were in Forsberg's room McGuinness whispered, "Look at his hands."

The orderly looked and she asked, "What do you think?"

"I don't know. What am I supposed to think?"

"Do you think the skin on them is getting more color?"

"I don't know. I never looked close before."

"But look at them. Compare the skin tone to that of the skin on his face."

"Well, that's easy. His face is splotchy. It has been since he got here. I can hardly look at it."

"Yeah, I know. But what I'm saying is…Well, and do you see…hairs have… um… sprouted up."

Lumley decided to poke fun at her. "Probably this has been going on for a while. You just didn't notice."

"But I *have* been looking," she said defensively.

"Well, it is difficult to look at him. Naturally, you want to look away. I think you can be looking but not seeing—if you know what I mean. I've done that with certain patients who are uncomfortable to look at."

She said impatiently, "I could have sworn that earlier tonight there was no hair there. It's new hair. It's rapid hair."

"Wait for the doctor. See what he says."

The nurse stood her ground, nervously. "There's more hair there now. There just is."

Lumley didn't mean to tease her, but his voice sounded like he was, "So there's more hair there now than there was five minutes ago?"

Fright swept across the nurse's face. She answered, "Yes, I think so."

"We'll go down and wait for the doctor to come back," Lumley said calmly.

When Tiller got back, he went upstairs with the nurse to Forsberg's room to have a look. He told her: "I'm not sure. It is possible to not notice things even if you're looking. We just might not have noticed hair was there before."

She'd still hadn't gotten over his cast breaking. Now this, the apparent growth of hair—and abnormally fast.

When she came in on her 10 p.m. round her glance drifted from the I.V. stand and over to Forsberg's arm. She noticed a patch of hair growing on his forearm that she hadn't seen before. The texture of skin was different as well—it looked tougher. Her eyes then darted quickly over to his chest. She saw it rise and fall with each breath—but his breathing was heavier than she ever remembered it had been.

She thought to herself: why am I noticing things now, but not earlier? She looked his left forearm and then his right one. The pores of the skin of both arms seemed darker, like dirt had collected in them. It seemed the patches of hair on both arms had widened—plus, the hairs had differing colors—some were dark brown, some black, some even white. The patches had spread to places on the arm where there is normally little or no hair.

She thought to herself, yes, usually I don't let my eyes stay on him long. I turn away as fast as I can. I know I'm supposed to look after him, but...

Then she noticed the pigment in his lips had blackened and his horrid grin had widened. Now you could see the color of his gums had vaguely brightened.

No, this was a new development. It definitely wasn't like this before. She shuddered. She left quickly to get the doctor again, carefully closing the door to the room so the MP guard could not get a glimpse into it.

A couple of minutes later Dr. Tiller, walking briskly in front of her, went in.

By now, the hair had spread to the inside of the captain's wrists. It covered the top of his hands profusely, and, with his hands resting by his side as they were, it was possible to see follicles had formed in his palms and short thin hairs grew from them.

Tiller moved his eyes to Forsberg's face; its flesh had acquired hair that didn't belong there; completely out-of-place tiny hairs grew on the back of the captain's ears.

What is this about the captain's hair? He remembered, after the cast had broken in pieces, noticing how fast the hair on Forsberg's head had grown back after having been shaved to treat the wound there.

Tiller could smell Nurse McGuinness's sweat. He sent her out of the room and told her he wanted to examine the captain on his own. He then looked at Forsberg's eyes which were half open (They weren't like that before, he thought). He believed he could see in each eye a yellow iris, and a black, not cloud-white sclera. The shape of the captain's eyes had changed. The edges of his eyebrows nearest his temples were raised, and below them, his eye sockets turned upward as well, giving his eyes an almond shape, as the shape that one sees with wolves' eyes.

Thoughts in his mind sped back to medical school and the thousands of pages he read so that he might acquire an encyclopedic knowledge of medicine.

He went back to his office to look at his books.

A mere ten minutes passed, and he was at the nurses' station telling Marcia Guinness, "Hypertrichosis." He sounded definitive. He explained quickly it was a condition where there is an abnormal amount of hair growth over the body. His words did calm her some, because having a diagnosis—even if it turns out to be wrong—is far, far better than having none at all.

"Underlying conditions can be involved. It can develop as a result of malnutrition, for example—I think that's the case here."

"But it's happened so fast, doctor." She didn't only mean the hypertrichosis, but also the cast breaking into pieces. She should not question the doctor's diagnosis, so she said no more than that.

"We *think* it happened fast, but sometimes we're mistaken. And once it appears… it says it can take days to clear.

He thought of the belt restraints fastened to the side rails of Forsberg's bed and said without emotion, "The patient isn't going anywhere soon…please, go and take a break. Go out for a moment and get some fresh air, if you like."

She left the nurses' station and went outside the back of the infirmary, where there was nothing but a small lot and some garbage cans.

Tiller went back up to Forsberg's room. The MP guard there was a short, thin man with glasses. He looked like he was on edge. Tiller thought to himself: that soldier looks like takes amphetamines.

Once inside the room, Tiller reached over and lifted the sheet that covered Forsberg. The captain was in the usual short cotton hospital gown. He saw that Forsberg's thighs, legs and feet were covered with a surplus of hair. He noticed that Forsberg's fingernails had turned yellow. Now *that,* he said to himself, is not part of hypertrichosis.

What a strange condition, he thought. The captain looks like he'd be welcome in a carnival sideshow.

As Beaumont had directed Tiller to contact him if something noteworthy about Forsberg's condition occurred, Tiller telephoned the major. It was fortunate for Beaumont that he was still in his office.

He hurried over to the infirmary.

Tiller told him it appeared Forsberg had a condition called *acquired hypertrichosis*—though he displayed other symptoms not normally associated with that condition. However, he, the doctor, was going to look more into the treatment of the condition, and causes of it, and he would initiate therapy when he felt sufficiently informed.

Beaumont thought to himself: this is good, Tiller's thinking within the confines of his professional training. He's staying within the system; when he needs to tell his staff anything, it'll be based in known medical experience and practice. This could keep people's minds from wandering.

Tiller told Beaumont Forsberg's hairy appearance had to be dealt with because those who were providing him with care would find it repellent. They wouldn't want to get close to him, let alone assist in the hygiene he required.

Beaumont asked, "What's your opinion on how to proceed?"

"Remove the hair."

"How?"

"Cut it, shave it. Surgical nurses routinely remove hair in the area where there's to be incisions."

"Do you have a surgical nurse?"

"We do have a surgical nurse on staff, Barbara Gregg. But there's hair all over his body. It's a unique situation and I'm reluctant to ask her. I've had the impression lately that she wants to quit—it's because she's homesick—it's a challenge for her to stay, poor girl. I wouldn't want this to be the final straw for her."

"What if I do it?"

"You?"

"Yes."

"You don't have any medical training."

"This case is secret." The major paused, then said, "Look, I've been on farms. I know how sheep are sheared. My grandmother had a long-haired dog. I saw how she groomed it. I'm… a man who shaves every day. I'm not uncomfortable with clipping hair. If I do it, it saves you a lot of trouble." There was no answer from the doctor. Beaumont went on, "I insist, I'll do it. I'll come over right now."

Tiller was speechless, except to say, "All right."

"One other thing," the major added, "Increase the dosage of codeine sulfate into his I.V. to sixty milligrams every four hours, at once." Inwardly the major reproached himself. He should have told the doctor to give Forsberg that amount to start with.

"Why?"

"Do it, please, right now. It's an order, doctor. From our superiors."

Beaumont excused himself and said he was going to get a drink from the water fountain.

Tiller asked himself: but isn't the hair still growing? Then he answered his own question by thinking: any positive advance is useful.

As for the increase in codeine dosage, his mind went back to a conversation he had in the infirmary, in Dr. Kalin's office, the day after Forsberg's cast broke into pieces and Beaumont prevailed upon him to give the captain codeine immediately.

"I was told last night that you had Captain Gideon Forsberg on daily codeine, for chronic pain."

"War injury-caused, yeah. There was blunt trauma. Nerve damage in the groin. Had a splenectomy," Kalin said collegiately. Kalin was both a G.P. and a specialist in internal medicine. "He still has shooting pains. No point in severing nerves—his feet would feel like they don't properly touch the ground; it would make it strange for him to walk."

"So he takes it every day?"

"Yes, anywhere between 180 and 360 milligrams per day. It depends on how much pain he's feeling."

"There's no non-opiate analgesic that doesn't alleviate the pain?"

"No, according to his records, and statements by previous doctors, codeine sulfate is the only thing that works for him"

Dr. Tiller raised his voice in exclamation, "I don't believe I could walk or think with 360 milligrams of it in my system every day."

Kalin responded, "Yes, but you're not getting the energy—if you want to call it that—from daily acute pain. It's a state I know I'd never want to be in." Kalin, at age forty-five, had been a doctor longer than Tiller.

Tiller then asked Kalin if he knew anything about Forsberg that wasn't noted on his medical record. "No," Kalin replied, simply.

Concerning the task of removing the captain's the excess hair, Beaumont was stoic. He felt it was good he could be there and save someone else from a traumatic experience. He at least knew what he was dealing with.

With scissors and an electric clipper, he hurried to finish the shearing before midnight, when the next shift would come on. It turned out to be impossible to finish before

12:45; the work shift change was delayed until then.

That night, before going to bed, Marcia prayed to God, imploring Him to see her through this job with its mysterious patient Forsberg. She asked Him to help preserve her sanity, and also asked that He let the captain recover fully. Marcia was brought up in the Catholic Church. She was a believer— though not a strict type—she believed there were modern factors to consider.

The next day after reading all the information he could find, Tiller devised a therapeutic strategy. He read that hypertrichosis could be the result of insufficient nutrition. He decided to add more protein, vitamins, and food of higher caloric value into Forsberg's feeding tube. "Amino Acid Requirements of Man," had been published the previous year. He let that scientific article guide him in creating a dietary regimen.

He also read that the unsightly condition could occur because of sensitivity to light. The doctor didn't want to darken Forsberg's room any more than keeping the main overhead lights switched off (the patient needed to be observed; there needed to be enough light to care for him and to write on his chart). Natural light would come in through the single window.

Tiller was pleasantly surprised. The patient responded well to the nutritional regimen. There was nearly instantaneous remission of the hypertrichosis, as well as the manifestations of morose bestiality in the captain's lips, gums, eyes and fingernails. He attributed these improvements to his self-devised treatment, i.e., the nutritional ingredients added into the feeding tube.

Tiller didn't make the connection that the excess hair growth and other manifestations started going away *before* Forsberg's body could metabolize the new nutrients, that his symptoms lessened with the increase of codeine in his body.

The doctor didn't believe the codeine sulfate had any rehabilitative effect. It was required as maintenance, he thought, because of Forsberg's preexisting daily use of it; he had a tolerance of it, a dependency on it; it needed to be kept up.

For three whole days the staff of the hospital had time to try to put Forsberg's bizarre symptoms behind them—though clearly, some of the symptoms Tiller connected to hypertrichosis weren't consistent with that condition.

Disappointingly, four nights after the flare up of hypertrichosis, with the distant moon's face still growing fuller outside the window to the right of the bed, new, unusual symptoms appeared in the comatose patient.

They were first noticed in his arms, which were uncovered, as usual (there was always an I.V. line in one of them, and the other rested and aired, after its previous duty, for several days, as the I.V. arm).

It occurred to Nurse McGuinness that this evening, there was something different about Forsberg's forearms and biceps.

She slipped out of the room, passed the armed MP guard posted outside, and went downstairs to Dr. Tiller's office.

"I just noticed, doctor, that Captain Forsberg seems to be putting on weight—or should I say, putting on muscle."

He smiled and said back to McGuinness, "Good, it means that his body is metabolizing the nutrients with efficiency."

"But building muscle without any exercise—is that possible?"

The doctor paused and then explained, "It's true we could be regularly massaging him and flexing his limbs. But I'm not allowing the staff to do that because of potential complications arising from his having had a concussion."

He didn't answer the nurse's question.

She and others who cared for Forsberg had to cope with not asking questions. Questions like, shouldn't he be under the care of specialists at another facility after his hypertrichosis scared everyone so much? (You couldn't blame the staff for wanting to avoid touching him.)

Tiller could see the frustration on the nurse's face. He said, "I'll go up to his room with you."

Her shoes were noiseless as they mounted the stairs to the infirmary's upper level. They got to the corridor… yes, it had a strange air to it, because the whole floor served only one patient—the captain.

McGuinness had only been out of the room for five minutes, but when she and the doctor came back, there wasn't time to examine Forsberg's arms to judge the muscle mass.

His body had shifted position: his back was arched; his chest was constricted. He wasn't breathing. His eyelids were almost closed. Underneath them his eyes fluttered. The doctor thought: Forsberg has a head injury. There's a lesion in his brain.

"He's in the middle of a convulsion!" he declared. He should pull the nasogastric feeding tube from the captain's nose. No, he corrected his thought, if I do that, his tongue might settle in back, and he wouldn't be able to breathe.

McGuinness needed instructions. "Quick, go downstairs. Get a needle, syringe, and phenobarbital. There's no time to put it in the I.V. It's all I can think of giving him right now," he said, almost shouting.

She hurried out of the room.

The doctor then heard a soft groan come from the captain's chest, and the body shook for an endless ten seconds, during which Forsberg tried to raise his arms, as if to get at him and strangle him.

Soon after the sound and the violent motions, Forsberg's body slackened. In less than a minute his back no longer was straining to push his chest upward. His regular breathing, though light, returned. His eyes ceased all rapid movements—these were positive signs. The doctor could only hope the neuronal activity that'd triggered the seizure had ebbed.

McGuinness came back, put the needle on the syringe.

Her hands shook, the doctor noticed. The underarms of her white uniform were moist with perspiration. After opening an ampul of phenobarbital, once she'd drawn up the plunger and brought the drug into the syringe, Dr. Tiller grabbed it from her to save her the trouble of having to touch Forsberg and inject him.

As he pushed the plunger down, he spoke calmly, "Would you please go downstairs again? I'd like you to bring me back some wrist restraints, as well as some mitts."

The doctor wasn't about to tell the nurse that Forsberg had a made a sound while she was away, and his body had moved spasmodically, even threateningly (the last couldn't have been the case, realistically, since he was unconscious) —it would only frighten her.

The wrist straps and mitts restraints he referred to were common supplemental restraints, used in addition to bed restraints attached to bed side rails; they prevented a patient from interfering with catheters, tubes, needles and other therapeutic gear, as well as unfastening the bed restraints themselves. The nurse knew what they were for. Forsberg was going to be fastened even more. This was good but it frightened her that such measures needed to be taken at all.

While Tiller was waiting for Marcia to come back with the items he requested, he glanced at the captain's arms and inwardly agreed with the nurse—yes, inexplicably, without exercise—but with more than adequate nutrition—his muscle mass had increased.

Tiller moved his hand under the bedsheet and lifted it to have a look at Forsberg's legs. They, too, displayed considerable development of muscle mass. He didn't know, but would have liked to know of any new medical articles that addressed a radical increase of muscle after an intensive nutritional therapy inspired by "Amino Acid Requirements of Man." Hm, he thought, this case of muscle growth with Forsberg might be something to write to the article's author, William Cumming Rose, about—clearly, the effect of the essential amino acids on Forsberg's musculature was extraordinary.

According to Rose's article, one could expect metabolic benefits to the patient's vital tissues and organs—the skin, brain, heart, and liver all would be helped. But rapid muscle growth?—that was intriguing.

When McGuinness brought in the additional restraints her face was white—not quite as white as her starched uniform, but it was getting there.

A few minutes later she was in a state of shock. The captain's condition was nightmarish. It was unbearable. She pictured herself standing on a lake shore or seashore on a summer day. She was in the county she grew up in. People were out in the water on a floating dock, sunning themselves on it and jumping from it into the water. She thought: my friends are out there and I'm going to swim out and join them. Once I'm there I'll be in a place where nobody can hurt me. I'm jumping in now. I'm swimming, I feel the cool water and splashing all around me.

In line with the command by Major Beaumont that his office be informed at once regarding any change in Forsberg's condition, the doctor called CI2. He couldn't phone sooner…he'd been too busy with the patient's treatment.

As it turned out, Beaumont was again in his office, working late into the night.

He came right over.

Tiller told him the captain had had a seizure; damage to the brain after being thrown from his jeep most likely caused the convulsions. He'd treated the patient with phenobarbital. Tiller hadn't decided yet how long to keep the captain on that drug.

That night before going to bed, knowing the person he wished to speak to on the phone couldn't be reached (because the professor was at that moment teaching in a classroom) Beaumont called the switchboard and read a terse telegram message out to the operator. It read: "A visit to Chitose is in order. You know who's best." The recipient of the telegram was Dr. Ilmar Hodinar, Washington D.C.

Early the next morning Major Beaumont phoned Major de Graff at his office. Beaumont had decided the commander of Logistics needed to be brought into the loop. More than the medical staff needed to be involved with Forsberg—much more. Dr. Tiller had served his purpose, but it was time for him—Beaumont—to take over.

Separately, the two majors each drove their jeeps out to a spot of hard mud ground next to Chitose River.

Beaumont showed de Graff the way. They took a path that local anglers used. It headed upriver. At this time of day, on a weekday, no one was around to hear them speak. Beaumont didn't tell de Graff that a third person would soon be joining them.

Tim wanted to get to the top secret matter right away. But there was a hurdle—the concept and the reality of Forsberg's condition. Of course, de Graff knew nothing about it. The hurdle needed to be cleared—and that was asking a lot.

They both wore light brown khaki uniforms. From a distance the two of them appeared to be identical, though Beaumont's hair was reddish and de Graff's was dark. The path wasn't wide enough for the two of them to walk side by side, Beaumont led the way; he gently craned his neck back when he had to speak.

"I asked you to come out here because I didn't want us to be seen together, if possible, for any extended time."

They walked. He kept talking.

"I'm going tell you something that sounds extraordinary. You can dismiss it on a commonsense level as something that's not possible. I understand that. I admit it sounds as crazy as UFOs."

Beaumont had to turn his head to look in front of him as he walked. After he could see where he was going, he turned back to de Graff and continued, "There's something called Operation Grendel and it's come to Chitose. Things will be happening over the next few weeks—and possibly months. It has to do with Captain Forsberg. As you know, he's in the infirmary, in a coma."

As Major de Graff tramped behind Beaumont in the morning sun, he knew that no response was expected of him. As for if anybody had spotted them, it could be thought they were on a break—admittedly unusual for this time of day, but nevertheless—and they were hiking near the creek, probably looking over places where they might go fly fishing later.

They walked a couple of minutes and a third man, coming from around a corner (there was a slight bend in the river and the path) abruptly appeared. Beaumont knew he'd be there. De Graff didn't and was surprised.

It was Captain Jake Torrington, walking toward them. He was in civilian clothes, brown slacks, a beige, long-sleeved linen shirt with pockets over each breast.

Major Beaumont glanced back at Major de Graff long enough to say, "Jake has been involved for some time. He even moved into the Quonset where Forsberg lives, but of course, the bird flew from there and landed in the hospital."

Torrington wanted to salute the two officers but knew he ought not to make a show. As he got closer Beaumont stepped out of the way to give de Graff room enough to shake Torrington's hand. The captain seemed nervous. Jake lowered his head slightly as they shook—a sign of respect—and said softly in greeting, "Major."

"Hello, Jake," de Graff said.

Beaumont said, "Jake was the right man to tell at the right time. Now, you are."

The two senior officers didn't notice, but Jake blanched at those words.

De Graff's response was a simple, "All right."

"I've just mentioned Operation Grendel," Tim

Beaumont said gravely to Jake, "to our new member."

De Graff still didn't know anything more than the name of the operation.

"First, Chris: there will be orders, paperwork. You both will sign paper that comes from me and sorry, there'll be no questions asked. I guarantee you, there're not enough answers to suffice. The orders'll concern Forsberg. Some will be unusual. They could give rise to talk about what exactly is the condition he's in, or even why I'm doing what I'm doing—and who am I to do it. I need such talk tamped down if it occurs."

Beaumont looked at the path ahead of them. A dwarf willow was just off to the side. Chitose River was behind the tall green reeds now. He decided they should remain where they were so he didn't move. He continued, "I'll be bringing new personnel into Chitose. For now, just one man. From Washington. I need your cooperation. Do either of you have any questions?"

Chris de Graff said, "Well, it's a top secret operation. I'm listening."

Torrington said to Tim, "If Major de Graff has questions for me, how much should I tell him?"

Major Beaumont replied, "Answer all the questions he asks you."

Beaumont then turned to Chris, "I caution you that any question you might put to Jake could result in a lengthy discussion with him. With all respect to both of you, I don't believe you don't have time for that."

Chris de Graff said to Tim Beaumont, "What can I say?— I'm sure you've thought this through."

Beaumont said, "Thank you, Chris, for your support."

De Graff responded, "I'll do all I can. Just let me know what you need."

Beaumont glanced downward. He saw iron-strong mahogany-colored vines. He raised his head and said, "Forsberg's in a room on the upstairs floor of the infirmary.

Away from the everyone in the facility. There's an armed MP guard on duty outside his room. Last night, as well as four nights ago, there were complications to his condition. I'm not going to go into them now. We need to provide one story, one explanation—if rumors start. The story is that he's in a coma. He knows a lot of government secrets and has to be isolated until he fully recovers. I'm flying in a medical specialist. He's an expert on Forsberg's condition."

That was the extent of the conversation—the ad hoc meeting that Beaumont had called was over.

Back at the base, Major Beaumont had a telephone installed in his quarters so he could be phoned directly by the infirmary when he was not in the office.

The evening, creatures stirred a little more than usual on base, in town, on farms and in the rising hills and mountains to the west of Chitose. The moon's plate, lucent and seemingly pasted in the afar, yet moving, so slowly, was almost round.

Forsberg could not be counted among the busy and sometimes agitated creatures of that night. He displayed no appreciable activity, yet his highly nutritious liquid diet was at work in parts of his body unseen.

The evening after a twenty-four-hour period of no unusual incidents, after Forsberg had been fed, his nasogastric tube was removed to give the mucosa of his nose, throat and esophagus a rest from being irritated.

Nurse McGuinness last looked in on the captain at 11:20 p.m. Throughout the evening she'd been marking time, keen to leave. It was now 11:40—the final time she'd have to check in on him that night; after that, her shift would be over.

Stepping noiselessly closer to the room, she heard disturbing sounds coming from inside.

It was unusual that the guard was not outside his door. Normally, if the soldier ever needed to use the washroom, for example, he always made sure that the nurse or an orderly was notified, and he'd head across the hallway to a room where there was a toilet.

When McGuinness crossed the threshold of the unguarded room she saw Forsberg's back bucking up. His body was thrashing. The MP on duty (tonight was his first time—he was a young African American G.I.—until now all the guards had been White) had rushed into the sick room, after hearing something inside and perceiving it to be trouble.

Forsberg was straining with superhuman effort at the straps that limited his motions. Underneath his half-closed eyelids, his eyes fluttered. His mouth opened again and again, quickly snapping shut each time afterward.

The guard thought the captain might try to bite through his restraints, so he put the steel outer barrel of his Colt M1911 service pistol crossways into the captain's mouth. He then pinned him down, putting one hand on the captain's left leg and the other on his chest.

There was little light in the room, but the nurse thought she could see excess hair again had sprung up on Forsberg's arms and face.

McGuinness couldn't help but scream when she saw it.

The MP yelled to her, "Get help! Get the doctor!"

Would the medical restraints hold? That was a question she felt burning through the whole infirmary itself.

She pivoted on her heals, slammed the door behind her, and rushed downstairs.

Dr. Tiller sent Corporal Lumley running upstairs. Roger grasped a Colt M1911. The pistol was a semi-automatic, it had seven bullets. It wasn't his, personally. There weren't many of them in the infirmary, but he'd found one.

Strange. There should be no call for guns. The patient was, after all, in a coma.

Lumley only stood and looked. He felt he couldn't do anything right at that moment. With the restraints still holding, and the guard pressing down on Forsberg's body, if he were to touch the patient he would only be getting in the way.

After a minute, Nurse McGuinness reappeared. Dr. Tiller had just unwittingly made the most brilliant decision of his career: he sent her back upstairs to the room with a syringe filled with fifteen milligrams of morphine sulfate. She instructed Lumley and the MP to pin Forsberg's shoulder as she injected the drug into the first vein she could find.

In two minutes, the positive effect took hold. Forsberg's back relaxed against the bed.

The MP took his pistol out of the captain's mouth. The jeering, ghastly grin fixed itself once more on the captain's hairy and dark face.

Downstairs, the doctor phoned Beaumont in his quarters. The major was in bed. He listened to the doctor's angry voice. Tiller had had it with being left out of the discussions concerning Forsberg's true condition and his treatment. This was an outrageous emergency, he said.

Beaumont then said, "Good. You've given him morphine. But now give him Thorazine."

"What?" asked the doctor incredulously.

"A whole ampul. Twenty-five milligrams."

"Do you know what you're saying?"

"I've been in touch with a specialist. This is the next step."

"But the man is in a coma. Thorazine is an anti-psychotic medicine!"

"I'm aware of that."

"You don't give a comatose patient an anti-psychotic. It just isn't done. It isn't necessary."

"In this case, give it to him. You don't want him breaking his restraints."

At this, Tiller blew his top. "What the hell is going on? You're telling me to throw half the pharmacopoeia at this patient while you're keeping his medical history secret. You know, it's not just me. The staff here is ready to mutiny. The army always talks about morale and keeping it up. There's a serious problem here, and it's not only with Captain Forsberg."

"Sorry, doctor. I'm sorry. I really am. Help is on its way… soon. That's all I can say except give him morphine and Thorazine as needed. Don't worry. This will be stabilized."

CHAPTER 32

Professor Ilmar Hodinar steered his gray 1949 Studebaker Champion out of the front gate of McNair and swung onto Potomac Avenue. He'd rolled his window down. It was a balmy July morning.

He took a quick left and went up to M Street. The street was broad and glorious. To his right, the whole length of the Navy Yard glided by. Its beautiful Latrobe Gate, smaller, but whiter than the White House, glistened as he passed it. He took M Street all the way to the Anacostia River. Then he turned right onto Pennsylvania Avenue, drove over the long and straight paved steel plate named John Philip Sousa Bridge. The wide, shallow river, whisked by, forty feet below him.

An Eastern European Jew who had doctorate degrees from two countries and spoke eight languages, he'd been employed by the U.S. Army for the last ten years. Early on in his career, his expertise in the psychological operations that the Nazis used had gained him the respect of Allied top brass at Supreme Headquarters Allied Expeditionary Force (SHAEF) in Teddington, England. After the war he worked for the army in the Allied Military Government in Germany; he helped design their denazification programs.

His car sailed through sprawling suburban land. On both sides of the road were big lawns, tall trees, generously distanced side streets and no business establishments. He went north on Minnesota Avenue. It was a windless day. Many people seemed to be out of town. It was the season for vacations.

He left Minnesota Avenue and continued north on Kenilworth. He got on the newly constructed Baltimore-Washington Parkway.

An each side of the four-lane parkway there was forest—thick with Eastern Seaboard hickory, beech, maple, oak and ash. The dew had evaporated. Bark and leaf scents were in the air.

Driving on this commodious swath cut through woodlands made you think you were in a national park—and it was true the National Park Service maintained the road, and no commercial vehicles were allowed on it. You were in paradisical corridor through Nature; it surrounded you all at once, but at the same time you were speeding along in a machine as if you were ridiculing it. Man had perhaps too much power to be setting things up like this.

A flock of warblers rushed overhead and then he passed the New Carrollton exit. His thoughts went back to the meeting he was at a year ago, at military intelligence at Fort Meade.

Then, the war in Korea had reached another critical point. There were atrocities, grisly deaths of civilians; the battlefields were lakes of gore.

At that time, the Chinese communists launched a huge offensive. The intent was to drive the UN Command Forces, many of which were American army, from the Korean peninsula. Military intelligence believed that the Chinese were overplaying their hand, that they'd already overextended themselves a few months before. The U.S. Eighth Army hit the Chinese army hard, inflicting significant losses, proving that the all-out attack was flawed and couldn't hold up. The enemy was forced to retreat to northern battle lines.

The UN Forces reestablished the Jamestown Line of defense and Seoul was back under UN control. Heavy fighting continued. There were no negotiations; the Chinese were not giving up. At the small meeting that previous July, Hodinar and five others from "The Frankfurt School," as Hodinar had dubbed the group, it was decided that Forsberg would be transferred to Korea so he could be possibly used as weapon. The American forces were not going to drop an atomic bomb on Korea. While that was mentioned, it was always realistically out of the question.

Yes, Forsberg was another possible form of weaponry. However, what wasn't clear—and as discussed in all previous meetings—was how to use him effectively. They still had no specific plan regarding that. It was thought something unforeseeable might likely inspire an effective use for him.

After Forsberg was transferred to Korea, he'd held his lycanthropy *mostly* in check. There was at least one occasion that Hodinar and his colleagues knew about where Forsberg transformed and an American army officer by the name of Charles Beswick was killed and mutilated.

Nine months into Captain Forsberg's assignment to Korea, The Frankfurt School had to move him; they changed his assignment: unit commander, MP Unit, Chitose, Japan— an army base that was peaceful, yet not too far away from the action in Korea. If he was needed back in Korea, he could be flown in.

The emergency meeting was being held at the U.S. Army Intelligence Agency, Fort Meade, Maryland. Professor Hodinar of ICAF (Industrial College of the Armed Forces) in Fort McNair, Washington, D.C., would be in attendance—he, of all people, was the one who needed most to be there. He wouldn't be teaching his 10 a.m. class today, and he might not be able to get back to the college in time for his 2 p.m. class either. It was an hour's drive from McNair to Meade.

He was now twenty minutes away from Fort Meade. The sun's radiant heat was laying into his Studebaker's roof, but gusts of air rushed in from his open windows to keep him road-alert. However, the alertness was also a day-dreamy kind.

His mind went back to the first-ever meeting of what was now called "The Frankfurt School." He gave the group at that meeting that name, using a name that was already that of a group of famous German sociologists and intellectuals who were active in Frankfurt, Germany in the 1930s. If anyone were ever to overhear someone speaking about this new "Frankfurt School," they wouldn't know it was a small group of army officers in Intelligence who had secretly taken it upon themselves to deal with the phenomenon that Gideon Forsberg was.

That first meeting was held in March, 1947 in a small conference room in the IG Farben Building (the U.S. Army acquisitioned it at the end of World War II) in Frankfurt, Germany. Those at the meeting either served in, or in some way were connected to, the 970th Counter-Intelligence Corps Detachment in Allied-occupied Germany.

Lieutenant Colonel Paul Scotto, commander of the 970th, chaired the meeting. He did not personally know Gideon Forsberg and had never met him, neither had Sergeant Major Wilson Simmons, the non-commissioned officer that assisted him and who was also at the meeting. The two men had been in the army over twenty-five years, were career officers in their late forties, as was Major David K. Mullins.

It was with Major Mullins that the connection to Gideon Forsberg became closer. Mullins' role in the 970th CIC was to supervise the men that undertook the huge task of microfilming pertinent official documents in defeated Germany. It was a young officer under him, First Lieutenant Walter Beutel, a German American—complexion not fair, eyes and hair dark, skin almost tan, fluent in German—who had requested a meeting with Major Mullins in a secure room (a room they were certain the Russians hadn't bugged) in the IG Farben building.

It was during their conversation that Lieutenant Beutel laid out everything he knew about Forsberg and his "illness".

Unsurprisingly, Major Mullins didn't believe Beutel at first.

Beutel reported in great detail the conditions of the corpses of the murder victims. Their wounds suggested that a violent animal had killed them, but careful inspection of the murder scenes indicated only a man could have been there and slaughtered them.

There was also a case where a German victim had survived and who had *seen* Forsberg in his werewolf shape. Lieutenant Beutel had interviewed the survivor; she gave him the details and said she would never speak of the attack ever again to anyone. Her mental health wouldn't permit it, she said.

Forsberg did not know Beutel, and Beutel was able to work behind his back.

Beutel discovered that Gideon was struggling to control his lycanthropy by using opiates, that he'd been permanently injured in combat.

Beutel had the idea that the army might in the future somehow be able to put Forsberg to use in some unique way. By the time the lieutenant had finished his one-to-one meeting with Major Mullins (which lasted ninety minutes), the major agreed with Beutel that something needed to be done with Forsberg—and it wasn't to arrest him for murder.

With Beutel and Professor Hodinar at the meeting, there were five Army Intelligence personnel—uniformed men, serious, almost faceless—at the latter-day Frankfurt School's meeting.

There was a sixth person present, though, as well. He'd been included in the meeting at the request of Lieutenant Colonel Scotto. He was a 970th CIC captain assigned to the Allied Military Government and had never crossed paths with Forsberg, though he might some day in the future, since he traveled a lot as part of his AMG assignment. A French and German speaker, this captain, named Beaumont, landed days after D-Day, interrogated captured Nazis and collaborators, and liaised with French locals. During the past two years he worked implementing de-Nazification programs that Dr. Hodinar had designed.

Paul Scotto had watched Beaumont for almost a year; he was impressed by his even-handedness and his shrewdness—and he took note of Beaumont's family connections to Europe. They both were West Point graduates, though Scotto was five years his senior and they'd never met there. Scotto, the son of Italian immigrants (their region in Italy was badly afflicted by malaria and they left, aiming to get as far away from it as they could) wanted a worldly, smart man of experience at this meeting—and somebody outside the chain of command of the microfilming unit—as an impartial, witness and assessor of the situation to be discussed. It was a plus that the captain, Timothy Beaumont, had been working alongside Dr. Hodinar in the Allied Military Government for the last several months and had gotten to know him—*and* that they worked well together—they might be working together for years, on and off, he surmised.

When that first meeting occurred, Dr. Hodinar had already had several private meetings with First Lieutenant Beutel—Paul Scotto and David Mullins had insisted on those meetings. They wanted Dr. Hodinar to know as much about this young sergeant Gideon Forsberg as he could tell them.

The lieutenant colonel sat at the head of the oval conference table.

> LIEUTENANT COLONEL PAUL SCOTTO: My view on the supernatural is that it doesn't exist. We've all had to challenge such views, and we're probably not entirely past the challenge yet. That's why I, in conference with Major Mullins and Sergeant Major Simmons, have invited Dr. Hodinar into our circle. One of the first things I'd like him to do is give us all a pep talk—that is, I think, a good word to use. We need to combine the inexplicable with logic, and make our plans from there.

I don't blame myself or you for being skeptical and dismissive. I first was, so too was Major Mullins. The sergeant major was, as well. I assume that Captain Beaumont, who is new to these discussions, is still having a hard time with the idea that Sergeant Gideon Forsberg turns into a werewolf and commits multiple homicides.

In my army career, keeping an open mind has been of great benefit to me, and I dare say others. I'm glad that First Lieutenant Beutel went to Major Mullins, who then came to me. If Lieutenant Beutel might have had a different superior officer than the major, Lord knows what would be happening now.

I'm now going to ask Dr. Hodinar to challenge our minds and convince us that there's a phenomenon… It is… powerful. It is… unbelievable—yet we must believe.

DR. ILMAR HODINAR: *(Animated; not nervous.)* Where to start? Yes, that's the thing. Where we've been has been in the dark. We must admit that. You would like answers, not questions, from me. I have answers that make sense to me. They aren't going to be ones that you're expecting. This matter is unexpected. The unexpected things I will say fit hand-in-glove with the extraordinary phenomena we're faced with.

My explication will likely seem strange to you. But we're talking about a strange matter, aren't we? What I say might *seem* disconnected or even irrelevant to the man-wolf, as it exists here, in our present day, and carries out violent murders. However, I foresee that what I say will contribute to your acceptance of Forsberg being a werewolf. Isn't that the reason why I'm here?

LIEUTENANT COLONEL PAUL SCOTTO: That's one of the reasons why you're here, doctor, yes.

DR. ILMAR HODINAR: My argument follows a consistent line. This line involves mythology. Now, when you hear the word, "mythology," I recognize I could be undermining my desired contribution to this meeting. You'll probably think, "What the doctor is saying is scholarly and interesting. It has some sense to it but it doesn't have anything to do with Forsberg."

LIEUTENANT COLONEL PAUL SCOTTO: Dr. Hodinar, don't be too concerned about that. You're the best intelligence analyst we have in Europe—or anywhere.

DR. ILMAR HODINAR: Thank you, sir. It's my pleasure to work for you. You can be sure I don't take lightly what Aristotle said: "It's the mark of an educated mind to be able to entertain a thought without accepting it."

So, I shall start. There's an ancient Roman author—if you don't know him, he's terrific: Ovid. When did he live? Well, twenty-three years of his life overlapped with the life of Jesus of Nazareth—I bring up Jesus only to give you the time period.

To stay on topic, Ovid of Rome—some of you here studied Latin in high school so you have a passing acquaintance with at least his name—wrote a book called *The Metamorphoses*. In this book he told seventy stories of people transformed, by powers exercised by the gods, into rocks, plants, animals and constellations.

Hubris was the moral theme dear to the semi-encyclopedic Ovid. His book, when you read it, is a little longer than the New Testament—I bring up the New Testament only to give you an idea of the book's length and breadth. In his stunning work filled with all sorts of havoc, Ovid railed against excessive pride and self-confidence—hubris, as I say.

What is extremely fascinating is that there are stories of seventy different punishments—the punishment was transformation. The first transformation-punishment is that of a man being turned into a wolf—these were Greek myths he was retelling, so you see, in the history of Western civilization, men being changed into wolves goes back to the beginning.

Zeus changed a man into a wolf because of the man's impiety and hubris. The man's name was Lycaon. That's how we got the word "lycanthropy," a word used when speaking of werewolves.

But please allow me to be pedantic for another moment. I must backtrack slightly and let you know that in his poetic almanac Ovid first recounted the creation of the world before discussing Lycaon's sin and transformation. Yes, there's something like the Book of Genesis in the *Metamorphoses*. I bring up Genesis from the Old Testament, but I'm not asserting that *Metamorphoses* was in any way a holy book—no, it was written to entertain and instruct his audience.

By the way, in the Graeco-Roman creation story that's retold, man is on earth, his power over the animals, plants, and Nature is growing; the culture of man has gone through various ages of development and progress. The author briefly describes how, with each age, man is slowing degrading the world around him. At the end of the Age of Iron, as the author calls it, less and less is regarded as sacred. So, the scene is now prepared for man to suffer for his sins against nature and the gods.

Enter the human named *Lycaon*. He's has been saying things highly critical of the Zeus and the gods. He says their claims of divinity are a lot of hot air.

Zeus is understandably angered. He dresses in disguise and pays Lycaon a visit. Words are exchanged between the two. To be brief, Zeus turns Lycaon into a wolf. It's not over after that, though. Zeus is so enraged by Lycaon's treatment—I left out the part where Lycaon approaches Zeus while he's sleeping and tries to kill him—he's so outraged by Lycaon's people's lack of respect for him that he decides to punish the *whole world* by flooding it and killing all humans

So right away, in unapologetic Ovid's *Metamorphoses,* we have the man-into-wolf story followed by the flood story—which has parallels with the Noah's Ark story in the Bible. In classic mythology, the man and wife are named Deucalion and Pyrrha. These two—like Noah and his wife—aren't killed in the flood that kills everyone else. They survive because of their piety. The Greek couple regenerates the human race, but unfortunately humans aren't cured of their evil ways. This gives our Roman author a chance to retell sixty-nine more stories full of sinful people being transformed into all manner of beings because of their wicked behaviors!

So what does this have to do with Forsberg? I tell you as a scientist that I find it, like you, nearly impossible that a werewolf can exist. The opinion of Leonardo da Vinci who hated superstition and the supernatural haunts me. One of the things he said was, "I look forward to the day when all astrologers will be castrated." That is a remark I do not brush aside! However, at the same time, I know as a psychologist, a scholar and a researcher that there's mythological "proof" that werewolves *do* exist. Therefore, as I am a scientist, psychologist, and have indulged myself in various disciplines, I see no point in holding to a position that is only one part of me, especially since First Lieutenant Beutel has presented a great deal of overwhelming, convincing evidence that Forsberg is a werewolf.

Gentlemen, what I've said... does this shore up a wavering acknowledgment that First Lieutenant Beutel must be taken utterly seriously?

There was silence as the attendees thought over the question. Major Mullins was the first to comment.

MAJOR DAVID K. MULLINS: If I may speak...

LIEUTENANT COLONEL PAUL SCOTTO: Please do, David.

MAJOR DAVID K. MULLINS: Before today's meeting I talked with Dr. Hodinar about accepting the unacceptable. I have come around to believing in werewolves—in this *one* case, at least. But since there is one person in this room who has only just been introduced to this situation—Captain Timothy Beaumont—I'd like to hear from him if what Dr. Hodinar has said has made an impact on him—one that's influenced him in such a way that he now accepts Forsberg is a werewolf.

CAPTAIN TIMOTHY BEAUMONT: I appreciate the thoroughness that First Lieutenant Beutel has displayed in gathering the evidence. I appreciate the Dr. Hodinar's honesty that he believes, on a certain level, in the existence of this werewolf. I have worked with the doctor for some time, and I would never dismiss anything he has to say. He's employing an intellectual rigor that listens to the World's Mind—if I may make up a phrase—as articulated through mythology. But I have to admit, I'm not sure my friend's argument leaves me convinced, probably because I don't buy that mythology can be a logical premise for an argument.

LIEUTENANT COLONEL PAUL SCOTTO: What if I told you, captain, two years ago, that a bomb smaller than the size of a car could flatten a city of half million people? Would you have believed me?

CAPTAIN TIMOTHY BEAUMONT: No, I would not have, sir.

LIEUTENANT COLONEL PAUL SCOTTO: So you admit that you would have been wrong two years ago to dismiss the existence and power of such a bomb.

CAPTAIN TIMOTHY BEAUMONT: Yes, I would have been wrong, sir.

DR. ILMAR HODINAR: I will take another tack if you permit me.

LIEUTENANT COLONEL PAUL SCOTTO: Please, we are all ears.

DR. ILMAR HODINAR: Captain Beaumont, you're a graduate of West Point where you majored in Chemistry. There at the Academy, as well as in high school, you were schooled in the Scientific Method. It has been an indispensable tool for scientists in the advance of science and technology.

The process involves gathering and examining evidence, ascertaining cause and effect relationships, then formulating a logical response after examining the data and phenomena. The Scientific Method inspires me; I'm not using it literally, but I'm using it as model to help steer me through my analysis of the mythology of the man-wolf.

But what about science—not mythology—but science, where the Scientific Method lets us down? I will tell you where it does that: when one is analyzing nonlinear systems.

I consider the lycanthropic Forsberg to be a *nonlinear* life system—that is, a system where the output change is not proportional to the change of input. There are many phenomena unleashed inside him; they are from a source we know nothing about. When he changes into a werewolf we cannot predict the damage he'll do—it's different each time and maybe even his shape is considerably different each time. The changes his body and mind undergo are counterintuitive to us. In linear systems, changes in systems are intuitive and predictable.

With many nonlinear systems we can just throw the Scientific Method away—unless we are using it to inspire us to analyze elements of mythology, as I have done.

My point, Captain Beaumont, is that nonlinear systems exist in the world. Seldom do we stop and think about them as such. They exist and if we stop to scientifically dissect them, we are lost. We don't have the tools to understand them. That's what I should emphasize with all of you here: we don't understand, we *can't* understand.

We know about the substance, *water*—for

example. We know that pure water, at sea level, freezes when the temperature goes below zero degrees centigrade—this is linear science.

But think of water, in a forest, flowing over a ledge to a body of water below. We have a 'waterfall,' in plain English. Yes, there are linear aspects to it: we know gravity causes the water to fall and that a spring melt will increase the volume of water going over the ledge, et cetera.

But what we're in the dark about, and what we will remain in the dark about, is the specifics of the water's movement—water above and water below—when falling water hits the pool beneath the ledge and creates splashes and contributes to churning the pool water. There are no equations that can be written to characterize all these movements. We don't know the tiny whirlpools and can't predict the pathways of the splashes. But what is undeniable is that water does fall. It splashes and churns. We see it; we accept it, and if we're scientists engaged in linearity, we stay above, before the water flows over that ledge, and we take measurements with instruments. We avoid the all the trouble that's going on below!

CAPTAIN TIMOTHY BEAUMONT: I think you could say I'm coming around, doctor. There are some things that we cannot know.

DR. ILMAR HODINAR: It would be hubris to think we know them.

MAJOR DAVID K. MULLINS: I must say, what you've just said has been a big help.

DR. ILMAR HODINAR: Furthermore, I must remind you: if the temperature of the water changes, if it lowers far enough, it freezes. It is in a new state:

ice.

LIEUTENANT COLONEL PAUL SCOTTO: (*After a silence.*) If you wanted to stop me from reflecting on what you're saying you've failed. Now onto the second purpose of this meeting: what to do about Forsberg? We are judge, jury—and *executioner,* if we decide to go down that road. Should he live after what he's done? Should we arrest him and put him on trial?

DR. ILMAR HODINAR: The prosecution would have to reveal that he's a werewolf. I see no way it could be avoided, given the condition of the murder victims' corpses. You, First Lieutenant Beutel, would be called to testify under oath. If you told the truth, you would be instantly discredited because Forsberg's defense would say that saying he's a werewolf and that werewolves don't exist is contradictory.

On the other hand, if First Lieutenant Beutel lied and said we have evidence that Forsberg is the killer and he doesn't mention that Forsberg is a werewolf, the judge is going to see no motive in Forsberg's actions. He could be acquitted.

MAJOR DAVID K. MULLINS: Then there's the issue that if the lieutenant tells the truth and says Forsberg is a killer werewolf, and some of the officers at the trial are convinced that a werewolf exists and is in our midst, the secret is out—and who knows what will happen. But there's no way any good can come of it.

DR. ILMAR HODINAR: I agree with Major Mullins. I'd like to provide more rationale why this should be kept secret—and kept a secret only among us.

LIEUTENANT COLONEL PAUL SCOTTO: Yes, that's

another reason why you're here, doctor.

DR. ILMAR HODINAR: We don't know what Forsberg did against God or the gods—did he, for example, deign to play God? *(Pausing briefly, then:)* All of us are guilty of irreverence. The way we live has its sins. I conjure that Forsberg is a sinner and that he is some other thing when he kills. Though I am Jewish, I know the New Testament. I'm sure you all do. When Jesus was asked if we should forgive those who sin against us seven times, he said to forgive those who sin against us seven times seventy. He also said, when he was at a scene where a woman was about to be stoned to death... he said to the woman's accusers, "he who is without sin cast the first stone." All this is to say, watch out, when you're in the position to judge; be careful. I say this when there are men continuing to be judged and sentenced still, even though Nuremberg is behind us.

LIEUTENANT COLONEL PAUL SCOTTO: So, Forsberg is to remain alive. There's ample rationale for that.

DR. ILMAR HODINAR: Yes, and the reason why I've added the words of Jesus to support my rationale is that I think we should use his words, as well as the counsel of other great and wise men, to guide us in our deliberations about what should be done.

LIEUTENANT COLONEL PAUL SCOTTO: So... please continue.

DR. ILMAR HODINAR: Captain Beaumont, who like me, welcomes the words of the great and wise, has admitted that there are some things that we cannot know. I myself have said it's hubris to think we can know everything, or many things, and I have lectured you on the impossibility of knowing nonlinear phenomena. Plato, in his book, "The Apology," writes that Socrates does not imagine that he knows what he does not know. *(Pausing only briefly, then speaking again.)* Yes, I've been rather circular, and yes, it's for the sake of emphasis. So, I've made my point: we are in uncharted territory. Now, what to do about uncharted territory? The circle has brought us to Socrates—he's the great mind I last mentioned.

Gentlemen, some of you are familiar with Socratic Questioning from courses you've taken in college. It's a method to examine an idea, a proposition or a truth. With an approach that mimics Socratic questioning, I propose that we shall arrive at what to do about Forsberg.

My first question is respectfully put to the lieutenant colonel. Please provide an answer if you think there's one.

Lieutenant colonel, you're aware that Forsberg is attempting to manage his episodes of transformations by taking codeine and other opiates. This appears to be working, to a certain extent. Are you willing to authorize that Forsberg be allowed access to codeine for as long as he remains alive?

LIEUTENANT COLONEL PAUL SCOTTO: Certainly.

DR. ILMAR HODINAR: So this means Forsberg will experience all the side effects of using opiates daily. The mental side effects, in particular, concern me. Forsberg is under sedation; he will daydream when awake, and when asleep will experience 'twilight sleep'—not as restful as the sleep people normally get. This means that Forsberg's mind is in a fog. Does the Army care about a soldier's mind being like that most of the time?

343

LIEUTENANT COLONEL PAUL SCOTTO: Yes. He would be an ineffective soldier.

DR. ILMAR HODINAR: If we take the codeine away, will he be effective?

LIEUTENANT COLONEL PAUL SCOTTO: No, because he'll experience transformations and kill people.

DR. ILMAR HODINAR: But don't soldiers kill people?

LIEUTENANT COLONEL PAUL SCOTTO: In combat, in war, soldiers kill people.

DR. ILMAR HODINAR: Would there perhaps be a situation that requires the U.S. Army to violently attack, and Sergeant Forsberg, as a werewolf, might play an effective role in it?

LIEUTENANT COLONEL PAUL SCOTTO: I suppose it's possible.

DR. ILMAR HODINAR: Now, if I may, I'd like to ask Major Mullins some questions. Major Mullins, has the group here decided not to turn Forsberg over to the pertinent authorities and have him tried for murder?

MAJOR DAVID K. MULLINS: It has been decided not to do that.

DR. ILMAR HODINAR: In other words, we're advocating that he be kept alive. But for what purpose? Man must have a purpose. Otherwise, the man risks illness and death. Do you believe we ought to establish a purpose for Forsberg?

MAJOR DAVID K. MULLINS: You've suggested that were he not to have a purpose, he would risk illness and death. I don't think you want that. I think you, of all people, would prefer to *study* him. I agree that if he's to live, he must be given a purpose, even if that purpose is a steady job.

DR. ILMAR HODINAR: But what good is a sergeant whose mind is foggy? But having said that, there are many opium addicts in history who have led productive lives, even though burdened with the side effects of opium. I'm attracted to your statement that his purpose could be to keep a steady job. It is for a lot of people. Then the question is, what kind of job? At present he's working as a microfilmer. But eventually, that job will end; we'll have processed the documents. Then what can we have him do? The work shouldn't be too strenuous. I'm not sure how his condition behaves. But I can imagine that stress would bring out the worst in him.

MAJOR DAVID K. MULLINS: So, you'd prefer a somewhat retiring job for him—not that he'll be retired. A job where no one's constantly checking on the work he's supposed to be doing. An army is strongest when all its soldiers are doing their jobs, working hard.

CAPTAIN TIMOTHY BEAUMONT: Excuse me. I have a suggestion—you've asked me here because I'm a breath of fresh air or possibly an impartial in some sense. I welcome you to shoot down my idea if you don't think much of it. It's only an idea.

DR. ILMAR HODINAR: Captain, this, as I see it, is a meeting of open minds. So, please go ahead.

CAPTAIN TIMOTHY BEAUMONT: It's wise to keep watch over him—I don't mean checking him once a day—that would not be enough. Major Mullins has remarked that you might like to study him. Is there some way you do that, Dr. Hodinar? Can we, at the same time, watch over him, track his movements?

DR. ILMAR HODINAR: I would need to keep some distance from him. I don't want him to know someone else is aware of his lycanthropy.

CAPTAIN TIMOTHY BEAUMONT: So it's impossible to study him?

DR. ILMAR HODINAR: Not impossible, but difficult. Lieutenant Beutel, you've accomplished a remarkable feat. You've gathered the evidence against Sergeant Forsberg and as far as we know, he's not aware that you know what he is. You've done impressive work.

So. *(After a pause to think.)* Where to go now? … Inventing a job for Forsberg—an easy one, at that. Then there's the aspiration that I study him scientifically—but the catch is I need to study him up close, and he must not be able to see me…

I think such a job…it will take some weeks to create it. *(Thinking aloud.)* We can rule out that I study him, somehow, in the dark, that I could approach him when he's sleeping, for example. When he doesn't sleep soundly? I couldn't even approach him to inject him with a sedative so I could study him when he's lost consciousness.

I need a repeating environment that keeps me not seeable by him, where I can study him for an extended period. A screen must stand between him and me—a screen that makes him not notice me.

People meet face-to-face in a variety of ways. Some are intimate meetings. Some meetings—you may not realize it—are face-to-face, yet the meeting is depersonalized, those involved in it have a weak sense of closeness and may actually feel distant from those around them.

(His ideas coalescing.) I've taught students in classrooms. The classroom is part of a school. The school is an institution. An institution can be a depersonalized environment. A professor may stand in front of his students, and especially in a room of over twenty students—many of the students—though they may be looking at and listening to the professor—don't feel—nor do some students even *want* to feel—any personal closeness to their teacher. It's not like an apprenticeship where there is working side-by-side, and there is some intimacy.

I'm not saying I could succeed in being anonymous while I'm a professor in a classroom where Forsberg is one of the students. However, I'm attracted to the idea of putting Forsberg in a setting that's depersonalized. The army has its institutions...

(With insight and inspiration combining.) My suggestion is to enroll him in OCS, at Fort Riley. I will also move to OCS—there are several subjects I can teach there. While Forsberg is taking his classes—I don't want him to be permitted to enroll in any course that I teach—I will find ways to get to know more about him. I will observe from a short distance. I will ask discreet questions. of those who come into contact with him. I will keep track of how he medicates himself. At the same time, I will strive to be aware to the best extent I can, of where he is—all the while being covert in my behavior.

I know this sounds extreme, moving him from Germany to Kansas—but after Fort Riley, he'll come back to Germany, a second lieutenant, to an easy position that we've created for him. And not one where a superior officer expects a lot of work from him; where those around him are led to believe that his real work, for example, is that of an undercover operative for Military Counterintelligence—you know, that he's focused on finding communist sympathizers and former Nazis. Naturally, in whatever position he has, we will watch over him.

After the doctor finished speaking, and a pause lengthened, Lieutenant Colonel Scotto finally announced, bluntly, "I like it." He waited to let the weight he was throwing behind Hodinar register. He then added, "We can put our heads together and arrange this."

Other meetings would take care of the finer points of the plan.

Colonel Scotto opened up the floor, for a final five minutes, to broad discussion.

Again, there were questions regarding how why Forsberg, out of a world of people, became a werewolf. Dr. Hodinar said he didn't know, maybe we would never know, but possibly he could find out more while he and Forsberg were at Fort Riley. Other questions naturally centered around the amount of control that Forsberg had over his lycanthropy.

Hodinar urged those at the meeting to not condemn the captain; he reminded them that the Soviet Union's stated desire was to spread communism throughout the world. That their system was antithetical to western democracy; that we needed to explore a range of weapons to be used against them, and yes, they were taking a great responsibility upon themselves and he didn't know what kind of weapon Forsberg could serve as. Again, hopefully, his observations of the soldier at OCS could help inform that idea.

Another question was, would Forsberg simply vanish one day, would he run away? Hodinar's opinion was he would not—this was only his opinion, of course, but Forsberg, by striving to control his condition, seemed not to want to run away. However, the doctor admitted that his opinion smacked of linear thinking, that there was no straight-and-narrow to this situation. It was not linear.

Sergeant Major Wilson Simmons, who had not once spoken up during the meeting, said, "I'm a Christian, a true believer. I believe this although there's nothing mentioned of this kind of thing in a *Christian* text. I can see that Greek mythology helps you in understanding Forsberg's condition, yet you can only understand it through an appreciation of things that are scientifically non-linear. What would you say to a Christian—because most of us here are Christians—to comfort them that this is not a work of God, but the work of the Devil?"

Hodinar answered with a collection of provoking thoughts. "I have thought about that. Forsberg isn't a being who brings to mind the "Lamb of God" metaphor—a soldier who is or has been active in combat is not an innocent fellow. On the other hand, I am reluctant to assign Forsberg the evil that gets ascribed to various figures at the end of the Bible's New Testament, in the Book of Revelation. For how can a thing that God creates be evil? Now, returning to the Greeks, the act of Lycaon being turned into a wolf points to more meanings than a god of the Hellenes reducing a man into a wild, meat-eating predator—a wolf. The Lycaon-wolf is a harbinger. Lycaon's transformation happens; Zeus gives humans beings another chance to be reverent; they are not. So then, Zeus unleashes the Flood, killing off humans so the species can start afresh. When we connect Lycaon with the ensuing Flood, we get a teaching of what happens to abject, incorrigible *sinners*, if you will. As I alluded to before, there's no shortage of the arrogant, the conceited, the self-important, and those who don't observe all the Ten Commandments among us. There has also been throughout history no shortage of apocalyptic beliefs and literature—

why shouldn't there be? The transformation of Lycaon, plus the Flood, means that too many people had lost their way, and that Zeus had had it with the whole race."

Hodinar started summing up, "All right, so maybe we have our modern Lycaon in Forsberg. Maybe the Devil isn't causing Forsberg's condition, but God is—yes, don't we flatter ourselves often, thinking we are good, righteous, and reverent?" He paused for a second, thought more, then added another idea. "Um…. maybe *we've turned ourselves* into animals with all our wars?—that's another interpretation." There was silence in the room. Hodinar said, "Yes, we must move forward, and as we do, we will learn."

A few words were muttered after it seemed he was finished. It did not amount to a discussion. The meeting finally came to an end after Ilmar suggested a code name for their operation: Operation Grendel. He said simply the word Grendel could mean "Forsberg." If anyone outside their group managed to overhear them, they wouldn't be able to easily decipher who or what was being talking about, since it wasn't a name used anymore.

When asked "Why Grendel… in particular?" Hodinar explained more. "It sounds like a word you're hearing incorrectly. Also, Grendel's the monster in the first epic story written in English."

Three months later, in mid-June 1947, Dr. Hodinar and Sergeant Gideon Forsberg, professor and student, respectively, were at OCS in Fort Riley, Kansas. Forsberg never met Hodinar, but the doctor had arrived two weeks before him and had made sure that the school's library lending stacks had in them some twenty books about The Wolf—its biology, anatomy, behavior, and habitat—as well as short stories and novels pertaining to werewolves—and folklore anthologies that contained articles about werewolves.

He also saw to it that the on-post movie house programmed movies that had werewolves in them. Hodinar's intuition told him that Forsberg would see the movies and read the books. Hodinar was right. In addition to learning about the properties and uses of aconite, Forsberg's side-education at OSC taught him about those of the yew tree.

During the soldier's seventeen-week course of study, he kept to himself. Hodinar found it difficult to learn much about him, but it appeared Forsberg was determined to keep up and surmount the side effects of codeine—he was sluggish and mentally in his own world, it appeared. There were many times that the doctor was at a loss for what might be done to get more information on what was going on inside Forsberg.

One thing was for certain: the young cadet was trying hard to stave off any transformations into a werewolf.

There was one time when Hodinar was given an opportunity to act. It was three weeks before the end of OCS studies and the weather—it was early October—was chilly and the winds rushed. Skies were grayer than those when the season first turned. Forsberg, drugged with codeine, looked haggard, yet there was a strange glint in his eyes. Looking at his body, it seemed he was straining under the pressure to complete his studies satisfactorily. His classes were a lot of work. Hodinar feared that the stress might weaken the deterrents he was using against the lycanthropic changes.

The professor decided it was time to experiment with aconite. He wanted to give Forsberg's body a shock. He wanted to "reset" it.

The doctor was able to surreptitiously place a small amount of aconite in Forsberg's food in the mess hall at OCS on a Friday.

It made Forsberg sick for two days—Saturday and Sunday—there were no classes on Sunday. Forsberg only missed one day of classes.

But the aconite had worked. After recovering from "food poisoning"—as Forsberg thought it was—the strange glint in the soldier's eyes was gone and the signs of tension and possible distress were no more. Hodinar had wished he had more chances to intervene and learn more about his subject, but he couldn't risk the cadet discovering him. During the professor's stay at Fort Riley he would get more rest and have more time for reflection than usual. He taught two classes—electives—one in international relations, the other in basic psychology. Forsberg wasn't allowed to register for either—and anyway, he showed no interest in either.

He graduated as a second lieutenant with no special distinctions—but at least he successfully completed the degree program. He took no leave to visit relatives in Minnesota while stateside. Upon graduation he was transferred back to Germany where he would spend the next forty-four months of his life.

After those months the "Frankfurt School" had "Grendel" transferred to a war zone: Korea. The werewolf's keepers had learned only a little bit more about him. But the attack on Korea by the Chinese and the Korean communists had shocked every echelon and organ in the military. The American military didn't see it coming. They were wholly unprepared for it, having drawn down large numbers of troops. In no small measure due to panic, Forsberg was assigned to Korea.

Now it was July 1952. Forsberg had been in Korea not quite a year. Time, attention and resources in the main fell to getting large units of troops on the ground in Korea as soon as possible; to prosecute a modern, conventional war. But the Frankfurt School wanted a possible secret weapon close at hand, in case they had few choices and losses were overwhelming. Captain Walter Beutel, unbeknownst to Forsberg, was his overseer. Forsberg was so self-absorbed that he never noticed Beutel. Beutel, unfortunately, was killed in an ambush in Korea. The Frankfurt school then transferred Forsberg to Chitose so Timothy Beaumont could watch over him.

Dr. Hodinar swung his gray Studebaker, back windows closed, front windows still open, onto the Fort Meade exit of the Baltimore-Washington Parkway and was in a secure meeting room in a building of the U.S. Army Intelligence Agency in fifteen minutes.

This was a meeting of the Frankfurt School. After 1947, these face-to-face meetings to discuss "Grendel" never took place more than once a year.

In the intervening years since the first meeting of the Frankfurt School at the IG Farben building, all the army men at that meeting had been promoted and had gotten new assignments. Just after North Korea invaded South Korea in June of 1950, most of the "members" of the school had been transferred to AIA at Fort Meade.

Former Lieutenant Colonel Paul Scotto, was now a full-bird colonel. The 704 Military Intelligence Brigade—the U.S.'s premiere MI Brigade—was stationed at Fort Meade, and he was its commander. Working with him was Wilson Simmons, the advisor he had alongside him in Germany, who was now Command Sergeant Major Simmons.

A new member of the school, and who was at today's meeting was Major General C. Holt Jamieson. He was the commanding general of the U.S. Army Intelligence Agency. Colonel Paul Scotto had brought him into the club. Also present was the general's Assistant Chief of Staff, David K. Mullins, now a lieutenant colonel.

Absent from the meeting were Walter Beutel—killed in Korea—and Timothy Beaumont, now a major, in Japan.

Another new member of the school was Command Sergeant Major Virgil Overbeck. The sergeant major was Lieutenant Colonel Mullins' right-hand man.

The group had come together to discuss what should be done with "Grendel" since he was in a coma. The consensus reached was they should do nothing at present, that if it lasted a year there should be a decision whether he should be taken off life support. There was also discussion of what to do with

Grendel if he came out of the coma (the consensus was to have him go back to "work"), as well as how to presently manage the body hair and skin changes.

The meeting only took twenty-five minutes. The group would be better informed, and in a much better position as to what next actions needed to be taken. First it was imperative that Ilmar Hodinar get to Chitose as soon as possible and see for himself.

CHAPTER 33

Various matters left unsaid before, but worth mentioning now.

i.

What caused those astonishing, emancipating cracks in the cast on his leg? After them, Major Beaumont, head of Command, Control and Intelligence appeared; he had the captain moved upstairs. He was now an influential advisor to the doctor. Prior to the trouble, Marcia had never seen the doctor with Beaumont. Had the major been a medical doctor before he went into Intelligence? She thought: am I having a crazy dream where bone heals miraculously because it's an Act of God? No… though I'm a believer; I don't believe that's the case.

Corporal Lumley recognized there was something strange about all of it. He kept his thoughts to himself, though.

He did his best to make it easy for McGuinness to approach him—she knew he liked her, probably he even lusted after her. His attraction to her meant nothing; she was not about to become involved with him. She wasn't overly attracted to G.I.s. Her heart went out to them; they had little control over their days, let alone their destinies. These men were generally a few years younger than her and there were so many of them; they outnumbered females on base more than a hundred to one. They were different human beings than her: they smoked, drank, paid for sex in town—and some of them had a venereal disease to prove it.

ii.

Protocol didn't expressly forbid McGuinness and the other nurses to say a few harmless words to the MPs on guard duty upstairs; they were only not supposed to talk about the captain and the state of his health. So, very limited conversation occurred between nurses and guards on occasion; it would have been stilted and absurd to remain silent.

Private First Class Stan Shuck, the soldier who wore glasses, was on guard duty. Marcia didn't want to talk to him, so she said nothing. (He'd been the guard many times, on various of the four six-hour shifts of each twenty-four-hour period.) She had easily noticed his addiction to pep pills. She was afraid that getting into a conversation with him would result in drawn-out talk she couldn't easily break away from.

The infirmary wasn't far from the post's bakery. Finding their way into the corridor upstairs that evening were smells of dough, deep-fried in shortening, vanilla, and nutmeg—hot doughnuts. A weak but insistent odor, wafting in from town, of burning wood—pollution—competed with the bakery smells.

Stan had very little to do, of course. He focused on the donut aroma. It bothered him. It made him feel hungry, but he really wasn't hungry. He didn't smell the pollution from town. He stood there irritated, nervous, high-strung on Benzedrine.

On Nurse McGuinness's 8 p.m. round to look in on Forsberg, she noticed his complexion had darkened. The skin tone of his hands, it seemed to her, had darkened as well.

But was she imagining these changes? Maybe the hormonal changes in her own body were affecting her judgment. There was gibbous moon on the rise. It was almost the time of her period.

She debated within herself whether she ought to ask the doctor to come up and see if he saw anything new—if she didn't approach him and something really had changed, it would be a serious mistake.

She went down to his office, but he was in the Officers' Mess for a quick meal. Hearing this, a thin film of sweat swept over her.

She found Corporal Lumley in a storage room that also served as an informal office and lounge. He was happy to with her to the room. He was in a good mood (it had been a fine summer day). If only he and the nurse could go upstairs, retire to the room across the hall that the guards use as a break room, shut the door behind them, throw off their clothes, peel off those white tights of hers, and have wild sex, he mused.

When they got upstairs, they greeted Stan Shuck with a brief hello and went into the sick room, closing the door behind them.

McGuinness pointed to the captain's hands and said anxiously, "Do you notice anything different about them? Do they look stronger …and hairier than you remember?"

"Aren't you answering your own question without letting me try?" Lumley asked, in his good mood.

"No, I mean it. I just want to be sure I'm not imagining things."

Lumley gazed at the hands with more attention. "I'm not sure I see anything different about them. I don't seem him as often as you do but I could think they've gotten hairier."

During the back and forth on the subject, Lumley was careful not to completely rule out Marcia's notion that there'd been a change in Forsberg—such a thing might cause her to not like him, and that would douse the flames of their budding romance.

The corporal persuaded her to simply wait for the doctor to come back. This was not to say that Lumley didn't feel there was something newly strange about Forsberg. Maybe it was just he'd had a pleasant day and didn't want any strangeness to cross his mind.

McGuinness was dejected after Lumley didn't agree with

her. She regretted bringing him upstairs. It had probably given him the false impression that they were friends. She needed to maintain a proper distance from him. Now he probably thought there was a personal connection between them. She was spooked—that's why asked him for his opinion about the captain's condition.

When Dr. Tiller got back, he right away went upstairs with Marcia.

He, too, wasn't sure he saw any significant change in the patient. That made Marcia sweat more. She slipped away from thinking about the captain and into self-analysis. She knew people noticed how easily she was prone to sweating. What was she like that? Did it happen because she was in some way acting against her will, her true nature? Was it that deep down inside she was an introvert who should only be surrounding herself with a few people? She was in the wrong line of work; it seemed her body was often on edge, that's why she perspired. She couldn't remember exactly when the abnormal sweating started—maybe in early adolescence.

Dr. Tiller no longer doubted the nurse after 10 p.m., that is, after her round at that hour to check on the captain.

After that he announced authoritatively that the patient was suffering from a hypertrichosis (he got this information from his reference books). Hypertrichosis is a rare affliction, he told the nurse. He'd never seen it before in practice but there are hundreds of medical conditions a doctor will come across for the first time in his life.

So Tiller had given a name to the condition. Naming it brought a smidgen of relief because a condition that can't be identified and named causes worry and fright (that it might be fatal or contagious, for example).

The momentary lessening of anxiety that came with the diagnosis quickly receded, however, when McGuinness sensed hypertrichosis couldn't explain all his symptoms. It would have been unprofessional of her to voice any doubts of the doctor's expertise, so she didn't say anything. Surely, hypertrichosis doesn't cause lips to blacken and cause wolf-like features (that's what they looked like to her) to form on a human face.

But then again, the doctor was saying malnutrition was behind the hypertrichosis and she was no expert on the ravages of malnutrition.

At any rate, the doctor said she should leave the room. Sometime later, downstairs (after Tiller talked to Major Beaumont, that shadowy figure), he informed her that from now on Forsberg would be given 360 milligrams, I.V., of codeine per day.

What did giving the captain so much codeine have to do with his health problems, she thought. She also was told that within minutes a cosmetic procedure (he would be shaved) would be carried out on him—but she wouldn't be needed to assist with it. The procedure would make the captain less difficult to look at, he said—seeming to assert that a modification of his outward appearance would have some benefits for not only the patient himself.

It was clear that though she was one of the attending nurses, she couldn't rely on Dr. Tiller for much support.

For Dr. Tiller, yes indeed, Forsberg was an uncommon patient. But then again, unusual things can happen when a patient is in a coma. Tiller did question why Forsberg's toenails and fingernails had yellowed. He put that down to malnutrition.

For treatment, he prescribed a diet (administered via the nasogastric tube) high in essential amino acids.

And no, Tiller did not much concern himself with the twisted and discolored appearance of Forsberg's face. To him there was no wolf-like aspect to the face. If he for a moment thought such an outrageous thought, he would clear it from his mind immediately. It was enough for him to keep up with the changes in his comatose patient's condition, to see what he could do in terms of diagnosis and treatment.

The night that Major Beaumont clipped off the

abundance of hair that covered Forsberg, the officer thought to himself: I made a mistake. No wonder Forsberg had developed a case of "hypertrichosis"—he wasn't getting enough codeine!

The situation wasn't one the Frankfurt School had foreseen. They'd never imagined they'd have a wolfen Forsberg under their direct control, that they would be tasked with controlling it. Beaumont thought: the "school" must meet again at once. We need to craft a plan.

The infirmary was not the perfect place for Forsberg— there was no perfect place for him.

Beaumont thought: I can't let this get worse. We cannot let what control we have slip away.

iii.

The last time they recruited, Nichols and Velchoffsky couldn't foresee they'd need to post a guard twenty-four hours a day at the infirmary. (Provost Marshal Major Tyler at Camp Crawford, to their mild surprise, approved this action the moment it was requested.)

Velchoffsky had prioritized. First, he'd sent his least favorite men there. Not many of his least favorite existed, however, so he was forced to assign highly trusted, smart MPs as well. It would be another three weeks before he could process a new group of candidates. A useless captain had not only been foisted on the unit; now he was costing it valuable manpower.

Since all his shifts at the infirmary had been boring, Stan Shuck expected this one to be like them.

However, Nurse McGuinness was rattled-looking after her 8 p.m. round to Forsberg's bedside.

A few minutes after she'd rushed downstairs, she was back—but with an orderly. You could tell she would've rather had the doctor with her, but apparently he wasn't available.

Their ministrations took place behind the closed door, so

Stan didn't know what was going on.

Soon, McGuinness and Lumley left and went back downstairs. A few minutes later the nurse came back with Dr. Tiller. They went into the room, closing the door as usual.

Shuck couldn't help but think to himself about these comings and goings—and the nervous look on the nurse's face each time. He knew she had to look in on the comatose patient every twenty minutes. This evening it seemed to be putting a great strain on her.

After her 10 p.m. round she darted downstairs and the doctor came back up with her. Stan smelled her sweat. Tiller and the nurse went into the room. After a few minutes, they left and went downstairs again.

It seemed to him that there might be some kind of emergency going on. He even asked, stupidly, the doctor and the nurse, when they left the room, "Is everything all right?"

Neither responded to him. He was out of line. This wasn't a battlefield or some family sickroom.

A few minutes later the nurse came up with some ampules of codeine in her hands and went in the room. (Shuck didn't know what she had in her hands.)

After spending a little time in the room, she left.

Stan's shift was ending. The methamphetamine in his blood was making him twitch and feel antsy. He felt his legs shaking and became convinced that he needed to walk to stop the shaking. With nobody around, he took a few strides down the corridor, away from the room and the spot where he usually stood. He paced back and forth. He knew, though, duty compelled him to come back near the captain's doorway and stand guard. So, he did, reluctantly.

He couldn't fight off his ever-increasing agitation. He shouldn't have taken that pill forty-five minutes ago. He was obsessed with the idea that something was wrong in the captain's room and things were getting worse, that the nurse had left and he hadn't seen her in more than twenty minutes.

What if things were getting worse in the captain's room and nobody knew it? (Yes, the Benzedrine was really stirring him up.)

He was convinced he had to go in there even though it was against orders. He couldn't fight off the idea that the situation could tip into being dangerously, fatally wrong, with no one there to save him. Somebody ought to be doing something, he thought. He knew couldn't raise the alarm by shouting—he'd been instructed that voices should always be kept low.

Then he changed his mind. He decided he wouldn't go in—but he'd at least open the door and peek in to make sure everything was okay.

He turned the knob and pushed the door open enough to see the bed and its surroundings.

Only moonglow provided the dark room with some light. (He thought: the overhead lights had been switched off, to help the patient to get a proper night's sleep.) All was quiet. There was only the sound of the patient breathing and it was neither soft nor loud. He was struck by the presence of belts that were stretched between, and attached to, the rails of the bed. Their purpose was clear. It was to limit the captain's movements. But did patients in a coma move that much? Weren't comatose patients unarousable and out like a light?

He thought back to the things that Forsberg had ordered him to get quickly, that first day he met him. A thought flashed through his mind: some of the items were ones used to restrain a person...what was it about Forsberg and restraints?

He tried to see Forsberg's face. He struggled to find the faint color of human flesh that belonged to his face but the room was so dim. It was clearer to see pale bed sheets, the metal side rails of the bed, the restraint belts, the lonely I.V. stand, the I.V. line, the nasogastric tube going into the darkness of Forsberg's face. It was so dark that he couldn't make out the face. It seemed there was a lot of hair there.

Shuck's eyes glided from the face area and to the captain's arm closest to him. From what he could see, there was an abnormal amount of hair on it.

Just then, Shuck thought he heard hard-soled shoes coming up the stairs to the floor. He pulled the room's door softly shut and took up his normal guard position.

But he'd been hearing things. Nobody came up the stairs—not at that moment. However, a senior officer (whose footsteps seemed to match those that Shuck thought he'd heard) did appear a couple of minutes later. The officer was Major Timothy Beaumont, commander of C2I.

Shuck knew who he was. He saluted him crisply, immediately. Beaumont said nothing and went into the patient's room.

Shuck thought: it's ugly and awful in there. I'm glad they didn't catch me looking in.

iv.

Velchoffsky sat in his swivel chair, his five o'clock shadow advancing to a beard.

Shuck had asked for a meeting with him earlier in the day. Velchoffsky said he didn't have time for him, that he would see him only at the end of the day.

Now Shuck was babbling crazy talk. He said he couldn't do guard duty anymore, that Forsberg was friends or enemies with the wanted Ainu man; that though he, Shuck, knew Forsberg's medical condition was top secret and would never say anything about it, that sooner or later theories would come out about it—because other guards and other people saw Major Beaumont from C2I visiting Forsberg and Forsberg really was suspicious and it was more than a medical condition and it had something to do with the attacks in Chitose.

The career sergeant thought to himself: these were the ravings of an amphetamine addict. He barked at Shuck, "You think I'm going to let you off guard duty because you're having hallucinations?"

What an insane, ungrateful, insubordinate soldier, Velchoffsky thought. I guess we're going to report his drug addiction.

"I can't do guard duty there, sir."

"That's the third time you've said that!" the sergeant yelled at him.

Velchoffsky calmed down. He then just stared at him and said, "Did you go into the room and see him?"

"No, sir."

Velchoffsky neither believed nor disbelieved him. How exasperating. Shuck's nerves were frayed—they shouldn't have been! His orders were easy. ...But, the sergeant thought, come to think of it, he's probably a lousy guard. In his condition, what use is he? If danger arose—and that's what he was there to watch out for—wouldn't he fail to prevent trouble and even add to it?

Shuck's head subtly bobbed forward and back; he said there were extenuating circumstances and he was ready to divulge them. "There's more to back up my story... but we can't tell anybody. But I can tell you things about Forsberg that are beyond army-secret. They're personally secret, things that only he and I know."

The sergeant's eyes opened big and skewed upward in disbelief. "You and Forsberg are close?"

"We were close the day he got here. I took him on a tour."

"Yeah, I know. The orientation tour." He growled derisively, "That made you two close, huh?"

"Yes, sir. He commanded me to get a few things for him—items that could be used to restrain a wild animal or a crazy man."

"He told you that specifically?"

"Well, no, not specifically."

"You're the crazy man! What the hell are you talking about?" His eyes narrowed, "Did anybody see you get those things for him?"

"Nobody saw me."

"So there's no proof. You're making stuff up, aren't you, Shuck."

"No, sir."

"Come over here, private. Let me look at your eyes." Shuck stepped to the side of Velchoffsky's desk where the sergeant was pointing him to stand. "Take off your glasses."

Shuck took off his glasses. Velchoffsky got up from his chair with disdain. He studied the younger man's eyes. "Your pupils are dilated. You're so high that I don't want you on guard duty anymore. There—you get your wish." He paused. He genuinely felt frustrated, wasn't putting on an act. "I don't know what I'm going to do with you. You're out of your mind. You have to stop taking Benzedrine or I will court-martial you. You'll get a year in the brig, then a dishonorable discharge." He paused for breath and continued, "If I hear you've said anything of the kind you've just said to me to anyone else, I am sure to prosecute you for drug usage and espionage and enemy propaganda. You're saying stuff that the enemy could only dream somebody would say! You don't talk about matters, true or false, black or blue, if they're about anything that's top secret, you got that!?"

Jesus, Velchoffsky thought. We don't have enough manpower around here. Taking him off guard rotation is going to mess us up.

At 5:30 p.m., when the office staff had mostly gone home, Velchoffsky was still trying to come up with a solution—who can I bring onto guard duty to replace Shuck? He didn't have an answer.

He knew Nichols was still in the office—neither he nor Nichols ever left the building for the day without letting the other know he was going.

He would ask Lieutenant Nichols. Maybe Nichols would think of something he hadn't thought of.

He went the few steps down the corridor to the lieutenant's office and knocked. No response. Often at this hour, Nichols was at secretarial services, proofreading orders and documents that had been written or processed during the day. Typewriters sat on four desks; two of these desks were occupied.

Velchoffsky saw Nichols sitting in a chair next to a male secretary who'd just finished typing out pages from shorthand. They were Nichols's dictations from the afternoon; he was proofreading them.

Velchoffsky came into the room and Nichols glanced away from the papers in his hand. He could see by Velchoffsky's look that the sergeant wanted to talk to him.

"What's up?" asked Nichols. His tone was friendly.

"Sorry to disturb you, sir. It can wait until tomorrow if necessary."

"It doesn't have to if it'll only take five minutes. I could use a quick break."

"Five minutes will be enough," Velchoffsky assured him.

He wanted to have the lieutenant's attention for every one of those five minutes, so he didn't suggest they go to his office to talk. Instead, he motioned for Nichols to join him just outside the room, out of ear shot of the young men—there were just two left, working.

v.

"There was an impressive lily that bloomed there last month," Beaumont said to Torrington, pointing to some flowerless green stems of knee-high wild lily plants.

He and Jake were out behind the officers club at Kumakawa's trading post.

"It had that red-orange color you see with tiger lilies, but the petals were broader and weren't flopped back. The stamens didn't stick way out like crooked teeth."

"Hm. Sorry I missed it," Jake said, somewhat interested. He took a step closer to the plants on their left, bent his head and peered at the stems and their blades. While studying them he remarked, "Strange. There's something like peach fuzz on the leaves and stems. Was it on the flower, too, I wonder?"

A mental picture of the lily he'd seen last month came to Beaumont. Yes, there'd been translucent, soft fibers—vellus-like hair—on the petals of the flower. The thought of hair made him want to shudder.

"I believe there was," he scowled.

Some twenty yards behind them was the back porch of the officers club.

The major had asked Jake to meet him here. Strain showed on his normally stalwart face.

Five minutes ago he'd told Jake about Forsberg's "hypertrichosis." Jake was shocked. Then they started to take a little stroll on the grounds of the club, which sided a bend in the river. Tufts of cogon grass and tussock sedge vied with patches of meadowsweet and aconite. The meadowsweet's tiny flowers were lavender; those of the aconite, purple-blue.

Jake Torrington thought to himself: I am an inadequate partner in the group managing Operation Grendel. (He didn't come right out and say it, however.)

Though after slightly recovering after being told of Forsberg's excess hairiness, one thing he did say to Beaumont was, "There's the 'Great Unknown,' with this, isn't there?"

To which Beaumont did not reply.

Beaumont's thinking went this way (but he didn't express it aloud): Jake's not an unreliable man or soldier. He obeys orders and provides advice and assistance. But he doesn't think Forsberg's existence is worth preserving. He thinks the world would be better off if Operation Grendel was terminated.

They lingered near the river. It was clear that Beaumont was going to say more. The leaves of the ash and maple trees were fully formed now. Normally this would raise one's spirits.

Beaumont said actions were being to be taken; that he

needed yet another ally on post. He needed one man in particular—and it was not Dr. Tiller. He wanted Major Christopher de Graff; he would tell him about Grendel.

Tim didn't want to discuss the matter of bringing de Graff into the loop. He just wanted to tell him he was doing it. He was guardedly optimistic—if those were the right words—that Forsberg could be kept under control.

Beaumont explained—and it wasn't a direct criticism of Jake—"De Graff is principled, calm. Complexity doesn't slow him down. He'll be a higher-up who'll challenge any hearsay. As head of Logistics, he'll be there for us, fast."

"Are you saying that we would move Forsberg out of Chitose fast? Jake asked.

"We need to be ready for any exigencies, don't you think?"

Beaumont said he was setting up a meeting with Major de Graff; that he'd like him, Jake, to join in it.

Jake said fine; then they both paused and watched the steady flow of Chitose River gently ease by.

Beaumont also said, "There's another man who'll be working on Operation Grendel with us. You have yet to meet him. He will arrive soon."

They were only out behind the club for ten minutes or so.

vi.

Nurse McGuinness had a nightmare where she was Little Red Riding Hood and instead of a wolf being in bed it was Forsberg. She talked only a little during her nightmare. She spoke to the furry creature in a kind of pidgin English and did not say, "What big eyes you have" or "What big teeth you have." She remembered saying, "Not take me. Not bake me." She was afraid Forsberg was going to snatch her up and put her in a large seventeenth century oven and bake her. Maybe this had something to do with smells from Chitose I's bakery wafting over to the infirmary.

Images from "Hansel and Gretel" also worked their way

into her dreams—she felt left in the forest to fend for herself.

On this evening's shift at the infirmary Lloyd Kelso was on guard duty. He'd been on guard duty twice before, so he had met him before. What a contrast the soldier from New York state was compared to Stan Shuck and the others. He was affable and seemed sensitive. They'd sneaked very brief chats together.

Kelso could see that Marcia's nursing duties were putting great demands on her—yes, the words "top secret"—that was why. Lloyd remembered the phone conversation he'd had with the captain when he thought ruined his chances to be an MP. He was grateful to him for giving him a second chance. The captain was a fellow that followed his own set of rules, it seemed.

The few times Lloyd spoke with Marcia he could tell it helped her relax. He felt she was merely being friendly to him—there was no attraction between the two of them. (He was still smitten with Kiriko.) He thought Nurse McGuinness to be pleasant and professional; a young woman with a strong accent he hadn't heard before.

Lloyd Kelso started his six-hour shift as the MP guard at 6 p.m. When she saw he was going to be on duty for the rest of the evening she greeted him with a spontaneous but tired smile.

When McGuinness checked in on Forsberg around half past ten, she was only in his room briefly. She left the room and went downstairs. Lloyd didn't know it, but it seemed to the nurse that Forsberg's bicep and forearm muscles had increased in size.

Downstairs she asked Dr. Tiller, "What if Captain Forsberg is putting on muscle? Can that happen? I just seemed to have noticed it."

The doctor answered, "Well, he's taking in more nutrition."

"But he hasn't had any exercise."

"True," he sighed. "Our patient is certainly unusual. I'll

go upstairs and have a look at him."

Once they opened the door, they knew it was an emergency. They slammed the door behind them. They were amazed. Questions about muscle growth would have to wait until later.

The captain's limbs were straining at the belts that were there to contain his movements. His chest was bent upward, his whole body jutted, contorted. Marcia tried quickly to take in what was going on. The doctor peered at the patients' eyes for neurological signs. He shouted at Marcia to go downstairs and bring back enough phenobarbital for a bolus. The nurse left the room, almost ramming the edge of the door into her forehead as she pulled it to open it. As she was going downstairs, perspiration, over her whole body, formed like dew.

The scene struck the doctor with awe. The captain's lungs weren't taking in air; he heard a groan or a creak come from somewhere in his chest cavity—Tiller was glad that McGuinness wasn't there to hear that. Right after the sound, the captain's upper torso quaked for ten seconds. It made the doctor step back instinctively to be safe from the patient's flailing, muscular arms. The arms couldn't get past the bed restraints, but nonetheless, the power in Forsberg scared Tiller.

The movements brought to Tiller's mind an image of a dead man in a casket in a funeral home—and then the soul of that man tries to lash out in anger, by using the corpse's arms. Though the captain was constrained by the belts, it did seem he wanted to punch the doctor—Tiller felt the captain was straining hard to raise a fist to strike him.

When McGuinness came back with the syringe of phenobarbital, he snatched it from her. As he injected the captain to sedate him, he told her to go downstairs and get wrist restraints and mitts.

McGuinness thought: what am I seeing? This is awful.

She went downstairs and got the additional restraints and

mitts. (The mitts would be put on the patient so he wouldn't scratch himself.)

While Tiller was fastening the new restraints and putting the mitts on Forsberg, McGuinness thought: the captain's muscles have changed, and he's almost strong enough to break out of bed… I know it's irrational, but I think he's going to kill people. She stopped herself from breaking into tears. She thought more: and I'm not allowed to talk to anybody! I can't even speak to the doctor about this, and I'm standing right next to him.

Lloyd, outside on guard, watched as she'd gone back and forth from the room to downstairs, seemingly more and more desperate, her face getting more ashen pale. He'd heard a few sounds in the room when the door was shut but he didn't know what they were. Each time the nurse passed him she said nothing. Lloyd thought: something dire was going on, but they're managing it.

McGuinness and the doctor left the room at the same time. As the doctor headed to the staircase to go downstairs he noticed the nurse wasn't behind him. She was still in the corridor, not far from the room. Then he saw she was heading down the corridor to its opposite end. Well, he, thought, I hope she can unwind.

Kelso's eyes followed her down the stark, cheerless hallway. She seemed fraught; she was a somber figure, head to toe in nurse's white. She wasn't saying a thing to anybody.

At the end of the hallway was a window. It was a multi-paned, metal-framed institutional kind. Its left and right sashes that opened outward. McGuinness undid the latch of the right sash and let it swing on its hinges out into the night air.

The patient was scaring her to death. She looked out the window and wanted to be a thousand miles away.

There was an infirmary at Chitose II. She must, she told herself, get assigned there. How could she?

They would probably say no. A nurse is supposed to be

able to put up with seeing and treating patients who have unsightly conditions.

She was desperate. She could lie, and insinuate that Roger Lumley was getting too close to her, and that she felt threatened. No, she couldn't lie, and also, her superiors would say the presence of bothersome G.I.s had to be tolerated while working on military bases, that the kind of thing she was complaining about happened all the time.

She certainly couldn't say she wanted to be assigned to Chitose II because she didn't want to care for Captain Forsberg anymore. It would be ridiculous to say that; it would be like saying she didn't want to be a nurse.

What if she'd been wrong about herself and going into nursing all along? Maybe she should have stayed home. She missed her mother's voice and advice, her siblings' everyday lives. But here, outside of work, there was a promise being able to experience new things. (She never met Bob Fernandez—but she did have wanderlust, just as that could be said of him.)

Kanashi ka na (which in Japanese means "Alas"), these thoughts made up only ten percent of what flashed through her as she stood before the open window. The rest of her thoughts were betokened by her eyes which had widened, transfixed in fear.

To her, Forsberg wasn't a man. He was a fiendish, virulent *thing*.

The trauma she felt being placed in the situation she was in was indescribable.

Somehow, after a few minutes, she left the spot at the far end of the corridor. Her cork-soled shoes touched the tiles of the hallway with dread as she stepped forward. It was like she was being pushed by an unseen force from behind. As she got closer to Lloyd standing guard, she began to stare at his sympathetic features. He stood there silently, trying to not look at her directly. She looked very bothered and he didn't want to bother her more.

She took two more steps and brought her body up against his. She pushed her head against his upper breast, just below his shoulder. It was strangely like they were about to begin a slow dance in a ballroom—her arms, though, didn't gently rest on him; instead, she threw them around him, clasping him, clutching him in terror.

Lloyd stood stock-still. His first reaction was not serious; he thought to himself: so much for the rumor that Lumley was bedding Nurse McGuinness (loose talk that Lumley did nothing to quash).

The nurse stood there trembling, terrified, and didn't say anything. Lloyd felt her body: it wasn't warm, it was clammy.

He didn't know what to say or do—it was a surprise to be confronted like this (if confront was the right word). He smelled her perspiring. He thought some more. Yes, he reflected, the condition of the captain has scared her, and she can't handle it.

He could sense her eyes had released tears, and she could do nothing to stop them from streaming down her face.

He just stood there straight, like a tree, with Marcia holding him in a tight, desperate embraces. His being startled had not worn off; she still was saying nothing.

He wondered how long they would stay like this. Strangely, it was as if time had stopped. But time being stopped is not always fortunate —for one thing, her right cheek was digging into the right side of his chest, and it hurt. Also, the fabric of her nurse's cap was scratching his chin, so much so, he thought he might have to move to stop being irritated by it.

He hoped she would say something soon. He didn't want to say anything or flinch—he didn't want to upset her any more than she already was.

Fortunately, she shifted her head to speak, and it against his chest with less force; her cap no longer scratched him.

When she spoke, though, it was with a voice that sounded far away. "I can't tell, I'm not supposed to," she whispered to his shoulder blade.

Lloyd considered her words. His orders were to ignore all aspects of the care Forsberg was getting, to never mention to anyone anything he ever saw in the infirmary. He whispered back, "I know."

She maintained her grip on him and whispered nervously once more, "They're not telling me the truth. His skin is gross and hairy. His face, his grin—it's awful."

She held back a sob. "I can't even talk to the doctor about it. Something wrong is going on. I can't take it any longer."

Lloyd comforted her, "There's always a guard here, someone always here to protect you, to stop any... there's always a guard to ensure that...

Marcia, in a spasm, whispered again with a disembodied voice, "Ensure that what?"

"That no intruders come," was Lloyd's reflexive reply.

"But the danger's inside!" Marcia cried out softly. His body looks like something I've never seen before. Nobody can explain it." Her voice dropped a little and darkened, "But Major Beaumont knows what's going on and he's not saying anything."

Lloyd could only find these words: "Try not to be scared. Lie to yourself: tell yourself you're overreacting."

"But I'm not," Marcia said, softly, coldly.

Lloyd felt her body shudder.

He wanted her to stop suffering. This couldn't last too much longer before someone would come up the stairs and see the shape she was in. He said quite innocently, "Please, tell me if you can: is there anything I can do to help?"

Marcia didn't respond.

He tried again. "You can tell me. I won't tell anybody else." After he said this, he regretted it. It was too instinctive to say that. He should have taken his time and thought about the implications of what he was saying.

She still uttered no words. Lloyd could sense her tears

renewing, uncontrollably.

After she cried in silence for a short time, finally she whispered, "I can't tell you, but I will. He's heavily restrained in his bed. That's proof that he's a monster—or a monster's inside him."

The words made Lloyd's mind flash back to when he'd had a panic attack on the street in Chitose after a night of drinking with Bob Fernandez. He paused to consider what he might say to her next.

It seemed she couldn't free herself, that she needed someone else to say the right words that'd get through to her and help her escape what was torturing her. It occurred to him that one tack to try was to accept her words at face value, respond with sincerity, and acknowledge the presence of a monster inside the captain.

He said to her firmly but softly, "Well, then we'll all have to be brave."

He knew she felt no courage when she rambled back in a series of murmurs, "I'm trapped here. I signed up. I can't walk away. I feel like killing myself because I'm not supposed to leave and there's no way out."

She choked back a crying sound and whispered and exclaimed at the same time: "I've prayed to God to give me strength. I'm supposed to nurse the sick—not to bring people into a situation where…" Her voice trailed off.

She clung to him in silence. Fortunately, she began again, almost letting out a gasp, "He's getting stronger but he's not waking up. It's horrible!"

Lloyd didn't know what she was talking about. He had no idea what to say or do.

He said impotently, "Please tell me what I can do to help you."

She protested softly, clutching him harder, "Nothing!"

He stood there, thoughts racing through his mind. A new idea came to him. He said softly, "I know what it's like to panic like you're panicking now. I've been through it. I still go through it. You're on a battlefield—or it's after the battlefield. The panic is hitting you, it's bitten into you."

She thought: it's more than panic.

He continued to whisper with care, "You can tell me anything. Move the panic out of your mind. Try not to be afraid."

She thought: that's impossible.

He continued, "Tell me things. Whatever you want. I'll listen. You'll be calmer. Give me some of the burden. I agree with you: there's a monster inside. The world's full of monsters. It's what makes the world awful and scary. But you can't live in fear twenty-four hours a day." He paused and whispered more, "Gather some strength. Tell me."

She murmured, "I don't have any more strength left."

"Every fear you have is real and it can be justified. That's because monsters are real! They do exist! They exist to destroy us. When we meet them, our natural reaction is to go crazy 'cause it's just too much to take."

More images from Lloyd's panic attack on the icy street in Chitose flashed through his mind—more of it than he'd remembered since then. He waited for Marcia, who was more than a head shorter than him (and four years older—at his age, such differences mattered), to respond to his last attempt at comforting words.

She pressed against him, not saying anything. She was damp and trembling less. She was thinking. She focused on stopping crying.

A half a minute passed, and her tears stopped. She spoke hastily, "I'm getting your uniform wet. Sorry."

She loosened herself from him.

Lloyd didn't know what it was that'd helped her to stop crying and move from him, but he was glad she did before anybody saw her. She spoke with a voice that was more "here" than far away. She was still afraid, it seemed, but not as afraid. "Thank you," she whispered and took a step back from him. Her face was red and moist from the tears.

She thought about her cap and how it must have dug into Lloyd's chin but said nothing about it.

vii.

Lieutenant Nichols and Sergeant Velchoffsky were in the corridor just outside the secretarial services room. They could stand there, on the other side of the door case, and talk and not be heard above the clattering sound of a typewriter that the second of two male secretaries was using.

Happy to be up on his feet rather than sitting, Nichols stretched his limbs now and again. This was supposed to be a break, after all.

Not realizing he was blankly staring into the secretarial services room as he spoke, Velchoffsky went straight to what was on his mind: "Damn that guard duty at the infirmary. It's driven Stan Shuck around the bend. I think he's told other men that Forsberg planned all the murders in Chitose. Or Lord knows what he's saying. I guess that's why now, when I mention guard duty assignment, any MP pretends they're not hearing what I'm saying at first. … Look, I cut Stan loose. He won't be doing guard duty at the infirmary anymore. I had to do it—there was no other choice. Now somebody else has to be found, and we don't have many available men. I'm stuck. I can't think of anybody off hand—we want to hold our best men in reserve for emergencies. Do you have any ideas?"

The rapid tapping of metal keys hitting typing paper continued with no pauses—that was because were no mistakes were being made. The man at the typewriter was a Black soldier, Thomas Delbert.

Lieutenant Nichols inquired, "Well, where will you send Shuck now? Wherever you're sending Shuck for his new duty, have the guy he's replacing go over to the infirmary and stand guard there.

"I can't do that."

"How so?"

377

"Shuck's not replacing anybody. I'm putting him on perimeter guard duty with Private Aiello. Aiello has to stay where he is because he's girl crazy. He would drive the nurses crazy at the infirmary if I put him there. That's the thing— so far, I've been able to staff the guard with guys who I think aren't going to bother the girls."

The expression on Lieutenant Nichols's told Velchoffsky he didn't have any new ideas about a replacement. Velchoffsky said, "I know you have to get back to work. Just wanted to let you know."

There was a pause in their conversation. Both men had fallen into peering blankly into the secretarial services room.

Nichols didn't move to go back into the room to go back to work. He liked being on a break, plus, he was still thinking. Velchoffsky thought maybe the lieutenant was going through lists of men in his mind. It was true. Finally Nichols said, "There is somebody that could do it. He's not going to bother the nurses. I think I know him well enough to say that."

"Who?"

"We're looking at him right now."

Velchoffsky refocused his eyes that were fixed vaguely in front of them. "Corporal Johnson?"

"No, not him," Nichols intoned. He's not the one.

There were two soldiers in the room: Corporal Johnson and Private Delbert. Even though Velchoffsky had Delbert in his field of vision, it would never occur to him to tap him for the assignment. You don't arm a Negro and let him stand guard around a whole bunch of White people.

"What?!" Velchoffsky winced.

Nichols turned his eyes sideways to look directly at Velchoffsky. "Eisenhower says we have to integrate the Army at all levels."

"But we decided to put him here, in secretarial services."

"Yes, we did. But he's needed elsewhere—at least for the moment."

Private Delbert sat at his desk, typing prodigiously, oblivious to being put under a microscope.

Nichols went on. "Not a lucky break for secretarial services because he's a hell of a typist." He held his gaze on the young man; he sighed and exhaled, "He'll be missed."

viii.

Marcia McGuinness had almost no contact with Black Americans her entire life. The Massachusetts South Shore where she grew up was White. In nursing school and in her short career, there'd been no Blacks. She wondered if their skin was thicker than Whites' skin, and if you had to press that much harder on the plunger of a syringe for the medicine to get into them.

She didn't know how insidiously conditioned she was, and had no idea how much Black life in America had given shape to American life in general. (Like many people, she could naïvely imagine that "She'll Be Coming 'Round the Mountain When She Comes" is not deeply meaningful. However, it's a Negro Spiritual, that crossed over into mainstream America—the "She" of the song is the chariot that Christ arrives on, when he comes back fulfilling the Second Coming prophecy.)

Marcia had a brief conversation with Lloyd when he first came on his shift. He mentioned his new friend, a young Black man from New York City—Thomas Delbert was his name—would be on guard duty the evening after he was.

She had no response to that. She only thought, well, the Blacks have arrived, and it won't be too long before I'm treating one of them.

She was still felt the terror of the previous night's ordeal with Forsberg (where he had to be given phenobarbital and she clung to Lloyd).

To survive, the solution was to mentally detach herself. She didn't want to be in the infirmary anymore; nonetheless she worked there, needed to be there. It's a summer day and

I'm on shore, she thought. There are people out on a floating dock, out in the water a hundred yards from shore. Sometimes they're sitting there, sometimes they're jumping off the dock and swimming. In a minute I'm going to go into the water and swim out and join them. The sun is warming me up. Now I'm ready. I'm jumping in now. I'm swimming, I feel the cool water and splashing all around me. I'm in control. Nobody will hurt me.

The evening was turning into night. The full moon had already passed Forsberg's window; it no long shone directly onto the patient's bed.

It was just before 11:40 p.m. when Private Delbert went in after hearing noises, thinking someone had broken into Forsberg's room from outside—they might have gotten inside by mounting a ladder against the wall, climbing it, he thought. (The window was small, though he didn't know that because he'd never been in the room.)

Though he wasn't supposed to, he felt he had no other choice but to go in.

The room's overhead lights were off. He'd had no time to switch them on because the second he entered he saw Forsberg was trying to free himself from his restraints. If there were restraints on him, there was good reason why he wasn't supposed to get out of bed.

The sound of thwacking helicopter blades making a night landing had escaped Thomas Delbert's notice—though he was only able to see the captain because of light coming from that very helicopter. Its headlights fleetingly streamed in, garishly lighting up the patient whose jaw looked deformed, whose mouth drooled and whose teeth champed ferociously while writhing to be free.

The captain's breath smelled to him like dog's breath; it struck unbelievable fear into Thomas.

Maybe the captain had rabies, the private thought. I've heard stories about rabies.

Because he could see, he was able to wedge the barrel of

his Colt M1911 pistol in the captain's mouth in such a way to prevent him from snapping more.

Outside of basic training, this was the first time he'd ever used a gun.

Thomas pressed down hard on one of Forsberg's legs with his left hand to hold it to the mattress. He bore down with his right fist on the captain's vigorously heaving chest.

He must stop the captain from getting up—he felt something awful—even somebody's death—would be caused if he were to escape his restraints.

On her way up the stairs just at then, Nurse McGuinness heard noises coming from within Forsberg's room. The door was open… No MP stood guard there. She hurried her steps forward, automatically, though if she'd been in full possession of herself, she would've turned and gone downstairs to get a man to go into the room.

But her body kept moving forward to her nursing assignment.

When she stepped into the room, she screamed a scream that switched on automatically—the sound ejaculated from her lungs without being commanded to do so by her brain. Though the room was half dark, she could just make out that, again, too much hair covered the captain. Instantly she let her mind make the whole scene blurry. (So blurry, that there could have been, for all she knew, a fire blazing in one of the corners of the room.)

But she could still see that the young Black soldier had jammed his pistol into the White man's mouth—though the White man was dark now, and looked like a beast…And this Black kid was frantically trying to contain Forsberg's movements and keep him in his bed—yes, this was an important thing to do—if only she could help—but there wasn't anything she could do.

When Thomas Delbert saw Marcia in the room, he yelled to her to bring help.

Marcia hurried downstairs.

Corporal Lumley came into the room carrying a Colt M1911 pistol.

In the struggle to keep the patient in the bed, Private Delbert was still winning. Forsberg had not yet managed to break his bonds.

Lumley only stood by. He didn't want to mix his hands or gun into the fray. There was another factor: the captain was abnormally hairy. It would be disgusting to touch him...Roger decided Delbert alone was doing a good enough job, at least until a tranquilizing dart could put the animal down.

Almost no time passed. A pallid, otherworldly-looking Nurse McGuinness came back with a syringe loaded with morphine sulfate. In a mechanical voice she said to the corporal, "Roger, you help hold him down, too, so I can inject him." Lumley winced—and he didn't like being given orders by Marcia, a young woman. Where was the doctor? he thought. Anyway, he obeyed her.

In a couple of minutes, the morphine, a fraternal twin to codeine, brought an opiate stillness to the hairy, repugnant body.

Once the captain was sedated, Thomas Delbert took his hands off him and removed his pistol from his mouth. He withdrew from the room discreetly, going back to stand guard in the corridor.

After Thomas left, the stupefied nurse closed the door quietly. She avoided eye contact with Lumley. During the brief lull it came to her that she must leave the room right away.

She left but didn't go downstairs. Instead, she walked down the corridor, to the same window which she'd taken refuge the night before. The guard Thomas Delbert's eyes followed her down that drab, bleak hallway.

Before she was halfway to the end, though, Roger Lumley came quickly out of Forsberg's room, shut the door behind him, and softly called out "Marcia!"

But Marcia didn't turn around. With her gaze on the window at the corridor's end in front of her, she made a gesture with her hand behind her for Roger to not come toward her, to stay away.

Roger then turned, and without looking at Thomas Delbert, went downstairs to report to Dr. Tiller that the morphine had taken hold.

Five minutes or so went by as Nurse McGuinness stood in a daze at the window she'd opened. During that time Private Delbert stood at attention outside the patient's room, struggling to smother his feelings: incoming waves of fear jolted him, he wanted to jump out of his body.

Dr. Tiller came up to the floor, said nothing, noticed the nurse had gone to the end of the corridor and the window there (how he hoped she would not attempt to quit her job).

He went into the patient's dark room and gave him a shot of Thorazine, an anti-psychotic medication not usually given to comatose patients.

To his chagrin, Keith Tiller's noticed tough, short hairs on the captain's body. He shook his head displeased, angry about how orders about how to treat Forsberg were coming from people who knew nothing about medicine.

He took the captain's pulse. It was normal. He left the room, shutting the door behind him.

Upon stepping into the hall, he heard a timid voice come from the stationary figure that was so close he could hear it breathe. "Excuse me, Doctor, sir," Private Delbert said, trying not to tremble, "You might have heard. I went into the room. Does the captain have anything that might be contagious? Could I catch something?"

The doctor rested on his feet, looked the guard up and down and said, "No, son, whatever he has, Black folk are immune to."

The doctor then walked to the staircase and went down, continuing to be peeved about being shuttled to the side regarding Forsberg's care.

Nurse McGuinness left her spot at the window at the end of the corridor after several minutes.

As she got nearer to Private Delbert, it came to her mind, again, that she lacked any familiarity with African Americans, and that moreover, she looked down on them as if they were an inferior race, dangerous and potentially violent.

With a brief glance at him standing there, she thought about the look she saw in his eyes. It was one of alarm and dread. The young soldier was horror-stricken, just like any White soldier would be. He'd been smart enough to risk disciplinary actions and go in there because he recognized the intention of his orders rather than obeying extraneous details. These were his orders: you are there, and you will protect people from monsters. He was brave. He prevented the captain from breaking loose... and killing.

CHAPTER 34

"If I can talk to him."

"But he's in a coma."

"Maybe he keeps himself there."

"What? …I don't understand you."

It was 10 p.m. Only the desk lamp was turned on in a room in the guest quarters at Chitose I.

Each man was seated in a folding chair. One was an officer—it was Major Beaumont. He was in fatigues. The other was the civilian Ilmar Hodinar. He wore a dark green suit, it was rumpled.

"The case could be that he *wants* to remain in a coma," Hodinar said with his light East-European accent. He was tired. His long trip from Washington, D.C.—the last leg of his trip was on a B11, from Tokyo—was at an end.

"You really think a person can choose to stay in a coma?" Major Beaumont asked. But he knew better than to be skeptical of any of the professor's hypotheses.

Hodinar paused to organize his thoughts, then spoke, "I had many hours to think during the trip. Let me explain what came to me while it's still fresh in my mind." Having said this though, fatigue caused him to digress momentarily, "When you fly halfway around the world your blood pressure rises. Did you know that? Of course, the state of our brain is affected as well. …My mind was freely associating. A new idea came to me about Forsberg."

Hodinar became instantly aware of his slight digression and said, "But let me get to my point." He paused again to gather his thoughts.

"There are times in the field—in the field of battle, that is—before or after shots are exchanged, when some men freeze up. They can't fire their guns and even much less than that. Some can't even move. Some have their minds stop. Their catatonia isn't fake. Their subconscious has taken over. That part of the person has directed his body to shut down. The condition is not unlike some comatose conditions."

Major Beaumont had been in the battlefields of World War II. He knew what Hodinar was talking about. He knew of soldiers who went blind temporarily or became rigid with paralysis—especially on the eve of a battle. Then there were the cases after the battle. Soldiers with no physical wounds would be insensate. They were traumatized and could not walk or speak.

Hodinar continued, "Well, just as sodium pentothal was used successfully in some cases to get some of these soldiers actually back on their feet—yes, it was an emergency measure that worked at times, it wasn't a final cure—I've decided the drug's worth a try with Forsberg. There's no risk with it. The worse that could happen is it sedates him and his body rests deeper, but not fatally deeper. The drug wears off in four hours."

For Beaumont, it was intellectually thrilling to be in the company of his old friend once more. Hodinar often came to problems with a new way of looking at them. The only new idea that Tim himself had come up with during Forsberg's episodes of "hypertrichosis" (and worse) was to cut off his food and let him die. But that wasn't a new idea. The thought had crossed the minds of the others—the nurse, the orderly, even Dr. Tiller when their patience was being tried. The only trouble was, Beaumont thought, what if Grendel realized it was being starved to death? What might it do to fight back to save its life?

Hodinar continued expansively. "Well, I did have another idea before I thought of sodium pentothal. I considered

386

shocking his body—not with electricity. …I was thinking about insulin shock therapy—it's worked in some cases of schizophrenia. You inject to induce an hour-long coma; you repeat this for a sequence of days; this treatment allows some patients to regain their mental health. So, this made me think I might chemically shock Forsberg out of his coma. I thought of using aconite—it's a poison found in nature that primitive hunters use. Do you remember I experimented with it on Forsberg at Camp Riley? Aconite, it's also called wolf's bane…"

Beaumont nodded.

Hodinar finished, "…it's a substance never to be underrated.

Beaumont asked softly, "But aconite…wouldn't that risk killing him?"

"If he's given too much. But in certain amounts it might be a useful therapeutic irritant—though on the other hand it might stimulate lycanthropic changes—you know, the body of the beast inside fights back, gathers whatever powers it can to stay alive… we will have produced a ferocious wild being who attacks and tries to kill us. So, there's a lot of risk with using aconite. There is, though, one known antidote to it—digitoxin. I thought of having some in a syringe, handy, if I tried the aconite on him."

Hodinar paused. He was tired. He needed it to stay alert. "Aconite is a powerful substance—but you see, it's just too powerful and unpredictable. Then it happened: on the final flight here, the thought came to me of coma-like trances and the use of sodium pentothal to get people who were in them out of them. …Doctors don't only inject pentothal; they *talk* to their subject; they're psychiatric explorers entering the patient's subconscious once that drug takes effect."

Hodinar shifted in his chair. He'd been sitting for hours and hours for the last day and a half. "In summary, the risk of aconite *causing* severe lycanthropic episodes was too great. Sodium pentothal is a sedative, however. It won't cause any violent reactions. It's injected and the doctor—in this case, I will do it—probes the mind, gently questioning the patient, who is in a state akin to being under hypnosis."

"You want to proceed on the assumption that he's put a block in his mind against being conscious?"

"Yes. Why be conscious when it's too painful? The coma gives him a way out. From what I observed of him at Fort Riley five years ago, and what I imagine of the life he's led since then, it's not unreasonable to think he feels his existence is wretched and not worth continuing—only that there's something in him that prevents him from taking his own life."

"I see."

"If I'm wrong, at least I've tried one way to end a stalemate here." Hodinar had said what he needed to. He touched the top of his forehead for a moment, pressed it, and yawned.

Major Beaumont couldn't help but ask, "When do you want to start?"

Ilmar Hodinar's face relaxed out of tiredness. "If we begin right away, I might have time to go into town and see the local *Obon* festival. It lasts for three days, I believe. I'd very much enjoy seeing some of it.

"You know about *Obon?*"

"I understand it's a Japanese Buddhist festival. I've read about it. I count myself lucky to be here when it'll be underway. Are you familiar with it? You were here last August."

"Yeah, I saw the *Obon* parade."

"I'm interested in seeing these celebrations."

The two men were referring to the Japanese festival in August which honored the spirits of one's deceased relatives. There were both public celebrations outdoors and private ones indoors—indoors an extended family would gather; a Buddhist monk might visit and recite a sutra and perform a memorial service. *Obon* was a happy occasion. The souls of the departed were welcomed back in joyous ways—reminiscing, food, dancing, singing. One did not want to scare the ancestors away with glumness—they'd stay away from a depressing place—where they were in the afterlife was depressing enough.

The major knew their conversation for the night had been concluded. He said, "I'll say *Gute Nacht,* now."

"Yes, good night to you, too, Tim. It's such a pleasure to see you again."

The major said, "Likewise." He rose from his chair, folded it up and set it against the wall in a space next to the guest room's closet. "See you tomorrow."

Beaumont opened the door and let himself out. Hodinar kept the room dim as he prepared himself for bed.

During the day before Ilmar Hodinar's arrival—he was a strange new figure for sure—Marcia McGuinness and others who'd been around Forsberg were talked to—individual apologies were doled out to each of them. Beaumont spearheaded the effort.

Beaumont charged Jake Torrington with making apologies to Marcia because any such expressions from himself, he felt, were useless. Beaumont couldn't be effective because Tiller had poisoned any well of good will Marcia might have had for him. The major assumed she didn't trust him, that she thought he was hiding the real story about Forsberg and was perversely exposing those in the infirmary to injury and even death.

"We apologize for putting you in harm's way and causing you fear." Captain Torrington said solemnly to Nurse McGuinness, following the playbook devised by Beaumont. "You should be provided a safe environment and we let you down. We want you to be able to take pride and pleasure in your work. We failed you."

How out of the ordinary. Someone who she'd never seen before was apologizing to her.

Who was this Captain Jake Torrington? The army could be a such a faceless monolith. Sure, he was from CIMIC. She could have cared less what unit he was attached to or what that unit did. It was all the same. He was a stranger.

Jake was glad McGuinness didn't know anything about him. Trying to use this to his advantage, he presented himself to her as an important higher-up who desperately needed to relay to her that the army was deeply sorry for its missteps. "The situations were frightful. Characteristics of Forsberg's body and condition are not to be spoken of, ever. We did not protect you as we should have. We've put in place measures that'll ensure such things will never again occur." He didn't mention to her any exact measures.

Torrington wasn't the only one Beaumont sent to apologize to the nurse—the major was right in believing she should get all the apologies they could muster—without appearing to go overboard, of course—that would then make her think they were being disingenuous. Beaumont asked Major Chris de Graff to visit the nurse after her meeting with Torrington was over. (Tim was so glad he'd brought Chris into the loop. He was perfect for the role; he reeked of authority. De Graff, too, was someone she'd never spoken to.)

De Graff, in a crisp uniform with gold oak leaf insignia on the shoulder bars, seemed severe to her (to anyone else he might have appeared gentle and steady). "I want to emphasize how sorry we are, Nurse McGuinness," he said, like a contrite but still mighty god.

Had Marcia been of good health and more self-aware, she would have recognized the officer speaking to her wasn't being stern. But she was in such a daze that she barely noticed anything about the high-ranking officer.

He continued soberly, "It was an unseen series of occurrences. I'm told that you stayed cool under fire. We thank you. We can't thank you enough. Please realize it wasn't our intention to distress you. Your service to our armed forces and our country is invaluable. There's no reason for alarm anymore."

McGuinness had to be handled with sensitivity; she wasn't a soldier in the army; she had no security clearances. She was psychologically injured. She might speak of her experiences to somebody. She had to be told she must remain silent. "You cannot ever speak of what transpired in that room. Descriptions of Forsberg's body and condition are not to be spoken of, ever. We understand your pain and suffering. But this is a top secret matter. Do you understand?"

The nurse muttered that she understood.

"If you have any emotional difficulties regarding your recent experiences, come to me—no one else. I will see to it that you're steered into a safe and confidential harbor. Remember, our nation's security is at stake."

The major then added, "I understand you're being given one week's leave and then you'll be stationed in the infirmary at Chitose II. I hope these things help."

It was the first time that Marcia had heard she was being given a short leave and she'd be transferred to the new infirmary.

Corporal Roger Lumley was spoken to by Major de Graff as well; de Graff was deployed for the same reasons that had sent him to Marcia and speaking to her. Lumley would need to be given a convincing apology, and Major Beaumont would not be well received.

Lumley knew Logistics was tasked with medical services in the army, and that de Graff was the big cheese there. The corporal, though shook up by the acute situations with Forsberg, had seen less than Nurse McGuinness in *that room;* he wasn't in the state she was in (though this was not to say, however, that the experience wasn't frightening, disgusting and weird) and he was, sensibly so, angry.

He was angry that whatever happened was being allowed to happen.

Lumley appreciated, on one level, the star treatment he got by Major de Graff visiting him. Forsberg was an important person the army was working with—otherwise, why would they be going to so much trouble to apologize to him? What Lumley didn't immediately get was that it wasn't only an apology the major had for him, but a warning, too—a warning to keep his mouth shut. The major was good at not sounding threatening. But it was there; it took Lumley half a minute to see it.

De Graff said to him right off, "Corporal Lumley, there's a top secret operation which you were never intended to be part of. You are to repeat nothing about it. Descriptions of Forsberg's bodily actions and his condition are not to be spoken of, ever. I regret that you experienced what you did, and I am sorry for the pain and suffering it has caused. But this is the army, son, and you and I remain alive—this is fortunate for you and fortunate for me. Now if you ever have any anxious thoughts that connect to the past few weeks, and you *must* talk to someone, come to me, and no one else. Is that clear?"

"Yes, sir."

"Good. Remember what we used to say during the war: "Loose lips sink ships. They do. I can't emphasize that enough. We who are concerned with this case will be keeping our eyes open and our ears to the ground, so take care to obey my orders."

While Major de Graff was in the infirmary, he circled back to visit Keith Tiller. He told the doctor plain and simple, much like he did Lumley, that Forsberg was part of an ongoing top secret operation. He said the army and he were sorry that Tiller hadn't been informed earlier but it'd been hoped it wouldn't be necessary to inform him of the special nature of Forsberg's "circumstances."

The doctor started to say something; Major de Graff perceived they would be words of protest. He cut him off. "I'm sorry but I need you to let *me* talk. We offer you our profound apologies. It turned out that Army Intelligence overplayed their hand—I am letting you know that much. I know this has caused panic and harm to you and your staff. We value your service and their service to our country. But I must emphasize an order to you: descriptions and discussions of Forsberg's symptoms and actions are not to be engaged in, ever. You are to remain silent of these unfortunate top secret medical incidences that occurred on your watch. A new team is in place and snafus such as those that have transpired won't occur again. We can be certain of that. You're assigned to Chitose II from tomorrow onward. You have a good working relationship with Nurse McGuinness, and we want you to continue in this regard. She has been given a week's leave and will join you at the new infirmary. If in the future any disquieting thoughts crop up in your mind related to these matters, report only to me—no one else. I will see to it that your cares are properly addressed. Also, as Nurse McGuinness's boss, please see to it if she has any worrisome concerns that I'm contacted right away, all right? She is not to talk to you about any of the events which grievously involved you and her. Do you understand? Don't attempt to countermand my authority. This is beyond your authority as a medical man. You are a military man in this case, and I am your superior."

Beaumont had no significant contact with the soldiers working as military police guards guarding Forsberg's room; he'd only passed them on his way into the sick room. Because of this there could hardly be any negative consequences of meeting with Stan Shuck, Lloyd Kelso and Thomas Delbert. Through Sergeant Velchoffsky they were summoned. Each young man reported to Major Beaumont's office individually. To each he said more or less the same thing: "The defense of our country and our way of life is in a critical state. We are at war. Officers subordinate to me do not have the clearances and are not in the know regarding the matter that brings me to you. As the commander of C2I, I must inform you that you were exposed to a patient whose is more than his service record, and that further information about him is top secret. We did not anticipate this. The patient in the infirmary whom you guarded…" (Beaumont did not speak Forsberg's name) "…has survived; he is a sick man, and he's been successfully protected—by you, in part. We thank you for courage and resilience."

When he met alone with young Thomas Delbert he added, "Your bravery carried the day, private, and I commend you."

To each of the guards he emphasized, "You are not to reveal any knowledge you have of the patient's health or any actions in or outside the patient's room. You are not permitted to speak of what transpired during your guard duty—ever. Even for civilian patients there are privacy laws—I say that just to compare this situation to more normal ones. We understand the situation brought pain and suffering to the infirmary staff, and that you yourself were not unaffected. But I must emphasize that the whole matter is confidential and classified. You are never to talk among the other guards, the military police, or the infirmary staff, about what you saw, heard or did. You will not be assigned guard duty at the infirmary, ever again."

He added, trying not to sound harsh, "We'll be monitoring your conduct to be sure our orders are obeyed."

After Beaumont spoke with the three guards, both he *and* Major de Graff drove over to military police headquarters. It was a show of strength and power to have them appear together.

When they got to the station, they both strode in and asked the clerk to put in calls to Nichols and Velchoffsky. Being visited by Beaumont and de Graff was an occasion. It was almost as if the base commander, Colonel Gerald Brewster, himself had come. This had to be very important.

They met in Nichols' office; the first lieutenant's secretary was sent out of the room. None of the officers sat down. It seemed the majors wanted it that way. They intended to stay for no more than five minutes.

Beaumont: "Sergeant Velchoffsky, thank you again for sending the young men over to me. I had a talk with each of them separately. I addressed behavior when faced with top secret matters. They are not to speak of their experiences as guards in the infirmary—ever—and neither are both of you to echo any of their sentiments. If you have heard talk coming from there, don't ever repeat it. As you know, the men are not volunteers. They never asked to be inducted into the army, or sent here. If someone mentions anything from their time at the infirmary, call me. Furthermore, the three young men in question—Shuck, Kelso and Delbert—I've told them they'll never be assigned guard duty at the infirmary again. I understand this may cause some scheduling difficulties, but I'm envisioning a day—soon—when Captain Forsberg no longer needs a guard."

Nichols and Velchoffsky continued standing, in silence.

Then Major de Graff spoke (the two majors had rehearsed it): "As you know, the army engages in research…"

"And intelligence gathering," Beaumont interjected.

De Graff continued, "Sometimes these activities are conducted right in front of our faces. I'm sure you've always had reasonable questions regarding Forsberg's transfer to Chitose. I can confirm that his transfer here was unusual and is part of a larger project. I'm not at liberty to speak to the magnitude of the project, but it's operational and you're not part of it, except that you provide cover. All that's been asked of you both is your cooperation, and you have given that unstintingly, and we appreciate your continuing cooperation."

Neither Nichols nor Velchoffsky asked questions of the two executive officers, so the brief meeting was over.

The senior officers left and the two top cops went back to work.

Out in the police station's parking lot de Graff said to

Beaumont: "Tim, do you think anybody who's been working at the infirmary is going to come to you—I mean, come to you because they're going crazy."

"That's a good question."

"What will you do if they do?"

"You're going to be introduced to Professor Ilmar Hodinar soon. He's arriving in one hour. He's the expert. I'll be taking advice from him."

Nurse Marcia McGuinness was not receptive to the apologies extended to her. She had been through too much. What a fate it had been to be assigned to the 120th Medical Battalion in Chitose. Now she was only going through the motions of her nursing job; her mind drifted to thoughts such as of the character Heathcliff in *Wuthering Heights*— Heathcliff becomes beastlike and is raving mad in that novel. Another thought that came to her—this was when de Graff was apologizing—was the image of Lot's wife (In the Old Testament, Lot's wife, never given a proper name, was only just "Lot's wife." When Lot's wife looked behind her to see God's destruction wrought on the wicked city of Sodom— against angels' orders to not look back—she was turned into a pillar of salt.

Chitose, too, was a place of wickedness for Marcia. And Beaumont was warning her to not look back, so to speak, at what had taken place in Forsberg's room.

When Major de Graff apologized to Roger Lumley, the corporal's reaction to the apology—and warning—was like Stan Shuck's reaction to Major Beaumont's apology to him: he thought it was standard army B.S., artifice and need to control. Shuck was more mind-scattered and less angry than Lumley. Shuck criticized himself for being stupid enough to sneak into Forsberg's room while on guard duty. Lumley thought they'd all been set up, and he didn't like having to bring a second loaded Colt M1911 into the sick room—a lethal sick room. He was bitter that Nurse McGuinness had been put through (look at what she'd become now) one traumatic experience after another. He felt that if they'd all found themselves in a dangerous, perhaps deadly, top secret situation—which they should never have been part of in the first place, according to the majors—why was Forsberg in the infirmary in the first place? Neither Beaumont nor de Graff could ever know what they'd been subjected to! There could be no apology for it! Lumley thought de Graff was Beaumont's stooge.

Lloyd Kelso—not having experienced the terrifying things that the others had—only sensing them from a distance, as when Nurse McGuinness was in a state of shock and came to him and clutched him—didn't know precisely what had happened. So when the apologies were being doled out, he didn't know what he was being apologized for; he hadn't spoken to Thomas Delbert about events in the infirmary—his barracks were far from his.

Private Delbert (what he experienced still scared him to death) would have felt much better if he'd been able to talk to *anybody* and get off his chest what some of his thoughts were. However, the meetings of apologies came before he was able to commiserate with anyone. Delbert was receptive to Major Beaumont's apologies. He was too inexperienced in the army to be any other way; plus, being Black, you accept what you're offered; you don't complain about it.

Captain Forsberg was handed over to the care of Dr. Hodinar thanks to the orders of Colonel Gerald Brewster, the base commander, to which Major Beaumont had appealed. Though Brewster didn't know anything about Operation Grendel he honored the special request without question since it was brought to him by authorities with top secret credentials.

Dr. Tiller, after having to be reminded by Major de Graff of his rank in the army and what *chain of command* meant, thought to himself: what qualifications does this Hodinar have? Is he a medical doctor at all? (Maybe he has a Ph.D., is a researcher, a book writer, not a licensed physician.)

None of that mattered much though, because Tiller was reassigned to Chitose II, where he was only to concern himself with cases there.

The MP guard new to his assignment stood at attention outside Forsberg's room. The guard, a White soldier from Nebraska named Berens, saluted Major Beaumont briskly. He wore no holster and carried no gun, though he had a service knife and a can of mace.

Major Beaumont opened the patient's door to first let Dr. Hodinar, who stood behind him, enter. After they were inside, Beaumont swiftly closed the door.

The overhead lights, as usual, were off, but morning light was coming in through the small window and Ilmar Hodinar could see Forsberg's closed eyes and revolting grin (Beaumont had ordered the feeding tube going through the captain's nose to be removed). It was difficult to see Forsberg's flesh because of the grotesque latticework—the various crisscrossing bed restraints.

Hodinar gasped quietly, "What a spectacle this is!"

Beaumont nodded silently in agreement.

Hodinar looked at Forsberg's face. He had a scraggly beard and more hair covered places on his neck and head than when he'd seen Forsberg years ago at Fort Riley. Under the current circumstances—coma, cords, ropes, and whatnot used to restrain him, along with the large cotton mitts on Forsberg's hands—it was a challenge to identify a human amid it all.

Hodinar had discussed his process with Beaumont before, so when Hodinar pulled up a chair, ready to insert the syringe's needle into the captain, the major knew he should stand by—not stand by the patient, but stand over near the closed door.

This would be in case the guard was needed because Forsberg was becoming violent.

The professor slid the needle into a vein in the captain's left arm and pushed down the syringe's plunger, injecting a third of its contents. He would see how effective the drug was; he'd inject more if the dose wasn't giving him the desired effect.

Ilmar alternated looking at his watch with looking at the captain's sleepy, horrific face. Seven minutes passed. Neither he nor Tim said anything the whole time. After Hodinar saw the hideous grin on the captain's face relax, he cleared his throat to begin speaking softly.

The doctor spoke with many pauses between his words.

"You, Captain Gideon Forsberg, are under medical care. You are in an infirmary. It is on a U.S. Army base in Japan. You, I repeat, are under medical care. You were in a jeep accident in Chitose, Japan. You suffered a concussion. You are restrained in a hospital bed in Chitose. You are isolated from other patients. I believe you understand why we are justified in using bed restraints."

The last sentence made Beaumont flinch. Ilmar had discussed with him the methods and logistics in general terms. But he hadn't mentioned what words he might say.

There was no response from Forsberg to the professor's words. Ilmar let three minutes pass. Forsberg did not stir. The professor pressed on the syringe, injecting the second third of the pentothal solution into Forsberg. He let another four minutes go by. The area around Forsberg's mouth relaxed so much that it no longer gaped; his lips were almost closed.

Professor Hodinar spoke softly again; taking his time, he repeated what he'd said before, exactly.

Still no response.

Hodinar paused and went right back to the same speech, repeating it yet once more, calmly. Beaumont thought to himself: it's a good try by Ilmar, but it's not working.

There wasn't a look of frustration on Hodinar's face. His face was still; evidently, he was mentally examining whatever options there might be.

He considered injecting the last third of the sodium pentothal into the captain.

Before doing that, though, something came to him. He thought of a different tack to try. So far, he'd only referred to short-term events in trying to get through to Forsberg. However, he'd read up on findings about long-term memory and coma. He thought, I should try reaching the ideas that have been living in his mind for a long time.

He paused and then intoned softly,

> "Ancient wolf
> who more than all other beasts,
> requires endless prey,
> hunger never satisfied…
> to the gloomy end."

Hodinar paused to take a breath, then repeated,

> "Once again,
> ancient wolf
> who more than all other beasts,
> requires endless prey,
> hunger never satisfied…
> to the gloomy end."

It seemed to Beaumont that Hodinar thought he couldn't get through to him because he wasn't speaking to his subconscious in the right way. It was as though the mundane information surrounding what the captain was now experiencing were of no great concern to his subconscious. What mattered were the primordial feelings: hunger, threat and fear.

However, there was no response to these words, either. Beaumont thought: he's doing his best but it isn't working.

Still, Hodinar persisted. He said the new words—the ones about the wolf—once more again, calmly. After he finished with the words, "hunger never satisfied… to the gloomy end,'" he asked the captain, keeping his voice constant, "I ask

400

you Gideon Forsberg, do these words speak to you?"

"Yes," Forsberg muttered.

A muffled shockwave went through the room.

Beaumont almost believed he was hallucinating, that Forsberg hadn't said a thing.

Hodinar was very, very pleased. He'd used a quote from Dante's *Purgatory*. He thought: I have everything to lose by not being able to get through to him.

He intoned, "If you will permit me to say, 'Oh, that which thou surveyest from thine unenvied throne!'"

Inside Forsberg's brain a storm of color raged. He saw fresh brilliant colors—it was almost like he was seeing color for the first time. After Hodinar intoned the words "unenvied throne," vivid colors coursed through him and his ears stopped hearing for a moment.

Hodinar waited for another verbal response.

He received none.

Ilmar thought back to Fort Riley. He recalled seeing Forsberg in the library there one day, sitting at a table in a daze, the narcotic effects of codeine overwhelming him, and not knowing what to expect from Forsberg and his codeine habit.

The professor, by saying "unenvied throne" was being sardonic. He believed Forsberg knew he wasn't sitting on an enviable throne, but that he was condemned to exist in a profoundly *unenviable,* violent existential *pit*. Ilmar could only guess; but he had to find a way to address Forsberg. (He took the "throne" quote from John Milton—or was it Percy Shelley—it didn't matter, it was poetry—poetry, not prose, nor conversational speech—he thought it help get him into Forsberg's subconscious.)

Beaumont, standing near the door, followed the ministrations with respect—he admired Hodinar, was in awe of the man's abilities—his methods were not readily clear and understandable at times, but there were times what he did astonished with remarkable results). The major did not realize that Ilmar, being neither a conjurer nor experienced hypnotist, could only experiment with words and his tone of voice.

Now that Hodinar had gained an initial "yes" from his subject a minute ago, he didn't want to lose him. He thought about using the "throne" quote again, but felt he needed to say something not sardonic, but sympathetic to him.

Calmly, slowly, he intoned, making sure to mark the rhythm and rhyme:

> *"Like one, that on a lonesome road*
> *Doth walk in fear and dread,*
> *And having once turned round walks on,*
> *And turns no more his head."*

Inside Forsberg the embellished language and its meanings had a calming effect. Though his face showed nothing outwardly, the colors that had been racing through his mind slowed. Then, there was a snap, a break in it all. The colors stopped. His eyes fluttered. In fits and starts they struggled and opened more than halfway.

Forsberg saw the drab room and the strange drab man sitting in a chair next to his bed.

Ilmar was so convinced of the power of his last quote (he remembered it from Coleridge's "The Rime of the Ancient Mariner") that he wanted to say it again. After all, it was pertinent to Forsberg's existence.

But then he saw... *Forsberg's eyes were open!*

The eyes only stared at him. The rest of the face had no expression.

It surprised Ilmar so much that he didn't know what to do next. Out of nervousness he spoke his last spell one more time, articulating it with outmost care:

> *"Like one, that on a lonesome road*
> *Doth walk in fear and dread*
> *And having once turned round walks on,*
> *And turns no more his head."*

A moment passed.

Forsberg muttered, "Yes."

The professor thought to himself: I have him and I must take it to the next degree.

"You are safe," Hodinar said.

Forsberg blinked.

"We're navigating downstream," the professor said in a quiet, almost conversational tone. "The problems are upstream and we're not up there."

The professor purposefully chose water imagery—after all, the body is made of much water and the brain can be felt to be an immeasurable waterway. There's something calming about water, about streams, the professor thought.

But then Hodinar led onward with a jolting, uncalming phrase—at least in Beaumont's opinion.

Ilmar said to Forsberg, "We've kept our distance but now it's time to acknowledge our relationship and work together."

Boom! Tim Beaumont thought. He cringed, perplexed. No, no, no! he thought. Ilmar's going to lose him for good. This step—it's extreme… it… the Frankfurt School hadn't discussed having one of its members tell Forsberg they knew he was a werewolf. Hodinar was changing more than six years of strategic practice when he said it was "time to acknowledge."

But the professor believed the pentothal could at any time turn less effective (even though he had a little more left in the syringe and could use it) and he needed to make solid progress toward his goal. What he knew about the use of the drug on soldiers was that the sessions hadn't dragged on. This was the moment to leap, he felt. The wall to the subconscious has been breached; I need to get fully through, to the inner sanctum.

"I believe you've been comfortable in your coma. I believe you've chosen the comfort of it. But there's another way. Please hear me out: you are safe. You just haven't known it, you didn't know that I know you. I, along with others, have protected you. You've been valuable to us—that's why we want you to live."

Beaumont's apprehensions ceased as he thought: it's been almost a miracle that our secret's been kept for so long; at some point, it was inevitable somebody would have to admit to Forsberg that they knew what he was—and they were assisting him so he might live, and the motives for this assistance would be revealed to him. This was only a matter of "when" not "if".

Forsberg's head moved ever so slightly; he was mentally digesting what had been said to him. He had trouble forming the words, but he asked, "How long have you known?"

"We knew almost from the beginning."

"You let me kill?"

"We saw no other way. Our aim was that you might kill as few as possible."

"You wanted me to stay alive?" The captain asked incredulously.

"Yes."

Beaumont was amazed they were having a conversation, let alone a meaningful one that straight away admitted Forsberg's condition had been known and he'd been helped.

The professor had been right—Forsberg had willed himself to stay in his coma.

Forsberg's eyes were fully open. Their aspect was natural. He asked, "Why?"

"We don't know the limits of your power, hence we can't predict the limits of your usefulness. We're at war with World Communism. We think you may be of great value to the United States. We can't easily dismiss a powerful force that could be harnessed to our advantage.

"So that's why," Forsberg spoke, sounding very much like a military man.

Ilmar wanted Forsberg to think with his conscious mind as much as he could; he waited a half minute to let Forsberg reflect on his surroundings and the realization that people knew what he was.

Letting the short pause dissipate, Ilmar then spoke protectively, "We and you share the same question: how is it that you even are what you are? …We have no answer for that."

There was silence. Ilmar knew he had to proceed quickly, that he had to persuade Forsberg to abandon his coma, his refuge.

The professor let his eyes drift over to Beaumont; he didn't indicate to Forsberg there was another man present. Timothy was silent and didn't move.

Ilmar's eyes went back to the captain. "Though we can only make surmises about how you are what you are, we're now facing a crisis."

Ilmar wanted Gideon to reply but he hadn't asked a question. Only the silence he let hang in the air told the captain that his interviewer wanted him to speak next.

Gideon said, "What crisis?"

"You're in a coma. You've chosen to remain in it. I'd like you to exit from it."

"Why would I want to leave it?"—this was said with such frankness that it made Hodinar shiver. No wonder some called sodium pentothal "truth serum."

"I can only appeal to your instinct for self-preservation. If you stay in a coma, you'll frighten enough people and they'll stop feeding you. You will certainly die. Do you want that?"

"So far… I've stayed alive.

"Yes, but it's not much of a life and the risk of death is real." He paused briefly to let his words sink in. "You want to live, right?"

There was a pause while Forsberg thought. He answered, "The life I was living…I couldn't take it."

"What can I do for you to leave your coma?"

The next thing Forsberg said threw Hodinar and Beaumont off balance with a jolt. "I want to live, but as a wolf."

It took a while for Hodinar to conceptualize what he heard. It seemed so out of the question, so impossible—but then again, being a werewolf itself is hardly a conceivable concept.

Hodinar had no immediate response to Forsberg; he needed time to recover, time to put together his thoughts.

But he *had* to say something. He didn't want to lose Forsberg. So, he asked, "What makes you say that?"

"Not live as man but as wolf... wolf not aware that he'll die, is not anxious. There is no cat-a-clysm."

"So, for you to leave your coma, you want me to guarantee you'll live as a wolf."

"No, I will be a wolf."

"That hardly seems possible."

"It happens. I've seen it."

Ilmar thought: What an astonishing remark.

Beaumont, by the door, mused to himself: it's probably true; the drug inhibits lying.

Hodinar asked carefully, "Are there other werewolves around?"

"I don't know," Forsberg said.

This surprised Hodinar and Beaumont.

"Then how can you say that you have seen a man change into a wolf?"

"Cannot talk about it. Upsets me too much."

Ilmar Hodinar took a breath and waited a few moments. He shouldn't have asked about other werewolves. That line of questioning could have jeopardized achieving the purpose of the session, which was to persuade Forsberg to come back to the world of the everyday.

"I'm sorry," he apologized. "Again, all I can do is appeal to your instinct for self-preservation. You'll certainly die if you stay in a coma. You understand that, I believe. Your first step is to will yourself out of your coma."

Forsberg didn't respond. He seemed to be thinking

consciously.

Ilmar added "We'll continue to do our best to protect you. We'll help you on your way."

"But you want… to control me."

The professor remarked, "Until recently you were doing a better job of that."

Forsberg didn't respond to Hodinar's remark.

Silence settled upon the room.

Hodinar was glad to see Forsberg drift off to sleep. There wasn't anything more he wanted to dare to say.

CHAPTER 35

Yokai means "mysterious apparition"—singular or plural. Whether one or many, they are spine-chilling ghostly entities. It took them some time, in Japanese tradition, to develop definite physical shapes.

They are rooted in human fear and awe; they are emotions, given form. They are a mix of the human and the animal; they're demonic, have supernatural powers that are sometimes downright quirky—the *ogama* is one example of this—it's a *yokai* that's like a giant toad. It comes from the deep forest. It walks upright on two legs and carries a spear. Its skin sags. It has a fish-like grin. Its breath has supernatural powers. It exhales disorienting, rainbow-colored breaths of air. Its victims are rendered defenseless by the breaths, and it snatches them up.

Like most *Obon* festivals, Chitose's included a street parade. As is the custom, it was on the third and final night of this festival honoring the spirits of one's ancestors that the townspeople—including children—marched, wearing costumes of supernatural beings including *yokai,* and animals that were believed, according to tradition, to have shape shifting abilities. Groups of participants wore holiday kimonos and danced folk dances; musicians wore light cotton tunics, played drums and flutes, shook rattles, and sang. The parade route in Chitose, just like in other places in Japan, ended at a carnival where there were festival foods, games, music, group dancing. The parade moved slowly. It lasted a half hour.

Toshi Nakano was at this year's parade. He'd been having the most unpleasant *Obon* he'd ever had in his life. Two days previously, his parents had told him:

"You cannot be here this year. The things you do dishonor us. We've put up with it for too long." Toshi challenged his parents by shouting, "I haven't done anything wrong. You can't do this." They responded: *"This is our house. You have your own apartment."* He shouted back, alluding to the holiday's family-reunion aspect, "You can't do this because no matter what I've done, we are family. We come together at *Obon* no matter what our differences are. We welcome back grandfather, grandmother, and the rest." Their response: *"We don't want you here. You're a lowlife. You take drugs. You sin—all the time."*

Sin is a large, integral concept in Buddhism. Toshi's parents weren't regularly practicing Buddhists, but *Obon* was a Buddhist festival and the monks who visited houses didn't shy away from speaking of Buddhist tenets.

Toshi shouted again, "How dare you do this. I want to pay respects to our ancestors. This is a holiday." As if he were an expert, and an innocent man as well, Toshi touched on the deep, ancient meaning of the holiday. "The holiday is about releasing suffering, not causing it. Are you spitting on this holiday?"

Abandoning the decorum he'd previously managed to preserve, his father declared loudly, "That's enough. It's not your holiday. It's the holiday of our ancestors. The holiday calls for a joyous atmosphere. They won't come into a house where there's no joy. They have enough sadness and distress where they dwell."

All this was true according to Japanese Buddhist beliefs.

Toshi shouted: "We will all be joyful."

"Your mother and I can't be joyful when you're here. You know, there is something more important than your joy. It's the happiness of the ancestors. If you're here, they're going to be scared off. And even if they weren't coming, even if this wasn't *Obon,* I don't want you here. You're a debauched hooligan. You breed hatred in others. You've never asked me permission for what you're doing."

"I don't need your permission."

"Apparently, you don't. That's why you're not welcome here. The bonds of family—you've broken them."

The row (his mother got upset enough to blurt out, *"You put yourself in rages. We all suffer for it."*) lasted a couple more minutes before Toshi gave up, jammed his shoes on and huffed out. His younger brother Noboru was upstairs in his room and listened to the argument. He did not come downstairs.

At the parade, Toshi, wearing black loafers, brown trousers and a white long-sleeved shirt with the top button unbuttoned, didn't stand at the same spot and watch the procession as it went by. Rather, he started at the town park where it ended, where there were carnival games, food stalls and the *yagura* (bandstand) for musicians; once the beginning of the cortège arrived, he began "walking" the parade. He would get to see as much of it as he wanted as he backtracked; he wouldn't have to be bored by the plodding spectacle; while walking the parade he could see who was in it, see who was there to watch it. He'd know who was back in town for *Obon* after being away. (There were those who moved to Sapporo or other cities.)

There were the groups of ladies performing the typical folk dances, to music from drums and castanets. A formation of farmers in samurai costumes rode atop their work horses, which were saddled for the occasion. A group of marchers wore *yukata*—light holiday tunics—marched slowly, struck drums, carried lanterns, and carried a large banner with the name of the department store where Kenshin Wada worked—they were employees—Wada was dissuaded from marching this year.

There was a gap in the parade for a moment. A portable shrine, set on a slab of wood, two long poles supporting it, went by. One man at the front and one at the back held in

410

each hand ends of the poles. Toshi heard *taiko* drums, *shinobue* flutes and *kane* bells but he couldn't see any musicians. He didn't know where the music was coming from.

Toshi looked around at everybody. There wasn't anybody who'd come back to town that he wanted to see.

It was not inappropriate, that given the trouble Chitose had seen, that *Obon* was proceeding as usual. The point was, *you must be joyful, we insist. If you are glum, the spirits of the ancestors won't come.*

Toshi's arms were twitching. He was still seething with resentment toward his parents. It was impossible for him to stand still for more than a few seconds at a time. He'd taken too much *shabu.*

Some people in the parade looked suspicious to him, especially those wearing costumes that covered their faces and bodies.

When a group of boys and men, dressed up as foxes, covered the breadth of the small street where he was at, he almost felt that they were real foxes—or rather half-human, half-fox. He wasn't imagining something his wits invented all on their own—no, the Japanese traditionally believed that foxes were shapeshifting beings, that they could turn into humans. They could trick you and do you harm.

After the foxes, three people followed, marching on their own, to no music. They were in the parade to show off their costume. It was a flimsy affair. Some of the cloth of it, olive drab colored, appeared to be discarded U.S. Army material.

Two people inside the dragon were doing their best to twist a little and keep the dragon's head bobbing out; a third person, in a *yukata* outside the costume, held up the tail so it wouldn't drag on the ground. 1952 was the Year of the Dragon in Chinese astrology (which the Japanese willingly adopted).

The dragon didn't scare Toshi but there was something about the people he saw across the street, on the other side of the dragon. Above them the sky was pallid and murky. There was little street light. The spectators on the other side looked like living corpses. Their faces were a bland, weak, gray; the spark of life was gone from them. Toshi gave his head a brisk shake to try to clear the awfulness of it out of his head.

A group of ladies in costume kimonos appeared after the dragon. The ladies' choreographed movements were to a coal mining work song known as *tanko bushi*. Everybody knew the common folk dance as well as the song.

He thought that every woman in the group secretly hated him. He didn't mind being hated by them. They were ugly creatures. White makeup was caked on their faces; they looked like kabuki figures—but garish, not delightful at all.

Toshi turned his eyes away from the parade, shook his head to clear his mind from what he'd just saw. He alternated between looking to his feet and then up to the shoulders of people gathered on the side of the street. He knew that wherever he was, somebody was probably looking at him, if not staring at him. He *did* have his enemies in town.

He continued to thread his way carefully through the clumps of spectators in front of the small shops watching the parade, walking against the advance of the parade.

The purpose of coming here was to see who was out and about. He still hadn't seen anybody he was interested in talking to. At one point he saw the motorized rickshaw driver Johnny on the other side of the street from him but kept his head down trying not to be seen. He hurried on. He saw small groups of G.I.s scattered here and there along the parade route with small cameras. But he could always find those stupid head-shaved mannequins at Tsuru Lanes.

He kept walking in the decrepit night. It was impossible for anyone not to notice the sixteen marchers coming into sight, who were dressed as *tanuki*.

As with the foxes, who are believed to be shape shifters, so too are the *tanuki*. These raccoon-like faced creatures are masters of illusion. They can turn into any form they choose: from a crooked old hag to a flask of *saki*. They like to use rhymes and sing songs. They trick people into touching enchanted objects, like rice cakes or parasols—all to lure people into their world. They can cast small curses. They can transport people into a distant wilderness.

They're not *yokai*—the ghostly entities spoken of above—but they can be just as dangerous. One of their favorite curses forces people to run around hills and do all sorts of things against their wills. Their victims are, in other words, possessed by them.

With all this in the back of his mind, *shabu* fueled Toshi viewed the parading *tanuki,* in long coats of fur, with paranoid eyes.

The *tanuki* revelers' masks had big friendly smiles on them—all to be attractive playmates for those in the crowd. They sang a tune of simple rhymes that invited them to join them in their magical games.

The crowd was entertained. When one of the revelers advanced into the crowd and tried to pull them into the parade, the crowd laughed as the spectator who'd had the tanuki's paws laid on him slipped away from its grasp.

The sight sickened Toshi; for a moment he felt he was choking. These creatures were real. They were not people in costumes. They would kill you if they could. It was no laughing matter. The people just didn't get it.

Toshi quickened his steps to get past these shocking creatures and their music.

There was a gap in the parade. He focused on his breathing. He forced himself to breathe regularly.

A group of men—there were thirty of them—appeared from out of the dimness in turquois and back garb. Their energetic movements were choreographed to *soran bushi,* a sea shanty that was banged out, strummed and whistled by drums, samisen, and flutes by some fifteen players. It was a familiar dance in Hokkaido. Toshi thought the gestures in the

413

dance, which depicted movements from a fisherman's job like net dragging and the hoisting of sails, were so quickly done that it made your head spin. He knew half the men in the group. He knew most of the men probably hated him. He didn't mind. They were losers.

He threaded his way through the crowd, continuing to scan the people around him when he could bare it. He saw no one that interested him. The temperature of the night was rising. He knew his parents had avoided coming to the parade because they wished to avoid him. His brother, Noboru, wasn't at the parade. He had avoided it for the same reason.

There were the *click-click toom* repeating sounds from the men beating sticks on their wood slabs and drums. They bored him.

Another portable shrine sitting on a slab of wood, mounted on two long horizontal poles carried by costumed men floated by.

By this time Toshi was at the edge of Shimizu, at a street corner on Koen Dori; the crowd on both sides of the street was shoulder to shoulder and three people thick. Movement was impossible. Toshi had to stand still. A shudder swept through him; he was hemmed in. There was no way he could move. He had to bite his lip, not lose control of himself. Pains surged through his body. He thought: it was a bad idea to come to the parade. But then again, it was a convenient way to make sure he knew who was in town.

After the portable shrine passed there was more *click-click toom* wood and drum sounds by six male musicians who weren't part of that group. Two boys broke out of the crowd, took advantage of a small gap between the musicians and the next figure in the parade, and lit off strings of firecrackers. The six male musicians added sporadic shouts in unison to their performance.

They were accompanying a solo highlight of the parade: a man in a costume who last year had come as an octopus.

414

The man, Mr. Masabumi Yamada, was a thirty-year old homosexual; the crowd had grown to anticipate his appearance in the annual parade.

This year Mr. Yamada had costumed himself as an *ogama*, the rainbow-breath-exhaling giant toad. Once the *ogama* came into view, some members of the crowd clapped in applause. The costume was clever and refined—it wasn't like the amateur ones others wore. They knew it could only be Yamada under the green and brown parachute silk that was fitted over chicken wire sculpted in the shape of an *ogama*. Yamada carried the spear that traditional lore said was the weapon that this *yokai* carried. Dangling from the mouth of his costume were strands of crêpe paper of different colors. Yamada's head was in the mouth of the *ogama;* he'd arranged things in such a way that he could blow into a tube and his breath would set the ribbons of paper flapping from the toad's mouth.

Toshi did not like animals and trusted them even less. His domain was the human world and town was Nature enough for him. Animals and anything that looked like them mortified him (though he never admitted this to anyone). He did not want any contact with any living fur, fin or fowl. It may have been entertaining for the crowd and the spirits of people's ancestors to see a huge toad parading on two legs, but to him it was scary, even shocking. For him the "skin" of the *ogama* was not green and brown. Rather, in weak light of the night he saw it as bubbly, with warts all over it, and it had the color of the inside of an oyster.

The two boys were still in the street. They lit off more firecrackers.

One part of him told him that Yamada was under the costume. He never liked Yamada. Yamada was too kind to old ladies; his gestures were effeminate; Yamada, in person, even without a costume, caused revulsion in Toshi to rise. There was that other part of Toshi—the methamphetamine-binged part—that believed that though there was the possibility that Yamada was inside the costume, maybe the giant toad he was seeing was real. Maybe it had eaten Yamada and was now going to breathe its rainbow breaths of air into the crowd, stun them and disorient them, snatch people up with its sticky tongue and smash them against buildings and the street and make them go crazy.

As this thought struck Toshi, two men standing on either side of him (he wouldn't have recognized the out-of-towners if he'd seen them) slugged him hard. He collapsed to the ground like a sack of rice falling from a bench.

The two thugs had been keeping up with him while he walked the parade, waiting for a chance to close in and land their punches.

The two resumed their poses of looking at the parade while Toshi groaned in a small dark space on the ground.

Mesmerized by Yamada's ingenious creation, the crowd near Toshi did not notice what was happening to him. They didn't see both assailants casually grind their feet into his face and stomach.

He could not yell. He could only groan. The groans were drowned out by the noise of the firecrackers, the sounds from the parading musicians' instruments and the cheers and "ahs" of the crowd.

However, there was one person standing closely by who did notice that Toshi had been struck and had fallen to the ground.

It was Jake Torrington. He was there as Ilmar Hodinar's guide tonight.

As head of CIMIC and an officer who spoke conversational Japanese, Torrington knew where some G.I.s got their amphetamines from—Toshi, for one. While *shabu* was technically illegal, the laws against having and selling it were not enforced.

A minute ago, he'd seen Toshi show up several shoulders away from him. The two Japanese fellows on either side of him… they must have squeezed into the crowd at the same time.

When out of the corner of his eye he saw Toshi's figure—or at least his head and shoulders—vanish from the crowd, he didn't say or do anything. He knew that Toshi must have been struck and was on the ground. He kept his eyes away from the direction where Toshi had been. He didn't want to mix into town affairs—not into town affairs of this sort.

An hour before the parade he and Hodinar, who now was at his right and engrossed in watching the parade, had been at Kumakawa's off-post officers club. They were alone in back, down at the river, each with a bottle of beer, Jake in civilian clothes.

"I'm interested in these animals, the *tanuki*," Ilmar said.

Jake had been telling him some of what to expect at tonight's parade. He'd been to two Chitose *Obon* festivals before. He told him about the animal and *yokai* costumes he might see. He said that as with Halloween in America, the costumes of scary beings "seemed to take away people's fright of them by making fun of them." Ilmar thought this was an astute observation.

Though Japanese folklore concerning the supernatural had some appeal for the professor, what most fascinated him was the biology of the *tanuki*.

Jake responded to Ilmar's curiosity about the *tanuki*, saying, "In what way are you interested in them?"

Ilmar began, "There's something called convergent evolution. The Japanese raccoon is called, by some scientists, a raccoon *dog*. It is neither raccoon nor dog, but its size and appearance are similar to the American raccoon. While the faces of these Japanese animals resemble raccoons, they're not related to them—they are more related to foxes. Why did it come to be that *tanuki* evolved to have masks of black fur that wrap around their eyes? The evolutionary progress to their features was separate from the raccoon's. How is it that animals develop such striking resemblances independently? This is the riddle of convergent evolution: analogous structures develop, have comparable form and function—but these characteristics weren't present in an archaic ancestor of either of the two animals."

Torrington responded, "It *is* interesting." He felt free to talk openly because they were on a spot of Kumakawa's property where nobody else was around. "It's like the riddle of the werewolf."

Though no one else could hear them, Ilmar was miffed that Jake had brought up the subject. Plus, they'd come to town to observe *Obon,* not to speak of Forsberg. There was annoyance in his voice, "It's not like the riddle of the werewolf. We don't have two creatures that look like werewolves and come from two entirely different evolutionary chains."

Jake was apparently thirsting for an argument. "You may find it easy to think there's only one werewolf. I don't."

"I don't rule out that possibility. But I'm still grappling with the existence of one."

"Maybe you should widen your view."

Ilmar was surprised at Jake's irascibility. And he wasn't used to being met head-on in such an aggressive way. Ilmar tried to remain polite, "It could be that I should, but for now, we have *one,* and it's an enormous challenge."

Jake wasn't interested in a soft-spoken debate. "You say *challenge?* I don't think you're afraid enough of what Forsberg can do. You don't fully understand the danger."

Hodinar was surprised at being called on to put himself on the defensive. He said courteously, "I am indeed afraid, sufficiently afraid."

Torrington did not like him using the word "sufficiently."

Ilmar didn't pause; he continued civilly, "I assure you I'm convinced of the extreme danger of the monster—just as those who served under First Mate Starbuck were."

The professor was referring to Melville's novel, *Moby Dick.* He knew Torrington had to know it. It was part of the English curriculum at West Point, as well as OCS.

Jake responded, "It concerns me, sir …that you're the one who's handling Forsberg. You intellectualize everything. Forsberg isn't an abstraction. He's dangerous beyond hope."

"Yes, I see you're of that opinion."

Jake declared confidently, but anxiously, "There's a strong probability that there's more than one werewolf in the world."

"Again, this is your opinion."

"Have you thought about the sequence of events in Chitose? Soon after Forsberg arrived, two men behind the bowling alley were murdered, mutilated. The same evening a young woman was maimed but lived. Some days later a little boy was brutally murdered in his neighborhood not far from Chitose I's front gate. These acts are blamed on Akiyama, an Ainu man in town, who everyone believes turned into some kind of violent animal. Yes, it's quite likely he assaulted a young man with a knife—that happened before Forsberg arrived. And that the Ainu man killed a policeman who was staking out his cabin—yeah, that fits. Taken in all, some of attacks in Chitose were more gruesome than others. You've just talked about convergent evolution. What if *two* different werewolves are the killers?"

"Yes, what if," the professor said with no emotion.

Torrington complained tersely, "We have no way of knowing if Forsberg was off post during the time of murders that occurred after he got here. That's because those who manage Operation Grendel haven't seen to it that there's a log that records his movements through the front gate."

"You know that's not possible. It's an absurd demand; a dangerous one."

"It's not the smartest way of handling the danger of Forsberg, is it? You're no genius!"

Up to this time, Torrington's genial communication skills and his being a team player had qualified him as gentleman. But he was not being one now. He'd had enough. He felt his fellow officers who were running the Grendel operation ought to seriously consider his reflections. They'd already made up their minds, though. He was expected to go along with their plan.

After his last barb the conversation between the two ended abruptly. Since Torrington had agreed to be Ilmar's guide at the festivities that night, they remained together, at Kumakawa's, waiting for the time they would head over to see the parade. There was no rapport between them. They lingered where they began their conversation, outside, just the two of them, saying no more words together, not leaving to seek out any other officers. The humid summer air and the flow of Chitose River engaged in its own self-sufficient conversation which they listened in on. The river did all the talking.

During the parade, Torrington said a few things to Hodinar. When the group of women went by dancing *tanko bushi*, he mentioned that the ladies' movements mimicked the digging, cart pushing and lantern hanging which are part of a coal miner's routine. After the singers in fox costumes marched by and the *tanuki*-costumed group appeared, Torrington, acknowledging the professor's interest in *tanuki*, mentioned that the "raccoon dogs," like foxes, do not bark; instead, they growl. When Mr. Masabumi Yamada appeared in his gloriously theatrical *ogama* costume, Torrington mentioned that the fellow was a small-town celebrity, at least as far as the *Obon* parade went. That was the last thing he said before the discrete assault on Toshi took place—which Dr. Hodinar, like the crowd, did not notice.

After the parade ended and before they left the street corner, Torrington mentioned to the professor that he'd just seen Toshi Nakano get beat up during a noisy part of the procession, and that whatever he'd done, he'd supposed the man had it coming to him. He mentioned, with a trenchant look in his eye, that Toshi's younger brother, an innocent seventeen-year-old, was the first victim he'd first spoken about, earlier at Kumakawa's, when they talked about the violent attacks.

Jake mentioned that since then, Toshi, a seller of black market methamphetamine pills, had been going around town accusing American servicemen of being behind the violent attacks. Toshi had no proof of what he was saying, but more than once he, Torrington, had to discuss accusations by Toshi and others like him with officials in town. It was part of his job, as the U.S. Army's liaison to the Chitose community, do dissuade people from believing such talk.

It had been part of the plan for Torrington to accompany Hodinar to the final event in the evening's festivities: *Toro nagashi*—the floating lanterns ceremony. However, since the two men had not taken to each other and Torrington had seen the ceremony before, and Hodinar could easily catch a ride back to the base after it, they parted with Torrington saying, "Then I'll go back without you," and Hodinar responding, "Thank you for all the information, and for showing me around.

A dozen townsmen busied themselves on a broad wooden deck that reached out from the shore and over the water of Chitose River. This was *Toro nagashi;* after lighting the inside candles (they used long sticks as matches to light them), they carefully placed the *chochin*—cube-shaped paper lanterns—upon the water one by one.

It was the time to show the spirits of the loved ones the way home.

Obon was at its close.

People stood quietly along the banks of Chitose river, their thoughts on their loved ones who would cross back to the Other Side. They did not break the taboo; they were serious and respectful but not sad.

Men and women continued to bring more white paper lanterns to be lighted and launched by the men on the wharf; their solemnity touched him.

Once in the water, the illuminated *chochin* moved slowly—

the current, at this time of year, was gentle. The river at this spot was wide. The lanterns edged their way away from the wharf naturally. Some lanterns were together in a mass of six or a dozen, others floated alone or in pairs. These meek shinings in the warm night, these miniature boats, spread across the flat, breezeless field of the river's surface. The lanterns would guide the spirits unhurriedly, unopposed. You almost hear a *shakuhachi* (Japanese bamboo flute) melody, but Nature had its own dignified melody.

Graciously, the brown-eared bulbuls—flocks of birds often seen flying over the river in circles—stayed away, and refrained from their high-pitched sounds. They remained in town, perched on electrical wires, hidden by the dark. Intuitively, the mind blocked out all peripheral views of Chitose's businesses' lights, its shacky buildings, its electricity poles and wires.

The number of *chochin* on the waterway expanded ever and ever. The waterway is the spirits' road. The lanterns, like so many tiny boxes that had spilled from some jeweler's cabinet, had miraculously landed—unharmed, radiant, secure. Guiding the ancestral spirits back to their permanent dwelling places, they glowed softly, with devotion.

They would be dearly missed, these spirits. A new *Obon* was a year away. May these guiding lamps flow every-so-slowly… yes, please, voyage as slow as the slowest of clouds, take as much serene, floating time—as much time as can be laid hold of.

As Ilmar Hodinar watched, he thought of the members of his extended family who lost their lives and the millions of other Jews who were killed in the Holocaust. And at the same time, tranquility, and a stateliness, too, surrounded him. So, the souls of our loved ones are being shown back to the after-home where all of us will someday go; these lamps flow downstream; after a curve in the riverbed… they vanish.

The scene evoked an atmosphere of dream.

He'd linger at the shore until it looked awkward to stay

422

any longer. But before then, he gazed at the sublime floating lanterns, watching them disappear into the void like the last ethereal notes of Chopin's *Third Ballade*.

But after five minutes he reproached himself; it felt disrespectful, superficial, to seemingly push members of *his* family—victims of genocide—away.

Then he thought of the world, in general—if such a thing can be done in a flash. He thought of Forsberg… Where did he come from? Where was he going? He also thought: what have we humans done to this world?…and what good, what indisputable goodness, can I, Ilmar Hodinar, do?

CHAPTER 36

There were no complications to Forsberg's recovery. After a week of being steady on his feet he was back in his office in serviceable health. He was again his usual, subdued self of the past six years, though liable to violently metamorphize at unpredictable times.

He was in a daze, sitting in his swivel chair.

The next time he saw Hodinar, he thought: I don't know what I'll say to him. I don't want to say anything to him. I know what I'm *not* going to say:

A man was struck down, but he didn't die.
After he recovered, he found
He was now a werewolf (whereas before, he was not).

What a change in him!
But it wasn't just one, but many changes.
They'd come in flurries.

He couldn't create any tools to fight them,
Any mental methods.

One day, he got a cold and a cough.
He took codeine to control the cough.
To his amazement, it fought the changes he'd sought to defeat.
There! Eureka!

But it wasn't perfect.
Though it helped, sometimes it didn't.
He didn't know why.

He soon recognized
That while he could fight,
He could not utterly conquer *it*.

His acceptance of that actuality was what he called
The Rule.

But now, *daydream… Forsberg was with his father.* His father
was out of a job. It was the Great Depression. They lived
with relatives out in the country.

They both wore dungaree overalls. His father laid the
rows of the garden out by pushing a stick into the ground at
one extreme and another into the ground at the other. Then
the string that was looped on the ends and tightened between
the two sticks to make a straight line.

His father picked up a spade and dug holes and put a few
seeds in them. Gideon wasn't old enough to ask his father
things like the correct distance between plants and at what
depth the seed needed to be planted. He helped by carrying
the watering can. After his father put a few seeds in the holes
and covered them with dirt, Gideon watered the spot.

He remembered the crinkling sound the paper packets of
seeds made when his father put his fingers into them to get
the seeds out.

His father wore an apron, made of heavy cloth, tied
around his waist with sturdy cloth strings. The long front
cloth pocket held packets of seeds. The only other time he
saw that carpenter's apron was when somebody had nails in
it, and they were nailing in boards.

Small events of childhood seemed huge then and they
were still huge now. The night before they were planting the
garden all the people in the area had gathered to watch a two-
story old wooden house burn down. There was nobody in it;
they'd all gotten out. The torrents of water couldn't save the
house. Everybody stood around in the cold night for hours
and watched until it burned to embers. It was quite the town
event.

A year before Europe went to war in 1939, Forsberg's father got his job back at the factory. He was killed the third month after returning. A large machine part was being brought down to the floor where his father worked. It came down a ramp, supposedly held tight by a strong chain. But the huge part was unsteady and fell onto his dad, crushing him to death.

After this memory flew from his brain, he thought: I wish I could know more about him—Akiyama, that is. Strange how his mind changed from thinking of his father to thinking of the Ainu man.

Beaumont held off introducing de Graff to Hodinar until the second day after the professor arrived. Tim was grateful he could get so much of de Graff's time.

As Hodinar sat down with the two majors, he thought: this is always a hurdle to clear. De Graff had been of great service to Beaumont—he'd apologized to Dr. Tiller and the orderly on his behalf—but he didn't know what he was apologizing for, and now this needed to be explained—and yes, the explanation would be implausible at first, just as it always was.

It turned out that waiting an extra day to meet with the dark-haired major whom he wasn't acquainted with was beneficial—Forsberg had emerged from his coma—this meant their meeting could focus on objectives which would entail a future that seemed now to be more distinct.

The three men's meeting place was a drab but tidy secure room (no windows, only the blare of artificial light) in the Command, Control & Intelligence Building at Chitose I. They sat at one end of a long oval conference table, farthest from the room's locked door. Beaumont, before turning the discussion over to Hodinar to lead, told Major de Graff that he'd met the professor almost six years ago, in Germany. He mentioned some of the professor's projects and accomplishments. He said their association was top secret, that they were close as friends, that they were two of a small group of military men responsible for the oversight and welfare of Gideon Forsberg, and that the operation was code-named Grendel. With that said, Dr. Ilmar Hodinar took over.

> DR. ILMAR HODINAR: *(To de Graff.)* Major, thank you. Thank you very much.

> MAJOR CHRISTOPHER DE GRAFF: Glad I can be of help.

> DR. ILMAR HODINAR: Up until now, some of what we've told you about Captain Gideon Forsberg has not been true. It's my turn to apologize to you: please excuse us. It wasn't possible to reveal the facts. Please discard the information that his hairiness could be attributed to an unusual medical condition. *(He hesitates.)* I'm going to tell you the truth but at first glance it's stranger than you could ever imagine. It may take you time to accept it or you may never accept it.

> MAJOR TIMOTHY BEAUMONT: *(To de Graff.)* Sorry, Chris, but I think it did only good, no harm.

> DR. ILMAR HODINAR: If we'd gone into the real particulars, it would have prompted too long a discussion. We're having part of that discussion now. It wasn't possible before… I couldn't tell you that Gideon Forsberg is a werewolf.

There, he said it, thought Beaumont. The professor didn't waste much time.

> DR. ILMAR HODINAR: *(After giving de Graff a whole ten seconds to think.)* Major, what do you think of what I just said?

427

MAJOR CHRISTOPHER DE GRAFF: I find it hard to believe. But on the other hand, it would take up a lot of time not to accept it.

DR. ILMAR HODINAR: So it saves you time to believe me? *(He looks at Beaumont.)* That is, me and Major Beaumont—

MAJOR CHRISTOPHER DE GRAFF: It does. Tim isn't the type to convene a meeting with someone such as yourself who's just flown in from Washington... just to pull my leg. Plus, the look on the faces of those I apologized to told me quite weird things had happened. You could almost smell it.

The major's favorable reception of what he'd said jolted the professor—it was a pleasing jolt.

DR. ILMAR HODINAR: *(Not verbally stumbling yet taking a moment from time to time to consider his next words.)* I didn't expect such rapid acceptance from you... I'm trying to change gears... what I thought I'd need to say—it seems I don't need to. *(He pauses and then announces quietly.)* We'd like you to be part of the discussion. We need to meet and examine our choices. A course of action needs to be decided on. We can't have that meeting right now because the only other member of our group is Captain Torrington and he can't be here at the moment—he's in town, testifying about a crime there. But he'll be back.

MAJOR CHRISTOPHER DE GRAFF: Torrington is part of your group?

DR. ILMAR HODINAR: Have you ever had any problems with him?

MAJOR CHRISTOPHER DE GRAFF: No, not at all. He's a likeable fellow.

MAJOR TIMOTHY BEAUMONT: And he can be trusted. Plus, he deals with the Japanese community effectively—he's good at his job— some think an American carried out the murders in Chitose. He's calmed some people down. That's why we brought him aboard. It wasn't hard to predict there would be some suspicions and accusations thrown at us.

MAJOR CHRISTOPHER DE GRAFF: *(Supportively.)* Okay, I think we get it.

DR. ILMAR HODINAR: *(After casting a glance aside for a moment—a nervous reaction to what de Graff just said.)* Forsberg needs to be removed from Chitose and sent elsewhere. It's no small business for discussion. We would like you to be here as a balancing influence. You could lend a fresh perspective, and if you should feel so compelled, be our cross-examiner. Those of us who've been occupied with Forsberg are close to this matter. We don't want our actions to be part of a vicious cycle. *(Hodinar suddenly feels woozy—the effects of jet lag. He is out of words but happy to run out of them—it allows de Graff to be free to talk.)*

MAJOR CHRISTOPHER DE GRAFF: *(To Beaumont.)* How many people know about this here?

MAJOR TIMOTHY BEAUMONT: Good question. Only a few. Camp Crawford doesn't know, and that includes Military Police Provost Tyler.

MAJOR CHRISTOPHER DE GRAFF: *(To Beaumont.)* What about Colonel Brewster?

MAJOR TIMOTHY BEAUMONT: As base commander,

I had to tell him something but he's in the position that you were at the beginning of our discussion before we informed you that Forsberg is a werewolf. So, he knows Forsberg is part of a secret operation, but the operation's details cannot be shared with him.

DR. ILMAR HODINAR: There'll only be you, Tim, myself, and Captain Torrington discussing Forsberg's future. The rest of the group that looks after Forsberg is not in Asia. I must tell you that our approach to the matter has been that a werewolf is an embodied force that's been sent to punish man for going against God and Nature, for exceeding his reach as a man. The natural order, if you will, is fighting back. A werewolf isn't just some violent being that's here for no reason. It has a moral, cleansing purpose that's not charitable toward those of us who are in its path.

MAJOR TIMOTHY BEAUMONT: We're not asking you to accept the moral ramifications right away. It takes some thinking about it, I understand.

DR. ILMAR HODINAR: By the way—and this is new—Forsberg now knows we know he's a werewolf. He didn't know that before he went into his coma.

MAJOR CHRISTOPHER DE GRAFF: Will he cooperate?

DR. ILMAR HODINAR: If our requests are reasonable, I imagine he will. When he's conscious, he doesn't appear to have anything against us. I know there's no joy within him regarding being a werewolf.

MAJOR CHRISTOPHER DE GRAFF: So there'll be only four of us deciding his fate?

MAJOR TIMOTHY BEAUMONT: *(Slightly defensively.)*

Well, his *next move.*

DR. ILMAR HODINAR: *(Slowly speaking, admitting frankly.)* —Which, granted, is linked inextricably to his fate.

It was the previous evening, at half past seven, before sunset. Nurse Mildred Castillano—who had not been apologized to because she'd never seen Forsberg in his worse moments—was checking in on Forsberg when she noticed his fingers moved sporadically but with a calmness. It wasn't the first time that the Filipina nurse had a patient whose condition she was not fully apprised of. Her American superiors and colleagues didn't always treat her as they might have treated a White nurse. Thus, when McGuinness had been sent away to Chitose II along with Dr. Tiller and Corporal Roger Lumley (and Marcia had been given a single room there) and nothing in the way of an explanation of why the changes had occurred was offered to Mildred, she took it in stride. It was just the way things were now: Dr. Ilmar Hodinar was supervising Captain Gideon Forsberg's care. She didn't know why, but Marcia had been instructed not to talk about Forsberg or his condition with her. So be it. There's such a thing as patient confidentiality.

Nurse Castillano was told to contact Dr. Hodinar directly if she saw a change in the captain's condition. This she dutifully did when she saw the captain's fingers moving.

Hodinar, after mistakenly appearing his first time in the infirmary without one, made sure to never be in the infirmary unless he wore a physician's white coat. With Nurse Castillano out of the room, he could now be alone and reflect on the success of his conversation with Forsberg.

Gideon's face was no longer frozen in a grin, thought there was a slight pull of muscles on the right side that drew his mouth in that direction from the still unrelaxed left side.

When Hodinar tried to carefully lift Forsberg's eyelid to check the size of the pupil, the captain wiggled his eye to prevent it and mumbled, "Don't touch me."

This threw the professor for a moment. But then he realized it didn't mean that Forsberg wasn't going to cooperate. It only meant he was sensitive to being pushed at and probed.

Less than twelve hours had passed; Forsberg's brain had rested, his heartbeat and breathing were regular. He was coming out of his coma.

In the medical encyclopedia in the infirmary, Hodinar had read the extensive entry on coma. Since Forsberg had been unconscious for ten weeks it was likely he might regain good control over his physical movements in less than a week.

Hodinar turned on the overhead lights in the room. They'd been switched off for how long? He didn't know. He was aware that light was a powerful stimulant but felt it would only cause Forsberg to wake fully, not to change into a werewolf.

He noticed a wince across Forsberg's face when the lights came on. Forsberg's lips and jaw moved. The captain was moving as though his mouth was uncomfortably dry and it needed to be moistened.

Ilmar shone light brown in the strong light. He said, "I can give you a sip of water if you think you can handle it."

"Yes," was Forsberg's only reply.

This meant Ilmar had to leave the room, go across the hall to the room with the bathroom.

In thirty seconds he was back. He raised the back of Forsberg's bed, causing a creaking sound because of the restraints affixed to the bed, before giving him tiny sips of water out of a full glass.

"The restraints on your bed are going to be taken away," he announced spontaneously. "You'll be kept on codeine, but there'll be no phenobarbital or Thorazine."

The professor spent the next five minutes giving him the tiny sips of water. Then he said, "I believe your rehabilitation will be swift. It has been ten weeks since you went into the coma. I'm prepared to stay with you for a few hours—in case you have questions." He paused, and then ventured, "I believe you might be able to speak—you spoke yesterday to me."

Hodinar knew it would be counterproductive to try to rush the patient. He would come around at his own time. To make good on his promise of being willing to stay for hours, the professor settled into a chair and cast his eyes down, focusing idly on a spot in a corner of the room.

Twenty minutes passed, and Forsberg spoke, abruptly, "I want these tubes, needles and pads taken off me."

Hodinar was pleased that Forsberg spoke in a fluent, complete sentence.

"I'm sorry, but in the morning. There's only so much we dare to do at night. Your diet will be organized. There'll be massage and exercise—but as I say, this will be a matter of days, not weeks."

A whole long hour passed since Ilmar's last words, during which both of Forsberg's eyes stayed open and the mild paralysis on the left side of his face disappeared, making his face look rather normal. It seemed Forsberg was busy internally retraveling pathways that had been dormant while he was in a coma.

"I told you. I want to live as a wolf." Forsberg spoke again, abruptly.

Hodinar thought long before he spoke. "I told you we would continue to help you. At the same time, you and I know you're not under our control. You are not, it seems, always under your *own* control. Of course, you're a living being, and it's in your makeup to fight to stay alive."

"You want me to stay alive?"

"Yes. But we can't do what is possible until it's possible."

"What does that mean?" Forsberg asked darkly.

"It means we have to function within our limits. You must survive, whether it's with two legs or four."

Forsberg said nothing in response.

Hodinar let him rest. It seemed there was a lot for him to think about. He'd only been in Chitose for a few months, and half of the time he'd been in a coma.

The professor let another twenty minutes in the well-lit room pass. Among other things, during this time the smell of Nurse McGuinness's sweat came in and out of Forsberg's mind.

The professor finally spoke. "Little by little, we let this happen. We had a hand in creating you."

It took a while for Forsberg to answer. "I don't see how that could be true."

Hodinar waited a moment. He was looking at Forsberg but not staring. "There's the story of Icarus. When most people think of it, they think of it as a parable. You're not to fly too high too fast. You're not to be godlike, or your wings of wax will melt; you'll fall into the sea and drown. Most people don't know the labyrinth part of the tale, or they've forgotten it. The whole reason why Daedalus, the father, and his son, Icarus, put on wings to fly was because they couldn't get out of the labyrinth. They were imprisoned in it. If there hadn't been the labyrinth and they weren't prisoners, they wouldn't have been motivated to take wing—literally. This man Daedalus, by the way, was a professional inventor. He himself invented the labyrinth. The king he served got mad at him, so he put Daedalus and his family in it. The labyrinth was so well designed, by the way, that even its maker— Daedalus—couldn't find his way out—on foot, that is. I say that little by little we created you, just like that myth that little by little took shape and wound up giving us a story that a man shouldn't try to do only what a bird or bat can do."

"You think this Greek myth has something to do with my situation?"

"It helps me try to get a perspective on what might have happened to you. I find there are no Judeo-Christian stories that fit—I mean, that can begin to explain you to me.

"It doesn't explain how you created me."

"While we humans are not your inventor in a precise Daedalus sense, we've had a huge hand in letting a labyrinth of a world develop. But I *like* the Daedalus comparison, though it by no means fits perfectly. It's easy to understand. You're the adolescent boy, Icarus. We—a group of people— adopted you as a son, more than six years ago, in Germany. We've been watching over you. It has taken some invention on our part of how to proceed."

"I think you're crazy. Don't I kill rather than fly? Does what you say fit all that much?"

"Well, what I can say helps me so I can help you. For example, when you're stuck, we always have to figure out a way to move you on. By the way, we, too, need not to get stuck."

"What would 'getting stuck' for you be?"

"One thing would be that people find out that you're a werewolf. That would be deadly for you and the least worst thing for us would be that people would write poems about it—like they did in 1685, when German villagers thought they had a werewolf on their hands in their town called Ansbach."

Hearing "Ansbach" instantly stung Forsberg. Hodinar saw Forsberg flinch and did not understand the reason why.

As for the captain, he wondered if Hodinar knew anything about Ansbach. But he kept silent.

Ilmar didn't enquire why Forsberg had flinched. The important thing was not to lose his attention.

Hodinar resumed, "Regarding not getting stuck—now, some people know you here, in a bad light, let's say—and we have to get you out. We can't help you to become a wolf— we don't know anything about that—but we must transfer you. You're our Icarus who we can give wing to." He spoke apologetically, "We can fly you back down to another labyrinth, I'm afraid, for the time being."

"You want to use me eventually as a weapon. I get that. That's why you want to keep me alive."

"I admit, that's why some people do."

"How many of you are there?"

"I can't tell you, it's a secret. There are only a few. Otherwise the secret would get out." After this apology, he sounded more positive, "Now, as two-way streets go, we're keeping you alive." He paused to take a breath; the jet lag tugged at him. "So far, we've had successes. We flew you out of Germany and into Korea. Then something happened in Korea, and we flew you here to Chitose. Now you will fly again."

"What happened in Korea?"

"An officer was killed."

"What officer?"

"An officer watching over you. He died in an enemy ambush. That's why you had to come here."

Hodinar waited while Forsberg digested the information. When in Korea, he had not sensed he was under surveillance.

After a drowsy while—the night, despite the bright lights in the room, seemed to bear down on them both—Forsberg asked, "So you're the chief planner?"

"I'm an important part of the group."

Forsberg fell silent. Hodinar made no motion to leave; the silence lasted ten minutes. The captain said out of the blue, "I heard the nurse speak your name."

"Yes."

There was silence again; it lasted five minutes until Forsberg said blandly, "I'm feeling tired now."

"I will go. Thank you," Ilmar said, collecting himself mentally. He was ready to rise from his chair when heard, "Do you know where you're sending me?"

"Not yet. There's going to be some discussion."

"With Major Beaumont?"

Ilmar tried not to show he was startled. "What makes you say that?" he asked.

"He was in the room when you injected me with sodium pentothal and persuaded me to come out of the coma."

Hodinar thought Tim had been adequately concealed. "Did you see him?"

"No, I smelled him—his cologne. I've smelled it before. He eats at officers' mess like all the officers."

After the professor got over his surprise, he asked, "Somehow, in Korea, for example, you never noticed the officer who was watching you?"

"Maybe he never got that close. Besides, a lot of people just use soap and water—like you—and there's nothing exceptional about that."

Hodinar rose from his chair and said goodnight, leaving the captain to have his first night of post-coma sleep. Because of the codeine in his blood, he would have no shortage of dreams.

Hours later, in a secure room at C2I, Chitose I. Three officers and Ilmar Hodinar:

DR. ILMAR HODINAR: First, for the benefit of Captain Torrington, I'd like to take up the notion that if we killed Forsberg or just let him die, the problems would be over. A useful position I've taken on this is that this would amount to shooting the messenger. My feeling is that Forsberg is possessed, that he has no free will, though he's by no means innocent. *(To Torrington.)* Sorry, captain, Major Beaumont has asked me to cover this in your presence because he knows, as I do, some of your feelings. *(Addressing everyone again.)* It would seem to be a solution if Forsberg was acting on his own. Yes, wherever he winds up, there are invariably victims. I don't want to disrespect them and I'm not treating the situation coldly—I believe that what we've been doing has been softening the brute in him. We know what he is. We mitigate the death and destruction.

MAJOR TIMOTHY BEAUMONT: *(To Torrington.)* Jake, the professor's idea is that we can only understand what Forsberg is by imagining a large picture—a large picture that Forsberg's a small part of.

DR. ILMAR HODINAR: *(Defensively.)* It may be a small part, but it's a part filled with horror—I am in no way rejecting that.

CAPTAIN JAKE TORRINGTON: So, you understand that he's evil—

DR. ILMAR HODINAR: Yes, but that he requires maintenance. We need to manage him.

CAPTAIN JAKE TORRINGTON: Why manage him? Why not stamp out evil?

DR. ILMAR HODINAR: Because evil will always be with us and if we try to stamp it out it will come back ten-fold and stamp us out.

CAPTAIN JAKE TORRINGTON: What makes you sure of that?

DR. ILMAR HODINAR: Everything that I've studied.

CAPTAIN JAKE TORRINGTON: No offense, there may be gaps in what you've learned.

DR. ILMAR HODINAR: There certainly are.

MAJOR TIMOTHY BEAUMONT: There are other angles to this as well, Jake. Forsberg is a... *phenomenon* worthy of scientific study. If one day someone can get close enough to him and he'll trust them...

CAPTAIN JAKE TORRINGTON: But people in town have died.

DR. ILMAR HODINAR: We don't take that lightly, I

assure you.

MAJOR TIMOTHY BEAUMONT: Another angle is that he may be of military use as a weapon. There are some who've advocated for his survival solely based on that idea.

CAPTAIN JAKE TORRINGTON: But there's no way of knowing what kind of part Forsberg is of a larger picture, is there?

MAJOR CHRISTOPHER DE GRAFF: *(Inserting himself diplomatically.)* One werewolf is a large picture in and of itself.

MAJOR TIMOTHY BEAUMONT: We should consider ourselves fortunate that we have him and the Russians don't.

CAPTAIN JAKE TORRINGTON: *(To Hodinar.)* Professor, you've talked to him. Have you asked him if there are others ...werewolves, I mean?

DR. ILMAR HODINAR: He was vague on that point. Though he did say that no, there aren't any others like him that he knows of.

CAPTAIN JAKE TORRINGTON: Yes, so, if there's only one, I don't see why we should keep him alive. He's a mutant. He's evil. He should be liquidated. End the aberration and the violence. Terminate the operation.

DR. ILMAR HODINAR: As I said, I don't believe you can end such things.

CAPTAIN JAKE TORRINGTON: We execute murderers in the electric chair.

DR. ILMAR HODINAR: That's a perfect example. It doesn't stop murder.

CAPTAIN JAKE TORRINGTON: So, we keep murderers alive? We show them mercy?

DR. ILMAR HODINAR: We recognize entropy increases with time in the universe—it's the second law of thermodynamics, unstoppable—but meanwhile we shore up existence—all existence in its many forms—because if we don't, our world is gone. When we understand this we know there'll be times when we have to risk our reputations, our comfort; we'll have to make sacrifices.

CAPTAIN JAKE TORRINGTON: I understand basic physics, but we're not making the sacrifices that people in Chitose who were attacked did. Some of them died.

DR. ILMAR HODINAR: Excuse me, I'll have to digress into a story, because stories are all I have... to comprehend Forsberg and the situation we find ourselves in.

It was less than a thousand years ago—not a long time in many contexts—that the Norse still believed in a giant wolf they called Fenrir. Fenrir was one of the sons of the god Loki. Loki himself was a real 'piece of work' as you say in English— his aim was to sow chaos in the world. But back to his son, the giant wolf. Fenrir's reason for existing was subtle and precise. It was he who was going to kill the leader of the Norse gods, Odin, on the battlefield during *Ragnarök,* which means the 'Doom of the Gods' and is the end of the world of gods and men. Can you imagine that? The Vikings believed there was a being who was going to murder their God and end the world.

Since this was going to happen sometime in the future you would think powerful Norse gods would simply kill the giant wolf—then their problem would be solved—their god wouldn't die and their world wouldn't end. But though Fenrir terrified the Norse gods, they knew it wouldn't solve anything to kill him. So, they captured him, found a piece of ground and chained him to that ground, hoping that this would keep him away from Odin.

But Fenrir was monstrously strong. He broke the chain. He was captured again, and they put ever stronger restraints on him. There was even an ultralight ribbon that the dwarves made in the underground world specially to hold Fenrir, and it worked for decades, even centuries, but eventually it frayed and broke. The giant wolf got free, and as was prophesized, Fenrir killed Odin. The great battles ended in fire. The world as they knew it ended. There was a flood to wash away the blood, the bodies, the sins.

CAPTAIN JAKE TORRINGTON: But couldn't your story be interpreted as that of a superstitious people who gave an evil god a sporting chance—and then paid for it?

DR. ILMAR HODINAR: If you're untutored and you don't understand culture or physics, perhaps. *(He paused to remain calm, then spoke more.)* Look, I'm certain that Norsemen weren't known for giving evil *people* a sporting chance. Their methods of torture and execution were gruesome.

CAPTAIN JAKE TORRINGTON: Forsberg's a person, so...

DR. ILMAR HODINAR: But that's just it, he's not a person, he's a werewolf.

MAJOR TIMOTHY BEAUMONT: *(Not impatiently, just*

firmly.) We could go around in circles on this for a long time. Jake, you know the man who lets us use his trading post as an officers club. *(Beaumont bent to Hodinar and spoke.)* His name is Tadao Kumakawa. He's an interesting man. He's an Ainu fellow. The Ainu are the indigenous people of Hokkaido. *(Beaumont directed his attention back to all who were present.)* Some of his people's ancient words of wisdom he said to me once—in a different context, of course—were, "Everything and everyone in this world has a part to play." So Jake, I have to say this: Forsberg stays alive, and that's that. *(He paused for a brief thought and spoke again.)* The question is, where to send him?

Torrington grumbled inside himself, thinking, *Put a steel collar around Forsberg's neck and chain him to the ground!* He did not voice the words because he knew they were childish and overly emotional and might indicate to the others he wasn't trying to be collegiate and problem-solve.

MAJOR CHRISTOPHER DE GRAFF: *(Adroitly inserting himself during the momentary lull.)* You, Tim, are in the only position to really decide that, aren't you?

MAJOR TIMOTHY BEAUMONT: Yes, I suppose I'm just thinking out loud.

MAJOR CHRISTOPHER DE GRAFF: Do you have an idea where you'll send him?

MAJOR TIMOTHY BEAUMONT: Yes, well, we've been giving the French army and navy a lot of equipment to fight the communists in Vietnam. We send officers there to keep track of how things are going. We call them advisors, but they're just watchers.

MAJOR CHRISTOPHER DE GRAFF: Who will watch the watcher if Forsberg is sent there?

MAJOR TIMOTHY BEAUMONT: I'll get to work on that right away.

CAPTAIN JAKE TORRINGTON: Do you think it's safe? Do you think he can do the job?

MAJOR TIMOTHY BEAUMONT: It's an easy job and not dangerous if you avoid combat zones.

MAJOR CHRISTOPHER DE GRAFF: Are there other choices under consideration?

MAJOR TIMOTHY BEAUMONT: The thing is we're not at a stage yet where we've figured out how to deploy him as some kind of weapon.

CAPTAIN JAKE TORRINGTON: We may never be.

MAJOR TIMOTHY BEAUMONT: That's true.

CAPTAIN JAKE TORRINGTON: Excuse me but I don't see why you're having this meeting with me and Major de Graff present. You and Professor Hodinar seem to be managing all right, just the two of you.

MAJOR TIMOTHY BEAUMONT: You didn't raise any real objection, nor did Major de Graff, to my idea of posting Forsberg to Indochina. Your reactions are valuable to me. It means I'm hoping that my way of thinking isn't way off the mark.

MAJOR CHRISTOPHER DE GRAFF: You're proposing yet another holding pattern to keep Forsberg in?

MAJOR TIMOTHY BEAUMONT: Yes.

CAPTAIN JAKE TORRINGTON: Will he murder again?

MAJOR TIMOTHY BEAUMONT: Probably.

CAPTAIN JAKE TORRINGTON: I just don't see the point in keeping him alive. There, you want my reaction; sorry, you have it.

DR. ILMAR HODINAR: We injure ourselves more if we kill him.

CAPTAIN JAKE TORRINGTON: I don't understand that, sorry.

DR. ILMAR HODINAR: How much of us can he destroy? He can destroy some of us, but he's not going to single-handedly end the world. It's not him that's the colossal danger—it's what comes *after* him.

CAPTAIN JAKE TORRINGTON: That's vague. I'm being asked to believe that, but I can't.

DR. ILMAR HODINAR: If we rid the world of this monster who's terrorizing us, it could be a step toward making us very proud, proud like Oedipus when he got the riddle right that the Sphinx told him, thereby ridding Thebes of its monster. There, I fixed it!—Oedipus said. He went on to become king—King of Annihilation.

CAPTAIN JAKE TORRINGTON: You're always falling back on pagan myths.

DR. ILMAR HODINAR: They help me to understand better—and I hope you, too.

CAPTAIN JAKE TORRINGTON: *(Referring to Hodinar being a Jew—not in a friendly manner)* We're Christians in this country—most of us.

DR. ILMAR HODINAR: The Abrahamic religions— Judaism, Christianity and Islam—don't provide material that gives me insight into what we face. Sorry, I must pause for a moment. I'm feeling the effects of jet lag.

The professor was lying. He felt he was on the verge of saying too much. I have to be careful of voicing my thoughts in public, he thought—I'm a Jew; what I say could be used in such a way that I'd be distrusted, could be harassed, and worse—it would be completely wrong, but easy, to call me an atheist, a communist—anything—by somebody who feels I'm endangering them.

But there were other more worrisome thoughts that had been crossing his mind for some time. The presence of Forsberg is a defeat of the Abrahamic religions, he thought. These religions have lost their usefulness; they are not legitimate. With Forsberg, there's no messiah, no heaven; there's a punisher who's a harbinger of our annihilation.

Ilmar had no contempt for religion. He credited it for many improvements. It contributed to the creation of art works of great beauty such as Christian hymns and chorales. They brought people together, peacefully. The phenomenon of group singing, whether accompanied by instruments or not, can be profound and uplifting. The words don't even have to be devotional. This is one of the endeavors that show humans at their best.

He understood he must control himself and not express views that would harm his chances of helping. People are born into their traditions. They don't readily accept that their traditions are examples of one set of traditions, and that there are others. All religions claim to be the *only* religion, and that just proves, as Bertrand Russell says, that *none* of them can be the only true one. Regarding Forsberg, Hodinar thought these critics who condemn religions because of their sacred scriptures claiming to reveal truth—truth, once and for all, in utter perfection, with no possibility for change—well, these skeptical critics do have their point.

The problem with Torrington was his mind couldn't accommodate change. He couldn't comprehend that the

445

more things change, the more things *don't* remain the same.

MAJOR CHRISTOPHER DE GRAFF: *(Quite sure that Hodinar's discomfort is not jet lag, wanting to keep the meeting going, addressing Beaumont.)* Tim, you're running an operation that hinges on a series of controls. Your control fails sometimes. When can it be fail-safe?

MAJOR TIMOTHY BEAUMONT: Maybe never.

MAJOR CHRISTOPHER DE GRAFF: Can we afford that?—I think that's what Captain Torrington's point is.

DR. ILMAR HODINAR: We have to.

MAJOR CHRISTOPHER DE GRAFF: Yes, it's clear that's your point. I understand the captain's anger and frustration. He works with the community. The community is going through a rough patch.

MAJOR TIMOTHY BEAUMONT: Forsberg will be sent away so he can do no further damage.

MAJOR CHRISTOPHER DE GRAFF: Yes, in Chitose community. But when does it all end?

DR. ILMAR HODINAR: I wish I could say.

MAJOR CHRISTOPHER DE GRAFF: One result of this meeting is—and thank you for including me, if only as a sounding board—that I know you're unable to guarantee when the violence and death from Forsberg will stop.

MAJOR TIMOTHY BEAUMONT: Just as we cannot state when all wars will cease on earth.

MAJOR CHRISTOPHER DE GRAFF: I think we've reached a standstill in this part of our discussion.

We should move on.

MAJOR TIMOTHY BEAUMONT: To what? As far as first meetings go, we've covered a lot. I move that we adjourn.

As it turned out there was no need for a meeting, later. Smart commanders know how to use their time wisely.

CHAPTER 37

Two weeks after the rains from Typhoon Karen ended, the rains from Typhoon Mary arrived and soaked Chitose for three days.

At the time, few scientists paid attention to the history of the earth's weather. A few remarked that global temperatures were, decade by decade, on the rise. Measurements showed that sea levels were rising as well.

Hokkaido had always gotten the tail end of typhoons, in the form of rain. It seemed more of those rains were the new trend; the rain lasted longer, too.

Sheriff Danjuro Fujita

Danjuro Fujita's mother had her copy of the *Ekikyo* in her hands. She was in bed, in her room.

The *Ekikyo* is the Japanese translation of the *Yi Jing,* or *I Ching,* the *Book of Changes*—the ancient Chinese divination text which is more than that—it's even a philosophical and religious text.

Her hand rested on the page that showed and explained the thirty-ninth hexagram. Her fingers had happened on this spot when she opened the book, searching for answers. A hexagram aims to address a current situation. It's a simple two-dimensional diagrammic drawing partaking of straight lines that aren't broken, and ones that are broken in two. These lines sit stacked neatly, equidistantly, on top of each other—or under each other, depending how they're looked at.

Both the six (hence, *hexa-*) horizontal lines and the whole hexagram itself are charged with meaning. Along with this visual configuration of lines is text that interprets and translates the hexagram and each of its single lines, and purports to suggest keys to solutions. The variations of all possible combinations of the six lines in the hexagrams total sixty-four. Thus, there are sixty-four possible hexagrams, and they all have titles.

The thirty-ninth hexagram is known in English as the hexagram for "Obstruction" or "Impediment" and announces that the present situation is difficult.

One of the reasons why is because progress is blocked.

Good fortune, as well, is not possible, because this is blocked.

Some experts contend that the *Ekikyo* is not a fortune telling aid for the superstitious but rather a guide to open a person's mind.

The top line of the thirty-ninth hexagram is broken in two. This signifies water. The line just below it is unbroken. This signifies mountain. The next four lines are as follows: broken, unbroken, broken, then broken.

This configuration of lines means that there's an abyss lying before us and a mountain rises at our back. We are trapped—at the edge of an abyss, no less.

The *Ekikyo* tells us that we need to think hard about the possibilities and synthesize the meanings of being stuck with seemingly nowhere to go. We must be patient; we must reach out; we must persevere; if we are earnest and devote ourselves to attaining a harmonious solution during the difficult period when we are striving to overcome the obstruction, our inner selves will grow, as well.

Danjuro Fujita had settled onto his knees at the edge of the tatami mat on which his mother's futon lay.

"Why are you looking at that?" he asked his mother. She lay there comfortably, her head propped up by pillows, studying the *Ekikyo*.

"It has something to say."

"Many things have something to say," he said ruefully. "It doesn't mean we should listen to them, especially if they have no expertise."

"I'm looking at the hexagram for Obstruction!" She held the book with steady hands.

"So you are." He was trying not to chide her.

With her eyes fixed on the page, she announced quietly, "You're impeded in your investigation of the murders in town."

"You with your book are stating the obvious."

Well, he was chiding her. She wasn't noticing.

She turned her eyes up to him. "Doesn't it bother you that something's in your way?"

"Of course it does." Did she realize she was annoying him?

She spoke almost like a schoolgirl. "It says here that you must not be afraid or too proud to reach out to other people who might be more expert than you."

Just a few more of her thoughts and I will get up and leave, Danjuro thought, restlessly. He responded, "I'm not afraid. I remain in touch with other sheriff's offices and with the Americans."

Her eyes went back down to the page. She read; the sound of rain continued. Her son's eyes drifted to the ceiling. It was dry and sturdy. No rain would get into the house. After a half a minute of reading silently his mother commented, "Brute force won't get you out of the jam."

"I don't need a book to tell me that," he murmured.

Her eyes clasped the page. She reported, "Present thought-patterns are quite likely due to stubbornness, stupidity, or ignorance. Ponder the situation; start over with fresh ideas."

"Not bad advice."

"You implement the fresh ideas and little by little the

bundle of things that make up the obstruction can dissolve."

So, Hisano Fujita and her *Book of Changes* is schooling Sheriff Fujita about how to do his job, he thought.

"I can imagine that," he said, agreeing with her. "But do tell me something I don't already know!"

She continued to peer at the book. "You shouldn't dismiss notions that your own errors have played a part in getting you into the situation you're in now."

"I am not." He tried to not let her irritate him. She didn't realize she was haranguing him. But that was nothing new.

"I'm not sure you can do it."

There is nothing like a mother expressing full confidence in her son when the chips are down.

Danjuro spoke dutifully. "Thank you for your confidence."

"You're welcome."

"My comment was disingenuous," he remarked.

His mother seemed not to hear these last words. She continued, "You're at the edge of an abyss and you must go forward, but of course you can't because you're at the edge of an abyss…"

He interjected, annoyed, "Yes, I need fresh ideas."

"…That's what the lines of the hexagram mean."

"Yes, precisely."

"There are steep mountains behind you, confining you, just like the Chitose landscape. So you're blocked both ways—in front of you and behind you."

He gestured toward himself with one hand. "Mother, I must go. Thank you for reading the things to me."

Talking with her was an important part of her life. Neither ever acknowledged this out loud. It fell to him to perpetuate it.

Suddenly she was wistful. She cradled the book gently. "Son, we must keep the traditions of Japan! The books, the music, the dancing. …Let no other culture take them away from us!"

She was referring to cultural incursions of the Americans.

"The book you have in your hands is not Japanese. It's Chinese."

"Well, it's Japanese, nonetheless," without skipping a beat.

Danjuro looked down at his knees, readying himself to rise.

"I understand," he said.

Then, as he was getting up, she said, "I don't know if you do, Danjuro."

He didn't know why he said it—it just came to him once he was on his feet. "Mother, we all float away like lamps into the sunset, and there we vanish."

Mommy Eri

I'm not the only one who has trouble with work. Look at the police. Akiyama attacked and killed people and got away with it. Where did he go? Why can't they find him?

That good-for-nothing Toshi Nakano: what do you expect? If you lead a life like that, things are bound to happen, especially with the kind of attitude he had.

Week by week I'm less afraid. I don't know why, but that's just the way it is.

There's nothing wrong with what I do. It's an honest business. It's a place where men indulge in earthly pleasures. People need pleasure. People need to earn money.

Soon I'll have earned enough so I can buy two buildings—with two apartments in each of them. It'll be a decent income, renting them out.

Not to Americans—they have to live on base. I'll be renting to Japanese people—who are in no way better than the Americans if you ask me.

Do things yourself. Never ask people for help—they will only humiliate you.

Kiriko

The small doses of phenobarbital she took for her seizures made them stop. What a relief to her.

Yokatta! (*Yokatta* means "fortunately.")

Sapporo, with its population of one million people—what a city—it's easy to be anonymous there.

She got a job in a ball point pen factory in Sapporo.

She left work a half hour early one day. She rushed out, didn't punch her timecard. Normally she'd never do such a thing, but her period came and she wasn't prepared for it. She was scared that if she stayed, something embarrassing might happen.

Mr. Matsumoto, her supervisor, noticed she'd left early. The next day at work he spoke with her. She apologized; there was an emergency she said; she would never leave like that again. Her boss understood it would make her uncomfortable and there'd be no point in asking about the nature of the emergency. He told her she had two choices: to work one of the next few days for an extra half hour or accept that she'd get twenty yen (a half-hour's worth of work) less next payday.

Matsumoto was a busy man. He told her that one time and that was it.

A whole pay period went by. Kiriko didn't stay and work the extra half hour.

On payday, he happened to come into the *genkan*—the entryway where everyone takes off their shoes, puts them in cubbyholes and puts on light footwear; in this case, to go into the factory proper. It was the end of her shift; she was putting on her sturdy boots—the Hokkaido climate calls for a good pair of them if you can afford it.

Matsumoto knew she'd been paid and that she hadn't worked an extra half hour.

After they greeted one another, he said, "Sorry couldn't make up that half hour. So they paid you twenty yen less."

She said nothing to him—a wall of silence.

She stopped looking at him. She bent and tied her bootlaces. They were a too long; they didn't fit the boots. As she yanked the laces to double tie them, Matsumoto noticed tears seeping from her eyes.

She came back to the factory the next day and worked. Nothing about the day before was mentioned. As the days went by, it was as if it had never happened.

Aunt Satomi

When the animal spirits who lived in the heavens saw the beauty of the world below, they begged the creator god to let them live there; God created fleshy animals in the image of their spirits; He allowed them to live on earth.

The first *people* on earth were *ainu*—a word which means "human being." These *ainu* had bodies of earth, their hair was of chickweed; God fashioned their spines from willow sticks.

God sent the divine man named *Aioina* down from the heavens to teach humans how to hunt and cook.

Aunt Satomi did not believe this necessarily. But who was she? What did she know? How much does it matter if such stories are true or not? The thing was not to tell Kiriko such stories. She always had enough on her mind.

Give your love and don't expect too much out of life. Loving, and being good in life, are rewards enough.

After Kiriko was treated by the doctor and it was clear the medicine had worked, Satomi arranged for her to go to Sapporo, live with a half-Ainu family.

Kenshin was pleased she was living in Sapporo. He made sure to let his co-workers at the department store know she'd left town.

From that time on there was less tension in the department store between the others and him. He was no longer shunned. People who had fruit trees in their yards shared the excess fruit with him, just like last year. The same thing happened for Satomi at her job at the telephone company.

Harvest time in Hokkaido is a bountiful time. Branches and vines are heavy with enough fruits and vegetables for everyone. *Kaki* (persimmons) and *nashi* (Asian pears) are abundant—there are almost so many that you can't give them away.

Never talk about personal happiness; one is not even to think about it.

Toshi

He didn't feel the insect biting the skin on his arm—he was dead. His slender corpse was in neat clothes—not too roughed up.

A few people saw his body on the muddy street. It had been dumped there. A man went to the police station to report it.

A hoodlum who had no qualms about abducting him and then strangling him, that's who it was.

Not long before it happened, Toshi, in a raincoat, in a surly mood, going out to buy cigarettes, had protested to a policeman on his beat that it looked like the police would never get the attacker who attacked his brother and murdered Chitose townspeople. It was as if he cared about his brother (Noboru had returned to work in a coal mine Muroran. Toshi didn't miss him in the least.)

He said to the cop, "You're not doing enough. That's why you haven't brought anybody in." The policeman, irked, said back to him, "Well, the violence has stopped."

Lloyd Kelso

(At first, Hokkaido's weather hadn't bothered Kelso. It wasn't that different from where he came from. But then he decided he didn't like it—especially the rain—because it drove him into himself.)

I assume something I'd never want to see… was going on

in the captain's room. You can be sure I won't ever speak to anyone about it, or about Forsberg himself.

I look forward to the day when the army is years behind me.

I'm never going to talk about Korea—to anyone. Anyway, no one could benefit from anything I would say. So it's locked up inside me.

I'm avoiding anything that's horrible. For example, I'll never see a horror movie again in my life.

The only kind of drama I want is what you get in sports. I'll always follow the Giants. If there's a game and Willie Mays is in it and I'm nearby, I'll go to the stadium and see it. I'll always keep an eye on the Dodgers, in memory of Bob.

I've done my part to help in the fight against communism. Communists enslave their people.

It's a quirk of mine. Sure, I like to introduce people from New York State to one another. Thomas had never met an American Indian before. He'd read magazine stories of the Mohawks working at tall heights building skyscrapers. One day I introduced him to Daryl Stonefish, a Mohawk, in the mess hall. The two shook hands, didn't say much to each other, and never spoke to each another again.

Oh, well, I tried. It was something I could do. If you introduce people to each other, they might become friends; there might be fewer ills all around.

I'm not much of a religious person anymore. One of the stories that Thomas told me was about a bunch of ex-Columbia students and one of them was religious—even though he smoked marijuana.

The guy he told me about was a writer, a French-Canadian American. The writer wrote a long book, inspired by a religious book he grew up with, called *En Route,* which was in French. He typed his book out on one long scroll—it was blank pages of typing paper pasted together. It was like his own Biblical scroll. He called his book *On the Road.* It was about traveling around America, looking for God. He drank coffee to stay up for ten nights and type out his scroll.

It sounded like a stunt to me. I said to Thomas, "You should have offered that guy to type up his book properly—on *separate* sheets of paper."

Thomas said, "Only after I was drafted, and they gave me a test, did I find out I could type so fast."

Thomas Delbert

Private Thomas Delbert was glad he was never put on guard duty again. It was partly because there was an additional equipment shack behind the station and sometimes you had to go there if you couldn't find something inside the station. The problem back there was the dog kennel was next to it; one of the German shepherd guard dogs seemed to only get aggressive when it saw Black soldiers. It never acted that way with White ones. Thomas thought the dog had an odd name. (Its name was "Newman.")

Though that dog scared him. It wasn't on the level of being scared that night when he struggled against Forsberg.

The only thing one could do with that episode at Forsberg's bed was bury it and forget it ever happened. He didn't want to know what it was all about. If he did, he doubted it would serve any good purpose.

Sometimes being with Lloyd was too much to handle. It wasn't that he was aggressive. It was that he could be cheerful, joking and inquisitive, but then his mood would shift. He'd say depressing things like, "Yeah, if we're still alive then."

Man, Delbert missed New York.

He had two new buddies, Michael and Clarence, both Black draftees. One was from Detroit, another from the South. They were in training and would be sent to Korea. Clarence spoke with a thick accent. It was hard to understand him, even if you slowed him down. It was a comfort to be around Black guys. You were always taking a chance being around Whites—you never knew which ones of them would just as soon see you dead because you were a Negro.

He was coming around to the idea of going to college— a *Black* college, not Columbia University. For all the talk about integration, universities we're getting it going. He had his eye on LeMoyne College in Memphis, Tennessee.

Nurse Marcia McGuinness

Her job is in the infirmary at Chitose II. She's always driven to work in a jeep by a sergeant unknown to her, who is not part of the hospital staff.

The jeep, in the lightest of rains, with her in the passenger seat, shifts higher. Now on the paved road, outside Chitose I. A quick drive over to Chitose II.

She has a runny nose. Her cold symptoms won't go away. She attributes them to stress. She's still trying to keep fright at bay.

"I am not worthy of so much attention though I'm thankful this is being done for me."

It was hard for her to speak, so she did not—these words were only ones that she thought.

Often she just wanted to shut her eyes and erase this place from her mind.

It was a bad dream where ghouls screamed, where buzzards fed. It was the land of the dead.

—So she thought, but never said.

Major Timothy Beaumont

If I'd never approached Torrington… never told him… he would have thought like the others, that Akiyama was behind all the murders and attacks. But we needed a new person in case of an emergency. Torrington's record of service is flawless.

His talents would have been wasted had I not used him.

There was a chance that Forsberg might strike in Chitose.

There is always a chance.

No, I cannot square the murders in Chitose so they come out being committed by just one individual.

We can't control everything—and this makes us feel small. We see those who have power; some need their power taken away because their power kills. Sometimes it's broader and worse than our little minds could ever imagine.

The French have an expression: *se jeter dans la gueule du loup*. The literal translation is "jump into the mouth of the wolf." It means to recklessly expose yourself to danger.

Of course we must not be reckless. But so too we must not act stupidly and think we can destroy evil. Even God can't do that.

A plane will fly over the mountains, a forest, fields of rice, peasant's huts and shacks, more than one shrine, more than one temple… It will descend from over a hill and it will land in a valley.

Captain Jake Torrington

They were in the officers' mess having lunch: frankfurters in buns, sauerkraut and pineapple cottage cheese salad.

It had taken some time, but Torrington was having a change of heart.

While he and Tim Beaumont were dining, much of their time was spent in silence. While the rain pattered on the roof, Jake thought:

This is a man who feels the weight of the world on his shoulders. He reached out to me, needed me. He respects me, my skills, my personality. I shouldn't be so quick to judge him. I should proceed carefully before I argue against him and I must have solid reasoning behind everything I say. But the problem has been how to reason when presented with an unreasonable situation. He, Hodinar, and the rest of the group have been living with Operation Grendel a lot longer than I have. It's harsh of me to think of Ilmar Hodinar as a "smarty pants" …to criticize him for it. That's what this operation needs: somebody like him.

Yes, Jake had been sometimes too uninhibited with his opinion. He'd thought of his own command, his expertise with working with the Japanese for a common good, his achievements. He'd patted himself on the back. But he was wrong to think he didn't have ingrained ways that could lead to mistakes. He had thoughts that were predictable because he'd taken certain ideas for granted! Now he'd been taught a lesson about how to consider—carefully. He now saw what he was answerable to. The Frankfurt School didn't have anyone they were answerable to. They were answerable only to their own consciences.

To kill Forsberg and his kind whenever they're found—he wasn't brought into the group to give advice of that sort.

Of course, it's easy to say nothing good can come from a werewolf. But since when was he an expert on them?

Maybe Beaumont and Hodinar had had similar ideas to his—at the beginning—but then their approaches evolved.

One of the few things that Torrington said to Tim Beaumont during their quiet lunch was, "I'm impressed that you permit debate. You know, I've... I believe I've... changed my... I can't now, but soon ...I might be able to explain."

Professor Ilmar Hodinar

There was a break in the rain. There might be sun for almost an hour; time to go out for a walk.

His stroll took him out past the buildings at Chitose I that included C2I. He headed for the farthest extreme of the parade ground; there he would turn back and return to the office.

It's not enough to observe. You must synthesize the meanings and act.

I am not a genius, and even if I were, a genius is not a god.

You can't help think that humans are on the wrong track, and they must change track, or else…

I have been accused of lacking a sense of urgency, even responsibility, regarding Operation Grendel.

My surname means "clockmaker" in Czech.

I know what the time is.

CHAPTER 38

Wolves live in packs of six to ten. They hunt together, bringing down large prey.

During their hunts, sometimes antlers and hooves kill them.

Wolves can die of starvation.

Their young don't hunt. They play.

Packs are family. When one of the family dies, the other wolves mourn for weeks, often visiting the place where the wolf died, even if the body has decomposed.

He was in the mountains, across the Ishikari Plain. Even so, he heard the high-pitched sounds of Kiriko at night.

The Akiyama wolf was old, had difficulty breathing. Being alone, he could only hunt small prey.

The day was clear. Birdsong was in the forest's laurel and pines. The terrain warmed. Oxygen from the trees and plants strengthened nature—the wolf felt it. His nose attended to the scents spread by the air currents.

Frost turned to dew. Water gurgled from the spring he knew, that he drank at, where other animals came to drink and sometimes were slain.

By mid-morning the warming day no longer strengthened the Akiyama wolf. He tired. Belched from volcanic crevices to the west, warm gasses drifted his way.

When the solstice passed and grasses withered, the high elms shed their leaves.

The Akiyama wolf wasn't going to live through the first

heavy snowfall.

The Norse gods wouldn't kill Fenrir. It would sully their honor. They let fate take its course, knew they had no power to stop it. They fed Fenrir, watched him get bigger and bigger. No wonder he had enormous strength.

The Akiyama wolf had little strength left.

He was going to die of starvation and cold.

After Fenrir did as prophesized—he killed the father-god Odin at Ragnarök—the god Vidar slayed Fenrir straight away. Foretold to the Norse, they knew it for centuries.

The Norse died. Another world without them came into being.

CHAPTER 39

On October 14, 1952, the air traffic controller at the French garrison at Nghia Lo—a town in the Muong Lo basin in northern highlands—radioed the go-ahead for the U.S. Army Cessna L19A Bird Dog to land on the short narrow landing strip.

His ninety-minute flight from Hanoi to this five-mile-wide valley in the mountains had not been without its dangers. The U.S. Army pilot had been obliged twice to fly his two-seater close to Highway 32 to get his bearings because of clouds; both times anti-aircraft fire missed him (with mountains as high as five thousand feet, it was easy for the expertly camouflaged Viet Minh to occupy niches in the terrain from which they could fire their Soviet-made cannons at airborne enemies).

Unlike Hokkaido, the geography wasn't conspicuously volcanic; it was more like that of the Alleghenies of West Virginia. However, terraces had been carved into some of the hills, and seeds, fecund land, subtropical climate, and agricultural know-how combined to make for paddies that yielded abundant crops of rice. The north highlands got plenty of rain, especially monsoon rain, and cattle grazed in clearings that rolled, were stony and not conducive to paddies.

As the Cessna descended to the airstrip, rows and rows of barbed wire fence directly below came into view. Alternating with these thin bands of strung wooden posts were seven-feet deep ditches that laborers employed by the

French Far East Expeditionary Corps had dug. This bristly and treacherous belt of armored earth, thirty yards wide, included numerous land mines. It encircled the entire garrison.

Just as the forbidding land moat ended and the Bird Dog was about to touch down, the two Americans in the plane saw just inside of the garrison's boundary a loose parade of thick-timbered blockhouses—soldiers would man these structures in the unlikely event that invaders breached the deadly "moat" and were attempting to seize the garrison. A double row of these small fortifications, each methodically distanced and angled to the other, extended around the inside edges of the military base. With this network of defenses, the French were taking no chances.

The Bird Dog touched down and its pilot and passenger watched ahead of them as a figure approached the airstrip's other end. The figure was that of Lieutenant Fabrice Lormer. The officer strode crisply through ragged grass. His gait did not reveal that his service in the military had become a repetitive process of playacting for him during the present year; he knew his country had bit off a lot to chew in Indochina.

Both the plane and the Frenchman reached the strip's other end in less than half a minute.

With its propellers twirling slower and slower, the craft rolled to a stop. Doors on either side opened and the American pilot and his passenger slid themselves out. The passenger carried an attaché case and a duffel bag. The pilot didn't carry anything.

Forsberg was struck by Lieutenant Lormer's dark blue kepi that sat on his head and instantly made him look taller than the Americans. He'd encountered, occasionally, French soldiers in occupied western Germany, but they wore peaked military caps like the Americans and British did. But Asia was different, evidently. The kepi is cylindrical in shape, its circular top reminded Forsberg of a short chunk cut from a stovepipe and covered in cloth with a visor placed on it to make it look real.

Otherwise, Lieutenant Lormer's uniform was khaki. He was a tall, slim, thirty-year old. With vigilant blue eyes he greeted the captain and his pilot on behalf of the Nghai Lo's base commander, Commandant René Thirion, remarking that he was sorry if they'd encountered any enemy fire on the way. The French lieutenant said he was to be Forsberg's liaison and guide.

They shook hands—first the captain, then the pilot. The American pilot was a curious figure. An analytical-looking kind of guy of thirty-five who wore army clothing but there was no insignia on it. After the pilot shook Lormer's hand, he shifted his shoulders and chest within his brown leather flight jacket and informed the French officer he was leaving immediately to fly back to Hanoi, to reach there before nightfall. Then he stretched his arms and legs a few times, saluted the lieutenant, walked back over to the Cessna, got in and turned on the engine.

The two on the ground waved goodbye; the plane turned around, sped down the airstrip and took off.

Forsberg said, "Interesting landscape you've got here."

They were talking inside Lormer's office. The garrison's daytime operations produced a din that made it difficult to have conversations outside. Forsberg had almost forgotten how noisy a military installation could get—the last time he experienced a post this loud was in Korea; Chitose had been a country club compared to this.

Lormer responded, "One is always surprised how a place so rural can be so important." The French officer shifted farther back in his armchair. "The population here is not Vietnamese, you know. They are Tai." He was saying "Tai", not "Thai". Although Nghia Lo was in Vietnam, the people who lived there were not *kinh* (the term for the ethnic group which was synonymous with Viet), but of Tai ethnicity. Tai and other non-kinh indigenous peoples had lived for centuries relatively free of nation-state interference in the highlands.

Suggesting that the Frenchman had misunderstood his English, the vaguely disheveled captain countered, "Actually, I mean the geography of the area." He was seated across from the French lieutenant in a foldable cross-frame chair with a canvas seat and back which was steadily acquiring the name "director's chair" in America.

"How so, 'interesting,' then?" asked Lormer.

"I would say, gloomy, but it could be just the season."

The Frenchman's eyes jumped at the word gloomy; he became defensive and parried instantly, "It's just the season, yes. There's a hint of autumn here, and now you come in when the hills cast shadows well before the end of the day." But then he added in a contradictory manner, words that weren't contradictory, "There are times that the elevations to the south and east of the garrison are depressing to look at," and tailed off to murmur, "but the village of Nghia Lo is something different, I hasten to say."

Right then Forsberg's strong senses picked it up, though six feet separated them. Almost from the start he'd felt there was something peculiar about this Frenchman.

Forsberg smelled the sweet but acrid stench of opium smoke on the man's breath. He gave no indication of his discovery to the Frenchman and ventured casually, "The landscape seems gloomy. Although you call it rural, I imagine it's still home to many wild animals."

Lormer said, "Rice terraces have been a signature of the region for quite some time. They look beautiful but farming drove all the elephants from these highlands."

"But I imagine many hills are still wild," Forsberg emphasized. "There aren't any roads. Your enemies can infiltrate such places and strike at you."

"You're correct."

The United States was paying forty percent of the French military's costs of fighting their war in Vietnam. Three months ago, French Minister of State Jean Letourneau had flown from Paris to Washington to ask for an increase in military aid. Forsberg's reports on Nghia Lo and other French installations had to speak to the readiness of the installations, as well as their current and future needs. The Americans were suspicious that a crisis was looming and that huge sums of money to the French might never be enough. Forsberg's reports also had to include his critiques of the French's own assessments of their strengths and their superiority. A vexing feature of the war was that the Viet Minh had no communication lines or military bases to guard, thus making it impossible to launch an all-out French offensive. The entrenched Gallic army had to play defense; the Viet Minh regiments' great advantage was its fluidity of movement.

"You say Nghia Lo village is something different. What do you mean by that?"

"Nghia Lo!" the lieutenant sighed, with a sudden dreamy look in his eyes. "You marvel at the clothes the people wear... they're a unique people, almost untouched by recent centuries... and the variety of items at their Muong Lo market is astonishing. This valley produces tangerines, oranges, peaches, and plums."

Lormer's brief monologue didn't provide the kind of response the captain was looking for. Forsberg comprehended at once that he was sitting across from an opium addict. Was the Frenchman taking opium to stave off lycanthropy? Had The Rule somehow paired Forsberg once again with a being that was close in nature to him? Forsberg instantly felt that none of this could be the case since he had no strong animal-like reaction to the lieutenant.

Forsberg pressed on, "I understand that you've recruited a hundred or so Tai men."

"Yes, guides for us in the mountains; reconnaissance, too."

"But you don't go into the mountains—"

"Not unless we have to. They can be dangerous."

"How so? Or is the answer obvious?"

"Yes, the bullets and bayonets of the Viet Minh can kill you. But there are also poison spears."

"The Viet Minh use poison spears?"

"No, the sworn enemies of the Tai people do."

"Who are they?"

"There are different ethnic tribes which vary from hill to hill. You don't want to get in the middle of things. Sometimes there are tensions over land. The Tai people also use poison spears. You want to be far away from them. They're tipped with aconite. It's fast acting and deadly."

Some of the color went out of Forsberg's face when he heard the word "aconite". Maybe he was wrong about Lormer. Was it really by chance that opium and aconite figured in his life and lycanthropy did not?

Lormer went on, "But one of the benefits—and I say this sarcastically—of having the Viet Minh as an enemy is that it usually unifies the *Montagnards,* the mountain peoples, against them.

"Yes, that's what I've been told."

The highlander natives understandably hated the Viet Minh—communists fighting to establish a centralized state run by the majority *kinh* population. The state would dictate to them the terms of their existence. The *kinh* were openly hostile to their culture and their religion.

"Yes, the *Montagnards* will fight to the death against the Viets. You know what the Vietnamese teach in their school about them?"

"No."

"They say they have long tails and are hairy all over; that they're essentially…

"I get it," Forsberg interjected speedily.

"Animals." The lieutenant finished his sentence.

Forsberg was made nervous, though not yet afraid. What strange land had he dropped into? Would this country be more dangerous to him than any French, Viet, Montagnard or American could ever imagine? Still, Lormer's presence was having no physical effect on him. Opium, aconite, and animal-people—so familiar to him—was it just a fluke they were there together? He shifted the conversation back to unambiguously official business.

"I understand that ten days ago your garrison got reinforcements—a unit of 250 Moroccan soldiers.

The lieutenant picked up on Forsberg's taking the wheel of the conversation. "Yes, the 5th Tabor Company was sent to us. Lieutenant General de Linares is right to bolster our numbers."

"But that's not enough, so more soldiers arrived five days ago."

"Yes, a heavy artillery company arrived, adding two more Howitzers. More petroleum came, more ammunition, more electric generators; three Foreign Legion platoons."

"Still, Intelligence counts that there are three whole regiments of Viets less than ten kilometers from here. My plane steered clear of them. They're marching on this fort. I don't intend to be here when they attack. I fly out tomorrow, or the next day, early morning."

"We understand that."

"You know the Viets will sacrifice themselves in large numbers. Do you think you're up to the challenge?"

"We're up to the challenge."

"One can hope. You're fortified and heavily armed. Washington doesn't want all their equipment to go up in smoke. Not to mention, they're concerned about loss of life on the French side."

"We'll do what we need to."

"Yes, we hope it will be enough." Forsberg shifted his gaze to the lieutenant's closed office door and said, "I'm ready to get started on the tour if you are."

"I'll show you all of the garrison, but because of the mountains it'll be *entre chien et loup* in less than an hour. Then we'll only see things in artificial light.

Forsberg didn't speak the language, so he snapped at Lormer, "Lieutenant, what did you say to me in French, please?"

"Oh, *entre chien et loup*—sorry, I couldn't think of the English word, so I used the French expression."

"What does it mean?" Forsberg asked testily.

"We say "between dog and wolf." It's for that time of day before nightfall.

"Oh," Forsberg frowned, "you mean the word 'dusk'."

It took the pale-eyed Frenchman only a second to recognize the English. "Yes, that's it. That's the word."

What kind of character was this officer-opium addict? thought Forsberg.

Was Lormer at all close to Major Beaumont? *Did he know?*

With shadows lengthening over the garrison, Lormer took Forsberg around to offices to introduce him to those on duty who were still at their desks. Forsberg meet the garrison commander (the aforementioned Thirion) and his staff; it seemed Lormer took great pains to locate any officer that could be found at any workspace, no matter if the room contained only a single desk or lone counter to stand at and write notes.

He was unenthusiastic about going outside. He told Forsberg that tramping about the garrison in the near darkness would be a waste of time, and that if Forsberg didn't mind, he would rather make the rounds to those in administration, and meanwhile he could mention a few things that Forsberg might find worth knowing as they did so.

Such things were these: that the valley floor on which they stood was at an altitude of 261 meters or 865 feet; that these highlands were an extension of the highlands of Yunnan, China (and of course, Communist China was the enemy; they funded the Viets while the Soviets and East Germany provided a few choice sophisticated wares); that since this was Tai Country, the Viet Minh had no better claim to it than the French—or the King of Thailand, for that matter; that yearly outbreaks of cholera were common in the highlands and Asian communists will never provide clean drinking water and adequate sanitation to drive out cholera among the people because, at heart, they didn't care about people. They only cared about their ideology and rising up the ranks in its political system; that though the officers he was being introduced to were French and were White, the majority of the one thousand foot soldiers and their sergeants he'd see tomorrow in the garrison were recruits from the Maghreb— Morocco, Algeria, and Tunisia—it was not good politically to have Whites in the infantry. Back home in France support for the war in Indochina was waning.

These data, comments, and their like, disgorged by Lormer, made Captain Forsberg look back at the Frenchman's dreamy short monologue about Nghai Lo with new tolerance; it came to him that he'd rather be hearing more about the village than the garrison.

Lormer finished with, "The thing is, imperialist aggression and rule is similar to domestic dictatorship, except with imperialists the force is from without, and with dictators it's from within." His eyelids drooped halfway; there'd be no more of the guide from him; he was floating away; it was time to report to his opium pipe to prepare for his next assignment—twilight sleep on his cot in his quarters.

At 6 a.m. a bugle sounded reveille, just as at any American base. Once it finished, a recording of an instrumental arrangement, heavy with drums and horns, of the French national anthem played. After *La Marseillaise*, a choral version of another rousing anthem, *Le chant du départ*, took its turn on the loudspeakers which were situated throughout the garrison.

Soon small areas around the camp one by one erupted with machine noise and the voices of groups of soldiers moving through sets of calisthenics or hand-to-hand combat drills. Beyond the boundaries of the garrison, above the forest hilltops' outline, a sky of gray mist was a stationary wall. Small clouds of a lighter shade sailed, from north to south, in front of it. It would take some hours for that moisture to clear if rain wasn't going to come.

Their breakfast together in the Officers' Mess was over. Fabrice Lormer and Gideon Forsberg began their circuit of the treeless garrison.

Nghia Lo garrison had two gates. They were near the south gate, located on the side of base where the land sloped gently up (the arrival-end of the airstrip sat on this uplift as well). The arrangement of buildings near the south gate followed a design of two rectangles side by side, forming a modest "village-green" square. These buildings were the nerve center of the post. Forsberg had been taken through this quadrangle yesterday. One rectangle was home to the Administration and Operations building and Headquarters; surrounding that building were the buildings and offices of Radio Operations, Translations and Tai scouts, the NCOs' mess, the officers' mess, the quartermaster's office and an officers club. The contiguous rectangle to the side of these hard-at-work day buildings consisted of a courtyard, officers' quarters, a first aid station, as well as a depot for provisions.

Forsberg had seen from the air that the areas on base used for drills, that had weaponry and equipment, could be toured in less than an hour. However, it was important to confirm what kind of ordnance was on hand and inspect its placement throughout the fort. Forsberg wasn't schooled to be a great military tactician and he didn't need to be. He needed to write a report.

These areas of the base were small enough to walk. The armory, machine shop, pads for generators, vehicle garages—glances and salutes by the French guide and the American were cast politely as they proceeded.

As they were treading the gravel (gravel, a good guard against mud) to acknowledge these necessities, Forsberg eyed where the howitzers and numerous mortars were positioned around the base, as well as spaces where Hotchkiss machine guns might be effectively shielded from enemy fire.

Forsberg reckoned that Nghai Lo could defend itself against a Viet Minh attack that numbered five thousand ground soldiers and had no air support (which usually was the case in the highlands).

Lormer remarked, "Yes, American aid keeps the garrison strong. We defend the highway, the two rivers, the village, and the hills.

As they ended Forsberg's confidential inspection of the garrison proper, the captain saw some Maghreb platoons engaged in guerrilla exercises and others in rifle drills. The soldiers wore white kepis—this was not a good idea, Forsberg thought. If they were transported, for example, in the backs of trucks, those hats could serve as targets.

Lormer quickly made his way over to a lot where a jeep was parked. He beckoned Forsberg to the passenger side, but the Frenchman delayed him before he got in, gently swinging his hand up and pointing to the tops of three buildings just outside the garrison's east gate, which was the fortress's main gate and the one closest to the streets and paths of Nghia Lo Village.

"We have a number of strongholds outside the fort. I'm going to take you to the two largest support points. The first is the village outpost."

It was a one-minute drive beyond the main gate. There wasn't much to see. The purpose of the outpost was to protect the short stretch of road and entrance to the main gate. A hundred men were crammed into the small area. Forsberg could see around fifty men engaged in unarmed exercises. Two howitzers were on the site. Tents were pitched throughout; there were no barracks. The two men stayed five minutes, then Lormer led the way back to the jeep.

He drove up to High Point—a ten-minute drive up a dirt

road. It was double the size of the village outpost. It sat on a compact plateau, covering the flat ridge's entirety; its rim was heavily sandbagged. It protected the east gate and the garrison itself—from high up. Its howitzers could more easily reach the enemy if they were to penetrate the hills. Seven oblong, one-story buildings surrounded a courtyard which was essentially an exercise ground. Barbed wire barricades, trenches and land mines surrounded the small complex. Upon seeing the outpost, Forsberg didn't revise his estimate that the French could survive a Viet Minh attack of five thousand. The reason was that if the weather was bad and time was on the side of the Viet Minh, this outpost could prove to be superfluous—in other words, not effective, because it could be taken out by a large force of Viet Minh. Then the Viets could wait a day and go after the main fortress—and then, one would think, they would be stopped there, from inside.

They arrived back at Nghia Lo garrison just before 10 a.m. Forsberg spent ninety minutes in his guest quarters, which smelled of rain-soaked wood and mold, writing his report on the conditions, strengths and needs of the garrison. He expected the French had organized his flight back to Hanoi after he and Lormer had lunch.

When he first sat down with the French officer in the officers' mess there was clearly a change in his mood. There'd been nothing unusual about his state of mind previously this morning. He was all business. His speech, movements, or disposition didn't reveal him to be a man with an opium habit. Yet something, it seemed, had happened since they'd separated and Forsberg had gone to work on his report.

Lormer told Forsberg that unfortunately, a few things appeared to be scuttling the plan to fly him out after lunch. First, there was the weather—there was still too much cloud cover between Nghia Lo and Hanoi. Second, there was the likelihood that the 6th colonial parachute battalion would be placed on airborne alert within the next twelve hours.

Forsberg asked what the battalion had to do with his flight back to Hanoi and Lormer responded that intelligence was reaching the garrison that the Viet Minh were moving quickly through the hills, that their numbers were larger than previously thought and that various garrisons in the area needed reinforcements.

Forsberg asked, "Does Nghia Lo need more reinforcements?"

"I don't know. What I do know is that the parachute battalion might probably be sent to Tu Lu."

"Not here?"

"No, not here."

"How far away is Tu Lu?"

"It's thirty kilometers upriver from here."

"It appears I should have arrived a few days earlier."

"Only now we can say, yes, probably."

Forsberg tried to make his sigh unnoticeable. "My life could end here if the Viet Minh's numbers are higher than five thousand. But then, I'm only thinking of myself, am I not?"

"Maybe later in the day you can leave or tomorrow morning. Anyway, we believe the garrison will hold in any case."

The situation was more serious than either man thought. What they didn't know was that an hour before, the Commander in Chief of French forces in Indochina, General Raoul Salan, based in Saigon, had sent a secret message to Lieutenant General François de Linares in Hanoi saying he believed Nghia Lo was very exposed and vulnerable; that army intelligence had said ten thousand Viet Minh troops were advancing in the direction of the garrison and it could be taken.

Though he didn't know specifically of that secret communication, Commander René Thirion had his own fears and at 11:30 a.m. ordered trenches be dug between the blockhouses lining the inner perimeter of Nghia Lo garrison.

Lormer said, "I'll take you to Nghia Lo village and show you the market."

Forsberg thought what a curious way to kill time while the fleecy canopy of opaque gray prevented his departure.

For the American, the hardy lunch of stroganoff, ham and bread, followed by coffee and imported Jura cheese, ended up being too drawn out. But there wasn't anything that could be done about it.

After leaving on foot the main gate of the garrison and then walking seventy yards on a gravel to reach the highway (the major truck route of the area), they crossed said highway (which ran roughly south to north through the wide basin valley) and were immediately in the village proper. Not only were they in the village, they were also at the nearest edge of Muong Lo Market. Overhead, at the beginning of the market, a sign and various colored flags hung from a wire that was strung between the tops of two telegraph poles on either side of the street. The sign, weathered but not too ratty, welcomed locals and soldiers; it was in French.

Lormer walked slowly, leading Forsberg by his side. The lieutenant clearly enjoyed looking at the people in their native clothing and took pleasure in casting glances at the thrown-together sheds and tiny shops that had congregated at this end of the village (in hope of being the first ones to do business with anybody leaving the fort). A few men called out at him in hawker's French, offering him services and merchandise. These native men were dressed in black shirts that had short, straight-up collars embroidered with discrete bands of color. It was still that time of year where they wore short black trousers with cuffs just below the knee, or even above the knee itself.

For a while, Lormer and Forsberg didn't talk as they proceeded. Forsberg was still surprised and unhappy at being delayed.

When Lormer next spoke he told the captain the Tai Dam people— *dam* means "black," in Tai—exclusively populated

Nghia Lo. He said both men and women dressed mostly in black and they referred, with no qualms, to themselves as Tai Dam—this designation helped them distinguish themselves from other Tai Highlands groups who had slightly different customs.

Upon reaching the boundary of the market Forsberg smelled hot cooking oil, then smoke from frying cabbage, eggs, and noodles.

The stall was intentionally positioned there for the benefit of any soldier who might want to, straight away, plunge into a dish of local food.

Across from that stall on the other side of the market street was a booth selling fried crickets, grasshoppers, and silkworms—again, a positioning of a kiosk to capitalize on the presence of a visiting soldier.

Lormer described what was on offer. The American thought to himself that the few insects flying around in the market didn't know how lucky they were not to be fried.

Advancing into the bustle of people and busy stalls with frames made of slight timbers lashed together, Lormer didn't hide his affection for the place and its barrage of odors. He mentioned right away that he found the Tai Dam also very interesting because none of the world's great religions had infiltrated their culture; they remained animists and ancestor worshippers. Their beliefs centered on spirits and life essences; they and their cosmology were ripe for study by scholars.

Forsberg thought Lormer had romantic ideas of the people of the area but there was no harm in it. He was convinced that the Frenchman made his ideas even more romantic during his reveries when he was high on opium.

The sellers in the market were reserved hill people; they did not shout out from behind their groups of baskets or their stands perched on trestles. A full range of goods were for sale: tea, spices, whole cloth, dyes for cloth, yarn; shoes, tools, knives, live chickens and ducks; sticky rice, noodles,

478

fruits and vegetables, pork; sheets of tin, animal skins and leather; books, amulets, beauty products, porcelain and ceramic kitchen ware, tobacco, and folk medicines. From time to time, sellers, when they saw Lormer and Forsberg, politely called out *"Bonjour!"* and *"Bienvenue!"* However, most of the merchandize offered at the market was for the local populace.

One middle-aged Tai woman, though looking wizened, dressed in black, wearing the characteristic headdress of the Tai Dam—the headdress consisted of thin black cloth wrapped over the top of her head (like two layers of a turban) which was then itself covered by a thick embroidered-patterned floppy kerchief—was the proprietor of a stall who sold silver accessories. She tried to get Forsberg's attention first by calling out "Hello" and "Welcome" twice at him in French. Somehow, he allowed his gaze to fall on her.

So… it might be said their "jaunt" to the market had a positive effect… it seemed to have at least half succeeded in drawing Forsberg away from taking worried glances up at the sky with its stubborn mouse-colored hue, wondering when he might be able to fly out. Indeed, after the Tai woman in her native headdress cried out to him, he diverted his gaze toward her. Seeing she'd gotten his attention, and hoping to get him to stop and buy from her—she seemed to be an uncharacteristically extroverted example of her people—she blurted out, in French, at a slightly lower volume, *"Je vous connais!"*

Forsberg, with a sour look still dominating his face, grunted to Lormer, "What does that mean?"

"It means, 'I know you.'"

What!? The captain's heart sank. *How* could she know me? *Does she sense* what I really am? Then he thought to himself: no, she can't know me, I've never seen her before…

Seeing the American flustered, Lormer chuckled, and told Forsberg with a smile—and with no ill intent—that the woman was using an old seller's trick. The trick was to forge quick intimacy, by insisting that they had once met. It was all so she could slow him down, pursue a conversation with him, and hopefully sell him something. Lormer said the Tai Dam didn't usually do it, but there were cases…

As Lormer was explaining to the captain, Forsberg could feel the woman's eyes remaining stubbornly on him, even as they moved forward and away. The captain fixed his eyes on a stall coming up on the left with nuts, seeds, jerky and dried herbs in crocks, boxes, and shelves. He could've cared less about them. He just wanted to show the woman "who knew him" that she didn't and he wasn't interested.

The woman saw exactly what he was doing to ignore her. Her voice rang out in the widening distance, *"Mais je vous connais!"* (But I know you!)

Forsberg shuddered to hear the woman's voice once more.

Lormer raised his eyebrows but didn't turn back to look at her.

Muong Lo Market didn't enchant the captain like it did his guide. In a military career, during peacetime, it was common for soldiers to stroll through a local market; they simply visited such places as a diversion—there often weren't many things to do outside a far-flung base abroad. Sure, this could be said to be a different kind of exotic. Forsberg had seen enough that was exotic—in Korea, in Japan, even in Europe sometimes. He'd gotten over it.

As Lormer led the captain forward still deeper into the market he began to talk about a man named tNoon (tuh-NOON), whom he apparently found to be an intriguing individual. It seemed he was on friendly terms with the local man, a Tai Dam whose brother was in the service of the French military (already six years now, chiefly in reconnaissance) and had risen to the rank of sergeant at Nghia Lo garrison. However, tNoon was not like his brother, Lormer pointed out. He did not work for the French, and he did little work at all. Lormer called him a "bit of a philosopher," saying that he was a reflective man, at turns comical and serious; that tNoon was apart from society and a thirty-year-old-man (though he couldn't tell his real age) who passed most of the daylight hours hanging around on the market street (he always seemed to be there) watching life happen as it happens and speaking to those who felt like speaking to him.

Until the subject of tNoon had been brought up—the local people had given the man this nickname because *tNoon* simply means "road" in their language— Forsberg had thought there was no particular purpose to his and the French lieutenant's walkabout. But the more that Lormer described tNoon, the more Forsberg discerned that they would be soon meeting this man; it wasn't going to be just a highlight of their stroll, but rather the real reason for it. (Though from the descriptions, it seemed to Forsberg that tNoon was nothing more than a garden variety idler, that the Frenchman was romanticizing him because he himself likely wished, deep down inside, to have no job and live the life of a dreaming loafer.)

Three minutes after they'd encountered the woman who claimed she knew Forsberg (strangely, the woman reminded Forsberg of the short, weathered crone outside Modena, Italy who herself seemed to know his secret and urged him to offer his soul up to God, but then wanted to involve him in a reading of Tarot cards), Forsberg found that Lormer had conducted him up the slowly inclining street, and after passing by stalls selling incense, horseshoes, saddles, Chinese lanterns, and sheets of tin, they arrived at a booth that sold pots and pans but that stank of burning poppies. Whether this stall was tNoon's own property was of no matter—he was there, ready to be spoken with.

Unsurprisingly, the man was a head shorter than the two officers. His trousers were cuffed just below his knee and he wore the black clothes customary of his people. He greeted Lormer with an animated face and jagged teeth but also with deep-seated eyes that appeared to be in their own world. Both men spoke in French and tNoon's French was more than adequate. Their friendly exchange of words included mention of Forsberg; soon after the captain heard his name, tNoon's hand stretched toward him and they shook politely. The Tai Dam's hand was that of a man who'd had labored many seasons in the hills. It was calm, as was the man. His breath smelled of opium and his eyes were in the place where opium transports its users.

With a brief glow flashing across his face, taking pride and pleasure in speaking the man's name in front of him, Lormer said, "So this is tNoon."

The Tai man made a remark and Lormer translated it. "He says, you didn't bring your ponchos? It looks like it might drizzle, fellows."

It was easy to see the leaden sky above the giant hill rising at the end of the market street; there was no reason to raise one's head.

Lormer responded in English, for Forsberg's sake, and then straight away translated his words into French, "We are hoping for quite the reverse. We'd like the weather to clear, so Forsberg can fly out."

tNoon frowned on hearing this. To downplay his forecast for rain, he added amiably, and Lormer translated it for the American's benefit, "The weather's very changeable here. We say here at Nghia Lo that the four seasons of the year can go by in one day."

This was of no comfort to Forsberg. What if the weather didn't clear today? What if it didn't clear tomorrow?

The conversation was wholly in French:

Lormer asked tNoon, "Why do you talk to us about weather?"

"Because you bring a visitor who is not French. So, he comes and then he will go. He can't fly in the rain."

"True."

"Has your friend come to buy anything from me?"

"No, I didn't bring him here for that."

"How much would you like? I haven't seen you for almost a week. You've been busy. Of course, there's a lot going on."

Lormer said nervously, "Please, a cigarette tin—full."

Forsberg watched as tNoon slipped a tin box of cigarettes out from his pocket, gave it to Lormer. The French officer then handed the Tai man several French banknotes all at once (The captain couldn't see exactly how many francs there were.)

Acting as though nothing unusual was taking place, Lormer said to Forsberg, "They make their own smokes at home, and it has more flavor.

Forsberg could smell that the illustrated rectangular French metal box did not contain eighteen cigarettes of Egyptian origin, but was full of balled up dried opium resin.

Since Gideon Forsberg needed opiates daily, it was wise to take note of a person such as tNoon. It was prudent to know where resources existed.

Did tNoon recognize that Forsberg was taking an opiate? That was impossible to know. He had the mien of a clever, observant man, and it was in his nature to keep some of what he perceived a secret.

Forsberg decided to take the lead. He said, "If we could, I would appreciate speaking to your friend. I recognize that his brother works for you, and I imagine he has many scouts in the field who help him with reconnaissance. But one never knows what might turn up today, at this moment... something that has not been in any report, or at least any report that's been available to me." It was, after all, Forsberg's mission to not only size up the garrison's capabilities and its preparedness, but to learn what he could of positions and movements outside the base.

So he engaged tNoon; Lormer translated.

"If you would be so kind to help me."

"I'm always here to help," said the man from behind

483

deep-set eyes.

"You know the United States army has invested in the French forces here. My bosses would like the best picture possible of how our money is being utilized. But though I say that, my questions aren't going to directly address dollars and francs."

"All right," tNoon said, awaiting the onslaught of questions.

"Would you help me if I came to you, and I was Viet Minh?"

"No."

"Why?"

"I'm sure that Lieutenant Lormer has explained that to you, and also you have your American research that tells you."

"Would you help me if I came to you, and I was American?"

"Certainly."

"How would you help me?"

"You only have to say what you want. I'll do it for you."

"You're vulnerable to enemy attack. How are you prepared for this?"

"Those of us who are not in the French army are not organized. Those of us who are unorganized will avoid doing battle with the enemy. We are what the world calls civilians. But don't misunderstand me. We won't collaborate with the enemy. We work... farming, hunting sometimes. We bide our time, going slowly. We move when we need to. Until now we have had a certain amount of independence.

"We want you to retain your independence. But the Viet Minh threaten it. They want to move you when you are living a peaceful life right here. Do you agree? Do your people agree?"

"Of course we do."

"We don't expect everyone to take up arms. You are farmers, I know that. What do you think is going to happen?

Is our investment in this place worth it?"

"It depends on who is stronger. Who is stronger will win. It will be army against army. The people here, who are Tai Dam, side with you."

"Can we win?"

"I hope so."

"Lieutenant Lormer tells me you're a bit of a philosopher. You've thought a lot about the situation here, I image. Is there anything you can tell me that might help me to further understand your people and their view of what's going on around them?"

When Lormer heard this, his facial features sharpened; he translated it with pleasure, for he'd had meditative conversions with the Tai *flâneur* that had fascinated him.

tNoon did not disappoint the Frenchman when he answered:

"When you're pushed against your will, the old ways go by the wayside—you aren't able to hang onto them because you're not moving at your natural pace when your hands are steady. You're driven so fast that your fingers can't grab them. You lose the old ways. Notice I say the word "fast." It's the *speed* at which you're forced to go—that's as bad as the move against your will. It's frightening! What you're left in is somebody else's vision of how they want the world to be. I said it's frightening… you can die of fright. You may not be killed instantly. It may take you some time before you die. But you die of the push and the speed of that push."

Forsberg thought about tNoon's dreamy answer and tailored his next question in more geopolitical terms—though tNoon wouldn't have seen it that way. "You feel great pressure, then?"

"Yes."

Forsberg couldn't think of anything more to say. He also didn't like that their conversation, for a moment, seemed to stop time. He wanted to get back to the garrison and fly to Hanoi.

As almost an afterthought, he put only last question to the opium seller.

"Can I find you here most of the time?"

The Tai man nodded.

"Good. Thank you."

Lormer recognized this was the end of Forsberg interviewing his friend. He spoke a few words in French that were clearly words spoken when departing. Both officers shook hands with tNoon.

The two stepped away from the booth selling pots and pans, and Lieutenant Lormer motioned to Forsberg to turn back with him, in the direction of the garrison.

They walked back through the market, with footsteps no longer pausing to allow for a glance at the sellers and their wares. Out of the blue Lormer remarked, "You know, tNoon has a wife. He speaks well of her but I've never met her."

It started to drizzle five minutes after they passed through the garrison's front gate. Once inside the fort men were continuing to work on the trenches being dug between the blockhouses. Lormer heard some soldiers taking about sandbags that would be stacked in walls by some of the trenches, with spaces in the walls being left for rifle rests. The talk was in French and Lormer did not translate it.

The clouds above were the color of the head of a hammer. Not only the garrison, but the giant hills outside it, which everyone had to admit were at dangerously close range, took on an eerie aspect for the Frenchman. He told Forsberg that the two of them could relax in the compound's bar for an hour or so and wait for the skies to possibly clear. He was lying. It was obvious the skies weren't going to clear. However, he was resolved to put on a good face. Forsberg knew he could expect a drastic reduction in translations today from the Frenchman. It was old hat to be in situations where he couldn't understand the language; when it came to matters that people tried to hide from him, he always knew when he was being deprived of such information.

With the drizzle—and dusk to appear in less than five hours—Forsberg knew no one would want to risk flying him to Hanoi. His lower abdomen, where the she-wolf in the Italian mountains seven years ago slammed into him, ached. The pain was there because of the tense circumstances occurring *now*—it wasn't there because it was chronic and never went away, as he told doctors.

Forsberg told his host he would wait for the summons to the airstrip (though he knew there would be none) back in his room where he would read and relax.

The first thing the captain did when getting there was to down sixty milligrams of extra codeine, in pill form. Dull the physical pain. Don't let the anxieties of those in the compound affect you. If you must curse a situation, do it after distancing yourself (at least in your mind) from it.

At that moment—Forsberg did not know it—a group of ten French soldiers showed up at Nghia Lo garrison saying they had just managed by a hair's breadth to arrive. They had abandoned their small observation post fifteen miles away to the east. Reconnaissance had told them that Viet Minh assault divisions 308 and 312 were in their area, that they were outnumbered one hundred to one. They were not the first group of soldiers to retreat to Nghia Lo. Lormer didn't mention it, but yesterday, just before Forsberg arrived, a dozen soldiers fell back to the garrison from their observation point eighteen miles away, again, from the east, near Vietnam's Red River. They fled, knowing that if they stayed, they'd come under fire and would not survive.

1:20 p.m. was the present time. Nghia Lo's commandant had just received word communications with the French fort at Gia Hoi, twelve miles north, had been cut off; that the Viet Minh might have even taken that fort.

With the current weather hampering reconnaissance, Commander Thirion at Nghia Lo couldn't know that skillfully camouflaged Viet Minh ground troops had quietly advanced and were now within ten miles of his garrison.

Forsberg sat in his room's rattan chair to let the extra codeine take effect. He thought about what he'd been shown, selectively, he thought, in the previous twenty-four hours.

He hadn't comprehended the scope of the threat. The French were too sure of themselves; now they were paying for it. Out of their optimism—which their securing the Tai hill people as their allies partially fueled—they hadn't acknowledged, or they'd acknowledged too late, the uncomfortable realities about the Viet Minh's numbers and their guerilla advantages—and they concealed those realities from him during his visit.

The image of the outpost at High Point came to his mind. It was a fine outpost, so to speak—well-built, commanding a strategic view of the area. But soldiers abandoned such outposts all the time when they were dangerously outnumbered and needed to save their skins. With trenches being dug *in the garrison proper*, it was clear to him he wasn't being told the true size of the Viet Minh's forces around Nghia Lo. He thought to himself: Every French stronghold for five square miles could be turned into a graveyard if the Viets take out High Point. One by one, all will fall, in less than a couple of days.

He mused, with half-shut eyes. Yes, he could see this all from a distance, but he had to remind himself he was not an onlooker; he was there in the middle of it, and could die.

Was I sent here to die? he asked himself. Was this the purpose of sending me here: to kill me? Does Lormer know Beaumont?

He didn't see how being sent to Nghia Lo was like being sent to Chitose. There were tantalizing suggestions, with Lormer and his opium, his talk of aconite and dogs and wolves. But so far he'd seen nothing he could consider as a manifestation of The Rule in action.

True, his now racing thoughts told him: The Rule could be mysterious.

Well, …death was mysterious. You die. You go

unconscious. Things you cannot imagine will happen to you.

He did not want to die.

I need to get out tomorrow, he thought. I will get out, even if I can't fly out.

A knock came on his door at 5 p.m. It was a Maghreb corporal speaking passable English. Probably the young black-haired man had worked on long-haul ships—he had that kind of sailor's English. The corporal came with the message that he could meet Lormer in the officers' mess at 6 p.m. for dinner.

The captain told his visitor to please tell the lieutenant he wasn't hungry, that he would stay in his room, good to bed early, and would very much like to meet him at 5 a.m. at the officers' mess in hopes of, after having a small bite to eat, flying to Hanoi.

The young man left Forsberg's door and Forsberg realized the rain had just stopped.

Too late. But now it was too dark to fly.

Yet having the drizzle end wasn't necessarily good. Drier weather would be advantageous to any Viet troops on the move.

After a fitful night of sleep, Forsberg rose, packed his things up and went to the officers' mess to meet Lieutenant Lormer. Lormer was already inside the sharply lit place (it was early; it called for bright lights). He was jittery. He didn't feel like sitting. He stood by the table where they'd sit. He'd spent the previous night in a twilight-trance, hallucinating, never descending to true sleep. Forsberg could smell the strong coffee on his breath.

"Good morning, Captain, I hope you slept well."

"Excellently, thank you." Forsberg lied.

"I did as well," Lormer said, without hesitating—though his voice quivered.

"Excuse me, but I have to get right to the point. How does it look?"

"Well, maybe we should sit down, sir." Lormer tried not

to fidget. "You can't depart until well after breakfast because we know there have been troop movements overnight. Our plane needs to go up and have a look at the area before your plane can go up."

The two men sat down, with the soldier who was to serve them pulling out their chairs for them. The mess was empty, except for the soldier and the staff of three manning the kitchen.

Forsberg asked, "Is it supposed to rain today?"

"The weather is going to be variable. There could be a time when the skies are clear enough for you to go."

Forsberg was disappointed with Lormer's tone, and especially with what he was saying. He'd half-prepared himself to hear the words.

He spoke without emotion, "All right, that sounds realistic."

"Of course we need to know where the Viets are. There are reports there are lot of them, and they have heavy artillery."

Forsberg said, irritated now, "It seems like they've appeared out of thin air. Didn't you know this yesterday?"

"We've had our suspicions, but the Viet Minh are well camouflaged and the weather's made it impossible for us to see. If they've taken certain positions, you won't be able to leave."

Without raising his voice, the American said, "It seems that my visit was entirely misconceived."

"As I said before, it would have been better to come at an earlier time."

There wasn't anything more to say. Lormer and Forsberg were army men. The overview of what needed to happen during the next few hours had been announced. All they could do was sit back and let various events unfold.

Five minutes into their breakfast—and with small talk about when the last time either officer had been back to visit their home country (Forsberg lied and said he'd been back

490

two years ago—he had not), and a comparison between the hills of Korea, Japan with those looming over Nghia Lo— the captain asked Lormer, "Do you happen to know Timothy Beaumont, he's a U.S. Army major."

"No, why do you ask?" Lormer countered, blankly.

Forsberg believed the Frenchman. It was that look on his face before he spoke.

"I've worked under him. He speaks French. His grandfather was a general in the French army. Major Beaumont has friends in the French army. He's an unofficial liaison; he does people favors."

"Oh," was all that Lormer could utter, not particularly interested.

Forsberg spoke gruffly, "It's a common name, isn't it?"

"Yes, but the name is not always everywhere. I personally don't know any officers with that family name."

"Do you know Professor Ilmar Hodinar?"

Lormer responded with an even more blank look than before.

"No." The name "Ilmar Hodinar" had an off ring to it, and it wasn't that Lormer wanted to smile at the sound of it. Rather, there was something almost extraterrestrial about its sound.

Forsberg thought to himself: I was sent here on purpose, I was put in a trap to be caught and killed—or on the other hand, both the French and American armies have bungled things to such an extent that all of us in this garrison are going to die, and I'm just here by chance.

When Forsberg thought it was the right moment, he mentioned tNoon. He asked how often the Tai man was at the market. Lormer responded with, "There is never a time I've gone there and I have not found him."

Walking back after breakfast to his guest room Gideon felt a tenseness gripping the garrison. Each man knew his life was in danger. Information was passed around—and the figure was correct—that the Viet Minh in the area were ten-thousand strong. That meant those at the Nghia Lo garrison were outnumbered ten to one. Each man on base snapped to work building final defenses. To be outnumbered ten to one was an astonishingly bad prospect.

Captain Forsberg spent the entire morning in and out of the rattan chair in his room. When on his feet, he paced the room, fear wracking his mind. There would be no sweating this out. It was suicidal to stay in the garrison. He had to run. He knew what he had to do was leave the garrison, in a jeep—or on foot, if necessary. But where would he go? And what point was there in taking a jeep?—the Viets would control the few roads. He'd be killed. It would be safer to just leave on foot, he reasoned. But then, what? What could he live on? Oh… he could ask to be taken in by the Tai Dam. They were on the side of the French, and from what tNoon said, it seemed they would extend their alliance so an American might be accommodated by them. Also, the Tai Dam grew opium…

After the sun was above the horizon, a reconnaissance plane went up. It stayed in the air barely ten minutes. It was fortunate to make it back to the airstrip undamaged.

The report was that there were likely ten thousand men and their march was bringing them ever closer by the hour. It was going to be an all-out attack.

Lormer stopped by Forsberg's quarters and apologized, saying it wouldn't be possible to fly out that day. The reason wasn't the weather, but that there were too many Viet Minh in the area. They agreed to lunch together at 11:30 a.m.

Forsberg went over to his bed and lay down. His thoughts swirled. He thought of Akiyama, his no longer being human, his change into an animal. Animals might go to mortal combat with one another, but they cannot know just how final death is, even though some animals do mourn their dead and come back to the carcasses of them even after they've disintegrated. Animals don't have the minds to know that death is the end of the cosmos for them individually, that those experiences their minds have placed in the realm of pleasure are erased; they can never feel the desolation that humans feel when realizing that death obliterates not only their bodies, but also the experiences and abundant extensions of experience that human life thrives on and often gives people cause to live (not that Forsberg could enjoy life—but he could see how others might).

He knew if he was captured by the Viets, whose continual saw was to label the French as lackeys of American Capitalism, he'd be locked up and nearly starved. But the difference between him and other prisoners was that he, without codeine, would take sudden and lethal action. There would be no time for false confessions and reeducation classes.

At their lunch, while going through the motions of dining, Forsberg said to Lormer that he wanted "the whole truth and nothing but the truth." It was pointless to keep him in the dark anymore; he wanted to know exactly what was going on around them.

Lormer acquiesced. He told him French army soldiers last night had destroyed their own posts in several hamlets nearby. Then they were let into the fort, in the dark. He said planes were dropping six hundred paratroopers into Tu Le, a French garrison forty kilometers to the northwest, but no paratroopers could be dropped into Nghia Lo, that Nghia Lo was blocked off by the enemy from Tu Le. They had to make do with the soldiers they already had on hand. "We are preparing for the worst," he said.

Forsberg asked, "Are we trapped?"

Lormer demurred, "It wouldn't be so bad if their numbers were smaller."

"They could overrun us, if their numbers are significant."

"Yes, it would cost them many lives, but they could do it."

"I would like to be of some use here. Is there anything I can do?"

"No, you don't speak French. I'm afraid you'll only get in the way."

That sounded disgraceful to Forsberg. His anger rose, "What good is High Point if there are so many Viet Minh? High Point will be overrun; it can't defend us."

"High Point will defend us. If there comes a time they can't, as a matter of course they'll destroy the station and come down to the garrison to fight with us."

After walking back to his room after lunch, Gideon Forsberg began to put his plan in motion. A U.S. Army canvas field bag was among his belongings. Its size: three or four cartons of a dozen eggs could be stacked on top of each other inside it—indeed, a rather small field bag.

As he put a canteen filled with water, all the codeine he had with him, a rain poncho and a tee shirt in the bag, his eyes fell on the information stenciled in black ink on the bag's olive drab fabric: "W.L. Dumas Mfg. Co. 1951, Pack, Field, Cargo, M-1945, Stock number 30 B. 10-16."

It had a tough canvas handle sewn on its top. Once outside his room, he walked with indifference, carrying his bag like a briefcase; he cleared the imperiled quadrangle of the command center, administrative and service buildings. He continued onward across the gouged and sandbagged grounds of the post to the main gate, the east gate that faced the town. As the gate opened for four workers to enter, each with wheelbarrows carrying freshly butchered goats from town, Forsberg raised his right arm in a half salute (the guard was there to control the entrance to the base, not to monitor the exits of officers from it). He sauntered away from the entranceway, his boots stepping lightly over the gravel of the short stretch of road that connected the army post to the main road, and over that road was town.

Cottony islands of calm white clouds floated soberly and steadily from north to south in the blue sky. Below, the giant hills were dark green—and somehow ominous. At the foot of the nearest giant hill lay the streets of Nghia Lo and

Muong Lo Market.

He crossed the main road and vanished into the market street.

When he wasn't at the officers' mess to meet Lormer for dinner, the Frenchman went over to the guest quarters to get him. Seeing he wasn't there, he wondered if the captain had scheduled a meeting with another officer.

Lormer returned to the officers' mess and had supper at a table for four. None of the officers in the mess that evening knew where Forsberg was.

In the hubbub of preparing the garrison against attack—and now it was dark—it was probably pointless to seek out Forsberg who might have, against the lieutenant's advice, volunteered to help and now was working somewhere to aid in strengthening the base.

The night passed with Lormer checking Forsberg's room twice to see if he was there.

In the morning the captain didn't come to breakfast and he wasn't in his room. The garrison was big enough that if you had to get from its southside to the rest of it in a short time, you needed a motor vehicle. Lormer took a jeep. He drove here and there, covering the garrison in its entirety. No one had seen Forsberg.

There was a curiously empty feeling throughout the fort even though there were many people where in it. The day was turning cloudy. The sky was the color of pus.

By mid-morning the French lieutenant left the front gate by foot. The market wasn't busy like it usually was. Some sellers hadn't shown up at their stalls. Everyone in town had apparently heard that a massive group of Viet Minh were on the march and were fast approaching.

Lormer walked two-thirds of the way into the market and got to the booth selling pots and pans—where he always found tNoon. He wasn't there. The Frenchman looked around and didn't see him at any of the nearby stalls. At the stands that were open, he asked if tNoon had come to the market today. He was told no. Strange. It was the first time ever he hadn't found the Tai man there.

This surprised and perplexed him; he was at a loss at what to do. He thought a moment and then went back to the people he'd talked to about tNoon; this time he inquired whether they'd seen an American army captain there, the previous afternoon, with tNoon. Everybody told him no. He felt they were lying to him.

He walked back to the garrison, keeping an eye out for tNoon but there was never any sign of him.

That evening, at 5 p.m., dusk was humid. The Viet Minh fired their Soviet-made cannons against the garrison. Their barrage lasted ten minutes. The artillery fire set off mines in the land moat of barbed wire fences and deep ditches on two sides of the fortress. A few shells fell inside the post hitting blockhouses, but no one was hurt. The French didn't want to risk sending up observation flares to locate where the cannons were. The flares would give the Viet Minh a better idea of where the French Howitzers were inside the compound. The French cut off all lights in the garrison. After the ten-minute barrage, the Viet Minh didn't fire again that night.

However, their soldiers encircled every small station the French had outside the garrison, and surrounded the large town outpost (which helped guard the main gate), and the outpost at High Point.

During the night heavy fighting ensued and one by one the French outposts, large and small, fell. Some French survivors were able to flee into the garrison by the south gate.

Preparations for an all-out attack by the Viet Minh continued at daylight. The sky was pearl and murky, but it did not rain. More earth was moved to protect ammunition stores and fuel stores. Machine gunners were positioned in every feasible place. Each cannon, howitzer and mortar was fully manned. Nobody could go to the land moat to make repairs. They'd be too easily picked off by Viet Minh gunners.

The attack by the Viet Minh did not come. French radio communications continued to be operational. The French Army in the whole of Vietnam knew what the men of Nghia Lo were up against.

The sky cleared a little; it was no longer opaque. French planes would try to provide some air support, but they couldn't guarantee much. While visibility was a factor, they knew the Viet forces on the ground were vast.

At 4:08 p.m. the Viet Minh finally began their attack. First there were cannon and mortar. The Viet's target was large and broad: their artillery pounded the land moat at all sides of the garrison. French artillery tried to respond. It was hard for the French to pick out with binoculars any single pieces of Viet artillery in the dim light. Along with the land moat, the Viets managed to hit two buildings next to the airstrip and smoke rose there.

The air all around thickened. Man-made thunder rumbled and cracked. Barbed wire fence posts in the moat leaped into the air like match sticks. With metronomic regularity, shells rapidly followed one another and exploded. Soldiers strained to see whatever they could; no matter what station a French trooper was at, he was mindful of the gun, knife, and grenades on his belt. He might be fighting hand-to-hand.

Each man on the Viet side threw himself into the attack without regard for his own life. Man-made thunder rumbled, cracked, and resonated through the valley; knowing the numbers of those in the garrison, every Viet soldier was confident the French would be annihilated.

At 4:30 two French-manned B-26 bombers appeared over the giant hills. They went to High Point and dropped napalm, strafing all beneath them as they flew. Lines of flames burst forth from the forest below them, burning everything in their path.

The spatter of machine gun fire—both French and Viet—took over from the sound of exploding land mines in the moat. Grenades ripped apart the flesh of the men on both sides.

Viet commandos crawled up and down through the wreckage of the land moat to reach inside the garrison. Some were cut down by remaining mines, the rest by machine gun fire and grenades, but then columns upon columns of Viet Minh soldiers poured forth from an infinity at the rear—there were thousands, predictably so—and many of them died and filled the ditches so that the ground was leveled by their corpses; the next wave of their comrades could proceed with surer footing to the French side and obliterate all men there.

It was like the hand of a clock clicking over into eternity. Abruptly, on the French side, death was on display. Lifeless sergeants slumped over their burning, smoking howitzers; Maghreb regulars sat with their backs against blockhouse walls, inert as scarecrows, their clothes picked at by bullets, not birds.

Before two hours passed, the inner sanctum of the garrison was breached. Dead bodies of legionnaires lay on top of each other in the trenches (dug only the day before) of the administration building's courtyard.

It was in the courtyard at around quarter to six that Lieutenant Fabrice Lormer faced a grenade. Suddenly his head was no longer there. His body was sprawled in a pool of blood.

In the end, nothing moved in Nghia Lo except smoke; smoldering oil tanks turned it blacker than night.

When they succeeded, several days later, in reaching the American army, the French reported Captain Gideon Forsberg as missing in action.

Thanks to: Ryusuke and Haruka Ito, Tenjinyama Arts Studio, Tetsushi Yuzaki, Ryoko Suzusappno, Yuji Yamada, Stevyn and Yukako Prothero, Kazumi Sasaki, Hokkaido Tourist Station, Chitose. The libraries at The Japan Foundation in Los Angeles, Sydney, Toronto and Bangkok. La Bibliothèque Centre Pompidou (BPI), Paris. Walter Teres, Frank and Jean Hoff, Bill Dunn, Gwylene Gallimard, Jean-Marie Mauclet, Leo Mac Dougall, Ariane Dubillard, Roland Dubillard, Bill Troop, Wanda Ivey, Todd and Lori Isaacson, Pip Chodorov, Michael Kewley, Maria Machado, Wangtae Lim, John Calder, Xiawei Cui, Byron Thigpen, Julek Kedzierski, Yvonne Shafer, Darko Suvin, Stephen Fitzstephens, Justus Rosenberg, Marie-Céline Courilleault, Marjam Oskoui, Sungtae Kim, Bérengère Pajolec, Linda Jamsen, The Taits, The Massaros, The Segarnicks, Yves Gaudin, Steve Koons, Isabelle Weingarten, Jason Eng, Ursula Werner, Elie Yarden, Ben Boretz, Natalia Golimbievskaya, Brian Keane, Jill Danger, Jim Haynes, Joseph Rowe, Catherine Bratslovsky, Jim Shutt, Bruce Boswell, Carey Downer, Damian Corcoran, Gordon Rogoff, Carlos Auckland, HaeJoon Moon, Ilmar Taska, Don Yorty, Patrick Graham, Graham Aid, James Graham, Grace Simpson, Kevin Lathrop, Susanne Palm, Hazel Lee, Kai Ephron, Vlanes, Boris Staroselsky, Justin Newcomb, Michael Stromme, Stéphane Taib, Scott and Babette Lithgow, Sheva Fruitman, Sally Young and Dave McFall, Jennifer K. Dick, Mark Teverson, Lucy Cook, Alberto Celletti, John Romano, Stephanie Schildknecht, Christian and Veronika Mahnke, Mark and Karen Lacheiner, Emily Rubin, Natasha Golimbievskaya, Jacopo Quintavalle, Corneliu Mitrache, Amine Sabir, Linda Scheuber, Kevin Flury, Khalan Morel, Lise Neer, Madeleine Barchevska, Marie Flageul, Virgil Zolyom.

Printed in Great Britain
by Amazon